DEAD FILES

Mike Smitley

Special thanks to Steve Sanders for the cover design.
Most importantly, thanks to my wife, Jana, for her patience and support.
The author, Mike Smitley, can be contacted at:

www.mikesmitley.org

This is a work of fiction. Names, characters, places and incidents either are the product of the author's imagination or are used fictitiously, and any resemblance to actual persons, living or dead, events or locales is entirely coincidental.

First printing, September 2006
© August, 2004 Mike Smitley
Printed in the United States. All rights reserved.

ISBN 10: 0-9779407-1-3
ISBN 13: 978-0-9779407-1-4

For more suspense, read Mike Smitley's other novels:
IMPLIED CONTRACT and *PREY*

Father's Press, LLC

Lee's Summit, MO (816) 554-2156
E-Mail: fatherspress@yahoo.com
www.fatherspress.com
www.mikesmitley.org or www.mikesmitley.com

DEAD FILES

A Novel

By

Mike Smitley

1

GABE KINNETT'S SALEM studio apartment was dark, with only the dim light from the street to illuminate the drab, dated interior. He rolled over on his well-abused sofa and stared at the lighted face of the alarm clock. It was set to go off in a few minutes. He thought, *10:00. Time to go to work already? I'll never make it through the night.*

He reached over to the orange crate that he used as an end table and pushed the alarm stem down. He was already awake, so there was no need to listen to the irritating buzz. Midnight shifts were murder, especially with no sleep.

Salem P.D.s midnight shift was his assignment, but his internal clock couldn't adjust. He had lain awake most of the day, napping only intermittently. He couldn't sleep now, but his body would start shutting down about 3:00 a.m.

The hours between 3:00 a.m. and 7:00 a.m. were torturous. He would fight hard, but could not fend off sleep. His eyelids would fall shut no matter how hard he resisted. He spent those hours trying to avoid Sergeant Shelley. He would not tolerate sleeping on duty.

When Gabe was that tired, he prayed that the dispatcher wouldn't give him calls. He didn't trust his judgment while suffering the effects of sleep deprivation. He certainly didn't want to make any critical decisions.

The guys on the shift understood what he was going through. They'd all experienced the same problem at one time or another. They were a close-knit group, mostly rogues and rebels, but they stuck together like glue. That cohesiveness was a lifesaver. Gabe was going to need someone to cover for him tonight.

He looked at the clock again. Ten minutes had passed while he'd contemplated his problems. His divorce was final two months ago. He had no money, furniture or food in the apartment. His car was worn out. He had no girlfriend, and his bitter attitude had placed his job in jeopardy. His only friends were the guys on his shift, guys who had lived through the same emotional torture that he was going through.

He slowly rolled off the sofa and staggered across the bare wood floor to the bathroom. He deliberately picked up his feet so he wouldn't pick up a splinter.

Once in the bathroom, he leaned over the rusty sink as he stared at himself in the cracked mirror. He shook his head in disgust and lowered his stare to the sink. He wondered, *How could my life have fallen apart so quickly? What did I do wrong? How am I ever going to get my life back on track again?*

The self-pity was hard to shake off. These questions had haunted him ever since his wife had announced that she was leaving three months before the divorce was final. Serious soul-searching had only brought him a headache and more bitterness. He didn't need either right now. He'd been late for work four times last month. If that pattern continued, Sergeant Shelley would send him home and dock his pay.

He hurriedly groomed and dressed for duty. There were no drapes on the windows, so he pulled the dilapidated shade aside and looked out to check the weather. It was foggy and drizzling rain.

He pulled the chain and turned off the only light bulb in the room, which hung from the ceiling on a frayed wire. He walked down to the street and contemplating if he should drive or walk.

As he stared at his car and assessed its condition, he kicked the front right tire, which was almost flat. He thought, *The body is rusted out; the valve covers leak; the exhaust system is shot; the tires are bald; it needs new ball joints and tie-rods; the battery is weak; the starter is shot; the radiator leaks; the transmission slips and the windshield is cracked. Other than that, she's cherry.*

There was time to walk to work if he hurried. He didn't like to drive unless he absolutely had to. He couldn't afford another car, and he couldn't afford to fix this one. As he hurried off to work he couldn't decide who he was angrier with, his ex-wife or the police department. He had been on the department only two years, but burnout was wreaking havoc on his morale.

Tommy Ryan closed himself in his room behind the locked door. He sat on his bed with his legs crossed and stared despondently at the pistol in his lap. Tears dripped from his eyes as he searched for another solution. He laid the pistol on the nightstand and walked to the door.

He stepped to the stair railing and looked sadly down at his father seated in his recliner watching television. His father had no idea of the pain and anguish that Tommy was suffering. He thought how hurt his father would be afterwards that he was so close and approachable, but Tommy couldn't come to him in his deepest hour of need.

As much as Tommy loved his father and didn't want to hurt him, there were things going through his mind that he couldn't share with anyone. At one time, he and his father had been as close as two people could possibly be. Now at the tender age of fifteen, he now thought that no one on Earth could understand what he was going through.

Grief overwhelmed him as he turned back toward his room and wept openly. He quietly closed his door so no one could hear him cry. The thought of the grief that he was about to cause his parents broke his heart, but he could think of no other alternative.

He sat back on the bed and stared at the pistol. His hand trembled as he picked it up and pulled the hammer back. He put the muzzle under his chin and cried as he pictured the grief that would consume his parents.

He applied gentle pressure on the trigger and held his breath, waiting for the quiet darkness. At the last second he relaxed his trigger finger. He put the gun back on the nightstand and took a few deep breaths. He would have to go through with it, but he didn't have the courage to do it tonight.

With trembling fingers, Tommy picked up the phone and dialed his therapist. She was the one person who could help him pull out of this emotional tailspin. After the fifth ring, he hung up and put his face in his hands. He cried harder as he realized that there was no one in the world who could save him.

Gabe hurried into shift briefing. Shelley looked at the clock on the wall as he slid into a chair barely in time. Shelley looked sternly at Gabe over the top of his bifocals and yelled, "Okay! Okay! Quiet everyone, let's get started." There were fourteen officers seated in front of Shelley's podium.

Len Shelley was one of the few blacks who had made rank in the department. Aside from being extremely capable, he'd never forgotten his roots. He was well-liked by his officers. He expected excellence from them, and in turn would go to hell and back for them. If they performed well and didn't get him in trouble with the brass, he overlooked minor policy violations and harmless horseplay.

He continued. "Listen up, you deviants! Here are the district assignments. Carlos is 131. Bigelow is 132. Gapky is 133. Lyzett is 134. Green is 135. Kinnett, you're the roving car, 136. Hallos, Ellis, Throckmorton and Schumacher, you guys partner up in two-man cars and work the projects. Reaves, Smith and Blackman are the traffic cars. Blauw, you're riding the wagon tonight."

The officers jotted down the district assignments so they could communicate car-to-car throughout the night. Shelley opened the pass-on book and read the intelligence information from the previous two shifts.

There was nothing unusual in the pass-on book tonight, just the usual warrants, house watches and department business. There was a general chastising from the Major about a policy violation that he had observed. His shotgun approached to discipline always irritated the officers. Rather than deal with the individual who had caused the problem, he would chew out the whole department.

4

Shelley closed the book and asked if anyone had anything for the good of the cause. With no response, he said, "Kinnett, I need to see you and Blauw after inspection."

The other officers jeered at Kinnett and Blauw, warning them that they had the right to an attorney. Blauw was unshaken by the teasing, but Gabe was worried.

Shelley walked into the garage and started down the line, inspecting everyone's uniforms and weapons. When finished, he dismissed the troops and had them stand beside their cars with the doors and trunk lids open.

After a thorough vehicle inspection, the officers left the lot and drove to their districts. Gabe lingered in the lot to talk to Blauw before going to Shelley's office. He didn't want Shelley to see them conspiring, so he waited for Shelley to disappear into the building before approaching Blauw.

Angus Blauw was the oldest officer on the force. He'd never risen above the rank of patrolman because of his brutal honesty, irreverence for rank and calloused indifference toward the public. Years of excessive drinking had taken a heavy toll. He was thin and his eyes were sunken. His voice was deep and gravelly. His face was wrinkled and his hair had long ago turned white. He kept it cut short in a flattop, which made his face look lean and gaunt.

After three failed marriages and more suspension days than even he could count, Angus was the informal leader in the patrol section. His prehistoric approach to police work had made him a legend with the officers and a nightmare for the staff.

Gabe met Blauw as he walked toward the back door of the station. He asked, "Any idea what Shelley wants, Angus?"

Blauw growled, "Yeah, kid, he probably wants to talk to us about that black preacher that we thumped the shit out of the other night. Don't sweat it, boy, let me do the talking. Shelley won't be doing the investigation, so he won't be taking formal statements. The ass-wipes in internal affairs will do that. We'll get together and get our stories straight before we talk to them. It'll be all right."

Gabe admired Blauw's arrogance as he swaggered into Shelley's office completely unafraid. Blauw sat in the chair directly in front of Shelley's desk, leaned back and put his feet up

5

on Shelley's desk. He nestled comfortably into the chair and said, "So, Len, old buddy, I suppose you're wondering why I called you here."

Shelley glared over the top of his reading glasses at Blauw and tried to appear angry, but he and Blauw had too many years of friendship under their belts for his facade to fool anyone. The anger slowly faded from his face as he shook his head. "Angus, you crusty old bastard, get your feet off my desk and show some respect. You're in real trouble this time, and I can't help you."

Angus put his feet on the floor and chuckled softly. "What kind of trouble, Len, has your old lady been calling out my name in her sleep again?"

As frightened as he was of Shelley, Gabe couldn't help but laugh at Blauw. The sergeant pointed his finger at Gabe and said, "Don't encourage him, Gabe." He turned to Blauw and said, "Yeah, but she was laughing at what a limp-dick you are. But that's okay with me, Angus. I don't care if she goes to bed with you. Every woman needs a good laugh now and then. You sure as hell couldn't hurt her any."

With the barbs exchanged, Shelley changed the tone of the conversation. "It's about that preacher you two thumped. I.A. called down and asked me what happened. They want statements from you two. I told them I didn't see anything, and don't either of you two fools get me involved in this mess. Someone's head is going to roll and it ain't going to be mine."

Angus knew the complaint was coming. He waited patiently until Shelley had finished. He examined his fingernails apathetically and growled, "Nothing out of line happened, Len. That phony black piece of shit resisted arrest and we used only enough force to overcome his resistance."

Shelley looked suspiciously at Blauw. "Don't give me that academy textbook crap, Angus. I saw him when you unloaded him from your wagon. He looked like he'd just crawled out from under a cattle stampede. He's a reverend, for God's sake! You've gone too far this time!"

Blauw frowned and snarled in his raspy tone, "Reverend! That phony bastard ain't no reverend, Len. There ain't a single ounce of reverence in his whole body. Why is it that you black people have to attach phony labels to your names to give

6

yourselves credibility? That asshole ain't cracked a bible open in twenty years, except to hide his dope in it."

Shelley sighed in frustration. "How the hell do you know, Angus? Maybe he has a church in his basement. Maybe he got himself ordained recently. Maybe he's stopped running whores and drugs and has turned his life around. Who knows? What difference does it make if he's legitimate or not? He can still cost you your job whether he's a reverend or not. You can't beat the shit out of everyone you don't like."

Blauw smiled at Shelley and defended himself. "I don't beat the shit out of everyone I don't like. I haven't kicked your ugly black ass yet."

Gabe cringed as he gritted his teeth. He turned his head away and waited for the sky to fall. A sense of indignation fell over Shelley as he shook a threatening finger at Blauw. "Why you senile old broke-dick, you ain't never won a fair fight in your life!"

As the exchange became more heated, Gabe became very uncomfortable. Blauw shrugged his shoulders and replied, "What's fair got to do with anything, Len? I'm too old to fight fair. Let me educate you, son. Age and treachery can defeat youth, strength and speed any day. Don't mess with me, boy."

Shelley stared at Angus apathetically. He gave up and shook his head in disbelief, realizing that a one-upsmanship contest with Angus was hopeless. He stopped sparring and said, "May be, old man, but when you climb on this ugly, black ass, you'd better bring your lunch. It's going to take you all day."

Angus chuckled softly. He thoroughly enjoyed pushing Shelley's buttons. Shelley continued, "All I can say, Angus, is you two had better get your stories straight. The major is going after your heads over this."

Blauw said as he stood to leave, "Fuck him, Len. He ain't got brains enough to get my job." He stopped at the door, turned and said sadly, "Now see what you've done? You've got me all scared and upset, you big bully. I'll be traumatized the rest of the night. You ought to be ashamed of yourself, scaring a frail old man like that. Meet me about three. You can buy me lunch to make it up to me, you asshole." Angus sniffled twice and wipes his dry eyes in a feeble attempt to act hurt.

7

Shelley glared at him as he walked out. He yelled after him, "Show some respect, Blauw! That's Sergeant Asshole to you!"

Gabe sat in disbelief as Shelley and Blauw exchanged insults. Although Blauw was a constant irritant to Shelley, it was apparent that both had great fondness for each other. Gabe said, "Listen, sarge, Blauw isn't worried, but I am. I've really pissed off the chief and major this last year. They'll hang me out to dry if they get the chance."

Shelley replied sympathetically, "Yeah they will, son, but make no mistake. You haven't pissed them off a tenth as bad as old Blauw has. Listen, Gabe, you've only been on the shift for a couple of months. You fit in well and we all like you. You're not a rat. You're a jam-up cop. You get with Blauw and do what he tells you. He's a complete disaster, but he's the best cop this department has ever seen. He knows how to write a report to cover his ass. He'll coach you through this. When you get your stories straight, get with me and I'll give you some pointers on how to get through the interview with the rats upstairs."

The sergeant's support reassured Gabe. He asked, "You known him long?"

"Blauw? Yeah, the old fossil broke me in when I got hired. I was one of the first black officers they hired, and Blauw bailed me out of a lot of tough scrapes. He saved my life twice. He's the most obnoxious old man that you'll ever meet, but he'd fight a grizzly bear at the drop of a hat. I love him to death. The staff hates him because he constantly points out what gutless paper-pushers they are. None of them were ever real cops, and Blauw rubs their incompetence in their faces. You guys stick together. You'll be all right. I know this preacher. He's just a militant, white-hating pimp. Every time he gets in trouble, he screams discrimination and hides behind his phony preacher title to get the blacks in the community in an uproar. He thinks if he stirs up a big enough stink, the department will drop the charges to shut him up. The sad thing is that sometimes it works. The good blacks in the community hate his guts. He gives all blacks a bad name. He's just a loud mouth nigger who runs drugs and whores. You guys can survive this if you stick together."

8

Gabe nodded and stood to leave. He turned and said, "You and Blauw sure attack each other's race a lot, sergeant. Doesn't anyone ever get offended?"

Shelley smiled and shook his head. "Nah, kid, it's all in fun. It's a stress reliever. We only insult the people we really like. If you can't poke fun at people, this job will eat you up. When someone uses a racial slur, we don't take offense. We know those terms don't apply to us. They only apply to the scumbags on the street. There are scumbags of all colors out there, but in here we're all one color, blue. One thing you have to be careful of though, kid. You have to learn who you can trust. Don't think that just because someone is wearing the same uniform that they're your friend. There are a lot of people in this department you can't trust. Some are on this shift. They'll try to warm up to you to make you think you can trust them, but when the chips are down, they'll sell you out in a heartbeat. I wouldn't say the things I say to Blauw to just anyone. Blauw is a dinosaur, but he's an old marine. He comes from the old school where you'd cut your arms off before you'd rat out another cop. Hang on to his shirttail."

Gabe considered Shelley's advice, then said, "Hell, sarge, sounds like I need to avoid him like the plague. He'll probably get me fired or killed."

Shelley seriously considered Gabe's remark. He slowly nodded his head and said, "Both are distinct possibilities, son."

Gabe stayed busy for the first four hours of the shift. As the roving car, he was sent to support the other cars when they needed assistance. When things slowed down, he called Blauw on the radio.

Blauw was driving the prisoner transport wagon and had been equally busy transporting the other officers' arrests to the city jail. He enjoyed the wagon. He got to roam the city, get in on some of the brawls, and had to do very little paper work.

He finally caught up with Blauw at an all-night diner where he and Shelley were finishing lunch. Shelley motioned for Gabe to join them. "Have a seat, kid. We're just arguing about who'll pick up the bill. Looks like you win."

Gabe blushed from financial embarrassment. "Sorry, guys, I don't have a dime to my name."

9

Shelley and Blauw looked sheepishly at each other. They'd known about Gabe's financial problems, but had forgotten when he sat down. Neither of them intended to embarrass him. Blauw motioned for the waitress to come over. When she arrived, he said, "Hey, baby, bring this snot-nosed kid a double cheeseburger and a load of fries, and put it on my bill."

Gabe shook his head and protested. "No! No, I can't do that! I ate before I came to work!" He really hadn't eaten for the last twenty four hours, but he was too embarrassed to accept charity.

Shelley leaned into Gabe and set him straight. "Listen, you little shit, no one can work eight hours without eating! No one on my shift is going to go hungry! Don't you ever let me find out that you can't afford to eat! We're family here! You let me know when you're so broke that you can't afford a meal! You got that, boy?"

The affectionate chastising touched Gabe. He nodded and mumbled, "Thanks."

Always one to stir the pot, Angus interjected, "Besides, I might stir up a shit-storm tonight. I've got to have someone who can finish the fights I start. You need to keep your strength up so I don't get whipped. We sure can't count on old Shelley here. Hell, we could all be dead before he'd get there."

Shelley stood to leave. He wiped his mouth on his sleeve and reached for his wallet. He said, "Hell, Angus, as pasty as your white ass is, no one could tell the difference anyway. You've looked dead for years."

He laid some money on top of his bill. He then took a twenty from his wallet and dropped it in front of Gabe. He leaned over Gabe and pointed his finger at him as though he were a small child. He said, "Here's your lunch money, little boy. If you don't want this big nigger all over your lily-white ass, you'd better say something next time you get hard up. Got me, kid?"

Gabe was embarrassed, but the sergeant was so forceful that it was pointless to argue. He didn't pick up the twenty, but nodded and patted Shelley on the arm. Shelley patted him on the back as he walked to the door.

Angus chuckled. "Hard to argue with, ain't he?"

"I wish he hadn't done that. I'm a big boy. It won't hurt me to skip a meal now and then."

10

"That's not the point, Gabe. He likes you. He's just trying to show you that you're one of our inner circle. It's hard to earn respect around here. You've showed us that you're not a rat and that we can count on you. Len's a little rough around the edges. When he wants to show affection, he does it with an ass-chewing."

"Yeah, I know. I'm flattered, but I feel uncomfortable taking money from people. He sure likes you, even though he doesn't act like it."

Angus leaned back and stretched. "I know. The big gorilla and me go way back. He's one of the few good blacks on the department. I'd take him over most whites I know. He rips my ass on a regular basis, but he knows it don't do any good. I just make sure I don't get him in trouble with the chief, and he leaves me alone. We plan to retire on the same day. We're going to buy cabins next to each other in the upper peninsula of Michigan and spend our retirement years fishing and deer hunting. Len already has land up by Scandia. When he gets pissed at me, he says he's not going to let me ride in his boat. I just tell him that I'll throw his big ass in the water and take his boat away from him."

"Angus, I hope you know that Sergeant Shelley could break you like a stick. His hands are as big as baseball gloves."

Angus nodded, "Ain't that the truth? He played for the Seahawks in the NFL before he got on the department. I like to be around when he goes off on people. He's put some serious hurt on people who've pushed him too far. If he gets a grip on your throat, you're worm food."

The waitress delivered Gabe's plate. He attacked the cheeseburger like a starving hound. He washed down a mouthful of food with a gulp of Coke and asked, "What's going to happen in the interview with the I.A. guys?"

Angus got the attention of the waitress. He held his cup in the air for a refill. He said, "Well, first of all, you have to understand a few things. The things that this phony preacher is accusing us of are criminal. The I.A. pricks are going to try to convince you that we're all cops and we have to stick together. They'll tell you to tell them the truth and they'll take care of us. They won't try that shit on me because I've been around the horn too many times. They're going to try to get you to say something

11

different than what I say. They'd like to catch us in a lie, then fire us for lying in an internal affairs investigation."

He leaned into Gabe and continued. "You gotta remember this, kid, we can be prosecuted and sued in different courts at the same time. We can be prosecuted and sued in state court for assaulting this fool. We can also be prosecuted and sued in federal court for violating his civil rights. The I.A. guys will try to get us to admit to doing something wrong and assure us that they'll keep everything in house. They'll tell you we might get a little disciplinary action, but our jobs will be intact and the department will take care of us. Don't you believe it! Those weasel-dicks will take our statements, then prepare criminal complaints on us. They'll go to the D.A. and ask him to file criminal assault charges on us. The chief will fire us, and they'll go to the U.S. attorney and ask him to prosecute us for violating the preacher's civil rights. Then they'll go to the preacher and encourage him to sue us civilly. You can't trust those rat bastards, ever!"

By now Gabe had stopped eating and was hanging on Blauw's every word. He put his cheeseburger down and asked, "So what do we do?"

Blauw leaned back and shook his head. "Easy, we don't trust them. We get our stories straight and don't deviate from them no matter what. Here's how it'll go down. First of all, the fifth and sixth amendments apply to us as well as the rest of society. We have the right to remain silent and have an attorney present in a criminal investigation just like the crooks. As long as there's a possibility of criminal charges being filed, they can't use the threat of termination to compel us to testify against ourselves. The most important thing here is to stay out of jail."

Gabe asked, "So, it's easy. We don't have to give a statement, right?"

Angus didn't speak while the waitress refilled his coffee cup. When she'd left, he said, "I wish it were that easy. The department can still do an internal investigation to fire us. They'll give us the Garrity Warning, which says that we have to give a statement, but they can't use it against us in a criminal proceeding. They can still use it to fire us. Make sure you insist that they give you the Garrity Warning before you give a statement. If you don't, they can fire you and prosecute you at the same time.

A sense of anxiety overwhelmed Gabe. "I can't lose this job, Angus. If I get fired, no other department in Oregon will hire me. I don't know how to do anything else."

Blauw glared at him and chastised him. "Ain't no one going to lose their job, boy. We'll get our stories straight and stick to them. First of all, you gotta remember, no matter how bad the chief wants to use us as his sacrificial lambs, he can't as long as we stick together. It's two words against one. That black doper ain't got no witnesses. You and I are going to tell the same story. We'll be fine."

Gabe finished the last bite of his cheeseburger and washed it down with the last swallow of his Coke. He nodded in agreement. "Hope you're right, Angus. So, what do we say in the interview?"

Angus looked around to make sure that they couldn't be overheard. He crossed his arms on the table and leaned into Gabe. "Okay, boy, listen up. Now! We can't use force against anyone unless it's in self-defense or to affect an arrest. It's simple. We told that Usher that he was under arrest. We tried to handcuff him and he resisted. He swung at me and I hit him. I'll defend my actions. All you have to say is that you saw him take a poke at me and I hit him."

Gabe glared at Angus. "Hit him! Come on, Angus, we stomped a mud hole in him! They'll never buy that! He had too many injuries! He was in the I.C.U. unit for two days! You know they'll interview the ambulance attendants who hauled him to the hospital from the jail! You know how firemen hate policemen! They'll burn us to the ground!"

Blauw growled, "I don't give a shit if they buy it or not, Kinnett! Their opinion doesn't count! They have to gauge their actions against what a jury would believe. If they fire us and we sue them, the case will go before a jury. They may not believe us, but if we stick to our stories, they'll be afraid to strap us on. If a jury determines that they fired us unjustifiably, they'll have to put us back to work, and we can sue their asses off for wrongful termination, defamation of character and anything else our attorneys can think of. If they pin you down, just say it was dark and you couldn't see everything. If you don't want to answer a question, just say you don't recall. Remember, preacher boy swung at me, and you only saw one punch. Anything else, you can't recall or you didn't see. Easy! Right?"

Fear was written across Gabe's face. He shook his head. "No, Angus, it's not easy. I'm not going to rat on you, but we've got to come up with something better than this. The injuries are far more serious than one punch would cause."

Angus leaned into him and growled, "No we don't, Kinnett! Listen, I'm not saying that one punch was all that was thrown. That's just all you saw. I'll take care of justifying the other punches. I can handle this, but you have to dummy up. They're going to interview me first. I'll hide a pocket recorder inside my shirt. I'll meet you after the interview, and you'll see how the interview goes. You'll see what I mean."

Gabe agonized over their dilemma. He sighed deeply as he hung his head and ran his fingers through his hair. "You sure this'll work, Angus?"

"Positive, son, you'll see. The only time we ever get confessions from crooks is when they don't realize what interview techniques we're using against them. We bluff our way through most of those confessions. I've been to the same interview and interrogation schools as those fools upstairs. They're not going to bluff me. You just be at your apartment when I'm finished. I'll meet you there."

As he stood to leave, Gabe squinted and glared suspiciously at Angus. "You'd better not get me fired, Angus."

Angus stood confidently and patted Gabe on the back. "You big baby, you just haven't been through enough of these yet. You'll see. We're right on this. It's no big thing."

Blauw was sitting in the lobby, waiting for Detective Lumas to call him in. He thumbed through a magazine and showed no emotion. The office door opened and Lumas motioned for him to come in. He escorted Blauw to the small interview room and motioned for him to sit in the chair across the table from him. He laid a *consent to speak* form in front of Blauw and said, "Sign at the bottom, Angus. Let's get this over with."

"Not so fast, Ezard, this is a criminal investigation. I have the right to remain silent under the fifth amendment. As long as this is a criminal investigation, I ain't saying shit. Now if you want

14

to give me the Garrity warning assuring me that nothing I say can be used against me in court, I'll talk."

Lumas glared at Angus, then slowly stood and left the room. Five minutes later, he returned with a Garrity warning. "Okay, Angus, I talked to the Major. You've got your immunity from criminal prosecution."

Angus signed the Garrity warning, then picked up the *consent to speak* form. He read it and signed his name. He then drew a line through the sentence that stated he would not hold Lumas or the department liable for any damage that he suffered as a result of the interview.

Lumas looked at the form and sat up straight. He glared at Blauw and barked, "You can't do that, Blauw! You've been ordered to give me an interview, and this is part of it!"

Blauw growled and shook his finger at Lumas. "I'll give you the interview, Ezard, but you can't force me to sign away my right to sue your ass if you damage me. Now, if you don't want to interview me, that's between you and the chief. You're the one who's backing out of the interview, not me."

Lumas gritted his teeth and tried to remain calm. He laid the form down and said grudgingly. "Alright, Blauw, let's get this over with." He turned on the tape recorder so the secretary could transcribe the interview later. After the lead-in identifying the case number, victim and person being interviewed, Lumas asked the first question.

Lumas: "Were you on duty the evening of November 2nd, 1996?"
Blauw: "Yes."
Lumas: "Did you come in contact with the Reverend Tyrone Usher?"
Blauw: "No, I didn't contact no reverend that night. I contacted a dope-pushing pimp named Tyrone Usher, but he ain't no reverend, Ezard. Hell, ain't you checked that fool's criminal record yet? What kind of a detective are you?"

Lumas stiffened his neck and became defensive. He left the tape running as he chastised Angus. "Blauw, that's none of your business! I'm running this investigation, not you! Just answer the questions and show a little respect!"

Angus barked back at Lumas and the interview went quickly down hill. "The hell it ain't none of my business! You're trying to railroad me and that kid, Kinnett! Where's your integrity, Ezard? You want respect? You got to earn it! No wonder they kicked your yellow ass out of patrol! Is this the only pigeonhole they could find to stick your sorry ass in? Better watch it, Ezard, you're going to get a bad reputation, head-hunting your own kind like this, especially over a no-good, phony, white-hating preacher."

Lumas rubbed his eyes. He knew from years of experience that he could not best Blauw. He calmed himself and repeated the question.

Lumas: "Okay, Blauw, did you contact Tyrone Usher?"

Blauw: "That's better, Ezard. Let's don't be trying to confuse the facts here. Yeah, I contacted him. I arrested him for D.W.I."

Lumas: "What was your probable cause for the stop?"

Blauw: "The car he was operating crossed over the centerline. It ran a stop sign, and when I approached Usher, his eyes were bloodshot. His speech was slurred and he had a strong odor of intoxicants on his breath."

Lumas: "How did you know the odor on his breath was intoxicants?"

Blauw: "Because I've smelled plenty of intoxicants in my career, Ezard. Hell, I smelled it on your breath plenty of times when we used to work together. Remember how you used to show up for duty drunk, and we'd cover for you and handle your calls so you wouldn't get in trouble? Remember that time when I pulled you out of that whorehouse when you were on duty just before the vice goons hit the door? Remember---"

Lumas held his hand up as he angrily punched the *Stop* button on the recorder. Rage slowly covered his face. He leaned back and stared at Blauw for a long minute. Angus smiled obnoxiously.

16

Lumas calmed himself enough to speak. "Look, Blauw, let's get something straight here. It doesn't matter what I did years ago. The question here is what you did to Usher. Are you going to let me do my job, or am I going to have to call the sergeant in here to finish this?"

Blauw opened his eyes wide and nodded. "Hell yes, Ezard, get the sergeant in here. I got more evidence on him than I do on you. As a matter of fact, why don't both you fuckers come in here at the same time? It'll save me from having to repeat myself."

Lumas folded his arms across his chest and shook his head. "You're going to make this difficult, aren't you, Blauw?"

Angus leaned over the table and snarled at Lumas, "No, Ezard, I'm not, but neither are you. Since we're cutting to the chase here, let's get all our cards on the table. You don't outrank me, so knock off this condescending bullshit with me. You're up here because you're a rat bastard who sold your soul to the devil. I know your past, and the only reason I haven't burned your dumb ass is because I've got only slightly more integrity than you. But don't push me. I'll answer straightforward questions, but don't try to badger me or put your own spin on the facts. Don't try any of your crooked tricks, and knock off this holier-than-thou attitude with me."

He leaned back in the chair and motioned for Lumas to turn the recorder back on. Lumas re-wound the tape to the spot before Blauw's comments about the whorehouse.

Lumas: "Did Usher comply with your request to exit the car?"
Blauw: "Yes."
Lumas: "Did you perform a field sobriety test on him?"
Blauw: "Yes, he failed the balance test, the heel to toe walking test, and he couldn't say his ABCs. I also smelled a strong odor of intoxicant on his breath and his speech was slurred."
Lumas: "Did you tell him he was under arrest?"
Blauw: "Yes I did. I tried to turn him around to handcuff him, but he tried to punch me."
Lumas: "Which hand did he use?"
Blauw: "Can't recall."
Lumas: "What did you do then?"

17

Blauw: "I punched him, and Officer Kinnett helped me force him to the ground and cuff him."

Lumas: "How many times did you punch Usher?"

Blauw: "I only used the minimal force necessary to affect the arrest."

Lumas: "How many times did you punch him?"

Blauw: "I don't recall."

Lumas: "How did he sustain his injuries?"

Blauw: "I saw no injuries other than those associated with being forced to the asphalt."

Lumas: "How do you explain the severe bruising to his back, ribs and legs?"

Blauw: "I have to assume that he had a friend mark him up before he contacted your office in an effort to lend credibility to his false allegations against me and Officer Kinnett. He's a pimp and doper, you know. He's not above lying to get retaliation against the officers who'd arrested him. He would also like to threaten the department with civil action to intimidate the chief into dropping the charges against him. The chief might role over for him, but I won't."

Lumas: "What force did Officer Kinnett use against Mr. Usher?"

Blauw: "I can't testify about anything that Officer Kinnett did. I was so focused on protecting myself from Usher that I didn't see anything that Officer Kinnett did."

Lumas: "What is Officer Kinnett going to tell me?"

Blauw: "You'll have to ask him that yourself. He and I haven't discussed the incident once we found out the complaint had been filed. We didn't have to. The truth needs no rehearsal."

Lumas rolled his eyes and shook his head in disgust. Getting a confession out of Blauw was like cutting through a bank vault with a butter-knife. He gave up and ended the interview.

As he escorted Blauw out of the office, he said, "That interview won't cut it. You're in deep shit, Blauw. The chief will want more answers than this. You haven't hamstrung me yet. You can't prove any misconduct by me after all these years. No one will believe you. The major will conduct the next interview, and we'll see how insubordinate you are with him. He'll bounce you out of the department on your ass. Anyway, Kinnett will tell the truth. He's not going to take a fall for you. This department doesn't need cops like you."

Angus poked Lumas in the chest with his finger. "There you go again, Ezard, forgetting the skeletons in your own closet. I suppose this department needs drunken, whore-chasing cowards like you. You're where you belong, Ezard, stuck up here in this rat-hole office where you can't get anyone killed. All you can do is try to ruin the careers of officers who are twice the man that you are. You'll never be a cop, so you might as well help other scumbags just like you go after those of us who are. Don't fuck with me, Ezard. I eat pussies like you for breakfast. You try to burn me or Kinnett and your career won't be worth two cents. Think you're safe after all these years? Think I don't have evidence? Try me! The department may not care, but your wife and the newspapers will. And there are still enough of your victims around that you'd stolen property from and falsified charges against that they'll come out of the woodwork once my allegations go public. Remember that high-school girl that you knocked up and paid for her abortion? She's still around. I'm sure she and your wife would have a few hoots comparing notes on how lousy you are in bed."

He backed out of Ezard's face and smiled. He waved as he turned to leave and said, "Say hi to the wife for me, Ezard, and tell her to quit calling me all the time. I'm tired of her begging me to bang her."

Lumas did a slow burn as he watched Blauw swagger arrogantly down the hall laughing. He thought how glad he would be when all the old-timers who remembered his past were gone, especially Blauw.

Gabe was sitting on his sofa when Angus knocked. Before Gabe could open the door, he yelled, "Open up, asshole, it's the vice squad!"

He jerked the door open and tried to silence Angus. "Shut up, Angus, you old fool, I've got neighbors, you know."

Angus laughed loudly and responded without softening his raspy voice, "Fuck-em! You ain't got no decent neighbors living in this toilet. They probably talk worse than I do."

Gabe quickly pulled him into the apartment and closed the door. He said, "Angus, you cuss more than anyone I've ever met. Can't you speak just one short, little sentence without cussing?"

Angus responded with a chuckle, "Fuck no." Gabe shook his head in frustration and motioned for him to sit on the end of the sofa. Angus looked at him sternly and said, "Kinnett, I knew you were hard up, but this is ridiculous. Ain't you got no furniture?"

"Nope, just this old sofa and an orange crate. My ex got everything else."

Angus sat on the end of the sofa said in a disgusted tone, "Boy, you're a fool. Why the hell did you give the bitch everything? You're entitled to half, you know."

"Yeah, I know. I thought we were going to get back together, so I gave her what she wanted. I took on all the bills and her nursing school loans. I thought she'd appreciate the gesture and come back. I didn't know she'd been seeing a doctor on the side. By the time I found out, it was too late. She'd already married him and moved out of the state."

The bitter memories of his own divorces came rushing back. Angus genuinely felt bad for Gabe. He reached over, patted his back and said, "Sorry, Gabe, I didn't know. If I'd been you, I'd have hunted the bitch down and killed her and her asshole doctor."

"I know. I'd planned to do just that, but every time I started planning it, my conscience bothered me. I knew there wouldn't be anyone around to keep you from getting your feeble, old butt kicked. I couldn't stand to have three deaths on my conscience. Besides, Shelley would never forgive me if I let you get hurt. You're his reason for coming to work each night."

A devilish smile turned up one corner of Angus's mouth. "Yeah, I know. I sure get a hoot out of watching him sweat every time he thinks I've gotten him in trouble."

"Okay, Angus, let's get down to business. What have you got for me?"

"Oh, nothing, I decided to sell your sorry ass down the river. I told Lumas that you were the one who beat the shit out of Usher. I had to tell the truth, professional ethics you know."

A sense of panic overwhelmed Gabe as Angus masked the laughter roaring inside. He finally burst out laughing at the shock on Gabe's face. He swatted Gabe on the back and said, "Relax, Kinnett, you know I wouldn't do that."

He gave a sigh of relief. "You better not, Angus. I'll erase my ex-wife's name off that bullet and use it on you. Quit screwing around and let me hear the tape."

Angus played the tape of his interview with Lumas. Gabe listened intently until he pushed the *Stop* button at the end. Angus asked, "What do you think?"

Gabe stared at him in disbelief. "Boy, you sure gave him a lot of crap. I can't do that. I don't know him as well as you do."

"You don't have to, Gabe. Insist on the Garrity warning and don't be specific in any of your answers. Just stick to your story that we only used enough force to affect the arrest. If he asks how many times we hit Usher, just say it was dark and you can't recall. I said I didn't see anything you did. Just say you didn't see anything that I did. It's our word against Usher's. They can't do anything to us."

Gabe thought for a minute, then said, "I don't know, Angus. I'm not going to burn you, but I don't think I can pull this off. I hate having to lie like this. I just hope the D.A. buys it."

"He probably won't buy it, but he's not going to prosecute us over a shit-bag like Usher. He has no jury appeal. No jury would take his word over two, clean-cut, gorgeous studs like us, trust me."

Angus got up and walked to the door. He turned and said, "If Lumas gets in your face, just tell him that I said I'd ruin his life if he screws with us. He'll know what you're talking about. Call me tomorrow and let me know how it went." He pitched the recorder to Gabe. "Wear this. I'd like to hear how you do."

When he closed the door, Gabe laid the recorder on the orange crate and went back to bed. Again, sleep would not come. In addition to the pain of his divorce, he now had the anxiety of the upcoming interview to rob him of sleep.

2

LEN SHELLEY FINISHED the car inspections, and the officers scattered to the ends of the city. Gabe was the roving car again, so he was busy. Shelley called him at 3:00 to meet him down by the lake.

Gabe drove down the dark gravel road to the lake. Shelley was sitting on a picnic bench eating fried chicken gizzards. Gabe shut down his car and strolled up to him. He sat on the bench by Shelley and waited. Shelley shoved the grease-soaked box toward him and asked, "Hey, Gabe, gizzard?"

He looked into the box and turned up his nose. "No, I don't think so. That's black people food. Us white folks don't eat entrails."

Shelley's belly bounced as he laughed. "Oh, yes you do, whitey. Don't kid yourself, boy, you white folks eat anything that we black folks do. It was a white woman who showed me how good gizzards are. I've been hooked on them ever since."

He again shook his head and turned up his nose. Shelley said, "Boy, let me tell you a story. I used to work traffic. We were evaluated on how many tickets we wrote. Not a good system, I know, but I used to stop over two hundred cars a month. I used to get a big box of fried gizzards and some onion rings. I'd dip the gizzards in gravy and eat in the car while I worked. Those gizzards and onion rings made my breath smell so bad that no one ever

23

argued with me. They wanted me to talk as little as possible. They just wanted their ticket so they could go on their way. It was great. All the other officers were getting cussed out and argued with. I had very few problems. The only arguments I got were from people with worse breath than mine, and that wasn't many. You'll never be a real policeman until you've been divorced, suspended, ruined your liver with liquor, and learned to like fried livers and gizzards. You're already divorced, just three to go."

A gentle breeze blew across the lake. Gabe sat quietly in the moonlight and listened to the crunching gizzards being ground up between Shelley's teeth. He finally said, "I'm worried about my interview in the morning, sarge. Blauw talked trash to Lumas and he backed off. That won't work for me. I'm not going to burn Blauw, but I know I'm going to draw some time off if they think I'm holding out on them. The chief doesn't like me. He hasn't forgotten the time that I arrested that councilman. He showed up drunk at the car stop and tried to make me let the councilman go. I had to threaten to arrest the chief to get him to back off. He's just waiting for a chance to rip me."

Shelley laid the box on the bench and wiped his mouth on his sleeve. As he wiped his hands on his pant legs he pondered Gabe's predicament. He said, "You know, Gabe, it was that incident that won you the respect of the other guys on the department. You did the right thing. That took balls. That's why we like you. You ain't afraid of anyone. I know Garrison holds grudges. I wish I could put your mind at ease, but I can't. You may draw some time off, but they won't fire you."

Gabe sighed and looked up at the stars. He shook his head as the lack of sleep and stress of the past few months raised a lump in his throat. He fought back his emotions and said, "I can't take a suspension, sarge. I'm barely making it from check to check. I've stalled off my creditors as long as I can. If I lose one day's pay, I'll go under. And why should I get time off? Angus is the one who wouldn't quit beating Usher when he'd had enough."

Shelley heart went out to Gabe. He put his fatherly arm around Gabe's shoulders and began his lecture. "Listen to this old black man, boy. I know what you're going through. I've been there many times. I use to be so poor that I couldn't afford to pay attention. Don't get discouraged. Those bill collectors will wait.

24

As long as you're making an effort, they'll wait. Just don't let them scare you. You need to sit down with me and I'll help you make out a budget. You're trying to pay everyone else and you're killing yourself. You gotta put yourself first. Those creditors ain't going hungry. You need to start paying yourself before you pay them. Figure out how much money you need to get by and hold it back. And listen, boy, don't worry about a suspension. We have a charity fund that the staff doesn't know about. When an officer gets suspended or hurt and hasn't got any sick days, we all chip in on payday to get him enough money to keep him afloat till he starts drawing his pay again. We'll do the same for you. And I know it's not fair, kid, but you can't rat out another officer, not ever! This suspension will be a badge of honor when it's all over. Just be the man that I know you are. Sometimes you have to take a bullet for another officer. That's what makes us heroes."

Gabe looked up at Shelley and said, "Thanks, I guess. I'm sure you know what you're talking about, but I can't take money from you guys, sarge. All you guys have wives and kids depending on you. I can't take food out of their mouths."

Shelley squeezed Gabe's neck and lectured him sternly. "You ain't taking food out of anyone's mouth, boy. You're forgetting, we may all have wives and kids, but you're family, too. I can't sit down at my table and enjoy a meal if I know one of you is sitting home starving. It breaks my heart. Now quit being a martyr. We're a tight family here and we take care of our own until someone demonstrates that he's not one of our family. He does that by ratting out another cop. You're one of us now. You're one of my kids just as much as my own flesh and blood. Let us help you, boy. It's as much for the officers' benefit as it is for yours."

He felt uneasy with Shelley's show of affection. He sat quietly for a few seconds, then said, "Thanks, sarge, but I'm still worried. Blauw told me to just be vague and say I don't remember the specifics. I don't think Garrison will let me get away with that."

"No, he probably won't, but just stick by your guns. You'll come out better than you think."

Gabe stood and looked out across the moonlit lake. He turned to go to his car, and Shelley picked up the box of gizzards.

25

Shelley gave him one last piece of encouragement. "Remember, boy, never let the bastards see you sweat. We've all been through the fire before and came through it okay. They haven't fired anyone around here in years, and I know guys who have done a lot worse than kicking the guts out of a shithead." Gabe didn't answer and waved as he walked away.

Gabe was numb from lack of sleep when the sun rose slowly over the horizon. His interview with Detective Lumas was scheduled for 10:00. It was purposely scheduled so late in the morning so Gabe would be at his worst. He sat in the waiting room for another hour. He could no longer keep his eyes open and drifted off to sleep.

Lumas checked on him periodically and decided that any sleep at all would refresh Kinnett to some degree. When he saw Gabe dozing, he stepped out and called him into the office.

Once in the interview room, Gabe saw the tape recorder on the table and Chief Robert Garrison seated against the wall. His anxiety level shot through the roof when he looked into Garrison's angry glare. Garrison was present purely as an intimidation factor.

Lumas asked, "Ready to start, Gabe?"

Gabe rubbed his tired eyes and said, "Not if this is a criminal investigation. I want to exercise my right to remain silent."

Lumas had expected this response. Rather than waste time arguing the point, he simply slid a Garrity warning across the desk. Gabe signed it and slid it back.

Lumas put the lead on the tape and began the interview.

Lumas: "State your name for the record."
Kinnett: "Gabriel T. Kinnett."
Lumas: "Were you present when Officer Blauw arrested the Reverend Tyrone Usher?"
Kinnett: "Yes."
Lumas: "Did you witness the events leading up to the car stop?"
Kinnett: "No"
Lumas: "Did you witness Officer Blauw attempt to arrest the reverend?"
Kinnett: "Yes."

26

Lumas: "Did you see the reverend resist arrest in any way?"

Kinnett: "Yes, he tried to punch Officer Blauw."

Lumas: "What did Officer Blauw say or do to provoke the reverend?"

Kinnett: "Nothing. Usher's attack was unprovoked."

Lumas: "What happened then?"

Kinnett: "Officer Blauw and I forced Usher to the ground and handcuffed him."

Lumas: "How many times did you punch or kick the r reverend?"

Kinnett: "None."

Lumas: "How many times did Officer Blauw punch or kick the reverend?"

Kinnett: "One that I know of."

Lumas: "Have you seen the injuries suffered by the reverend?"

Kinnett: "Only those injuries suffered at the scene. I have no idea what injuries he may have inflicted upon himself to strengthen his claim of excessive force."

Lumas slid some photographs across the table and instructed Gabe to look at them. Gabe shuffled through them quickly and slid them back to Lumas. The questioning resumed.

Lumas: "Did you see these injuries the night of the arrest?"

Kinnett: "No."

Lumas: "I'll ask you again to tell the truth. How many times did Blauw hit Usher?"

Kinnett: "I told you the truth the first time, I only saw one."

Lumas: "Are you aware of the penalty for lying to internal affairs?"

Kinnett: "I assume it's the same penalty as for an internal affairs investigator who conspires with a suspect to manufacture false charges against a police officer."

Lumas: "Why are you lying to cover for Officer Blauw?"

Kinnett: "I'm not lying. Why are you assisting Usher in making a false complaint against one of your own? You're certainly not being objective."

Garrison had heard enough. He motioned for Lumas to stop the tape recorder. Lumas pushed the *Stop* button and Garrison stood so he could tower over Gabe. He gritted his teeth and growled, "Who do you think you are? You're a punk! You're not fit to shine Detective Lumas's shoes, let alone accuse him of corruption."

Gabe was exhausted and not prepared to battle the chief. He just wanted to survive the interview so he could go to bed. He was furious, but had to choose his words wisely so he didn't give Garrison cause to suspend him for insubordination. "With all due respect, Chief, Detective Lumas is the one who's making the false accusations. He's clearly not objective in this investigation. That's evident by the way he's structuring the questions. He deliberately scheduled this interview to cause me the maximum discomfort. He knows I work midnights and this is the middle of my night. You and he also made me wait an extra hour to cause me more discomfort from lack of sleep. No, Chief, I think my accusations are accurate. As far as his record goes, I can produce several witnesses who will attest to his past performance if you'll let me make a phone call. They've assured me that they would be here in five minutes if Detective Lumas's character came into question."

Garrison slammed his fist down on the desk and yelled, "His integrity is not in question here! Yours and Blauw's is! If you or anyone else had evidence of misconduct by Lumas, you should have brought it to my attention at that time! I won't even listen to it now! You either quit lying in this interview or get out of here and take your lumps! This is your last chance to tell me the truth about what Blauw did to the reverend!"

Gabe leaned back in his chair as Garrison yelled at him. When Garrison had finished, he stood erect with his hands on his hips, waiting to see what Gabe would do. Gabe slowly stood and turned to leave. Garrison stopped him before he could get out the door. "Before you go, leave your badge, commission card and weapon on the desk. You're suspended until I decide what disciplinary action is appropriate. Before this thing is over, Kinnett, I'm going to show you how the big boys play hardball."

Gabe pulled his badge case from his jacket pocket and laid it on the desk. He said, "You can take department issued property, but the gun is mine. I'll hang on to it." He walked out the door with no further comment.

Lumas looked at Garrison and said, "He's not going to crack, Chief. We may have made a mistake by interviewing him when he was so tired. He's not thinking straight. Maybe if he'd had more sleep, he'd think clearer and fess up."

Garrison grumbled, "Maybe you're right, Ezard. I thought he'd scare easier if he were tired. I'll give him a few days to worry. He'll soften up."

Gabe went home and collapsed on his sofa. He was surprised at how well he slept. Although his job was at stake, not having to work that night eliminated the pressure to sleep. If he couldn't sleep, he would have a few days to rest up. He was almost happy to be on suspension. The break would do him good.

Gabe awoke at 4:00 in the afternoon to pounding on his door and a barrage of swearing in the hall. He instantly knew Blauw was outside. The profanity and deep raspy voice left no question as to his identity.

He didn't bother to put on his pants. He stumbled to the door in his underwear and jerked it open without looking through the peephole. Blauw and Shelley were standing there with big smiles on their faces.

As they charged in, both patted Gabe on the back. Shelley said, "Congratulations, Kinnett, you've just taken one more step toward becoming a real policeman. You're suspended."

Blauw laughed as he picked up the tape recorder on the orange crate and turned it on. "Hey, Len, let's hear how our boy did."

After Garrison's threat, Blauw pushed the *Stop* button and growled, "That phony prick. He didn't have the nuts to sit in on my interview. I've got too much shit on him."

Gabe pulled the covers up to his waist. Seeing no other place to sit, Shelley and Blauw sat on the edge of the sofa. Gabe said, "Angus, I'm not sure it does any good to keep a little black book on people. If you don't use it at the time, it doesn't do any good. No one listens if you wait too long. I don't think anything you say about Lumas would make a difference to Garrison."

Shelley agreed. "That's right, Angus. If you're holding on to some old trump card and counting on it to bail you out of a pinch, you're making a big mistake. If you got something on someone, you'd better use it when you get it. You lose all of your credibility if you wait too long."

Blauw shook his head arrogantly. "Nah, that's just for little stuff. I've got some big hammers hanging over Lumas and Garrison. There's no statute of limitations on the shit that those guys have pulled. They won't tangle with me."

Shelley rubbed his eyes and shook his head in frustration at Blauw's stubbornness, then turned to Gabe. "Remember our conversation last night, boy? Don't worry about this mess. We'll take care of you until you get on your feet."

"You can't take care of me forever, sarge. If Garrison fires me, I'm through."

"Ain't gonna happen, boy! Garrison's just bluffing you. He'll let you sweat for a few days, then interview you again. Just do this. Ask him if he's going to ask you different questions than the ones he asked you today. If he says yes, go in. If he says no, tell him to refer to your original answers. You gotta follow orders, so if he orders you to come in, you gotta do it, but just use the same answers as this morning. If you give different answers, they'll hang you for lying for sure."

Gabe stretched and yawned. "Well, sarge, at this point, I don't care. I'm going to catch up on my sleep and take my lumps. You were right. My creditors will take what I can afford to send them. I'm going to start taking care of me."

Shelley slapped Gabe's leg. "Good boy! Listen, tonight if you can't sleep, come out and ride with me. I don't want you sitting here getting depressed."

He and Blauw stood and walked toward the door. Gabe pulled the covers up under his chin and didn't respond when they said goodnight and closed the door behind them.

Gabe walked into shift briefing his first night back. He was two minutes late, so everyone was already seated when he walked in. Everyone in the room stood and applauded as he hurried to his seat.

Although embarrassed, he bowed to the crowd and sat down. Shelley stopped applauding and yelled, "Okay! Okay, that's enough! We're making the lad blush. Let's get shift briefing over so you guys can get on the road."

Shelley hurried through the pass-on information, then walked to the rear lot to inspect the cars. When he returned to his office, Gabe was waiting. He sat down, leaned back and said, "Evening, bad boy, how does it feel to be back to work?"

"I don't know. I'm a little embarrassed I guess."

Shelley sat down and glanced over his payroll sheet. He smiled and said, "Don't be embarrassed, kid. You did the right thing. No cop worth his weight in salt can go his whole career without getting a suspension or two. I drew a few days off myself a few years back."

"You did? What happened?"

"Wrecked a car while I was in a pursuit. I busted a stop sign and wiped out a bread truck. Totaled my car. The chief back then was a crusty old fart named Bella. He climbed up my black ass with a chain saw and cut his way out, then gave me three days off for careless operation of the police car. The city bought the bread company a new truck and paid the driver's doctor bill. If you're trying to do a good job, things will go wrong sometimes. It's just going to happen. You shouldn't be embarrassed, you're a hero."

Gabe stared at the floor and sighed. "I don't feel like a hero. I feel like a fool. Angus beat the brains out of the guy and he got off with nothing. I just refused to sell him out and I got a day suspension. Doesn't seem fair."

Shelley leaned forward and placed his arms on the desk. "It's not fair, Gabe, but that's just the way Garrison is. He isn't fair or consistent with his discipline. He lets his personality override his good judgment. Blauw got off because there wasn't enough evidence to warrant suspending him. You got suspended because you pissed off Garrison. He kept your suspension under three days because you can't appeal anything less than three days to the city personnel board. He can do anything he wants and no one can challenge him as long as he keeps his discipline less than three days off. That's why I knew he wouldn't fire you. He couldn't make a long-term suspension or termination stick with the personnel board. He couldn't justify it, and the members of the board hate his guts."

Gabe considered Shelley's explanation. "So, why didn't he hammer Blauw? He could have given him a short suspension without the personnel board knowing about it."

"Yeah, he could have, but Blauw has something on him. I don't know what, but Garrison is afraid of him. You may not know it, but from the day that Blauw got hired, he's spent all his time following staff officers around when they were off duty. Since he works midnights, he's working when they're out carousing. When he sees one of their cars, he parks his car and tries to find them. He's caught some of these guys in some pretty embarrassing positions. He even bought a video camera and taped them. I don't know what he's got on Garrison and Lumas, but they're afraid to strap him on."

Gabe said, "I wish he would have called in a few markers for me this time. I can't afford this suspension."

Shelley leaned into Gabe and chastised him. "What did I tell you, boy? Didn't I tell you we take care of our own?" He opened his center drawer and removed a white envelope. He flipped it across the desk to Gabe. "Now, open that, boy, and don't ever doubt me again."

The big smile on Shelley's face made Gabe suspicious. He opened the bulging envelope and removed a thick stack of twenties. He choked up and asked, "Where did you get this?"

"The charity fund. Your family here took up a collection and made up your lost pay. Even that old wreck, Blauw, felt bad. He gave most of it out of his own pocket. I think the old corpse felt guilty about getting you in trouble. He'll never be able to force himself to apologize, but I know he feels bad. I guess he thinks he can make it up to you by paying for your suspension. There's even some extra. Take it out and buy yourself a bed. I felt like a flaming queer sitting on your sofa with you half naked."

Gabe tried to talk, but Shelley cut him off. "I know what you're going to say, boy, and I don't want to hear it. Just take the money and get your young ass out of my office. Get out in your car and go to work."

He was truly humbled. He stood and walked toward the door. As he walked out, Shelley stopped him and said, "Boy, you were late for shift briefing again. Get to work on time or you're going to have some more suspension days on your record. Got me?"

He turned and smiled at Shelley. "Sure, boss, I got you."

So far, the night had been quiet, and a cool northern-Pacific drizzle drove everyone inside, making the city look deserted. This was the kind of night that the officers enjoyed. After they had checked their businesses, they would pair up and shoot the breeze.

The rhythm of the windshield wipers made Gabe even sleepier. He had been on the road for about an hour when the radio silence was broken. The dispatcher's voice quivered with stress as she sent Ramón Carlos and Deloris Gapky to investigate a homicide.

He heard the sirens sound off in the distance. The dispatcher said the paramedics and the sergeant were also responding. Being the roving car, Gabe felt obligated to assist. He notified the dispatcher that he was responding also.

The dispatcher told all officers that the suspect was still at the scene. Reaves and Blackman volunteered to respond and were not called off by Shelley. With an armed murder suspect at the scene, too much help was better than too little.

Gabe arrived just as the first two officers parked half a block down the street and ran toward the apartment building where the homicide was reported. It was called in by a neighbor who had heard a gunshot and reported that the suspect was sitting on the front steps.

All units shut off their lights and sirens several blocks from the scene so the suspect would not get spooked. Gabe drove to the rear of the building to block the suspect's escape. He took up a position just outside the rear door. He cracked open the slide of his .45 to make sure there was a round in the chamber.

Seeing no one inside, he entered and walked down the hall until he could see out the front door. Through the front door glass, he saw a white teenage boy sitting on the top step. He was crying and rocking back and forth.

Ramón yelled orders at the boy to drop his gun. Gabe moved to a position of cover just inside the front door behind the suspect. He wanted to keep the boy from re-entering the apartment building and taking a hostage.

He was only about three feet inside the glass door and could hear the boy clearly. He was crying hysterically and repeating, "Why did I do it? Why did I do it? I can't believe I shot him!"

Ramón was saying all the right things, but the boy was not responding. Shelley arrived and was positioning officers where he needed them. The ambulance arrived and staged a block away.

Ramón was having little success establishing a dialogue with the boy. Frustrated by the boy's hysteria, Shelley joined in and tried to bring the boy back to reality.

Finally, the boy responded to something that Shelley had said and looked at him. Shelley seized the moment and instructed everyone else to be quiet so the boy wouldn't be confused about who to talk to. He pleaded, "Son! Son! Now listen to me, son! Everything's going to be alright! My name is Len. You remember me, son? You used to be my paperboy. Talk to me, son!"

The boy continued to cry hysterically and moved the muzzle of the pistol under his chin. Gabe could tell by the position of the boy's arms that he had the gun under his chin. The boy looked at Shelley and cried, "I killed him! I killed him! Why did I do that? I didn't even know him! I can't believe I did that! I'm not that kind of person!"

The boy cried uncontrollably. Sensing his intent to kill himself, Shelley's voice cracked with emotion as he pleaded frantically. "No! No, son, you're not! Just listen to me! I know you! You're a good boy! I've known you a long time! You're not a murderer! We can sort this thing out! Just don't pull that trigger!"

Gabe saw the terror on Shelley's face when the boy pulled the hammer back. Shelley was losing his objectivity and getting emotionally involved. He was the wrong person to be trying to talk this kid down. Gabe wanted to get Blauw on the scene, but he was on his night off.

Shelley continued to plead with the boy, but to no avail. The boy cried that he'd killed someone that he didn't know and had let his parents down. Shelley had unconsciously forgotten his own safety. He'd stepped out from behind cover and was inching closer to the boy.

Carlos and Gapky yelled at Shelley to come back, but he couldn't hear them. In addition to tunnel vision, he had developed auditory exclusion. He could not see or hear anything except the boy. The scene was utter chaos, intensified by total panic. The boy was crying hysterically. The officers were yelling at Shelley, and Shelley was yelling at the boy.

Gabe wanted to intervene, but knew if he stepped out the door, he would be in the direct line of fire from the officers on the street. He tried to get the boy's attention through the glass, hoping he could distract him long enough for Shelley to tackle him. His shouts went unheard. There was too much noise and hysteria on the other side of the glass.

By now, Shelley was running toward the boy, screaming, "No! No! No!" Gabe knew Shelley would be killed if the boy changed his mind about suicide and turned his gun on Shelley. Shelley had holstered his pistol to demonstrate to the boy that he meant him no harm.

Someone had to intervene. As Gabe grabbed the handle of the door the whole world seemed to stop turning. Everyone moved in slow motion, and sounds were amplified. He heard a muffled pop as the back of the boy's head exploded. Blood and tissue splattered on the glass door. The boy fell back on the landing, lifeless with his eyes fixed on the sky. Gabe jerked away in shock.

Shelley stopped yelling. He staggered to a stop and collapsed to his hands and knees in grief. Reaves and Blackman had been running toward Shelley to tackle him for his own safety. They staggered to a stop and leaned over Shelley to comfort him.

There was complete silence as the finality of the shot sank in. Everyone looked at each other in disbelief. Gabe staggered toward the back door and cried. The boy reminded him of his younger brother.

Shelley slowly stood with the assistance of Reaves and Blackman. He leaned his head back and let the rain splatter in his face, then staggered over to a row of parked cars and beat the side windows out of a truck with his forearms and elbows. Reaves and Blackman charged him and seized him by the arms so he wouldn't injure himself.

The crime lab showed up to process the scene. The murdered man was lying just inside the front door of his apartment. The coroner's assistants transported the bodies to the morgue. Len Shelley was taken to the station to recover. The detective sergeant assumed command of the scene, and Charlie Schumacher assumed command of the shift until Shelley could regain his composure.

The murdered man was Jonathan Lynch. He'd been a prominent Salem divorce attorney who had made a name for himself by handling high profile divorces. The boy was Tommy Ryan. He was an unassuming kid with no arrest record or history of violent episodes. At last, his torment was over. He had been right all along. His parents were devastated.

Gabe was in the station when Tommy's parents came in to talk to the detectives. He'd held over his shift waiting for the records unit to open. He needed a case file for an upcoming court appearance. He found himself sitting a few feet from Tommy's parents. He didn't want to appear nosey, so he pretended to read a magazine.

Both parents were almost dysfunctional from grief. Mrs. Ryan couldn't speak a complete sentence without falling to pieces. Mr. Ryan was bitter and angry. He looked like a man who was shell shocked. His eyes were red and open wide. The grief poured out of them and consumed everyone in close proximity. Gabe choked with emotion as he was drawn into their pain.

He thought about leaving and coming back after the records unit opened, but he was mesmerized by the Ryans' conversation. He had seen parents who'd refused to admit that their child could do anything wrong and blamed the world for their problems, but most of them knew deep inside that their kids were wrong.

These people were different. They'd never had an ounce of trouble with Tommy. He'd never even talked back to them. He was a little paranoid, but he was genuinely a good kid who could never hurt anyone. Murdering someone was completely out of character for him. Mr. and Mrs. Ryan were at a loss to explain what had gone wrong.

He listened as both parents tried to figure out who Lynch was. They had never heard of him and couldn't figure out how Tommy had come to know him. Both were still in the denial stage of their grief. They refused to believe that Tommy could murder a complete stranger for no reason.

Mr. and Mrs. Ryan moved like two people who had been paralyzed by strokes. Tommy was their only son and their reason for living. The pain emanating from them was overpowering and infected everyone in the room.

The oldest detective on the department was handling the case. Ben Hire had been a homicide investigator for over twenty years and was highly respected in his field. Even as he ushered the Ryans into his office, he took the time to speak to Gabe. "Hi, Gabe. Sorry to hear about your problems. If you need to talk, let me know."

Gabe was sincerely touched. He and Ben had never talked, and it surprised him that a stranger would show him such compassion. Ben was certainly no Ezard Lumas. He gratefully thanked Ben and went back to reading his magazine.

After getting his files for court, Gabe walked home totally confused. Why would a good kid like Tommy kill a total stranger? He hadn't seen many murders in his short career, but this one puzzled him. There had to be a connection somewhere. The Ryans were right. Tommy wouldn't do something like that without a reason.

Gabe was in the garage two nights later talking with Victor Lyzett about the shooting. Victor had been off that night and wanted the gory details. Shelley was late for inspection, so Gabe stuck his head back in the station to see where he was. Shelley and Hire were standing inside the squad room. He couldn't help but overhear their conversation.

Hire said, "Len, I've been a detective for twenty-five years and never seen anything like this. That kid had never heard of Lynch and had absolutely no motive to drop the hammer on him like that. I can't figure out what made him do it. He was a little paranoid, but not severe enough to send him over the edge."

Shelley was shaking his head as Ben talked. "I know, Ben, I've known that kid since he was a runt, and that was not

37

something that he would do. I saw him just before he killed himself. It was like he'd been in a trance and suddenly snapped out of it when he realized that he'd killed Lynch. He was absolutely shocked that he'd do something like that. It was like he'd just awoken from a bad dream and realized it was real. I don't care what anyone says, that kid would never do something like that. There's something spooky about this."

Ben nodded in agreement. "I know, but I don't know what we can do about it. He killed himself before we could talk to him. We interviewed his parents, but they had no idea who Lynch was, and couldn't believe that Tommy had killed him. There is no link between Lynch and Tommy. Usually a random murder without motive is the work of serial killer, but this beats anything I've ever seen. There has to be a connection somewhere. I'm going to work on this for a few more days. I just can't put it to sleep without hooking those two together."

Gabe met Shelley after inspection and said, "Sarge! I didn't mean to eavesdrop, but I couldn't help overhearing your conversation with Ben Hire. What's going to happen with that shooting?"

Shelley shrugged his shoulders. "Probably nothing, Gabe. The suspect is dead and there's no one to prosecute. No point wasting resources on a case that won't go anywhere. I'm sure puzzled though. I knew that kid, and unless there was something I wasn't aware of, he just wasn't capable of hurting anyone. I saw his eyes just before he pulled the trigger. He acted like he'd been under a hypnotic spell when he killed Lynch, and woke up when the gun went off. We'll probably never find out what set him off."

A knot swelled up in Gabe's stomach from the fear of what he had to say, but he had to get it off his chest. "Listen, sarge, I know what I'm about to say is going to piss you off, but I've got to say it. You've told me that we're all family. Sometimes family members have to tell other members when they're screwing up because no one else will. You were way out of line the other night. You gave up your position of cover and could have gotten yourself killed. You endangered the lives of the other officers who gave up their position of cover to save you. I know you cared about that kid, but you could have got yourself or other officers killed. I'm sorry, but you need to hear that."

Shelley stared at Gabe in shock. Gabe gritted his teeth and waited for the explosive retort from the big man. It didn't come. Shelley affectionately patted Gabe on the back and said, "Why, thanks, Gabe. You're right, I was out of line, and I'm touched that you think enough of me to say that. I would string another officer up for doing something like that, but when I looked in the eyes of that boy, I saw my own son sitting there. I appreciate you telling me that."

Gabe gave a visible sigh of relief as he broke into a nervous smile. "Boy, that's a relief, sarge. I thought sure you'd bite my head off."

Shelley shook his head. "No, I was out of line. I'm just glad none of the ladder-climbers were there. You know, the chief would have my stripes if he found out about this. You wouldn't say anything about it to anyone, would you?"

Gabe chuckled, "Not even if they tortured me. If I wouldn't roll over on Blauw for stomping the religion out of the pope, I wouldn't burn you for trying to save a kid's life."

Shelley laughed and patted Gabe hard on the back. "Attaboy!" He instantly frowned at Gabe and growled, "But make no mistake, boy, don't you never let me catch you doing something like that! I'll kick your young ass up between your shoulder blades, boy!"

Gabe reached over and patted Shelley's protruding stomach. "I'm not worried, boss. I don't think you can get your foot up that high." Shelley stopped in mid-stride and glared at Gabe as he walked away laughing.

Ramón Carlos turned off his lights and coasted quietly up beside Gabe's car. He positioned his car so that the driver's window would be next to Gabe's window. He knew this was Gabe's favorite sleeping place when Sgt. Shelley was at the station.

It was overcast and drizzling rain very lightly. There were no streetlights to illuminate the cruiser. Ramón rolled his window down and waited for his eyes to adjust to the darkness. He was going to pound on the driver's window to startle Gabe, but he had a better idea.

When his eyes adjusted, he quietly wiped the water off of Gabe's window so he could see inside. As expected, Gabe was seated behind the wheel with his chin on his chest. He was out for the count.

Ramón turned on his spotlight and focused it on the side of Gabe's face. From two feet away the 230,000 candlepower light shining through the wet glass created intense heat on the side of Gabe's head.

Ramón could no longer contain himself as sweat poured down Gabe's face. He was laughing so hard that he was snorting as he gasped for air.

Gabe was sleeping soundly, so it took a minute for him to awake. His face, hair and shirt were drenched with sweat. He could no longer sleep through the intense heat. He jerked his head up and stared straight ahead for a few seconds, trying to figure out why he was dripping with sweat. He suddenly realized that there was a bright light to his left. He jerked his head quickly and screamed.

The light was so close that it appeared to be a large vehicle heading straight toward him at a high rate of speed. He opened his eyes and mouth wide, covered his face with his arms and laid over in the seat, bracing for the impact.

When he felt no impact, he unclenched his teeth and opened his eyes. All he could hear was a man laughing hysterically. He sat up quickly just as Ramón flipped off the spotlight. He rolled down his window and yelled at Ramón. "You asshole! You trying to give me a heart attack?"

The drizzle had stopped. Ramón was laughing too hard to answer. He finally caught this breath enough to say, "That's what you get for sleeping on the train tracks, man. You had to know there'd be a freighter coming through here sooner or later. Just be glad it was a train and not Shelley."

Gabe shouted, "Pull up so I can get out for a minute!"

Ramón wiped the tears from his eyes and asked, "Why?"

He looked sternly at Ramón. "So I can wipe the sweat from my face and kick your greasy Cuban ass all the way back to Castro's jail where you belong." Ramón again broke into hysterical laughter as he pulled forward enough for Gabe to step out.

Gabe stripped his utility belt and laid it on the hood of his cruiser. He then removed his uniform shirt and opened the back door. He reached into his exercise bag and got a clean towel. As he stood there wiping himself off, Ramón came back and stood beside him. He leaned against Gabe's cruiser and said with his thick Cuban accent, "You know, Gabe, I've been watching you. You're a good officer, man. You're also a good person. Why did your wife leave you? She must have been a real gold-digging bitch, man."

Gabe leaned against the car beside Ramón as he looked up at the clouds. "Well, Ramón, I guess she figured she could do better in life than me. I've asked myself that same question a million times. I don't have the answer."

His under shirt splattered sweat as Ramón reached behind him and patted him on the back. He said, "That's her loss, man. Listen to me, man, I know human nature. I know good people when I see them. She'll never do better than you, man."

The show of affection touched Gabe. He hung his head and said, "I don't know, Ramón, sometimes I think she was right. I've been screwed up for so long that I'm not sure what's right or wrong anymore. All I know is that I hate crooks and staff officers. They're all cut out of the same cloth. I'd just as soon put a bullet in all of them. You guys are the only family I have. Well, the other guys are, you're a sneaky piece of crap."

Ramón bent over and laughed hysterically. Between heaves he muttered, "Man, you should have seen your face! You thought you were dead meat! I wish I had a video of that! That's the funniest thing I ever saw!"

Gabe finally chuckled. He shook his head as he looked at Ramón. Ramón laughed even harder when he again saw his sweaty face. When the laughter died, Ramón took on a serious demeanor. "Listen, man, the real reason I want to talk to you is I know you're having some problems. Me and other guys want to help. We chipped in and paid for your suspension, but that's not enough."

Gabe was embarrassed. "Yeah, I know. I never would have accepted the money if Shelley hadn't been so forceful. I want you to know I really appreciated that."

41

Ramón held his hand up to stop Gabe. "No need for thanks. You're blood, man. Blauw told us how you stood up to Lumas and Garrison. You got steel balls, man."

Gabe wiped his face and head with the towel, then looked at the ground as he wiped the sweat from the back of his neck. He said, "I'd trade them for steel brains. I've shot myself in the foot with Garrison. I'll never get ahead in this department."

"What are you saying, man? You wouldn't give up one of your own kind, would you?"

"No, but I should have done things differently. I should have been more tactful and diplomatic. Staff officers take it personal when you insult them."

"Yeah, I know what you mean, man. Garrison would like to ship me back to Cuba on a leaky boat after my last reprimand. But things will get better someday, man. When guys like Garrison, Richey and Lumas retire, guys like you and me will get promoted. Things will get better then, right?"

Gabe sighed and shrugged his shoulders. He looked at Ramón and asked, "What if guys like you and me become guys like Garrison and Lumas when we get promoted? Maybe Garrison and Lumas were jam-up guys when they were on the road. Maybe there are reasons they become cannibals when they move up the ladder. What if they have no choice? What if they hate what they've become, but can't control it? What if a set of stripes or bars automatically turns you into a shark?"

Ramón thought for a minute, then said, "Can't be, man, look at Shelley. He wouldn't sell out one of us. He's black, but he treats us all like family, no matter what color we are. He loves us like his own kids, man. He'll never be a rat, no matter how much rank he gets."

Gabe nodded as he considered Ramón's analogy. "I'd like to think your right, but who knows? Maybe he'd have no choice. A man can only take so much heat before he has to pass it on. I don't think even Shelley would give up his stripes for one of us. If we put him in a bad position, he'd do what he had to do."

"I don't know, man, I liked you better when you wanted to shoot them. I don't believe you ever have to compromise your convictions. I think you can be a staff officer and still have some compassion for your officers. You may have to suspend a guy, but

42

you can at least act like you're sorry you have to do it. You can let him know that he's still a valuable employee and not make him feel like it's a personal grudge. I wouldn't mind if you were a captain or major and had to suspend me. I know you'd feel bad about it and wouldn't hold it against me for the rest of my career. These guys get it in for you and you're scum for the rest of your life. The only way to get back in their good graces is to kiss their ass. I can't do that, man."

Gabe folded his wet towel and laid it on the roof of the car. He said, "Well, pal, I'm having a pretty tough time with that myself. Can't say I blame you."

He picked up his dry shirt and put it on. Ramón said, "One other thing, man, I want to help you with women."

He looked confused at Ramón and laughed. "You want to help me? What qualifies you as an expert?"

Ramón looked sternly at him and patted himself on the chest. "No! Seriously, man, I am an expert. Listen, man, I've watched you. You're a lonely guy. You want a woman, but you're just not confident enough. I don't know about many things, but let me assure you, my sweaty little Anglo bro, I am an expert on women. Let me give you some pointers, man."

Gabe laughed and shook his head. He unzipped his pants and opened the waistband so he could tuck in his shirttail. Ramón continued, "Listen up, bro, you got to understand women like I do. Women are emotionally weak, man. They need a man in their life to feel complete. All this women's lib shit is just a smoke screen to try to convince themselves that they don't need men. You know, *I am woman, hear me roar*. They won't admit it, but it's true, except for the lesbians of course. They're just that way because they never had a man like me in bed. But that only goes for the good-looking lesbians, man. Most of them are so butt-ugly and obnoxious that no man can stand to be around them. They have to settle for someone like them if they want sex. Here's some sure-fire ways to get a woman, man."

Gabe was laughing loudly at Ramón's philosophy and gyrations. Ramón continued, "No! No, listen, man, first of all, you got to set your sights high. It's just as easy to get a good-looking woman as it is to get a cow. Don't settle for ugly or fat women, man. Foxes need love, too. Also, don't chase these street queens or groupies. They'll just drain your checking account and give you the clap. Besides, they'll screw around on you and drive you crazy with jealousy, man. Find yourself a good-looking, professional woman. Always date women who have more money than you. You ought to see this good-looking psychiatrist that I've been hitting on. I'm this close to parting her thighs, man."

Gabe continued to laugh as he said, "Good for you, pal, but finding a woman with more money than me won't be hard. A homeless bag-lady has more money than I do."

Ramón's Cuban machismo surged as he continued, "And listen, man, you gotta make women feel special. Even if you don't love them, you have to tell them you do. Tell them they're beautiful, even if you don't think they are. When they start talking about their problems, you gotta learn how to look at them and nod your head, even when your mind is a million miles away. If they cook you dinner, you gotta close your eyes, smile and moan with ecstasy, even if it tastes like shit, man. When you have sex with them, you gotta learn to perform oral sex on them. Women love that, man. That's why it's important to get yourself a good-looking, clean woman. Don't settle for some nasty old douche bag, man. Dirty women are nasty in bed. Now! You gotta pretend that they're the best piece of ass that you've ever had, at least until you're ready to dump them. When you've had all of them you can stand, then you can tell them the truth, but it's not a good idea to dump one until you have another lined up. Always keep a future first-stringer warming up in the bull-pin. Trust me, man, I know. Have you ever seen me with an ugly woman? Not on your life! Stick with me, man, I'll get you a fine looking woman!"

After a minute, Gabe finally stopped laughing at Ramón. He said, "You know? I don't know how I ever managed without you. I appreciate your guidance, Casanova, but I think I can do okay on my own."

Ramón threw his hands up in frustration. "Okay, man, but I'm telling you, you need my help. If I had been in your corner when you picked out your wife, you wouldn't be going through this shit now, man. By the way, since we're on the subject, I've got a good girl for you. She's lonely and very sweet. She's my sister, man. She's beautiful, and you'd like her very much. How about it, man?"

The idea caught Gabe off-guard. He jerked his head toward Ramón, totally surprised. "Why, Ramón, I'm flattered. Thank you, but let me ask you something. Do all the rules that you just gave me apply to your sister?"

Ramón stood up straight and squared off at Gabe. He glared at him and yelled, "Hell no, man, that doesn't apply to my sister! That's just for other women! Louisa is different! You gotta treat her like a lady, man!"

Again, Gabe broke into hysterical laughter. He gasped for air and said, "Oh, I see, she's the only woman in the world who deserves to be treated with respect?"

Ramón shook his head in frustration. "Nah, man, you know what I mean. It's not being disrespectful to control the relationship. That's what women want. They want men to control them. Louisa is a good girl, but she needs a man she can respect and look up to. I don't want you to hurt her, but there's nothing wrong with letting her know who the boss is."

"Well, Ramón, that may work for the type of women you date, but I've never met a girl that would put up with that."

"No, man, you don't understand. You don't let them know you're lying to them. The key is to pull it off without letting them figure you out until you're through with them. When you have another one lined up, it's okay if they get mad, man." Ramón quickly caught himself and added, "But you can't do that to my sister, man!"

Gabe fastened his duty-belt as he said. "Funny you put it that way. That's just what my ex-wife did to me. You reckon women get together and talk like this about us men?"

Ramón's eyes widened as he was overcome with anger. "You know, bro, I'll bet you're right! I'm telling you, man, we can't trust them! No wonder we men are so suspicious! They started it, man! We men have to stick together!"

He got angrier with every word. Gabe laughed again and patted Ramón on the back. "Okay, Ramón, whatever you say. But I think I'd better wait to meet your sister. She sounds like a great girl, but I'm not ready to get involved again. I still need to get my finances straightened out. It's not cool to take a lady to your apartment when your only pieces of furniture are an old sofa and an orange crate. It's a little embarrassing, you know. But of course, you would know that, being the expert that you are."

Ramón nodded his head and said in a smug tone, "That's right, man, I am an expert, and don't you forget it. You'll come crawling to me someday to salvage your love-life. That reminds me, whatever you do, don't put the moves to any of these women on the department. Everyone will know about it the next day. You should never dip your pen in the company inkwell, man."

"Now that's the first thing you've said all night that I agree with."

Ramón continued, "Watch Deloris Gapky, man, she's a man-hating muff-diver. She thinks she's a better man than we are. She's shacking up with some other lesbian from city hall, man. She talks tough like a man until someone gets up in her face, then she tries to get the men to fight her fights for her. She's a coward. You gotta watch what you say around her, too, man. She's looking to sue someone for sexual harassment. She can't find legitimacy for her perversion any other way, so she wants the courts to give it to her. You also gotta watch Carla Ellis, man. She's screwing Major Richey. He's promised her the next sergeant's promotion."

Gabe was confused. "She's black, but isn't Richey white? Or do I have him confused with someone else?"

"No, you're right. He's white, but he likes that chocolate pie, man. She's peddling her ass to get to the top, but you can bet your ass on one thing, man. If she doesn't get that promotion, she'll play the race card or scream discrimination and sexual harassment. Richey is playing with fire, especially with that bitch. She's useless as an officer, but she's vicious, man. You say anything to her and it goes right to Richey and the chief. Whatever you do, man, don't make any comments about race around her. Even Shelley has to be careful. She'd burn her own kind in a heartbeat."

Gabe snapped his keepers in place and opened his car door. Ramón stepped away and said, "Careful tonight, bro, don't want you to get your dick shot off before you meet my sister. You'd make a good brother-in-law, man, but she don't want no eunuch for a husband."

The light drizzle began again. Gabe patted Ramón on the shoulder. "Thanks, Ramón. I'm flattered, but if you ever scare me

46

like that again, we won't be brothers-in-law. I'll be humping your sister and you'll be pushing up daisies. You'll be the one with his dick shot off." Ramón burst into laughter and staggered to his car.

3

DUTCH WINDSOR WAS a local radio personality with his own trash-talk show. His shock-jock tactics offended the upper crust, and many regional celebrities refused to be interviewed by him. His chauvinistic bashing of women had alienated the feminist, but had made him a star among the local rednecks who found his open warfare with women amusing.

He'd finished proofing the script for his next show and had walked down to the basement garage where his Porsche was parked. He inserted the key in the door lock, but froze when he heard the tapping sound of approaching heels on the concrete floor. He looked in the direction of the footsteps, which grew louder as they approached.

In the dim glow of the neon lights, he saw a tall, athletic woman with a short, skin-tight skirt walking slowly toward him. Her thigh muscles flexed and her hips shifted from side to side with each step. Her high heels made her appear about 6'3", but she was actually about 6' tall.

Stunned by her physique, Windsor removed his key from the lock and stood erect. The brunette stopped about a foot from him and stuck out her breasts as she smiled and spoke in a soft, deep voice. "Mr. Windsor? You're a hard man to get an audience with. I've wanted to meet you, but you won't return my calls."

She allowed her coat to gap open, revealing her unsupported breasts through a V-cut, sheer, red blouse. Her make up was excessive, but Dutch barely noticed her face.

Totally confused and almost salivating, Windsor replied, "Oh, baby, that can't be true. I'd never ignore a beautiful woman like you. You're magnificent. My secretary must have lost your messages."

She frowned and said in a seductive, Marilyn Monroe tone, "Well, you have, and my feelings were hurt. I was about to think you weren't interested in meeting the most beautiful woman in your fan club. I hope I was wrong. Are you interested in a rumble?"

The brunette wore a large, waist-length, fur coat which concealed the proportions of her shoulders and arms. As she opened her coat wider and exposed her breasts, Windsor could not restrain himself. He stepped back and conspicuously ran his eyes down to her hips and back up to her breasts. He stepped into her and said, "A rumble? Oh you sweet, sweet thing, I sure am! I'm sorry we haven't connected, but we're going to make up for it tonight. Get in."

As he offered his left elbow to escort her to the passenger's door, the brunette grabbed his jacket above the elbow with her right hand. She jerked hard and spun Windsor around as she stepped behind him and encircled his neck with her left arm. She released his sleeve and applied a lateral vascular neck restraint.

Shocked by the maneuver, Windsor tried to yell, but the brunette applied bone-crushing pressure with her arms and cut off his wind. Windsor was stunned at the size and power of the arms crushing his neck.

The mass and power of the woman's arms made him think that his attacker must be a male bodybuilder. The perfume, soft face and large breasts pressed against his back confirmed that she was indeed all woman.

He struggled for a few seconds, but the years of inactivity, booze and cigarettes had left him in pathetic condition. He was like a child in her coils and lost consciousness within five seconds.

When he could no longer stand, he slumped to the floor in a seated position. Concealed between the cars, the woman dropped to one knee and continued the pressure on Windsor's carotid artery. A minute later, she released her hold and checked for a pulse. Finding none, she stood, pulled her tight skirt back down over her hips, closed her coat and strolled back into the darkness from where she had come.

Gabe and Angus were exchanging friendly barbs in the rear lot of the station when Shelley ran out the back door. He yelled, "Kinnett! Blauw! Dead body in the parking garage of the McManus Building! I've got the lab techs coming! Get your asses over there and protect the scene! Gapky and Bigelow are on their way!" Both ran to their cars and sped out of the lot behind Shelley.

As they skidded to a stop in the garage, Bigelow was stringing crime scene barrier tape between the support columns close to Windsor's car. Gapky was standing by Windsor writing down the information from the driver's license that she'd removed from his hip pocket.

Newspaper reporters had heard the call over the scanner and were gathering outside the crime scene tape. Windsor was not the last employee to leave the building, so Shelley yelled to Gabe, "Kinnett, start interviewing those people. Find out who saw this guy last and who found him."

Gabe began at one end of the crowd and Angus began at the other. By the time the lab techs had arrived, there was a large crowd gathered. Deloris Gapky was showing little respect for the dead. Shelley walked up as she was telling Bigelow, "Yeah, this woman-hating asshole finally got his just reward. He was the most obnoxious bastard I ever saw. I hope it was a woman who got him."

Shelley looked around and saw the close proximity of the crowd. He cautioned Deloris, "That may be, Gapky, but your voice echoes in this concrete garage and someone's going to overhear you. Keep your opinions to yourself and do your job. Your opinion of this guy isn't important. Besides, there aren't any marks on the body. It's a natural death." Deloris glared at Shelley and prompted a glare back. Incapable of intimidating Shelley, she wisely chose to back down.

The lab techs began photographing the scene and taking measurements for their sketch. They called a tow truck to take Windsor's car to the police garage for processing while the

51

coroner's team stood by patiently to transport Windsor to the morgue.

Shelley called Bigelow and Blauw to a huddle. He instructed them to coordinate with the security officer and conduct a search of the entire building in case the killer or other witnesses were still inside. He was interrupted by Gapky's loud voice echoing through the garage. Her derogatory comments were offensive enough, but her apparent elation over Windsor's death was written all over her face.

From the back of the crowd, a hysterical woman ran under the barrier tape and screamed. Gabe grabbed her and Shelley ran to help. She was Mrs. Windsor. The death of her husband was shocking enough, but Gapky's defamatory comments and apparent glee were more than she could stand. Mrs. Windsor screamed at Deloris, "What's so funny? You got something to say about my husband? Here I am! Come say it to me! What's your problem?"

Shelley's eyes burned a hole through Deloris. She could tell by his glare that she'd crossed the line. Benny Green pulled up and wandered into the scene out of curiosity. Shelley yelled at him to come here.

Green walked up to Shelley who was stomping up to Gapky. He ripped into her. "You dumb-ass, I told you to shut up! Your man-hating comments just cost you three days off for conduct unbecoming an officer! You think you're a tough guy? I'll turn the dead guy's wife loose on you and let her kick your brains out!"

By now, Shelley was yelling, so everyone including Mrs. Windsor heard. "You give your notes to Green! Green, you're the reporting officer! Gapky, you get your ass to the station and wait for me in my office!"

Deloris masked her humiliation as she walked past the crowd. Mrs. Windsor glared at her, but Deloris could not look her in the eye. Bigelow hurried to the stairwell before Shelley unloaded on him.

Angus loitered for a few seconds until he could get Shelley's attention. When Shelley looked at him, Angus gave him the thumbs up sign, signaling his approval of Shelley's butchery of Gapky.

Shelley didn't have the time or patience to put up with Angus. He pointed to the ceiling of the garage, signaling Angus to get upstairs like he'd been told. Completely unfazed by Shelley's anger, Angus smiled from ear to ear and walked slowly to the stairwell.

From the street entrance of the garage, Gabe saw a lone figure walking down the middle of the drive. Ben Hire had parked on the street and walked in to confer with Shelley. His dress and bearing had a calming effect on everyone. He had a presence about him that exuded confidence.

Hire first walked up to Mrs. Windsor and put his arm around her. He said, "I'm so sorry, Mrs. Windsor. There's nothing anyone can say right now to make you feel better, but when I'm finished here, we'll go to the station and talk. We'll call your family and do anything we can to make this easier for you." Mrs. Windsor laid her head against Hire's chest and nodded as she cried.

Hire then went to Shelley. Both walked to a quiet corner of the garage so they could confer. Shelley ran down the crime scene protocol checklist. "Secured the scene, got the lab techs and medical examiner on board, we're clearing the building, we're identifying all persons at the scene, Green is taking your report, anything else you need from us, Ben?"

Ben was rubbing his chin as Shelley ran down the protocol list. He slowly shook his head as he said, "No, I don't think so, Len. Sounds like you've covered all the bases. We're sure going to a lot of trouble for a natural. Doesn't look like a murder."

"Yeah, I know, but this guy was a big shot. I thought we'd look better if we went through the motions."

"Well, Len, as usual, you're right. Certainly can't hurt. This guy had a lot of enemies. Who knows? All this fuss might pay off if the coroner determines that he was murdered."

Ben looked around and continued, "Would you please get the media liaison officer here to prepare a press release for the hounds? Call the D.A. for me, and we might also want to get the major and chief notified on this one. It's going to be a high profile case. They'll want to get in on this at the ground floor."

Shelley said, "Oh yeah, I forgot that." Shelley immediately keyed his portable radio and instructed the dispatcher to make the notifications. He then left the scene in Hire's hands and drove to the station to dismember Gapky.

Family members arrived to escort Mrs. Windsor to the station. That freed Gabe to tag along with Hire as he surveyed the scene. Hire instructed the building security supervisor to pull all the video surveillance tapes for the past week and bring them to the station the next day.

Gabe didn't want to annoy Ben while he was in deep concentration, but he wanted to help if possible. "Ben, is there anything else I can do to help?"

Ben smiled and shook his head. "I don't know what it would be, Gabe. It's a natural, not a mark on the body. Must have had a heart attack or stroke. If the coroner doesn't find poison, we'll close it out as a natural death and release him to the funeral home."

The elaborate measures seemed unnecessary. Gabe asked, "Then why are we going through all this crap if it's a natural? We don't do this for everyone else who drops over dead."

Ben smiled and patted Gabe on the back. He looked around the garage to make sure their conversation couldn't be overheard. Like a grandfather talking to his small grandson, Ben explained, "Politics, my boy, politics. We know we're wasting our time, but it makes the family and media think we're thorough and professional. It makes the big shots of the world think they're getting preferential treatment. The poor slobs of the world don't know any better. Besides, if we went through all this for every poor working-stiff that dropped over dead, we'd have to hire fifty more officers and the city would go broke. Get the meat wagon in here to haul the body off. We'll shut this thing down and get out of here."

The coroner's assistants were waiting patiently. Gabe motioned for them to bring the gurney in. As they were approaching, Ben walked over and examined Windsor. He pried open one of Windsor's eyes and stared for a minute. Gabe saw the confusion written across Ben's face and leaned over him while he thought. He said, "The coroner is ready, Ben, everything okay?"

Ben stood and put his hands in his pockets. He looked around to make sure he couldn't be overheard, then shook his head. "No, it's not. Something's not right."

Gabe looked at Windsor in shock. "What, Ben? I don't see anything."

Ben bent over and motioned for him to follow. "Look here." He opened Windsor's eye again. "See those little red dots on his eyeball?" Gabe nodded. "Those are petechial hemorrhages. They're little blood vessels that rupture when a person is suffocated. Old Dutch here was strangled."

He examined Windsor's neck and said, "No ligature marks on the neck, but his air supply was cut off somehow. Maybe his airway closed during a seizure or something. It'll be interesting to see what the coroner says. Maybe Shelley wasn't wasting our time after all."

The hair on the back of Gabe's neck stood on end as he realized that he may well be staring into the dead eyes of a murder victim.

Because of the high profile of the death, the coroner posted Windsor the next morning. Hire strolled into the coroner's office about 8:15. The assistant had just wheeled Windsor out of the cooler and had set up the tool tray beside the autopsy table.

Artie was sixty-five years old and had been the coroner's assistant since he was nineteen. He'd worked for eight different coroners and had become desensitized to the sights and smells of death. He asked, "Hey, Ben, donut?"

Ben shook his head and turned up his nose. "No thanks, Artie, I can't handle anything in my stomach during one of these. I'll wait." Artie laughed and shoved a donut in his mouth with the same ungloved hand that he'd used to hoist Windsor's chilled body onto the autopsy table.

The Marion County Coroner, Dr. Cletus Hendrichs, walked in and greeted Ben. "Morning, Ben, looks like a natural, huh?"

"Well, I thought so at first, Cletus, but I saw petechial hemorrhage in the eyes. I'm not so sure now."

Dr. Hendrichs looked concerned as he immediately bent over and pried open both of Windsor's eyes. He then pried open Windsor's mouth and pulled out his tongue. "Yep, your right. Artie, let's begin."

He pulled the large light down from the ceiling to Windsor's neck. He examined it closely and said, "Boy, Ben, I don't see any bruising on the outside of the neck. If he was strangled, the suspect used a very broad ligature. Let's open him up and see what we find."

The doctor recorded Windsor's vital information for transcription later, then made a Y incision the length of the torso. He removed and sectioned the organs like loaves of bread. Artie drew blood from the pool in Windsor's aorta for the toxicology analysis.

Dr. Hendrichs collected the contents of the stomach for analysis and found nothing unusual with the condition or orientation of the organs. He then opened the esophagus. "Well, Ben, we don't have strangulation. No trauma to the esophagus or larynx. Old Dutch here was killed by someone constricting his carotid artery. They cut off the blood supply to his brain. I can't see any bruising on the outside of the neck, but that's probably because he died too quickly for the discoloration to permeate all the layers of the skin. This is strange, not like an amateur killer."

Ben moved close as Dr. Hendrichs photographed Windsor's neck. He rubbed his chin as he said, "Hey, Cletus, you don't reckon this was a professional hit, do you?"

Dr. Hendrichs shook his head. "No, I don't think so. Mob and gang hits are usually messy, gunshots in the head, shotguns at close range, ice picks or knives in the heart, strangulation with piano wires. You know, all that grotesque stuff that leaves blood everywhere. They want to send symbolic messages. They don't care about being neat. This guy was neat."

Ben walked around the table, studying Windsor as he talked. "I can see that, Cletus, but how about a professional killer who was trying to make this look like a natural. Maybe he thought if he didn't leave marks on the body, we'd chalk it up as a heart attack. Maybe he thought we wouldn't post him and would release him to the funeral home."

Hendrichs straightened up and conceded, "Maybe, Ben, maybe. But why would a professional killer care what the autopsy revealed?" He looked at Artie and said, "Artie, let's have a look at the brain. Pop the skullcap."

Artie picked up a scalpel and made an incision around the back of Windsor's head. He peeled the scalp forward to Windsor's forehead and left the scalp hanging in Windsor's face. Dr. Hendrichs snapped photos to document the absence of trauma to the skull.

Artie picked up the bone saw and started cutting. Ben stepped back as Artie worked so the bone-dust that filled the air wouldn't settle on his suit.

Artie pulled the skullcap off as Dr. Hendrichs bent over and studied the brain. He removed the brain and sectioned it, but found nothing unusual. He looked at Ben and said, "Nothing here, Ben, but I'm sure he had his blood supply to the brain cut off." Ben didn't respond.

The doctor made linear incisions down the right and left sides of Windsor's neck, then peeled back the skin. He found slight bruising under the skin. He finished the autopsy, then dropped the plastic bag containing the organs into the chest cavity. "It's a homicide, Ben. Close him up, Artie."

Artie replaced the skullcap, stitched the scalp together and closed the Y incision in the torso. Ben followed Dr. Hendrichs into his office and sat opposite the doctor's desk. Dr. Hendrichs shook his head with apprehension. "I hate to say this, Ben, but I think you're dealing with someone who knows what they're doing. Most strangulations are down and dirty. They use a rope or hands around the neck and crush the larynx. This has a much different look to it."

Ben sighed. "Spit it out, Cletus, we both know what you're getting at."

"Okay, Ben, you remember that young cop who accidentally killed the meth-head with the lateral vascular neck restraint years ago?"

"Yeah, I remember. Johnsmeyer was the meth-head. He'd kicked the officer's ass for about ten minutes. When the officer finally got on top, he applied the neck restraint and was afraid to let go. He left it on too long."

"Well that's what this looks like, Ben. I'm not saying it's a cop who killed Windsor, but it's someone who knows that technique. There are no marks on the outside of the neck because a broad object was applied across the carotid artery, a broad object

57

like an arm. If that arm was padded with a coat sleeve, that would reduce the potential for bruising even more. This guy's a badass, Ben. It takes a set of rocks to go after a full-grown man with your bare hands. Most people wouldn't know where to start. Most people would use a weapon to give themselves an advantage and keep from getting hurt. This guy had to train for this. You don't get good at this technique without lots of practice."

Ben nodded as he sighed and looked up at the ceiling. "Boy, this is all I need right now. I'm six weeks behind on my cases. The chief and mayor will be crawling up my ass to solve this. This asshole had more enemies than Adolph Hitler."

Dr. Hendrichs laughed at Ben's analogy. "Yes, Ben, he did. Just look at the bright side. If you don't solve it, look at how many people you'll make happy. My wife is one of them. When I wanted to irritate her, I would tune in his show on the radio."

Ben stood and walked toward the door. Dr. Hendrichs said, "I don't want to add to your workload, Ben, but you need to remember something. This is the same way the Benson girl and Roger Moesen died. Remember them? We never solved those murders either. They may not be linked to this one, but this technique is a very rare M.O."

Ben stopped and pivoted. He glared at Dr. Hendrichs and ordered, "Yeah, I remember, Cletus, but you remember this! I'm up to my ass in alligators right now! Not one word about a serial killer in this town, hear me!"

Dr. Hendrichs leaned away from Ben and looked surprised. "Well, Ben, let's see here. What's in it for me if I keep my mouth shut? You buy my duck stamp on our next hunting trip? You pay for my share of the gas and food? You sell me that old Winchester double barrel that I've been admiring? Help me out here, make me an offer."

Ben glared at Hendrichs and patted himself in the chest. "Me pay you! Why you old tightwad, you make more money than I do! You're rolling in money, and I'm barely making it from check to check! And I ain't parting with that old Winchester! That was my dad's gun!"

Hendrichs laughed and patted Ben on the stomach. "Yeah, you poor thing, you're missing a lot of meals. I'll keep this to myself, you big crybaby. Call if I can help. I'll send you the report and the toxicology results." Ben waved as he shook his head in frustration and walked down the hall to the exit.

Bishop Aqui had been a petty meth distributor for the local biker gang. He'd fallen out of favor when he'd rolled over on a gang member to work off federal charges filed by the drug task force. He'd been lucky and was staying barely one step ahead of the hit man.

He had been a difficult informant to control. His agent on the task force no longer wanted to work him, so he cut him loose. Aqui would never give up his major sources, and the case agents grew tired of the little cookies that he threw out to make them think he was trying to cooperate.

Aqui wanted a downward departure from the mandatory minimum sentencing mandate that he was facing in federal court. Since he wouldn't give up a bigger fish than himself, the task force told the U.S. attorney to go ahead and file charges. He was facing twenty-seven years. Aqui was dodging the police as well as the assassin.

One good thing about working informants is that they have no ethics, and there is never a shortage of associates to roll over on. One of Aqui's girlfriends had been caught shoplifting enough merchandise to constitute a felony. She was a meth-whore and was teetering on the brink of having her probation revoked. To avoid losing her children and a lengthy jail sentence, she flipped and gave up Aqui.

Aqui needed cash to support his own meth addiction. He'd recently found a new source of meth who wouldn't rat him out. It didn't make sense to allow Aqui to get killed. He was a good source of income. He was dropping one hundred and fifty dollars a day for crank.

He needed large amounts of cash on a daily basis, and robbery was the quickest and easiest way to get it. Since Aqui was a prolific armed robber, his girlfriend had insight into his plans. She gave her controlling agent the date, time and location of the liquor store that Aqui had targeted for his next robbery.

It would be easy to stake out the liquor store and arrest Aqui as soon as he showed up, but by letting him go through with the robbery first, the robbery charge on top of his drug warrant would get him additional jail time.

The task force guys got into a turf-battle with the robbery unit. Although they wanted to exact some retribution against Aqui for jerking them around, they reluctantly turned the stakeout over to the robbery detectives.

Len Shelley walked into the briefing room of the detective unit. Captain Ritter was the criminal investigations commander. He said, "Hey, Len, have a seat, we're just going over the ops plan for tonight."

Ritter turned back to the chalkboard and continued the briefing. "The target is Burk's Liquor Store. Beth Lloyd will be the clerk. The owner took the night off so we could have the whole store to ourselves. Beth, you need to wear the owner's white smock to look the part and cover the top of your vest. Weder and Paulson, you two will be in the stockroom with shotguns. I'll be in the cooler so I can watch. It has a mirrored window so I won't be seen. I'll call out instructions to you guys in the stockroom. When you come out, you'll have a direct line of fire on Aqui in case he wants to dance. Everyone make sure you have your headphones on. I don't want Aqui to hear any portable radios. Lloyd, make sure you hit the deck before the guys light him up. Everyone note the location and shortest route to the closest hospital in case one of us takes a round. Remember, no talking to the press afterwards and meet back here to write our reports."

Ritter turned to Shelley. "Len, I'll need a couple of your goons. I want one man with me. No one works alone on this. I'll also need a marked cruiser to be the chase car if Aqui makes it outside to his car. If we have to chase him, we'll stay off the air and you'll coordinate the chase."

Len nodded. "Your inside man will be Kinnett. Your chase car will be Blauw."

"Thanks, Len. Everyone make sure you have your vests on and your equipment works properly. Read your ops plan so you'll know what everyone is doing. No screw-ups tonight!"

Gabe and Angus met the robbery detectives in the back lot. Angus couldn't resist the opportunity to poke fun at the detectives. "Hey, Paulson, you big pussy, who you going to get to shoot that mean old shotgun for you? Last time, it spanked you and you cried like a baby."

Paulson laughed. "I was crying, Angus, but it wasn't because the shotgun kicked. I'd just polished off your old lady and found out that you hadn't left any beer in the refrigerator for me."

Weder chimed in to support his partner. "Yeah, Angus, she was pretty good stuff."

Angus laughed and said, "That's okay, boys, I'm glad someone was getting a little off of her. The bitch wouldn't put out for me. How was she Paulson?"

Paulson smiled. "Not bad. It was like having a virgin once I got past that little, short used part."

Angus cringed as he conceded defeat. "Ouch, you insensitive fuckers, now you've hurt my feelings. I may not be able to save your fat asses tonight when Aqui opens a can of whip-ass on you."

Weder and Paulson laughed as they got in their car. Gabe was leaning against the cruiser when Angus turned around. Shaking his head, he said, "Man, I hope you guys never start on me about my ex-wife. You're brutal. I don't think I could take teasing like that."

Angus said, "Give it time, boy, you'll be the same way. It's just the way we show you that we like you. Those guys wouldn't have said anything if they thought it would have hurt my feelings."

Gabe and Angus talked while they followed the robbery detectives to the store. Angus gave him some last-minute advice. "Now, listen to me, boy, these guys know what they're doing. You'll be in the cooler with Ritter. He's a good guy, but I haven't worked with him for a few years. I don't know if you can trust him or not. He'll take care of his own men, but don't say or do anything out of line. I don't know if he'll do the same for you. Paulson and Weder are good. They'll shoot first and ask questions later. They'll blaze Aqui if they get the chance, so you make sure you're behind something solid when they jump out of that stockroom. Ritter will be hidden, but you don't want to be standing out in the open if a load of buckshot comes through that cooler glass, hear me, boy?"

Gabe was puzzled and asked, "They won't shoot Aqui if he gives up, will they?"

Angus smiled. "Probably not, but I doubt if he'll be able to give up fast enough. He's an evil bastard anyway. The courts will just slap his hands or give him a little shock time. He'll be out in no time wreaking havoc on society again. We're doing society a favor if we put his greasy ass in the ground."

"I don't think so, Angus, he's got a drug warrant. With an armed robbery charge on top of it, he should get a life sentence. We don't have to kill him."

"Ah, don't count on it. He could get out early for good behavior or some bleeding heart federal judge could decide that the prison is overcrowded and release him in a few years."

Gabe was confused. "I don't know, Angus, you guys don't do things the way they taught us in the academy. We're supposed to identify ourselves and order the suspect to drop his gun before we shoot."

Angus reached over and thumped Gabe in the chest. "Listen, you dumb-shit, those idiots who teach at the academy ain't never been cops. They're academy instructors because they never could cut it on the street. You're just supposed to listen to what they tell you and regurgitate it back on the tests so you can graduate. Once you're on the street, you forget all that academy bullshit, and we'll teach you how to do things right. All that warning stuff is just something you do in the academy or if there are television cameras around. In real life, you shoot these dirty fuckers every chance you get. They'll do the same to you and never lose a minute of sleep. The department will give you a nice funeral and tell your family what a hero you were for getting your dumb ass killed. Deep down inside, the courts, lawyers, citizens and staff don't care what happens to us as long as we don't get them sued. Hell, if we get ourselves killed, the city can hire someone else to replace us at lower pay and save money. You watch Paulson and Weder. They're a couple of dirty fighters like us. They'll seize every advantage and make sure they go home at night. They'll show you how it's done. After they blow Aqui's ass off, they'll show you how to make your reports sing so you don't get indicted."

Gabe sat quietly in shock for the rest of the trip. At the store, he and Angus exited the car and walked up to Shelley. Shelley said, "Gabe, you're with Ritter over there. Now remember, you're assigned to him, so he's your boss. Do what he tells you. Angus, you're the chase car. Don't park and sit. Aqui is smart enough to circle the store a few times to see if it's being staked out. Rove around, but be close when this thing goes down. I'm getting out of here so Aqui won't spot me. Good luck, boys. Gabe, shoot low in case he's riding a Shetland pony."

Shelley chuckled as he got back in his car and sped away. Angus patted Gabe on the back and said, "You lucky shit, you get the fun job. Wish I could trade places with you. Good luck, and give the greasy bastard a double tap for me."

Angus got back in the wagon and drove off. Gabe introduced himself to Captain Ritter who said, "You're with me, kid, stick close." Everyone took their positions. They checked their radios and weapons, and waited.

Bishop Aqui was at his wit's end. He was hiding during the day and moving in the shadows at night. He'd stopped seeing the girlfriend who'd given him up to the task force. She was too unreliable. He'd suspected that she was selling him out.

His new girlfriend was a heavy meth user with connections. She muled for her supplier, and got her daily supply as a commission. She was getting Aqui's supply at a reduced price, but his habit was still expensive.

Aqui climbed down the fire escape and eased down the alley behind his girlfriend's apartment building. He jogged the three blocks to his mother's house and tapped on the back door.

Elaine Aqui quickly opened the back door and jerked him inside. She wrapped her arms around her son's head and hugged him tight against her breasts. "Bishop, Bishop, my boy! Where have you been? I've been so worried about you! Why doesn't your girlfriend tell you when I call?"

Bishop hugged his mother back. "She does, Ma. I've just been busy. I just need a little more money, then I can move out of town."

Elaine went to the kitchen to check on Bishop's supper. She yelled, "Bishop, you have to promise me that when you get out of this town, you'll get yourself straight. I'll help you, but you have to get off this stuff that's ruining our lives. I can't sleep for worrying about you. Shame on you for taking years off my life like this!"

She returned to the dining room with tears in her eyes. Aqui hugged her again. "Ma, Ma, come on, Ma. I'm through with this life, Ma. I got one more paycheck coming tonight, then I'm out of here. I'm going to a new town where no one knows me. I've checked myself into a rehab clinic under a false name. Thirty days from now, you'll see a new man. I'll get a job, change my appearance so these people can't find me, and you and me can start over. I'm so sorry, Ma. You'll see, everything is going to work out for us."

Elaine nodded hopefully as she turned back to the kitchen. She pulled Bishop's dinner out of the oven and sat it on the table in front of him. She turned to him and ordered, "Sit! Eat, and tell me about your new apartment."

Aqui ate hungrily. Mom's cooking tasted better than ever. He explained his plans and assured his mother that he was getting his life in order. Ten minutes later, Bishop pushed his plate away and leaned back in his chair. Mom picked up his plate and patted his head as he rubbed his distended stomach. Aqui proclaimed, "Delicious, Ma, you're the best."

She dropped Bishop's dishes into the dishwater to soak. She opened the refrigerator and pulled out a dish of cream cheese dessert. She placed it in front of Bishop and said, "That's right, and don't you forget it, little Bishop. You're the only son I have left. You brother's death almost put me in the grave. I'm not going to lose you, too. You've got to make me proud."

He nodded his head as he overfilled his mouth with dessert. As soon as he could swallow, he said, "I will, Ma, you'll see. I'm tired of this life. We're going to start over."

Bishop kissed his mother goodbye and looked before he exited the back door. He hid in the shadows as he crept to his car. His paycheck was waiting.

Angus had circled the store several times. He was bored, but suddenly looked ahead and saw Aqui's old car sitting at the intersection and heading for the target. Angus made a quick right turn so he wouldn't be spotted.

He got on the scrambled frequency and notified Ritter that Aqui was two blocks away. Everyone in the store scrambled for cover. Lloyd buttoned up her smock and unlocked the front door. Angus bounced as he laughed at the look he'd imagined on Aqui's face when he found himself staring down the barrels of Paulson's and Weder's shotguns.

Gabe pulled his .45 from its shoulder holster and cracked the slide open slightly to make sure there was a round in the chamber. He'd recently switched to Hydra-Shok ammo, which used a bright nickel case. The nickel gleamed in the dim light of the cooler, putting Gabe's mind at ease.

He tested the thumb safety to make sure it was on. A quick flip of the safety downward would make the big automatic battle-ready. His conversation with Angus left no doubt that Aqui would never see another sunrise.

Aqui sat a hundred feet down the street watching the store. He studied the perky blonde behind the counter. He'd cased the store many times in the past and couldn't remember seeing her. His concern faded when he assured himself that liquor stores have high employee turnover, and she didn't look threatening. Besides, he needed the money, and she looked like she would be a fun toy after the robbery.

It took about thirty minutes for Aqui to smoke his last rock. With his courage fortified, he exited his car and looked around as he approached the store. He put his hand in his coat pocket and gripped a cheap imported revolver. He stopped at the front door and took one last look around before going in.

Angus positioned his wagon just out of sight. He jerked the shotgun out of its rack and chambered a round as he ran toward the store. He hoped to get into position before the robbery went down.

He positioned himself behind a parked car on the opposite side of the street. If the robbery detectives missed, he would have a clear shot at Aqui as he exited. He chuckled as he again imagined the surprise on Aqui's face. He hoped Gabe was enjoying this as much as he was.

Aqui entered and casually looked around to see if any other customers were in the store. He walked the isles and picked up a bottle of wine. Ritter whispered a detailed narration of Aqui's movements. "He's moving back toward Lloyd. Get ready--- ready---"

Weder had his shoulder against the stockroom door. Paulson had his hand on the knob so, upon Ritter's signal, he could turn the knob and he and Weder would rush in with no warning. They had rounds in the chambers of their shotguns and the safeties were off.

With fingers on the triggers, they waited and snickered quietly to themselves. Paulson whispered, "Man, is this asshole going to be surprised."

Beth Lloyd played her part perfectly. Before the detail, she'd carefully applied her brightest makeup and primped for Aqui. As Aqui sat the wine on the counter, she asked, "Is this all, sir?"

He smiled sadistically. "All for me. Is there anything you'd like?"

Beth feigned surprise and answered, "Why, sir, I don't know what you mean." Aqui became aroused as pretentious fear draped Lloyd's face. Robbery alone would not satisfy him now. He needed the cash, but he now wanted more.

As his pulse quickened, he breathed harder. His eyes widened as he lowered his gaze and fantasized about the large, firm rewards waiting for him under her smock. He had no intentions of leaving a live witness, but he would savor this fine trophy first.

Lloyd played Aqui like a fine violin. She gasped and bit her lower lip as she nervously raised her arms and covered her breasts. She whimpered, "Oh, please don't hurt me. I'll do anything you want."

He could stand no more. He produced the .38 and kept it low so it couldn't be seen from the street. "That's just what I want to hear, bright eyes. First the cash, then shed that coat and come with me. We're going to party."

Ritter couldn't see the pistol from inside the cooler. Lloyd was obstructing his view. He couldn't hear the dialog, but knew by the look on Aqui's face and Lloyd's body language that it was time. He keyed the mike and whispered, "Now!"

Paulson turned the knob the half-inch necessary to allow Weder's weight to swing the door open. Both charged out of the stockroom and shouldered their Remingtons. Ritter stepped back behind the corner of the cooler. Gabe did the same.

The commotion behind him made Aqui turn quickly. Lloyd proned out in mid-air and fell flat on the floor behind the counter. Before Aqui's body had completely squared up with Paulson and Weder, he recognized the two large muzzles charging him. He didn't recognize the goons behind them, but the shotguns were unmistakable.

Aqui tried to drop his pistol, but his finger was too deep in the trigger guard. The pistol rolled out of his hand and dangled on his trigger finger. Before he could shake it loose, Weder yelled, "Surprise, mother fucker!"

He knew now who the gunmen were, but couldn't act quickly enough. Weder and Paulson fired simultaneously. The Remingtons roared and the muzzle flash lit up the store like flash bulbs. The muzzle blast was horrendous and deafened everyone in the store. Both rounds of 12 gauge 00 buckshot hit Aqui in the chest. He flew backwards over the counter and landed on top of Lloyd. She was crawling to the end of the counter to get a shot at him in the event that her partners missed.

Gabe and Ritter peeked around their cover simultaneously, but could see nothing. The glass was covered with blood and tissue. It was also cracked in several locations by buckshot that had passed through Aqui.

They quickly ran out of the cooler, hoping it was Aqui on the window and not Beth. Paulson, Weder, Ritter and Gabe all converged on the counter together and looked over. Lloyd was covered in blood and tissue and was struggling to get out from under Aqui. The three detectives broke into laughter as Lloyd let loose a barrage of profanity.

Gabe stepped away to recover from the shock of seeing a man blown almost in half. He feigned a pretentious smile so the others would not think him weak.

Lloyd finally freed herself. All holstered their weapons and unloaded their shotguns. After congratulatory pats on the back, Ritter called for an ambulance. Gabe was sticking close to Ritter as instructed and asked, "Why do we need an ambulance? He's cut in half."

Ritter smiled and patted him on the shoulder. "I know, kid, we'll have the paramedics run a strip on him to cover our asses. Makes it look like we give a shit about this scumbag. Looks like we really didn't want to kill him and we're trying to save his life. You know, political correctness. It keeps the minorities off our back."

As in all police involved shootings, the lab techs responded. They processed, diagramed and photographed the scene. The coroner's office collected Aqui's parts and transported them to the morgue for an autopsy.

The assistant chief responded, and internal affairs took statements from all involved. The department chaplain took a backup officer to Elaine Aqui's house and informed her that her only surviving son had been killed trying to collect his last paycheck.

Gabe hustled through the station door so he wouldn't be late for shift briefing. Directly inside, he ran into Angus Blauw. He feigned a look of anger and yelled at Gabe, "Hey, you ungrateful little shit, what's the big idea of blowing that greaser away without giving me a shot at him?"

Gabe shook his head in disgust as he hurried by. "Ain't got time, you senile old liver-spot, Shelley will have my ass if I'm late." Angus laughed and strolled into shift briefing with total disregard for the clock on the wall or Shelley's wrath.

After shift briefing, Gabe grabbed his equipment bag and headed for the back lot. At the door, he was intercepted by Ezard Lumas. "Hey, Kinnett, I need to talk to you."

Gabe asked, "Officially or unofficially?"

"You ought to know that whenever I want you, it's official, Kinnett. My office in five."

Gabe shook his head. "I'll have to run it by my sergeant."

"No, Kinnett, the chief is waiting for you in my office. You don't have to run anything by your sergeant."

He thought about Lumas's order and decided to go rather than incur the wrath of Garrison again. Len Shelley came out just as Gabe was being led upstairs. He yelled, "Lumas, what the hell are you doing?"

"I'm taking your protégé upstairs to talk to the chief. If you've got a problem with that, you can come, too."

Shelley stormed up the stairs behind Lumas and said, "Think I will!"

In the internal affairs unit, Garrison was seated with his feet up on a desk. Shelley stormed in and protested loudly. "Listen, Chief, I've got a shift to run! I don't appreciate Lumas intercepting my men without going through me!"

Garrison looked up at Shelley with a feigned look of concern. He said with an evil, sarcastic tone, "Yes, Len, I can see how you would be upset. He's just doing what I asked. I should have called you first. I'll go through you next time, but this time I wanted to talk to Kinnett without tipping him off first. I've got some things to ask him and I don't want him coached by anyone."

Shelley resented the implication. "What do you mean, coached? Are you insinuating that I would encourage him to lie?"

Garrison gave Shelley a sinister grin and replied sarcastically, "Nah, Len, I know you midnight guys would never get your heads together and fabricate the same story. He'll be down in a few minutes. Go back down and run your shift. They need you more than we do. You're excused."

The message was clear. Shelley was powerless to help Gabe. He stared at Garrison, then wisely chose to leave before compromising his own career.

Garrison smiled at Gabe and motioned for him to sit in the chair next to him. Lumas remained standing against the wall as Garrison ran the show. "So, we meet again. Have a seat, Kinnett." Gabe remained standing in conspicuous defiance of Garrison.

He continued, "Looks like we have a slight problem. I've read the statement that you gave Detective Lumas the night of the Aqui shooting. You said the exact same thing the other officers said."

Gabe shrugged his shoulders. "So, why wouldn't I? It was the truth."

Garrison held his hand up to stop him. "You know? When five officers all say the exact same thing, I have to wonder if they got together and fabricated their stories before they gave their statements. When everyone writes up their own version without talking to the other participants, there'll always be slight discrepancies. That's expected. It actually lends credibility to everyone's statement when there are minor discrepancies. As long as there aren't any major contradictions, little discrepancies can be explained as differences in perception. How about it, Gabe? Is that what happened?"

He didn't respond. Garrison continued, "Cat got your tongue? You're acting pretty suspicious. Why don't you tell me what really happened? I know it wasn't a righteous shooting. The coroner wrote in his report that the buckshot entered Aqui from the side. He wasn't facing Paulson and Weder when they fired. They didn't warn him, did they? They shot him without announcing their presence and identifying themselves, didn't they? They murdered him, then agreed on a fabricated version of what happened, and you went along with it, didn't you?"

Gabe stood quietly as fear gripped his throat. He tried to muster some saliva so he could speak. He looked over at Lumas, who smiled sadistically. He finally took a deep breath and said, "I was in the cooler with Captain Ritter, sir."

Garrison took his feet off of the desk and sat up. He patronized Gabe with an evil smile. "Yes, I know, Kinnett, I read your statement. I'm not saying that you conspired before the fact to murder him. I'm just saying the shooting wasn't righteous, and Paulson and Weder killed Aqui before giving him a chance to surrender. They had their minds made up before they ever got there that they weren't going to take him alive. You and Ritter weren't a part of the killing. I'm saying that afterwards, Weder and Paulson convinced you and Ritter to go along with their version of the story to cover their asses."

He leaned into Gabe and pasted on his most sympathetic facade. He softened his voice and said, "Listen, son, you're a good kid. You have a promising future here. Don't get wrapped up in this brotherhood of blue bullshit that your friends are trying to sell you. It's one thing to stick up for each other when you're right, but it's sheer stupidity to take a bullet for another guy when he's wrong and wants someone else to take the fall for him. There's no honor in conspiring with a criminal to cover up a crime. That'll get you a trip up the river. I know what Blauw tells you, but he's not a healthy role model. He'll get you fired. This is your chance to clear your conscience and save your career."

He shook his head in frustration and continued. "Look, Gabe, I'm not going to fire or prosecute Paulson and Weder. This is a training issue. They just got scared and shot too soon. We'll give them some remedial training and counsel them about the criminal and civil liability associated with the use of deadly force. We're all on the same team. Believe it or not, I care about my officers as much as you do."

Gabe knew Garrison was lying through his teeth. His face showed no emotion as he stared at the chief, but his mind was racing. Was Garrison bluffing? Had he already talked to one of the other officers and found out what had happened? Had one of the other officers already broken down? Was he committing professional suicide by remaining silent? What should he do? Time was running out.

He took a deep breath, choked back his fear and said, "I'm not trying to cover anything up, sir. I don't know what happened at the time the shots were fired. I was in the cooler and didn't see anything. If you'll check the crime scene photos, you'll see that the glass of the cooler was covered with ---"

Garrison closed his eyes and held up his hand to stop Gabe in mid sentence. "I saw the photos, son. I'm not saying that you had any control over Paulson and Weder. You and Ritter are just covering up for them. Now, this is your last chance. The first person who tells the truth gets the deal. You can either be a friendly witness or a co-defendant. Show me what kind of man you are. Send a message to the rest of the department that you're an ethical cop who won't tolerate corruption. Make your family proud of you. Do the right thing and help me move you up in the organization. I need good commanders to take the place of the ones who are going to retire in a few years."

Gabe nodded that he understood. He looked at the floor and pondered his options. He knew his every thought was written across his face. He decided that silence was more incriminating than his weakest attempt at self-redemption. He looked down at the chief and said, "I want to cooperate, Chief, but there is no conspiracy. I don't know what Ritter and the detectives discussed. I wasn't a part of that. I've told you all I know, sir."

Garrison sat quietly and stared at him. He slowly rose to his feet and towered over Gabe. He laughed softly and said, "Ready for another inning of hardball, bright boy?"

Gabe refused to be intimidated. He mustered every ounce of courage he could and replied, "Yes sir, I am."

Garrison smiled and patted him on the shoulder. "Hit the road, Einstein. I'll have your lesson typed up first thing tomorrow." Gabe left the office. He could only imagine what Garrison had in store for him.

Len Shelley was waiting for Gabe in the back lot when he walked to his car. Gabe was still in shock and had a bewildered stare. Shelley motioned for him to come to him. As he walked up, Shelley asked, "What did that asshole want?"

"He thinks we all fabricated our reports on the Aqui shooting. I guess the coroner's report said Aqui was shot in the side. Garrison thinks Paulson and Weder shot him without giving him a chance to surrender."

Shelley shook his head angrily as he leaned against his car. "Those dumb-asses! What do they know about police involved shootings? When they worked the road, you couldn't find either of those white assholes when things got scary. It's cowards like them that give you white people a bad name."

His anger surged as he talked. "Hell, if they'd think about it for a minute, they'd know that just because his body wasn't fully turned doesn't mean that his head wasn't looking at them. If he was looking at them and didn't drop his gun, it doesn't make any difference what position his body was in. It's okay to shoot an asshole in the back if he poses a threat."

Gabe nodded confidently as Shelley's rationale flipped on the light switch in his head. "Yeah! Yeah, that's right! Police snipers shoot people all the time who aren't looking at them. Most of the time, the suspects don't even know there's a set of crosshairs on them. I wish I'd thought of that a few minutes ago. I'd like to put Garrison and that piss-ant, Lumas, in their place."

"Someday, maybe you can. Just remember this night if you ever find yourself in a position to send those two hiking. And listen, kid, I'm sorry I couldn't help you up there. I just don't have enough rank."

"Ah, don't worry about it. They don't scare me. I can handle those two minor-leaguers." As he was speaking the words, Gabe hoped the tremor had dissipated from his voice.

As the sun rose, Gabe again found himself numb from lack of sleep. He dropped his activity sheet, reports and citations on Shelley's desk. He was too tired to walk home, so he flagged down one of the day shift officers for a ride. Once home, he stripped off his uniform and gun-belt and collapsed on the sofa. He had barely enough strength to pull a blanket over himself.

About 10:30, his phone rang. After several rings, he stirred and dragged the phone to his ear. He mumbled, "Hello."

A familiar voice startled him. "Hey, Einstein, you awake?"

Gabe rubbed his face and tried to collect his thoughts. He knew he was in for a battle. "Yes sir, Chief, what can I do for you?"

Garrison grunted an evil laugh. "You can get your conniving ass down here to my office, now! I've got your hardball lesson typed. See you in fifteen minutes."

Gabe wanted to ask more questions, but the chief terminated the call. He panicked and jumped from the sofa to dress. He hoped the chief was not going to fire him.

He didn't know what the chief had up his sleeve, but it couldn't be good. He had just served a one-day suspension. If the chief was following a progressive discipline plan, this action would be three or five days off. The one-day suspension had almost broken him. If the guys hadn't chipped in to cover his lost pay, he would have gone under. Three or five days would be more than he could survive.

Gabe rushed into the secretary's office and asked her to announce him to the chief. As he entered the chief's office, he saw Detective Lumas and Major Richey seated around the chief's conference table. Garrison didn't bother to stand, but motioned to a chair by Richey and said, "Hey there, Einstein, have a seat."

Gabe hated Garrison's sinister condescension. He'd made it painfully obvious that he relished the opportunity to terrorize subordinates. Gabe sat quickly, hoping to soften the chief's anger. Garrison slid a sheet of paper across his desk to Gabe. He picked it up and read. The title of the document was *Transfer*. Garrison smiled and asked, "Any questions?"

Gabe's heart sank as he finished reading. He then asked, "Transfer? To the cold case unit? What's a cold case unit?"

Major Richey laughed and asked, "You don't know? Well, Kinnett, cold cases are cases that have been investigated and remain unsolved. We call them cold cases because they're so old that there are no leads or witnesses. They're also called dead files. We store them in a special unit until we find an officer with the special talents to review them and look for clues that the detectives might have missed. You're that officer, Kinnett. You're just the man to solve all those unsolved cases."

Emotion swelled up in Gabe's throat. He loved his job and the guys he worked with. His shock intensified as more details were revealed. Garrison said, "You see, tough guy, these are mostly murder, rape and robbery cases that have no suspects. It'll take real stubborn tenacity to clear them up. You're just that stubborn officer that I've been looking for, someone who can't get along with others or be a team player, a real lone wolf. That's you, Einstein. Major Richey will show you to your new office. Have a nice career. It's been nice knowing you."

Richey stood and waited for Gabe. He was in shock and couldn't think. Richey patted him on the shoulder and said, "Let's go, bright boy, your office awaits." Gabe rose slowly and followed Richey.

He led Gabe to the elevator and pushed the *Down* button. The door opened on the bottom floor, and Richey led Gabe to a stairwell that descended one floor below the basement. They walked down a dusty concrete hallway and stopped at a metal fire door. Richey opened the door, reached in and turned on the light switch, which illuminated a lone light-bulb in the center of the concrete room.

Gabe stepped in and looked in shock at the cold, dusty, concrete bunker that was going to be his office. At the rear of the room was a row of shelves that contained stacks of dusty file boxes. Richey patted Gabe on the back. "Here's your future, son." He pointed at the boxes and said, "There's your cases, have fun."

With that final gesture of support, Richey turned and left the room snickering. He stopped outside the door and turned to

Gabe. "Oh yeah, if you'll read your transfer order, you'll see that you're still working midnights and your off-duty employment permit has been revoked. No off-duty jobs. Go home and come back tonight."

Gabe's eyes watered. He fought back the tears as he surveyed his new assignment. He wadded up his transfer order and threw it in the corner. One third of his life now consisted of shelves of dusty cold case files, an old metal desk, a chair and one light bulb.

He milled around for a few minutes, trying to find some redeeming qualities in his new assignment. He had never been a detective before and had no idea how to open a cold investigation. As he surveyed the room, rats scurried around the shelf legs and ran in and out of the vents.

Overwhelmed by the hopelessness of his predicament, he slammed the door as he left. He avoided the other officers as he walked home. His anger was more than he could contain. This would be another sleepless day. His job was all that he had left, and now that was gone. He had nothing else to live for.

Len Shelley stepped to the podium to conduct his shift briefing. As he surveyed his shift, Gabe's empty chair was conspicuous. He looked around the room and saw the rage in the eyes of his crew. He knew what was on their minds, but wanted to get business out of the way first. He began reading the pass-on information, but was rudely interrupted. Angus blurted out, "Fuck the pass-on, Len, we don't give a shit about that. What's going on with Kinnett?"

Shelley looked calmly over the top of his reading glasses and said with angry determination, "In a minute. Don't interrupt me again, Angus." He dutifully finished reading the pass-on book, but no one was writing.

When finished, Shelley closed the binder. He slowly removed his glasses, put them back in their case and braced for the attack. "Okay, first question."

Blauw spoke for the other officers. "What's Garrison's beef with Kinnett? That chicken-shit wouldn't make a pimple on Kinnett's ass."

The other officers chimed in and Shelley had to hold his hands up to stop the barrage. He restored order and said, "I know, guys, I know. I agree with you. Kinnett got screwed, but that's the chief's prerogative. He can assign any of us anywhere he wants. The thing for us to do is to stick by Kinnett. He's going to feel like he's been thrown away. We have to let him know that he's still family. Now, go to work. I'll let you know more after I've talked to him."

The officers grumbled among themselves as they headed to the parking lot for inspection. Blauw eased up to Shelley and said, "I'll meet you after inspection. I want to see Kinnett, too. I feel partly responsible for his transfer."

Shelley snarled, "You are! We all are, Angus! It's hard for these new kids to step into a shitstorm like this and know who to listen to. We tell them to not be rats, and the staff tells them they have to squeal on their brother officers if they want to get ahead in the department. Then they make an example of someone like Kinnett and that scares the hell out of the rest of them. We should have found a way to fight our battles with the staff and leave Kinnett out of it. We own this."

Angus disagreed. "Nah, that's not right, Len. We can't control what battles we have to fight. That prick, Garrison, drew the line in the sand on this one. He went on a fishing expedition over the Aqui shooting. It was a righteous shoot. So what if Paulson and Weder blazed his ass before he could drop his gun. He shouldn't have been armed and robbing the store in the first place. If Lloyd had been a real clerk that night, he would have raped and murdered her without a single ounce of remorse. There's nothing we could have done to shield Kinnett from this. He was just in a bad place at the wrong time. That's life."

Gabe wanted to avoid his old shift so he wouldn't have to answer embarrassing questions. He entered the basement through a side door and hurried directly to the concrete bunker. Once inside, he dusted off his desk and made a list of things he'd need to make his existence tolerable.

When he answered the knock on the door, he found Shelley and Blauw on the other side. They wanted to cheer him up, so they acted happy to see him. He knew what they were trying to

76

do and appreciated it, but he couldn't mask his anger. He slumped into his dusty chair and stared at the floor.

Shelley and Blauw looked at each other to see who would take the lead. Because of his rank, Shelley felt compelled to start. He sat on the edge of Gabe's desk as he tried to think of the right words. "Listen, Gabe, I'm not going to sit here and pretend that this isn't a shit detail. The only reason you're here is because the chief wants to make an example of you. He sees you as a threat for some reason."

Gabe leaned his head back and stared at the ceiling. "I gathered that much, but what does he expect me to do here?"

"Nothing, Gabe, that's just the point. You're not here to be productive. He knows there isn't anything anyone can do with these cases. You aren't expected to produce. This is a jail. Look around you. This is just like a prison cell, except it's bigger and you can open the door. You're here to serve time. He's just locked you in a jail cell for eight hours a day. It's different from prison in that you can let yourself out each day, but if you want a paycheck, you have to stay in your cell for eight hours a day."

Angus got angrier as Shelley talked. He interrupted, "Yeah, Gabe, Len's right. What's even worse is that Garrison knows what shambles your life is in right now. He knows you're not sleeping, so he assigned you to work midnights so you can't sleep or have a personal life. He revoked your off-duty permit so you can't earn any extra money and dig yourself out of debt. He's doing everything he can to make you quit."

Shelley said, "Yeah, that's right, but you're not going to quit! You're going to hang in there and do your time! One good thing about this is that you'll be out of his sight for a few months. He can't keep track of all his enemies. You just wait, he'll get pissed at someone else before long and forget all about you. Garrison has such a long shit-list because he adds someone else to it several times a day. Give it time. In a few months, there'll be someone else down here, and you'll be back on the street with us."

Angus agreed. "That's right, Gabe, so here's what you're going to do. Just come in here and make yourself comfortable. Bring a TV and some books. Entertain yourself for eight hours. Every night, one of us will pick you up and take you to lunch.

You're still one of the family, and we're not going to forget you just because you're in cop jail."

Shelley laughed. "Hey, that's good, cop jail. He's right, Gabe, and there are a lot of cop jails in the police department. You're not the only officer who got sentenced to cop jail. Look at all the guys who got transferred to records or the property room. Old Schneider maintains the equipment room. What a shit job that is. And don't think you're the first officer who ever got assigned to the cold case unit. Others have been here. They just served their time and eventually got out when Garrison got pissed at someone else. The good thing is that there aren't enough cop jails for everyone that he's pissed at."

Shelley stood and towered over Gabe in his most intimidating pose. He growled, "But you listen to me, boy! Don't even think about quitting! You're a cop at heart! I've seen a lot of guys who got mad and quit! Every one of them regretted it later! Some of them were able to get back in law enforcement somehow, but some of them couldn't! You're one of us and you'd be letting us down if you quit! Now, don't worry about money. We'll make up what you lose from the loss of your off-duty employment. You just survive this and get back on the street."

Gabe stood and shook his head. "I can't let you guys pay my bills, sarge. You've got kids and---"

Shelley cut Gabe off abruptly. He put his hand in the middle of Gabe's chest and pushed him back down in the chair. He leaned over Gabe and poked him in the chest with his finger. He barked, "Listen here, white boy, it's our fault that you're in this mess! We ain't going to let you take the fall for this all by yourself! We can't serve your time, but we can help you pay your bills! All the guys want to chip in and get you back on your feet, so don't throw that gratitude back in our faces! We take care of our own, and you're going to take what we give you or you're going to have 320 black pounds of irate sergeant all over your snowy white ass! You got me, boy?"

Gabe saw the futility of arguing with Shelley. He was too overpowering. He sighed and shook his head. "I hear you, sarge, but it makes me feel bad to take charity."

Angus said, "Hell, it wouldn't bother me. If you don't want the money, give it to me. I'll spend it and won't feel a bit guilty."

Shelley glared at Angus. "That money is Gabe's! It ain't gonna be spent on toys, booze and whores for your decrepit old ass. You'd hurt yourself with the toys and kill yourself with the booze and whores."

Angus frowned and retorted, "Maybe, but I could still whip your big ass after I was drunk and half dead."

Shelley turned toward the door and shook his head in frustration. Once again, he realized the futility of trying to out-insult Blauw. He turned back to Gabe. "Hang in there, son. You just entertain yourself and keep your sanity. We'll be here for you."

He patted Gabe on the back and motioned for Angus to come with him. Angus patted Gabe on the back as he passed. "Remember, kid, never let the bastards see you sweat. Make them think you happy as a queer in a peter tree."

Gabe shook his head and laughed quietly as Angus closed the door. Angus's metaphors never ceased to amuse him. That was one of Angus's endearing qualities; probably his only one. He had offended every person that he'd ever met. Gabe wondered about his own character. Anyone who could find any humor or redeeming qualities in Angus had to be deranged themselves.

He walked over and opened the door. He yelled at Shelley, "Sarge!" Shelley stopped and turned around. Gabe was choked up by Shelley's clumsy show of affection and said, "Thanks! Keep Angus out of trouble."

4

GABE'S FIRST FEW nights in the cold case unit were hell. He sat in his dingy cell and went stir crazy. He had grown more depressed over the tailspin that his career had taken. He had to pull himself up by his bootstraps, so he resolved himself to make the most of his assignment. The next night, he came prepared.

He brought a folding cot that he'd found in his camping gear, which was left from his divorce. He brought a pillow and blanket so he could sleep when he got bored, which would be soon after starting his tour of duty. The cot, pillow and blanket folded up neatly and stored undetected behind the shelves of dead files.

He'd also dug around in his closet and found his fifty-pound dumbbells. His new assignment provided an excellent opportunity to get back in shape. He brought his exercise bag, which contained his running shoes, shorts, sweats and a change of underwear.

It didn't take long for him to settle into a routine. He began each night with sit-ups, push-ups and a vigorous weight workout. He then changed into his running shoes and sweats and went for a thirty-minute run.

The city was busy at that time of night. He wore a hooded sweatshirt to mask his identity from the officers and any staff who might be prowling around. His only concern was that Garrison or Richey would stop in and find him gone. He guessed he could get away with an apology and feigned ignorance the first time. It is sometimes easier to ask for forgiveness than permission.

After his run, he went to the officers' locker room to shower and dress. He wore jeans and casual shirts since he was not meeting the public.

About 3:00 a.m., he would meet one of the midnight officers for lunch. From 4:00 to 7:00 he would unfold his cot and sleep. Life was starting to look up. He was getting more sleep and the exercise made him feel better.

Two weeks into his new assignment, Gabe heard a knock on the door just as he was preparing to leave for his run. He panicked, thinking it was Richey or Garrison. He leaned against the door and asked, "Who is it?"

The voice on the other side replied, "Schneider from the equipment room."

Gabe quickly opened the door and stepped back. There stood a thin, elderly man pushing a large cart. He stuck out his hand and introduced himself. "Ray Schneider."

Gabe shook his hand and invited him in. "What have you got there, Ray?"

Ray pushed the cart in and stepped around it as he slapped his hands together to shed the dust. "Well, Ben Hire told me about your predicament. He asked if I had some things to make your life a little easier. I got hold of Mullens in the property room and he gave me some recovered stolen property that no one ever claimed. We thought you could use them until someone claims them, which will probably be never."

Gabe was ecstatic. He smiled from ear to ear like a kid seeing his Christmas gifts under the tree for the first time. "You bet! What have you got?"

Ray took items off of the cart and laid them on Gabe's desk. "Let's see here, note pads, calendar, desk lamps, paper clips, stapler, telephone, phone book, rolodex, pens, pencils and a sharpener. That's it for me."

He reached under the top shelf and pulled the big items off of the second shelf. "Mullens sent you a television, VCR, an old PC, monitor, keyboard, power strip and some pictures to hang on the wall. You'll have to plug the TV into the department's cable jack. If you don't, you won't get decent reception down here. Now remember, if someone wants these things back, he'll have to take them."

Gabe said, "I understand. This is more stuff than I have at home. I don't know what to say."

Ray smiled. "No need to say anything. This is just a gesture of support from two screw-ups to another."

Gabe was puzzled. "Screw-ups? What do you mean?"

Ray sat on the edge of Gabe's desk and explained. "Well, kid, years ago, I was a road officer. As time went on I found that I didn't have the heart for a good fight. I found myself avoiding activity and arrests. I got to where I dreaded coming to work because I was afraid of getting hurt. The guys began to suspect that I was a coward and I lost their respect. I didn't realize I was afraid of getting hurt until after I'd gotten on the department. I didn't belong on the road. I didn't want to get anyone hurt, so I went to the chief and asked to be reassigned. He put me in the equipment room to get me out of everyone's hair. I've been there ever since."

He hung his head in shame as he confessed his secret. He took a deep breath and continued. "Mullens was different. He hurt his back when he crashed during a pursuit. He couldn't work the streets anymore. They put him in the property room taking care of the evidence and recovered property. At least he got pigeon-holed for a good reason."

Gabe's heart went out to him. He patted him on the back and said, "Listen, Ray, you're no coward. It took courage to admit that you weren't suited for the street. At least you had the good sense and compassion for your fellow officers to admit your fear and do something about it. I admire that."

"Thanks, but I accepted my lot in life years ago. I'm just hanging on till retirement in two years. Mullens is doing the same. By the way, Mullens said if you need anything else, contact him. Same goes for me. We think you got screwed and we don't like Garrison anymore than you do."

Ray stood and pushed his empty cart to the door. Gabe hurried ahead and held it open. Ray said, "Later," and shuffled back to his own jail cell.

Angus shut off his lights and coasted to a stop. He got out of his car and closed the car door quietly. He crept quietly down the dirt lane leading to the shore of the lake. Ahead in the darkness, he heard the crack of a police radio.

In the moonlight he could see the rotund figure of Len Shelley sitting on a bench. Angus eased up behind him and gave an impressive impersonation of a snarling dog. His deep gravelly voice added realism to the growl.

Shelley levitated off of the bench and yelled. He drew his pistol and swore like a drunken sailor as he turned to fire. Angus howled with laughter and ducked behind Shelley's car to avoid being shot. Shelley heard the laughter and instantly recognized Blauw's raspy voice. He relaxed the tension on the trigger just in time to halt the discharge.

Shelley was furious as he holstered his pistol. He stomped over, jerked Angus up by the shirt and slammed him against the car. Angus was laughing so hard that he couldn't resist. Resistance would have been futile anyway. Shelley outweighed him by 170 pounds.

Blauw felt like a rag doll in Shelley's massive fists. Shelley yelled, "Angus, you crazy old corpse, you almost got your scrawny ass shot off! You know better than to scare a nigger like that! I'd pop your ugly head for you, but I'd just have to call someone in on overtime to finish your shift!"

He released Angus and returned to the bench. "Look at this, you old sack of wrinkles, you made me spill my gizzards." Shelley picked up the box and looked inside. "Good thing I was almost done. I'd really be pissed if you'd made me waste the whole box."

Angus finally stopped laughing and said, "That's what you get for sitting out here in the dark like some fat old deviant. You ain't fooling anyone. You're out here in the dark jacking off."

Shelley shook his head in disgust. "You sick old bastard! Don't you ever have anything nice to say to anyone?"

Angus chuckled. "Yeah, I say nice things to nice people. I just don't know any nice people. Let's get Kinnett and go to lunch."

"Nah, I just ate these gizzards. You take him."

"Oh bullshit, those gizzards won't hold you over. You'll be looking for something else to eat in thirty minutes. You'll be digging through the trashcans like some old, mangy dog. Come to lunch with us. I'm buying tonight."

Shelley perked up. "It's about time, you cheapskate. I'll go along just to get a free meal out of you. I'll meet you at the station. I need to see how Kinnett is holding up anyway."

Angus pounded on Gabe's door and yelled, "Open the fucking door, you pervert, and don't tell me to be quiet because of your neighbors! You ain't got no neighbors here, just a bunch of rats that have higher I.Q.s than you!"

From inside, a voice yelled, "Come in!" Shelley and Angus entered the pitch-black dungeon. The distant light from the garage was the only light that pierced the darkness.

Shelley's heart instantly sank. He whispered, "Shit, Angus, he's lost it, sitting in the dark like this. He's probably sucking on his gun barrel."

Angus growled, "Kinnett, you psychotic fucker, where are you?"

"Over here. Be quiet, you'll scare them off."

Angus fumbled around until he found the light switch and turned on the lone light-bulb. He and Shelley were shocked to find Gabe seated behind his desk with a rifle supported on his elbows and a contraption on his face that resembled something out of Star Wars.

Shelley slowly walked over to Gabe and rubbed his face. He asked, "Boy, what are you doing? You gone plum crazy?"

Gabe pulled the apparatus off of his face and smiled. "No, sarge, I'm hunting. Didn't you ever hunt when you were a kid?"

Shelley picked up the apparatus and said, "Yeah, but what are you hunting down here?"

Gabe put the rifle down and leaned back in his chair. "Rats, sarge. Those are night vision goggles. This is a .177 caliber pellet gun. I got them from Mullens in property. They were recovered stolen property that no one claimed. He let me use them to shoot rats. Look here at this rifle, it's a dandy. You break open the barrel and put the pellet in. When you close it, it fires the pellet at 1000 feet per second. No noise and it's deadly on rats."

85

Shelley's eyes opened wide with excitement. "Oh, man, I gotta try this! Turn out the lights, Angus." He put the goggles on and cocked the barrel of the rifle. He picked a pellet from the open container on Gabe's desk and put it in the chamber. He closed the barrel and looked around for a rat.

Turning on the lights had sent the rats scurrying for cover. It only took a few seconds of darkness for the vermin to show themselves again. Shelley put the front bead on the rat's shoulder. With a gentle press of the match-grade trigger, the silence was broken by a sharp crack. The rat jumped straight up in the air and fell dead to the floor. Shelley laughed with glee. "Ah man, I forgot how much fun it was to shoot rats. You guys go to lunch, I'm going to stay here and kill some more."

Angus busted Shelley's bubble. "Now, Len, you got a shift to run. What's going to happen if Richey or Garrison finds you here? Even if they're not out, one of the snitches will rat on you."

He realized that Angus was right. He removed the goggles as Angus turned on the lights. He laid the rifle down and nodded his head. "Yeah, I guess you're right, but don't you kill all the rats, boy. I'll be back when the ladder-climbers aren't working. Come on, boy, let's go to lunch. Angus is buying and that don't happen often."

Gabe perked up and grabbed his jacket. "Okay, I can't miss a thousand-year event like that."

Angus looked around and asked, "Hey, Kinnett, you little sneak-thief. Where did you get all this stuff? Pictures, TV, VCR, a computer, night vision, pellet gun, you been burglarizing businesses while you're working?"

Shelley interrupted, "Hell, Angus, you deadbeats on this shift couldn't catch him if he was."

Gabe answered, "No, not at all. Mullens and Schneider gave me this stuff. They heard about my transfer and wanted to make me more comfortable."

Angus shook his head. "Boy, that's a surprise. I didn't think those two had any feelings for anyone. They never did anything nice for me."

Shelley pointed his finger at Angus and chastised him. "That's because you treat everyone like dirt, Angus! Mullens and

Schneider are good guys. They just had some bad luck, that's all. They may not work the streets, but they're good cops at heart."

As they headed out the door, Gabe said, "Hey, sarge, pay raises are coming up soon and I was wondering who evaluates me in this position."

"Well, boy, I guess Major Richey will."

Gabe was confused. "How can he evaluate me if I don't have to do anything and he never sees me?"

"Good question, boy. You see, the way our performance appraisals are set up, if an evaluator checks the *Satisfactory* category, he doesn't have to justify it with a comment. He can just check *Satisfactory* in all the areas of your evaluation and never comment on how you're doing. He only has to comment if he checks *Above Satisfactory* or *Below Satisfactory*. He'll just check *Satisfactory* and you'll get an average pay raise."

He thought for a few seconds and said, "So, if I solve these cases, he'll have to give me an *Above Satisfactory* or *Outstanding* evaluation, right?"

Angus and Shelley both laughed hysterically. Shelley said, "No, he won't, because you'll never clear any of these cases. Don't frustrate yourself by trying. Just get your sleep, exercise, shoot rats and do your time. You weren't put here to clear cases. You were put here to force you to quit. Stick it out and get back on the streets. Don't make waves, boy, or you'll spend the rest of your career like Schneider and Mullens, wasting away in some corner office."

Angus slapped Shelley on the back and prodded him further. "Yeah, Len, he needs to be successful like us, stuck on midnights forever with no chance of promotion or getting the more desirable shifts or assignments."

Shelley frowned at him and retorted, "Hey, you old broke-dick, this is a great job! We get to throw shit-heads in jail and don't have to put up with the staff breathing down our necks. It's a great life. Look at all the fun we're having."

Angus responded sarcastically, "Yeah, and since we work nights, look at how much money we save on suntan lotion, not that you'd ever need any on your black ass."

Shelley laughed and slapped Angus on the back. "That's right, you shiny old fossil, I don't need no sun. I'm tanned

87

naturally. You white folks spend a fortune trying to get dark like me."

At the diner, Blauw, Shelley, Kinnett and Arvid Hallos sat together. They laughed at some of the humorous calls that they'd handled in the past few months. Gabe missed the excitement of the streets and needed this camaraderie to remind he him that was still one of the guys. As he glanced toward the door, he saw Ben Hire walk in. He raised his hand and motioned for Ben to join them. "Hey, Ben, how's it going?"

Ben replied, "Good, the wife is over in Bend visiting her sister, Pam. I couldn't sleep and thought I'd come see what you zombies are up to. I never see you guys any more."

Angus said, "Just dodging all you day-shift rats. How's that prick, Garrison, doing?"

Ben mumbled in disgust, "Okay, I guess, I spend all my time trying to avoid him."

Gabe interrupted, "Hey listen, Ben, I want to thank you for putting in a good word for me to Mullens and Schneider. They took good care of me."

Ben smiled as he scanned the menu. "Ah, don't mention it. We all fall from grace now and then. I may be taking your place down there before long."

Shelley looked concerned and said, "Now, Ben, I don't like the sound of that. What have you done? You get caught knocking off some strange tail?"

Ben shook his head as he poured sugar into his coffee. "Nah, nothing fun like that. I haven't done anything. That's the problem. Garrison is going to be crawling up my ass before long, and I don't have the answers that he'll be looking for."

"About what?" Shelley asked.

"Well, I think there's a connection between some of these old murders, but for the life of me, I can't find it. If Garrison gets wind of it, he'll expect me to put it all together, and I don't have a clue what it is."

Angus asked, "What murders, Ben, we've just had two."

"Yeah, I know, Angus. The Ryan kid might not have been connected, but the Windsor case stinks. We've had other people killed the same way, but I can't find a connection."

Shelley asked, "What did the coroner say about Windsor, Ben?"

"He'd had the blood supply to his brain shut off. Someone applied a lateral vascular neck restraint on him. Good thing you jumped through all the hoops that night. We'd have egg on our faces if you'd passed it off as a natural."

Angus said, "Hell, Ben, I've read all the dead files. There ain't no connection."

Gabe looked at Angus in shock. Angus snarled, "Yeah, that's right, asshole, I was in the cold case unit once. Think you're the only guy who ever shit in his own nest? Garrison wasn't the chief back then, but he carried on the tradition."

Gabe and Shelley leaned back and laughed. Shelley said, "Yeah, Gabe, who do you think that assignment was created for. Blauw here was the first inmate in cop jail. He started the whole tradition." Everyone at the table laughed at Angus, who was unfazed.

"I just can't figure it out." Ben said. "Most serial killers are pathetic, inadequate losers who victimize people weaker than them. This guy strapped Windsor on with his bare hands, and Windsor was a big man. He manhandled Windsor like a baby and killed him with a lateral vascular neck restraint. It takes some real balls to go after someone with your bare hands."

Gabe thought for a minute, then asked, "Ben, I'm dying to find some way to break the boredom. Would you like for me to look through the old cases for you?"

Ben shook his head. "Nah, kid, I've been through them myself. If Blauw and me couldn't find anything, it's not there."

Shelley said, "Yeah, Ben, we have to find something to entertain Kinnett here. He's running out of rats to shoot."

Ben looked puzzled and asked, "Rats? Oh no, don't tell me you're shooting my rats! I use to feed them! They're my pets!"

Gabe's mouth dropped open in shock. "You, too?"

Ben smiled. "Yeah, I relieved Blauw. I was the second guy to royally piss off the chief."

Gabe said, "Boy that makes me feel better. Now I know there's hope for me."

Ben reassured him. "Sure, kid, just do your time. Garrison will find someone else to focus on. You'll be out of there before you know it."

"That doesn't make me feel better. I wouldn't wish that assignment on anyone."

After lunch, Gabe settled in for his nightly snooze. He'd bagged up the dead rats and cleaned the blood off the floor. He pulled a blanket over himself and didn't awaken until he heard a knock on his door about 7:00.

He quickly folded up his cot and slid it behind the file shelves. When he opened the door, he immediately saw the stripes. He thought he'd been busted. He stepped back and allowed the sergeant in.

The sergeant stuck his hand out and introduced himself. "Hey, kid, Joe Rand. I run the records unit. I came in a little early because you're always gone by the time I get here at eight."

Gabe motioned for him to sit in his only chair. "Have a seat, sarge, I'm just finishing up here."

Joe remained standing as he looked around and asked, "Finishing what? What have you got to do here?"

Gabe looked around searching for an answer, then shrugged his shoulders. "Well, sarge, nothing. I don't do anything here, but that just means it doesn't take me long to finish up."

Joe laughed. "I know, kid, that's okay. I just wanted to tell you that I was sorry to hear about your assignment. I don't know you, but I hate to see anyone pull this detail."

Gabe smiled and shrugged, "Oh, that's okay. I've got more comforts here than I do at home. I'll be okay."

"Yeah, I know you will. I've heard good things about you."

Gabe couldn't resist the urge to quiz Rand. "Listen, sarge, how did you wind up in the records unit? I thought that was a civilian job."

Joe leaned against the wall and replied, "It was. I got in trouble several years ago, so they pigeon-holed me in the records unit. I'm out of sight and off the street. I guess I was the department's screw-up of the year."

"How do you mean, sarge?"

"Years ago, I was working the streets. I got a call to investigate a domestic assault over on Boice Street. When I got there, I got jumped by the old man. He was high on meth and thoroughly kicked my ass. He was bigger and stronger than me, and I wasn't a very good fighter. It was all I could do to keep him from taking my gun. I got lucky and wound up on top of him. I put him in a lateral vascular neck restraint, but held on too long. When he went limp, I thought he was faking it to get me to let go. I didn't think I had applied it properly and knew as soon as I let go that he'd get me down again. I was out of gas and knew I couldn't survive another round, so I held on till backup arrived. He was dead, and I caught all kinds of hell for killing him. The D.A. refused to prosecute me, but the chief transferred me to records to embarrass me and force me to quit."

Gabe listened intently and sympathized with Joe. "Well, sarge, you got promoted. You must have done something to redeem yourself."

Joe shook his head. "Nah, I just played the race card. I found a black attorney and sued the department. I claimed that I was being discriminated against because I was black. The chief wasn't impressed, but it was an election year. The mayor didn't want the negative publicity in the black community, so he overrode the chief and settled with me out of court. They promoted me to sergeant, but that didn't get me out of records. The mayor promoted me, but the chief still made the assignments. I got my stripes, but the chief left me in records."

Gabe was puzzled. Joe said, "I know what you're thinking, kid, but I did what I had to. I got used to working in records and I actually enjoy it now. I know you think I should be ashamed for getting ahead by playing the race card, but trust me, everyone plays the hand that they're dealt. I've never had the luxury of a college education. I couldn't screw my way to the top like some of the women on the department. I couldn't get any dirt on the staff, so I used the only asset I had, my color."

Gabe didn't speak. Joe said, "Don't judge me too harshly, Kinnett. Take some good advice. If you're ever lucky enough to have life deal you an ace card, play it. Life may only deal you one, and you'll hate yourself if you don't use it. Yeah, I got my stripes because I'm black, but I don't feel guilty. I'm good at my job and I take care of my employees. I'm not some incompetent token nigger that everyone has to cover for. I carry my load and I run a tight, efficient unit. I'm not sorry for the way I got my stripes."

Gabe sensed that Joe was getting more and more defensive. "I don't judge you, sarge. I haven't walked in your shoes. I've heard nothing but good about you."

Joe relaxed. "Well, the reason I came here was to tell you that if you need anything from my unit, it's yours. Let me know if I can help."

Gabe smiled and extended his hand, "Thanks, sarge, I appreciate that. Listen, you won't say anything about all the stuff I have down here, will you?"

Joe looked around and smiled. "What stuff? I don't see anything."

He turned to leave, but Gabe interrupted him. "Hey sarge, since you're here, maybe you can educate me on something."

"Sure, if I can."

Gabe pointed to the rows of dusty files on the shelves at the back of the bunker. "You're the records sergeant, so why are all these files down here? Why aren't they up in your unit? Why do we have a cold case unit anyway?"

"Good question. First of all, there's no such thing as a cold case unit. This is just the graveyard for dead files. You're just a caretaker. You see, by Oregon state statute, every police department has to have a records retention schedule. That's the policy that dictates how long we'll retain records. The statute suggests seven years, so that's what we've adopted as our policy. That means that we only retain records like offense reports, accident reports, payroll sheets, etc. for seven years, then we destroy them. If we didn't do that, we'd be overrun by boxes of old reports that no one needs any more."

Gabe nodded. "Makes sense, sarge, so why are we keeping these?"

"Simple. Some cases are serious and there's a slight chance that some of them will be cleared someday. We keep murders, rapes, kidnappings and armed robberies. There's no statute of limitations on some of them and there may be evidence that we'd collected years ago that we didn't have the technology to analyze or a suspect to link it to. As technology improves, some of that old evidence might be analyzed and used to indict a suspect. You never know when some convict might confess or roll over on a cellmate who confesses. A lot of old cases were cleared when they perfected DNA comparison."

It all made sense to Gabe. "Okay, I guess I see why I'm here."

Rand stepped toward Gabe and pointed at him. "No, Kinnett. Make no mistake about it, you're not here because of those cases. You're here for punishment. Those cases aren't just cold, they're dead. We're just keeping them to comply with policy. No one expects you to read them. You're just here to rot away. Don't embarrass yourself anymore than you already have. Don't give Garrison something to laugh about. Just pass the time until someone else falls from grace and replaces you here. Put this behind you and go on with your career."

"Yeah, I guess you're right, sarge. I just get so bored. You can only watch so many late-night movies and shoot so many rats."

Rand smiled. "Yeah, I know. All of us who got stuck in the dark corners of the department felt the same way. You'll adapt. You're lucky, your sentence isn't permanent. You'll be out of here soon, but we never will. Hang in there and call if I can help you with anything. And remember what I told you, Kinnett, if you ever get some leverage over those assholes, you'd better use it. If you wait too long, it won't do you any good. Get ahead any way you can."

He closed the door behind him. Gabe knew he'd never be able to look at himself in the mirror if he used blackmail to get ahead. He had too much pride. He knew of other officers on the department who felt the same way as Sergeant Rand, but that was not in Gabe Kinnett's character. He would get ahead by solid, hard work.

After Rand left, Gabe stared at the case files. He wondered what secrets they held that might help Ben Hire. If he opened them, he would have to keep it secret. If it got around that he was trying to investigate them, he would be the laughing stock of the entire department.

Swede Boreman drove back to the shop as fast as he could. He was a heavy equipment mechanic and had just finished replacing the fuel pump on a Caterpillar earthmover. He was late for his birthday party at the Last Drop Lounge, and nothing else mattered.

He threw his tools back in their bins without cleaning them. He didn't remove his oily coveralls before climbing in the driver's seat or de-grease his hands before touching the interior.

Swede dialed his home number on the cell phone and waited for his wife to answer. When Linda answered, he began his tirade. "Linda! The guys are having a party for me at the bar tonight. I'll be home late."

Fearing Swede's anger, Linda tried to ease into the issue gently. "Swede, we're having a party for you here. Mom and Dad are here. Kevin has been excited about this for days. I think your friends will understand if your family comes first."

Swede's anger erupted as he roared, "Maybe they would, but I won't! This is what I want! I don't give a shit about your mom and dad! Kevin doesn't care about my birthday! I don't give a shit about you or your damn party! I'll be home when I get there!" With that, he turned off the power to the phone and threw it across the cab.

Linda stood silently, then quietly hung up the receiver. She erased the humiliation from her face and turned to make Swede's excuse for him. "Son, dad has to work late. We'll have the party without him. We'll save him some cake."

Kevin angrily shook his head. "Mom, when are you going to quit making excuses for him? He's not working late. He's getting drunk again. He doesn't care about any of us. Why do we even stay here?"

Linda's mom and dad tried to act like they hadn't overheard the conversation, but they couldn't pretend any longer. Linda's dad said, "Linda, you've done all you can here. Why don't you and Kevin move in with us? He's going to kill you someday."

Linda fought back the tears as she shook her head. "No, not yet, Dad. Maybe the counselor can help. I want to give it more time."

There was an awkward silence in the kitchen. Linda choked back her tears, forced a pretentious smile and said, "Okay, so let's party." Kevin and the grandparents moved to the table and pretended to have a good time so Linda's feelings wouldn't be hurt deeper.

Swede bought the first round of drinks even though it was his birthday. Good friends were hard for a man like him to find, and he needed to buy as many as he could. The party didn't involve cake and gifts, but several rounds of bourbon.

After the sixth round, Swede looked around the bar to see if anyone he recognized had come in late. At the end of the bar, his eyes met those of a tall, thin woman of thirty-five years with reddish-blonde hair. She lifted her glass in a toast and smiled seductively at Swede.

The challenge was hurled. Swede suddenly lost interest in his newly purchased friends and eased to the end of the bar to investigate further. As he slid up on the stool, he motioned for the bartender to refill the lady's glass.

Swede had no time for tack and diplomacy. He pressed his unshaved face in the woman's and flashed his tobacco-stained smile. "Hi, beautiful, haven't seen you in here before."

The woman leaned away from Swede's foul breath and replied, "I haven't been here before. I just heard it was your birthday and thought it would give me an excuse to meet you. I've heard a lot about you."

Swede's curiosity shot through the roof. His ego wasn't far behind. "Really! You're kidding! You wanted to meet me? Lady, you didn't need an excuse to meet me. We should have met years ago. Listen, this ain't fair. You know my name, but I don't know yours."

The woman feigned an embarrassed smiled. "In good time, Swede, in good time. So, happy birthday. What's your wife getting you?"

He looked around to make sure no one was listening. "A divorce, I hope. I'm bored to tears with that bitch. Besides, it doesn't matter what she gets me. What matters more is what you're going to give me."

The woman blushed. "Oh, Swede, what could I possibly have that would interest a man like you?"

Swede rolled his eyes. "Oh, baby, let's get out of here. We'll find something." He slammed his shot and the woman sat hers on the bar. He encircled her shoulders with his arm and escorted her outside. She became frightened and tried to stay on her stool, but Swede was too strong. He lifted her to her tiptoes and hustled her out the door.

On the way to the truck, she tried to slow things down. "Swede! Stop! Wait a minute, I'm not ready for this!"

He laughed, turned her toward him and kissed her hard on the mouth. His foul breath and sandpaper face made her pull away. "Yeah you are, sweetheart. If you're not ready now, you will be in a few minutes."

He dragged her to the tool truck, opened the door and pushed her in. Once he was in, he pulled the woman close to him and tried to kiss her. She turned her head and acted like she wasn't disgusted. She said in a frightened tone, "Swede, this is too public. I'd be embarrassed if anyone saw us here. Let's go back inside and talk." She wanted to get back to the safety of the crowd without angering Swede. Without so much as a word, he started the engine, put the truck in gear and sped out of the parking lot.

As he drove, Swede pulled her close to him. He tried to move his hand higher up the inside of her thigh. Although under the numbing influence of heavy medication and alcohol, she was gripped with fear. She allowed him limited access, hoping he would not explode with anger and hurt her. Finally, she closed her legs tight before he'd reached his goal.

Swede said, "I can't believe we've met like this. This is the best birthday I've ever had. You and I are going to be great friends, you know that?"

The woman flashed a brief, pretentious smile and said, "Oh, Swede, you say that to all the women you pick up in a bar. You probably told that to Linda when you first met her."

Swede looked at her suspiciously. "How do you know Linda? I never told you her name."

The woman's eyes were glassy and unresponsive. He assumed it was from the drinks. "Oh, I met her briefly in passing once. We've not talked since. We didn't have a lot in common."

He didn't want to frighten the lady anymore than he already had. He didn't want this to turn into a wrestling match, so he tried to keep her anxiety level low. He wouldn't pry further until after he'd had sex with her.

At the end of a dirt road that ran along the river, Swede threw the truck in park and turned his attention back to the woman. "Now! If we're going to consummate this new love of ours, I have to know your name."

The woman gazed at Swede through watery eyes. She sighed deeply in an effort to fight back her fear. "Well, lover, you can call me Sarah. I'm a good friend of Linda's."

He jerked away in shock as he stared at her. "What is this, some kind of joke or something? Who the hell are you and what are you on? You're all fucked up!"

Sarah smiled as she produced a .380 automatic pistol from her jacket pocket. "Yes, I may be, but not over you. You're a pathetic, revolting pig. You've treated Linda like dirt for years and have the nerve to think that a fat slime-ball like you could have a woman like me. I wouldn't have sex with a greasy, obnoxious pig like you if the whole human race depended on it."

Swede panicked as he reached behind him and groped for the door handle. He couldn't turn from Sarah because he was focused on the muzzle of her Colt automatic. He found the handle, opened the door and slid out. Sarah slid behind the wheel and said, "Come get your birthday present, Swede."

He continued to back away, so she cautioned him, "One more step, Swede, and I'll blow your head off. Come here!"

Hoping to delay the inevitable, he stopped his retreat. As he slowly stepped up to Sarah, he knew his only chance of survival was to grab the pistol before she fired. She smiled and said, "That's a good boy."

Sarah opened her coat with her left hand and exposed her breasts. She said, "I want these to be the last sight you see on earth, and know that you'll never have them."

Before Swede could lunge for the gun, Sarah fired at his abdomen. The hollow point struck Swede's spinal cord, dropping him to his knees as he grabbed his stomach. She then stuck the muzzle to Swede's forehead with deliberate determination and executed him. The back of his head blew out and his brains splattered on the ground behind him. He fell backwards with his legs curled under him, and never flinched.

Sarah closed her eyes and regained her composure. She looked around the cab and saw the ejected shell cases in the passenger side floorboard. She leaned over and picked them up.

She put the Colt and fired cases back in her coat pocket, closed the door and put the truck in gear. She drove back to the bar and parked the truck on the street. She walked to her car and drove home.

Arvid Hallos chuckled every time he thought about Angus Blauw telling how he'd scared ten years off Len Shelley's life. Shelley wouldn't tolerate sleeping on duty, but even he couldn't stay awake all the time. Since his encounter with Blauw, Shelley had changed his hiding place. Arvid had made it his mission to find it.

He was driving the desolate roads that ran along the river and circled the lakes. As he bounced along an overgrown dirt road commonly used by parkers, he encountered a log lying across the road. He slammed on the breaks, not wanting to damage the undercarriage of the car.

When he got out to move the log, he stopped dead in his tracks. It wasn't a log at all. He leaned closer and shined his flashlight on the log. He took a step back in shock as his light illuminated the bloody face of Swede Boreman. Arvid recognized him from their many encounters on domestic abuse calls and D.W.I. arrests.

He noticed that the back of Swede's head was missing. He followed the spray of blood and tissue on the ground with his light back to his own feet, then realized that he was standing in Swede's brains. He quickly jumped to the side and wiped his feet in the grass as he cringed. He grabbed his portable radio and called for Sergeant Shelley to meet him there.

When Shelley pulled up, Arvid's cruiser blocked his view of Swede. He berated Arvid as he stormed past the cars. "Arvid, what the hell you doing way out here, boy? You tore up your car, didn't you? You hard-headed little shit, I told you guys to be careful on these old roads!"

Arvid laughed and replied proudly, "No, sarge, I didn't tear anything up. I was just out here looking for your new sleeping spot."

Shelley stopped in his tracks and glared at Arvid. His glare had no effect. His men had long ago pegged him as a big softy. "Okay, Arvid, you got my big ass out here. What do you want?"

As the last word had rolled off Shelley's tongue, he jumped as though he'd spotted a coiled rattlesnake. He fell back a step as he saw Swede on the ground in Arvid's headlights.

Arvid laughed hysterically. It had become a shift tradition to startle the sergeant. Arvid now had something to humor the other guys with.

"Arvid, you asshole! Next time, warn me when you find something like this! You scared ten years off my life!"

Arvid stopped laughing and said, "Hell no, it's too much fun watching you jump."

Shelley studied the corpse closely. "Who is he?"

"Swede Boreman. I arrested him a few months ago for thumping his wife and kid. He's a real piece of work."

Shelley stepped around the blood pool and eased closer, "Not any more. Looks like someone did a real piece of work on his head. Bet it was his wife, what do you bet?"

"I ain't taking that bet, sarge. If she did, I wouldn't blame her. If it were up to me, I'd classify this as the weirdest case of suicide I've ever seen and release him to the funeral home."

Shelley leaned over and squinted his eyes as he took a closer look. "Hmm, one in the belly and one in the forehead." He looked around and didn't see a gun. "Not a suicide, Arvid. Looks like old Swede here finally paid his dues. Probably his wife. Can't say as I blame her. Better call Ben."

Ben showed up an hour later with the lab techs. After a cursory search of the immediate area, Ben turned the scene over to the techs and returned to the station where he contacted Shelley in his office. "Okay, Len, the techs have the scene. We need to make the notification to Linda Boreman. I hear our victim was a fine example of manhood."

"Yes sir, he was. Fine piece of work. Probably his wife or kid who shot him."

Ben rubbed his fatigued eyes. "Yeah, that's my guess, too. I want to deliver the notification myself so I can gauge her reaction. I should be able to get a feel for her when she hears he's dead. Could I have one of your guys accompany me?"

"Sure, I'll have Arvid go with you. He's just finished his initial report."

Gabe was adjusting to his new job. He was getting a few hours of sleep each night. That held him over until he could catch a nap in the early afternoon. He was feeling better, losing weight and firming up from his runs and weight workouts on Garrison's time.

He looked at the clock when he stirred from his afternoon nap. It was 4:00. He hurriedly dressed, hoping to catch Ben Hire before he got off duty at 5:00. He slipped on his sweats and ran to the station.

As he entered the detective unit, he was met with laughter and cutting remarks from the other detectives. He let it roll off his back and hurried into Ben's office.

Ben was poring over case files, hoping to find a common factor in the recent killings. He looked up as Gabe walked in. "Hey, Gabe, what are you doing out this time of day? Don't you midnight guys know that you'll burst into flames if you get caught in the sunlight?"

"That would suit Garrison and Richey just fine."

"Ah, don't let those guys bother you. They've pulled some pretty devious shenanigans in their careers. What brings you here? You get enough sleep today?"

Gabe strained his neck to see what Ben was reading. "Yeah, sure, I'm adjusting. Hey listen, Ben, I heard we had another killing last night. Any idea who did it?"

Ben laid the files down and leaned back in his chair as he rubbed his eyes. "No, I thought I'd get a clue when I talked to his wife. She was shocked and genuinely traumatized. His son was also upset. If I'm any good at reading people, I'd say they had nothing to do with it. They were both at home with her parents celebrating the asshole's birthday. He was at a bar getting soused. The other patrons at the bar said he left with a blonde, but no one had ever seen her before. His truck was parked on the street, so they must have left in her car."

Gabe asked, "Did the lab boys find anything in his truck?"

"Nah, we didn't tow it. It may have been a mistake to release it back to the employer, but I looked inside. It was so dirty and greasy that you'd never find anything of value in it. Besides, I'm sure they left the bar in her car. This gal was classy. It's likely that she would never be caught dead in a grease bucket like that. I described the woman to Mrs. Boreman, but she didn't recognize her. We don't know if she killed him or not. She's just the last person that he was seen with. For all I know, the blonde's jealous husband could have killed him. It's hard to imagine any gal that good-looking screwing a greasy slime-ball like Boreman. I guess we'll never know until we find her."

Gabe thought, *Ben's a top notch detective, but he really screwed up by not towing that truck. It was a mistake to make assumptions like that. Oh well, Ben is the expert. He must know what he's doing.*

He turned toward the door, "Well, Ben, I was just curious about the killing. I know you don't need my help, but I have a lot of time on my hands. If I can help, let me know."

"Thanks, Gabe, but if Garrison found out that I was using you in any way that got you out of your prison cell, he'd have my head on a platter for robbing him of his revenge. Thanks anyway."

"Sure, I understand, but tell me something. Just where do you start in a homicide investigation anyway? I'm just curious." Gabe had an ulterior motive for asking. He wanted to know where to start with the dead files, but didn't want Ben to know it. He had taken enough teasing over his transfer already.

Ben looked a little surprised, then began. "Well, I start with the crime scene. We interview all the witnesses and make sure the lab boys do a thorough job of processing, photographing and diagramming it for court. I then go to the coroner's office. They determine the cause of death, then photograph and collect vital evidence from the body. I then do a thorough background on the victim. That usually leads to at least one person who wanted them dead. When you trace the victim's footsteps a few hours before their death, you'll usually be able to focus on a suspect."

Gabe listened intently and asked, "That didn't happen with those cases in the basement?"

"No, those cases led nowhere. I'm afraid that's where this case and the Windsor case are going to wind up. Sometimes

101

suspects and motives just aren't obvious. Like the attorney that Ryan kid killed a few months ago. That kid had never heard of Lynch. I still don't have a clue why he targeted him. There has to be a link somewhere. That kid was too good a kid to kill someone at random for no reason. I guess we'll never figure that one out."

Gabe shook Ben's hand. "Okay, Ben, thanks for your time. If you can't sleep at night, come on down to my dungeon. We'll snipe some rats."

Ben glared at him and ordered, "You leave my pets alone!"

Gabe laughed as he walked through the gauntlet of derogatory comments from the other detectives. As he got to the hallway, he held his middle finger up in the air for all to see. He was proud of himself. He was getting almost as calloused as Blauw and Shelley.

Gabe hit the office with a renewed sense of purpose. He had all the time in the world, so he felt no urgency to push himself hard. He still wanted to do his nightly runs and weight workouts. He would read files until the need for sleep overtook him.

After his run and weight workout, he turned his attention to the case files. He began with the oldest, but they were thirty years old. He scanned the classifications on the file covers. After the first few files, he could scan the files and see that no leads existed. He wasn't sure he trusted his ability to identify leads. He'd never investigated a case before. He was sure the detectives would have a good laugh if they could see him now.

Most of the files were unsolved robberies and sex offenses. Since he couldn't see a connection between old robberies, sex offenses and the recent murders, he abandoned the idea of reading every file and concentrated on the homicides.

He found only five homicides before 1985. Two were domestic related; husbands who'd killed their wives. Both were tried and convicted.

One was a murder-suicide involving a disgruntled employee who'd killed his supervisor. The other two were robberies that had gone sour. One was cleared by the confession of a man serving time in a neighboring state. The other was cleared when the suspect confessed in a suicide letter just before he'd swallowed a .44 hollow point. His drug and alcohol addiction had become more than he could deal with.

After several nights of unproductive reading, Gabe returned to the first puzzling murder. It took place in 1985. A tool and die maker from Harbaugh Industries was killed by another employee.

Jared Cutchall was killed one night on his lunch break. He'd been working the night shift and was walking out of an all-night diner next to the plant. Paul Siles walked up to him, shot him in the face and walked away.

Witnesses described Siles and he was apprehended an hour later. He confessed and said that he'd killed Cutchall because he'd gotten the supervisor position that Siles felt that he should have received. Throughout the interview, Siles kept shaking his head and mumbling through his tears that he couldn't believe that he'd killed Cutchall. He was truly shocked at his behavior.

The case file contained videotape of Siles's interview. The grief and demeanor of Siles during his interview bore an eerie similarity to Tommy Ryan after killing the attorney. Siles never went to jail. He committed suicide two days before his trial.

The opinion of the psychiatrist who had evaluated Siles was that the murder created such a conflict with his moral values that he couldn't reconcile his actions with his conscience. His guilt overwhelmed him. That, combined with his paralyzing fear of prison, prompted him to take the only avenue of escape available. He was, however, judged mentally competent to stand trial.

Gabe was able to complete one thorough case study each week. Between his workouts, lunches with the guys and naps, he usually had about two hours a night to devote to the dead files.

Each homicide was set aside for comparison later. He made a fact sheet for each case, which listed the circumstances, evidence, all the players and a synopsis.

The next puzzling case was in 1986. A college girl stabbed a psychiatrist to death in his office. Nat Benson was a student at the junior college. She'd requested a consultation with Dr. Albert Sabre about her manic episodes and bipolar disorder. She'd attempted suicide twice, and her parents were at the end of their rope.

Benson had walked into Sabre's office, but never sat down. As he turned his back to sit at his desk, she produced a knife and stabbed him in the back just below his heart. When he dropped to his knees, she stabbed him three more times and left the office.

Sabre's secretary thought the counseling session had ended rather abruptly and went to ask Sabre how it went. She found him bleeding on the floor and called paramedics. He was dead when they arrived.

Benson's videotaped interview revealed a completely different demeanor than Tommy Ryan and Paul Siles. She showed no remorse and seemed completely unaware that she'd done anything wrong. She had to be reminded several times by the detective why she was in custody. He had to tell her repeatedly that she'd killed Dr. Sabre.

In September of 1986, Nat Benson was remanded to a psychiatric hospital for evaluation. She was judged competent to stand trial, but the judge mistakenly set bond too low and released her into the custody of her parents. Benson herself was murdered two weeks later. Her murder was the next case file that Gabe ran across.

In January 1987, Nat Benson was found in an alley. She was totally nude and wrapped in a towel. At first, detectives thought she might have overdosed on prescription drugs, stumbled out into the cold and frozen to death after taking a shower and being high on crystal meth, which was her ride of choice.

The coroner later determined that she'd died as a result of having the blood supply to her brain cut off, just as Dutch Windsor had. She had apparently been killed during a shower or immediately afterwards. She was covered with a thin layer of ice and had ice in her ears.

On his fact sheets, Gabe listed the cause of death for each victim. The similarity between Nat Benson's and Dutch Windsor's deaths rejuvenated him. His chest swelled as the excitement of making the connection filled him.

He wondered if Angus and Ben had made the same connection. They must have. The lateral vascular neck restraint was a technique of incapacitation taught to police officers and martial arts students. It was not commonly known by the general public and certainly not a common means of murder.

In May 1987, an assistant district attorney, Tim Allis, was murdered. He'd been eating Italian food with his wife at his favorite restaurant. A twenty year-old man suffering from manic depression shot him in the parking lot as he left the restaurant.

Roger Moesen shot Allis and tried to shoot his wife, but she ran back into the restaurant, screaming for help. Moesen panicked after missing her several times and fled the scene. It took the police several weeks to focus on him, but eventually a tips hotline call dropped Moesen's name to the detectives. When they went to his apartment to question him, they found that he'd been murdered.

He'd been killed like Windsor and Nat Benson. The blood supply to his brain had been cut off. Mrs. Allis identified a photograph of Moesen as the man who'd shot her husband. A background check of Moesen revealed that he'd had a history of schizophrenia. There was, however, nothing in his background that indicated that he'd ever known Allis.

August of 1987 began a series of related killings. Three elderly ladies were all killed by the same means. Eleanor Rudder was found dead in her house by her daughter. She'd been raped and strangled by a large powerful male, judging by the bruises left on her neck by his fingers.

In September of 1987, Grace Lindsey had been killed the same way. She was found in bed strangled with powerful hands and raped.

In January of 1988, Lois Andover was found in her bathroom strangled and raped. All three case files were rubber-banded together indicating that Ben had worked them simultaneously. He determined that the same person had killed all three women, but never found a suspect to compare the hair and semen samples with. The killings stopped after the third murder.

Gabe easily saw the similarity in the cases. The killer had posed each woman after killing her. He'd used duct tape to tape their hands on their hips and hold their eyelids open. Ben suspected that the killer had taken photographs of the posed women as souvenirs, but he never found the photo lab that had developed them.

Ben had solicited the help of the FBI's behavioral science unit at Quantico, Virginia. They had provided a psychological profile of the killer. They said that he'd been abused as a child and had vented his frustration on others. They estimated him to be six feet tall and about two hundred pounds. He had no college education and was unable to sustain personal relationships or employment. They said nothing that Ben didn't already know.

Ben knew this guy was a sick, masochistic thrill-killer, but was never able to find him. The FBI suspected it was because the killer had an enabler who supported him and kept him out of sight. Ben never located anyone who matched the profile.

Lois Andoever was the last woman murdered before the killer disappeared. The killer had died, gone to prison or moved away. Ben put out a nation-wide alert for any agency investigating similar homicides, but received no response.

In July of 1988, a local drug dealer was beaten to death in an alley behind a nightclub. The alley was Lucian Green's preferred location for illicit drug transactions. It was dark, impossible for the police to surveil, and easy to see someone approaching on foot or in a car.

Apparently one of Green's customers had objected to the quality of the product or the terms of a transaction. The murder weapon was a length of pipe that was wiped clean and left at the scene. There were no witnesses and no tips from informants. Ben had worked that case, too, but the file was noticeably thin. There were either no leads or Ben thought Green deserved little consideration.

5

THREE MONTHS AFTER Gabe had begun his case review, he visited Joe Rand. He awoke from his afternoon nap and walked to the station. As he entered the lobby he felt the penetrating stares of the office staff who looked at him as if he were a leper. He hoped to avoid Garrison and Richey as he hurried directly to Rand's office.

Rand was on the phone when Gabe knocked. Rand motioned for him to come in and finished his call. "Hey, Kinnett, have a seat."

Gabe sat down. "Thanks, sarge, I hope I'm not keeping you from anything important."

"Nah, just answering some records requests. Some people think they're entitled to more than they actually are. Everyone's a big-shot. So! What brings you out of your hole?"

Gabe looked around Rand's comfortably decorated office. "I wanted to ask you something. Didn't you tell me that we retain all records for seven years, then destroy them?"

"That's right."

"All except the serious crimes? Those are in the dungeon, right?"

"Right."

Gabe thought for a second, then said, "So, you've got the last seven years of homicides here in the records unit?"

"Yep, sure do."

Gabe tried to think of a tactful way to ask for those files without raising Rand's suspicion. "Well, sarge, I don't suppose you would let me read them, would you?"

Rand looked suspiciously at him. "Hey listen, you're not launching your own investigation are you?"

His guilt was written across his face. "Well, sarge, I can't lie to you. To tell you the truth, I've been bored to tears. I've been reading those old homicide files and I'd like to read the recent ones. I don't want to put you over a barrel, so if you can't let me, I'll understand."

Rand smiled. "I can certainly understand the boredom. I'll let you see what we have. I can't let the originals out of the unit, so I'll have to make copies. Whatever you do, don't let Garrison know I did this. I used to think there wasn't anything worse that they could do to me than sticking me in the records unit, but I was wrong. I could be stuck in your place."

Gabe assured him, "Don't worry, sarge, I wouldn't say crap if I had a mouth full."

Rand laughed and reminded him, "Yeah, kid, that's what got you in this mess in the first place. You don't talk."

Gabe stood and shook Rand's hand. "Thanks, sarge, I appreciate it." He laid a key on Rand's desk. "I made you a copy of my key. If you would, just leave the files on my desk. I'll see them when I come in at night. It's not a good idea to leave them outside my door."

Rand picked up the key. "You got that right, boy. Garrison would have both our heads if he caught me doing this. I wouldn't do it for just anyone. I'm only doing it because you don't rat out other cops. I respect that."

"Thanks, sarge, if I can ever return the favor, let me know."

Rand was able to copy only one case file per week without arousing suspicion. Gabe carefully read the files as they came in and continued his runs, weight workouts and naps.

The next five homicides were all cleared by arrest, except one. They began in 1989 and ended in 1992. Two were domestic disputes, and two were robberies that resulted in killings.

108

In 1990 though, an eighteen year-old high school student, Mickey Clearey, was killed in his home. He'd been strangled with a length of clothesline cord.

His parents had left him alone while they'd gone out to dinner. No signs of forced entry were found. He had apparently known his killer. He'd let them in the house and escorted them to his room. No suspect was ever identified.

In 1993, there was another strange killing. Howard Wilcox had been the president of the school board. He had no enemies that anyone knew of. He'd been shot to death in his car behind the health club.

He didn't come home one night and his wife asked the police to try to locate him. A midnight officer found him. He apparently hadn't seen his killer. He'd been shot through the driver's window in the side of the head. No suspect was ever located.

There were two more homicides in 1994. One was a local businessman who was having an affair with the wife of one of his disgruntled employees. The employee caught them in the act and killed him in the saddle. The other was a neighborhood dispute that ended in one neighbor shooting the other. Both killings were cleared by arrest.

1995 saw two more killings. One was a drug store robbery that ended with the clerk being shot. The police responded to the silent alarm and rolled up as the suspect was exiting the store. He was convicted and sentenced to life in prison.

The other killing was a high school assistant principal. A special education student had stabbed him. Bruce Webster had been working in his office when Sammy Pritchard asked to see him. When Webster approached the counter, Pritchard leaned over and stabbed him in the chest without warning.

The knife lacerated Webster's aorta and he bled to death before reaching the emergency room. Sammy was only sixteen and was declared mentally incompetent to stand trial. He was remanded to the state mental hospital.

When Gabe lined up the data sheets, he discarded the cases that had been cleared by arrest. The domestic disputes and robberies had understandable motives. The other killings had suspects, but were conspicuously absent of motives. He listed fifteen murders that made no sense. His data sheets were brief summaries of those cases.

1985:   Jared Cutchall: Harbaugh Industries supervisor killed by Paul Siles. Siles had been passed up for the promotion that Cutchall had received. Siles was declared competent to stand trial, but committed suicide two days before trial. Ben's background investigation of Siles revealed that the killing was out of character for him.

1986:   Dr. Albert Sabre: Psychiatrist killed by Nat Benson. Stabbed in his office. Benson had never met Sabre and had no motive.

1986:   Nat Benson: Killed by a lateral vascular neck restraint, probably in the shower. Dumped in an alley. Wrapped in a towel. No suspect identified.

1987:   Tim Allis: Assistant district attorney killed by Roger Moesen. No evidence that Moesen and Allis had ever met. No motive.

1987:   Roger Moesen: Killed in his apartment by lateral vascular neck restraint. No suspect identified.

1987:   Eleanor Rudder: Elderly lady killed in her house and found by her granddaughter. Raped and strangled, with hands and eyes posed. No suspect identified.

1987:   Grace Lindsey: Elderly lady killed in her house. Raped and strangled, with hands and eyes posed. No suspect identified.

1988:   Lois Andoever: Elderly lady killed in her house. Raped and strangled, with hands and eyes posed. No suspect identified.

1988:   Lucian Green: Drug dealer killed in alley. Beat to death with metal pipe. No suspect identified.

1990: Mickey Clearey: Eighteen year-old high school student found dead in his room. Strangled, no suspect identified.

1993: Howard Wilcox: School board president shot in the side of the head. Found in car behind the health club. No suspect identified.

1995: Bruce Webster: High school assistant principal stabbed by Sammy Pritchard. Pritchard was mentally retarded. He'd had no behavioral problems or prior altercations with Webster. No motive.

1996: Jonathan Lynch: Divorce attorney shot at his front door by Tommy Ryan. Ryan then shot himself on the front step of Lynch's apartment building. Ryan had not known Lynch and had no motive to kill him.

1996: Dutch Windsor: Radio talk show host killed in parking garage by lateral vascular neck restraint. No suspect identified.

1996: Swede Boreman: Heavy equipment mechanic shot in secluded area by the river. No suspect identified.

With the list of murders with no apparent motive complete, Gabe looked into the background of each player. After several nights of study, he'd found no motive strong enough to justify murder. One existed. It just wasn't evident in the case files.

Aside from the distinct lack of motive, one similarity did stand out. It was the fact that some of the suspects had had mental disorders. That was not unusual, however. That affliction is common among the criminal element. Ben, Blauw and Rand were right. He had wasted four months of hard work.

Ben Hire eventually closed the Lynch investigation. He re-interviewed Tommy Ryan's parents, who still contended that neither they nor Tommy had known Lynch. There was nothing in

Tommy's past that would explain the killing. Ben put the case to sleep, as baffled as ever.

The Windsor case also stalled. No leads came in through crime stoppers, and no other police departments in the area reported similar killings. Windsor was laid to rest with no idea who had strangled him, Nat Benson and Roger Moesen. Ben was sure that the same person was responsible, but found no connection between the three.

Swede Boreman also joined the ranks of unsolved killings in the records unit. Ben thought the killer must have been a family member, but the wife, son and in-laws all had air-tight alibis. They were together at the time of the killing.

Ben found several people with motives, but could find none who had the opportunity. If Linda Boreman or her parents had hired someone to kill Swede, Ben was unable to find out who they'd hired.

Gabe put the files away, each in the appropriate box. He went back to his exercise routine and met the midnight guys for lunch to stay in touch.

He did, however, leave the data sheets taped to the dungeon wall. He periodically reviewed them and struggled to make sense of it all. He wished that he'd been a detective. If he'd had more experience, he might have seen something that Blauw and Hire had missed.

Ben Hire stepped out of the station at 5:05 and walked toward his car. As he looked up, he saw Gabe leaning against his car. He extended his hand and greeted him. "Hey, Gabe, how's life in the sewer these days?"

"Gets better all the time, Ben. I'm getting worried about myself. I'm starting to like it."

"Ah, don't worry. That just means that you're adaptable and you don't let little setbacks get you down. What's up?"

"We haven't talked for a while and I thought you might like to get a bite of supper. Is your wife expecting you?"

Ben threw his brief case in the back seat. "Not tonight, I have to fend for myself. Want to come over and raid the icebox with me?"

Gabe looked surprised. "Sure, but I wanted to buy."

"No need, climb in. We'll see what kind of leftovers Mama has saved. Besides, you can't afford dinner." Gabe gladly accepted and jumped in the passenger seat.

After hanging up their coats, Ben opened the refrigerator and browsed the leftovers. He cracked open a couple bottles of beer and gave one to Gabe. Thirty minutes later, dinner was served.

Ben leaned back and smiled at Gabe as he attacked his food. Ben remembered when he was young and single. He remembered how he cherished a home-cooked meal. As Gabe used his bread to sop up the last drop of gravy, Ben chuckled. "You know, Gabe, there is more on the stove. You don't have to eat the plate."

Gabe nodded, but couldn't talk. His cheeks were bulging. After a couple of swallows, he said, "Sorry, Ben, I guess I forgot my manners."

"No need to apologize. I know how good a home-cooked meal can be when you're single. So what brings you out of your tomb?"

Gabe didn't want anyone in the department to know that he'd been reading the dead files, but he knew Ben would understand. "Well, Ben, to tell you the truth, I guess I need some advice. I went against everyone's advice and read the homicides in the dead files. I also got copies of the most recent cases from Sergeant Rand. I made data sheets on the cases and taped them on the wall. I've gone over those cases with a fine-toothed comb, but I'm stumped."

Ben said, "Yeah, I knew it wouldn't take you long to dig into them. I knew you were too nosy to leave them alone."

"Okay, you had me pegged, but help me out here. I've made data sheets on all the cases, but I don't know where to go from here."

"There's no place to go, kid. That's why we call them dead files. I've looked at those cases from every angle. Don't worry yourself about them. There are a lot of murders in this country every year that are never solved. It's just a fact of life."

Gabe sat silently for a few minutes, then asked, "Ben, doesn't it seem strange for a town of a hundred thousand people to have so many killings that don't make sense? Some of these people might have had a motive, like Siles when he got passed over for promotion. But Nat Benson, Sammy Pritchard, Roger Moesen and Tommy Ryan had absolutely no reason to kill, other than some mental problems. They didn't even know their victims. Pritchard knew Webster, but just barely. They'd barely spoken and had never had an altercation. Does this happen everywhere or is there something about this town that I'm missing?"

Ben folded his hands behind his head and leaned back in his chair. He stared at the ceiling as he shook his head. "No, kid, you're not missing anything. I've racked my brain for years about this. You're right, it's odd that a town this size would have so many killings without motives. It's logical to think that there has to be a common reason, but I've checked those personal backgrounds thoroughly. None of them knew each other. There's just no reason for these things to happen. I know psychotic and schizophrenic people sometimes kill, but that doesn't happen this often. It's got to be a fluke. I thought it would stop on its own, but Tommy Ryan proved me wrong."

Gabe listened to Ben's frustration, then continued, "I can understand the three old ladies killed in their homes. They were all killed and posed the same way. The same guy had to have killed them. The only reason we never caught him is because he must have died."

Ben agreed. "Yes, I think you're right on that one. A guy like that doesn't stop killing just because he moves away. If he were still alive, we'd have had some other city calling us with similar murders."

"And some of those old killings never had a suspect. I can even understand the Boreman, Wilcox and Clearey cases. We just couldn't find the suspects."

"Yes, that's right, Gabe, but the cases that baffle me as much as the ones without motive are the ones killed with a lateral vascular neck restraint. Benson, Moesen and Windsor were all killed by the same person. I can't believe that there's more than one person who kills like that. The old ladies were killed by one person, and those three were killed by another. It sure would be nice to clear those up. I don't think we'll ever find our old lady killer, but the psycho who killed Windsor, Benson and Moesen is still here in town and will probably hit again. There's a connection between those three, but I can't find it. It was no coincidence that three people with mental problems all killed people, then were all killed themselves by the same neck restraint. I'd really like to catch that asshole."

Gabe thought for a minute, then asked, "Listen, Ben, I remember that you'd instructed the security supervisor of the McManus building to pull the surveillance tapes of the garage where Windsor was killed. Did you see the killer on the tape?"

Ben shook his head. "Nah, there were so many people leaving the building just before he was killed that I couldn't make head or tails of the tape. The only thing that struck me as strange was a woman who was on the tape after everyone had left. She'd walked toward Windsor, then walked past the camera as she left. I backed the tape up, but couldn't match her to any of the employees. She had a coat on, and the camera didn't get a good look at her face. She also didn't match the description of the woman that left the bar with Boreman. I've pretty much forgotten about her. There's no way that a female could have manhandled Windsor like that anyway."

"That might be a dangerous assumption, Ben. The academy teaches our female officers how to use the neck restraint. It's not out of the question for a woman to take Windsor out if she knew what she was doing."

Ben thought as he nodded quietly. "Yeah, I thought of that, kid. If we just had a suspect, we could background her and see if she'd ever had that kind of training. Without a place to start, it's pretty tough. We can't background every woman in the city."

Gabe again asked, "So, Ben, like I asked before, where do we go from here?"

Ben yawned. "Well, kid, you can go wherever you want. I'm going to watch TV and go to bed. I've beat my brains out for years over those old cases. I'm not going to lose one more minute of sleep over them."

Gabe stood to leave and Ben reached for his coat. "That's okay, Ben, I'll walk."

"Oh no, kid, that's too far. I'll give you a lift."

He motioned for Ben to sit back down and said, "Not at all, Ben. I run that far every night. The walk will do me good. It'll help my food settle."

Gabe closed the door behind him and headed home through the slow drizzle. As he splashed through the puddles at a slow jog, he rolled the dead files around in his head. He felt lost. If Ben Hire couldn't make any progress, how would he?

As he jogged up to his building, he decided that Ben was right. He would serve his time in confinement and go back to being a policeman. The dead files would be someone else's problem.

Weeks passed, and the city was in the grip of winter. Temperatures dipped below zero at night, and Gabe could no longer stand to jog outside. He bought a weighted jump rope and found that twenty minutes of jumping rope was far more punishing than the slow jogs that he'd been used to.

Most of the rats had been killed or had moved on to other remote corners of the complex where they would be treated with more compassion. The concrete bunker was cold, and the nights were becoming intolerable.

Gabe looked for ways to pass the time. Exercise, movies and naps helped, but he found himself staring hopelessly at the data sheets on the wall. With no loose ends to tie up, he had no idea how to jump-start the investigation.

After finishing his workout and shower one night, he walked by the data sheets and gave them their nightly stare. As he scanned by the data sheet of Bruce Webster, he stopped quickly.

He remembered that Sammy Pritchard had been committed to a psychiatric hospital. A quick check of the case file failed to reveal what hospital Sammy was in, but his mother's address was there. Would an early morning visit with Mrs. Pritchard be productive? After all, Gabe had no idea what he was looking for. He hoped he could pick her brain without upsetting her.

He was too nervous to sleep. When he got off work at seven, he drove by Mrs. Pritchard's house on Felton Street, hoping she was awake.

Her house was a small, white-framed bungalow. The lights were on in the kitchen, so he parked in front and sat for a few minutes. After long deliberation, he finally mustered enough courage to knock.

Mrs. Pritchard was a small-framed woman about fifty years old. She opened the door and greeted Gabe with a pleasant smile. Her smile relaxed him and made the questioning easier.

After identifying himself as a police officer, Gabe explained his business and tried to mask his true agenda. "Listen, Mrs. Pritchard, the reason I'm here is because I've been assigned to review all of our old homicide cases and see if there's anything else that we can do with them. I just wanted to drop by and see how you and Sammy are doing. I hope this isn't too difficult for you."

Mrs. Pritchard smiled. "Oh no, son, it's so nice of you to check on us. Have a seat."

He sat at the kitchen table and refused Mrs. Pritchard's offer of coffee. After pouring herself a cup, she sat across the table and began. "I'm doing well. My husband died the year after Sammy went into the hospital. Sammy is doing fine and will be getting out in a few months. The doctor says he's not a threat anymore. I've petitioned the court to release him into my custody. He'll always need a guardian, but he's so much better than when he went in."

Gabe asked, "He's been in how long?"

"A year and a half."

Gabe really didn't know what to ask and let the conversation ramble. "So, Mrs. Pritchard, did anyone ever figure out what made Sammy stab Webster?"

Mrs. Pritchard thought for several seconds and shook her head. "Well, officer, the only thing I can think of is maybe Sammy's medication was clouding his judgment. Sammy was always an impulsive boy. His doctor at the hospital said his doctor here had messed up his medications. When they admitted Sammy, the doctor got his records and changed his medications. He's been fine ever since. He's had no more violent episodes, and they think he's ready to be released."

Gabe was taking notes as Mrs. Pritchard talked. He caught up his notes and asked, "Who was Sammy's doctor here?"

Mrs. Pritchard looked surprised as if Gabe should have known Sammy's doctor. She said, "It was Doctor Maura Loar of course. She's well respected, but wasn't having much luck with Sammy. His mood swings weren't improving. We were going to take him to another doctor, but he loved visiting her. He had a fit when we suggested switching doctors. The attack on Mr. Webster was such a shock. Sammy was unpredictable, but had never been violent before. I felt so terrible about Mr. Webster's death. I wish there was something I could say or do for Mrs. Webster."

Gabe kept writing and asked, "What did the hospital's doctor do different than Dr. Loar had done?"

"Nothing that I know of. He adjusted Sammy's medication, and he's been fine."

Gabe thought for a minute, trying to imagine what questions Ben would ask in this situation. When he found himself at a total loss, he began to feel nervous with his clumsiness. He stood and said, "Thanks, Mrs. Pritchard. I just wanted to see how you were doing. May I call again if I have any more questions?"

Mrs. Pritchard stood and shook Gabe's hand as she said, "Of course, officer. Thanks so much for your concern."

Gabe didn't have business cards, so he wrote his name and phone number on a piece of paper and gave it to her. "Here's my name and number. If I can help you with anything, would you please call?"

Mrs. Pritchard assured him she would and escorted him to the door. As he stepped outside, he turned as an afterthought and asked, "Listen, Mrs. Pritchard, what hospital is Sammy in?"

"Beacon South State Hospital down at Corvallis." Gabe waved as he walked toward his car. He hoped it would start.

The drive home gave him time to think about the interview. He'd been so clumsy. He knew he hadn't asked the right questions. The interview was far too short. Mrs. Pritchard was cooperative, but she hadn't given him anything that would help. Or had she? Would he even recognize anything significant if he'd heard it?

When Gabe walked into his dungeon the next night, he paper clipped his interview notes from Mrs. Pritchard to Webster's data sheet. Sammy was the only survivor of the collection of motiveless murders. He contemplated a visit with Sammy, but doubted that Sammy would tell him anything different than he'd already told Ben at the time of the homicide.

After a couple of nights of boredom, he decided that he had nothing to lose. The next day, he called Ben at the office. "Morning Ben."

Ben greeted him and asked, "Make it home okay the other night?"

Gabe assured him he had and asked, "Listen, Ben, I need a favor."

"Sure, anything."

He swallowed hard, then asked, "Well, Ben, I don't want to put you over a barrel, but I need a car. I'm going down to Beacon South to interview Sammy Pritchard, and my car won't make it. Can I use one of the detective cars this weekend?"

Ben cringed at the request. "Oh, Gabe, I don't think so. Garrison will have both our asses if you take a city car. What do you want to interview Pritchard for? He's retarded and won't tell you anything. We interviewed him after the killing and he didn't make a lick of sense."

"Yeah, I know, Ben, but the doctor has changed his medication since then. He might make more sense now. I'd just like to see if he remembers what made him kill Webster."

Ben thought for a second. "I'd like to help you, kid, but sure as I give you a car, you'll have a wreck and we'll both get fired. Listen, come over to my house Saturday morning. You can take my car. I won't need it."

Gabe hesitated, then asked, "Are you sure, Ben? I'll put gas in it and be real careful."

"Sure, kid, see you Saturday."

Gabe rose early Saturday morning and walked to Ben's house. Ben met him at the door in his robe and handed him the keys. Gabe felt a little embarrassed and asked "Ben, you think I'm wasting my time, don't you?"

"Yep, sure do, but I understand how those dead files can eat at you. Go ahead, kid, knock yourself out."

"Want to come, Ben? You're a lot better at interviewing than I am. Might be interesting."

"Nope, I interviewed that kid once and got nowhere. Besides, Mama woke up in the mood this morning. I'll have a lot more luck here than at Beacon South." Gabe smiled understandably and left.

Gabe approached the admissions desk at Beacon South. The receptionist asked him if she could help him. He said, "Yes ma'am. I'd like to visit Sammy Pritchard."

She asked, "Family or friend?"

Gabe thought for a second and replied, "Police."

As the word passed his lips, he knew that he'd said the wrong thing. Sure enough, the receptionist said, "Oh, I'm sorry, sir. If you're going to question Sammy, I'll have to clear it with his doctor. Please have a seat."

He knew he'd screwed up. He should have said he was a friend, but it was too late. Five minutes later, he was facing Sammy's doctor. The doctor extended his hand. "Doctor Gandmeten. How can I help you, officer?"

Gabe shook the doctor's hand and searched for the right words. "Doctor, I'm assigned to the department's cold case unit. I'm checking on the Pritchard family to see if they can offer us any more information that might help us understand the stabbing. I'm also interested in Sammy as a victim. I spoke with his mother and she's doing fine. I'd just like to see how Sammy's doing."

Dr. Gandmeten squinted his eyes suspiciously at Gabe. He didn't believe a word of Gabe's story. "Long way to drive just to see how Sammy's doing. A phone call would have saved you the trip."

Gabe searched for a better explanation. His clumsiness was apparent. Dr. Gandmeten sat down and asked, "Why do you really want to interview Sammy? The case is closed. He's not facing additional criminal charges, is he?"

Gabe shook his head. "No! No, nothing like that." He knew he couldn't fool the doctor. Dr. Gandmeten made his living in the human mind and had faced much better liars than him. He decided to shoot the doctor straight from the hip. "Listen, Doctor, I don't know if you can let me talk to Sammy or not, but I've been assigned to the cold case unit. My job is to look into our old homicides and see if there's anything we've missed. Sammy can't be charged again, but I'd like to talk to him. I want to see if I can make some sense out of Webster's killing. I've read the case, and it seemed so out of character for Sammy to have stabbed him. I guess I'm here for my own curiosity."

Dr. Gandmeten listened intently. "I see. First of all, I can't let you talk to Sammy. I have an obligation to protect his rights. If he is going to be interviewed, a juvenile officer has to sit in on the interview. Surely you know that."

Gabe was surprised. He didn't know that. He suddenly realized that he was making a fool of himself. He shouldn't have come here. He looked at the floor and hoped the doctor didn't ask him what questions he wanted to ask Sammy. He had no idea.

Sensing Gabe's awkwardness, Dr. Gandmeten set aside his professional demeanor. He leaned back in his chair and asked, "Officer, what are you really here for?"

Gabe stared at him, then shrugged his shoulders as he confessed, "I really don't know, Doctor. I've been put in charge of our cold cases, and to tell you the truth, I don't have a clue where to begin. I've never been a detective and I was hoping Sammy could tell me something that would make sense of some of our motiveless killings. We've had so many. They just don't make sense. Sammy's the only survivor. The others were either killed or committed suicide. I guess I'm on a fishing expedition. I'm sorry I wasn't up-front with you."

Dr. Gandmeten nodded as he contemplated Gabe's confession. "I thought so. I'd like to help you, officer, but I can't let you interview Sammy. I do, however, appreciate your honesty. Most people who come in here are writers or students wanting interviews for research papers. You wouldn't believe the scams that I've seen in the past years."

Gabe said nervously, "Well, as you can tell, I don't think fast enough on my feet to scam anyone. I'm sorry I wasted your time. Please forgive me."

He stood to leave and the doctor stepped around his desk. As he shook Gabe's hand, Dr. Gandmeten pulled him back into the office. "Have a seat, officer, maybe I can answer some of your questions."

Gabe was shocked and replied enthusiastically, "Oh, Doctor, that would be great!"

He sat back down and Dr. Gandmeten took the chair beside him. Feeling more at ease, Gabe began. "Listen, Doctor, I really don't know where to begin here, but we've had a series of killings with no motive. The confusing thing about them is that none of the victims knew each other, and only one of the suspects knew the person that he'd killed. I can see one killing where the suspect has nothing against the victim, but we've had several. Sammy killed Webster for no apparent reason. Nat Benson killed Dr. Sabre for no reason. Tim Allis of the D.A.'s office was killed for no reason. There were others, but none of them make sense."

Dr. Gandmeten listened intently, then sat silently for a minute. He looked at the floor as he organized his thoughts, then said, "Sounds puzzling, officer, but let me assure you of something. People don't kill without a reason. They either have some emotional or monetary reason to kill or the killing satisfies some compulsion that the killer cannot suppress. If a serial killer didn't do these killings, then there's a link somewhere. You just haven't found it yet. I can't speak for the others because I haven't been privy to the case files, but I can speak intelligently about Sammy."

Gabe listened intently as Dr. Gandmeten continued. "Sammy is not a killer. He operates on the intelligence level of a five year-old child. He'll be able to communicate and take fundamental care of himself, but he'll always need a guardian. When Sammy killed Webster, two forces were at work. First of all, Sammy was bipolar schizophrenic and emotionally impulsive. He was under the control of medication that had leveled out his mood swings. He was taking Lithium. The usual dose is twenty-five milligrams three times a day. He was on one hundred and fifty milligrams a day. That was way too much Lithium for Sammy. His previous doctor was overdosing him on Lithium, then stopping the Lithium and allowing the mood swings to resume. The trip down from one hundred and fifty milligrams was far more severe than if he'd been taking the seventy-five milligrams like he should have been. It takes one to three weeks for the Lithium to normalize a patient's symptomology. His doctor was not giving the Lithium time to normalize Sammy and was taking him off of it after only one week. That was combined with the fact that Sammy didn't have the I.Q. to realize that the stabbing would cause Webster's death. He'd never seen anyone die before. He'd seen people shot and stabbed on television for years. Then, by the end of the episode, they were back on their feet again. Sammy didn't understand that death is permanent, and he didn't associate death with the stabbing of Webster. He had no idea that stabbing Webster would kill him. That's why he wasn't competent to stand trial. He didn't know the consequences of his actions would cause death. He also would not have understood what was going on in a court proceeding. He's not mentally capable of understanding all that. Keep in mind that Sammy was also taking Thorazine. That has a numbing effect on the senses. It was like his mind was detached from his body. He should not have been taking Thorazine and Lithium simultaneously."

Gabe thought for a minute, then asked, "So, Doctor, why did Dr. Loar have him on so much Lithium in the first place?"

He shrugged his shoulders. "I suppose she felt that it would make Sammy easier for his parents to control. Sammy had reached the age where he was getting harder to control. I can't believe Dr. Loar had miscued so badly in this matter. She should have known better than to stick Sammy on such a high dosage, then jerk him off of it so suddenly. She should have begun with a low dosage and worked up if circumstances warranted. If she had bothered to read her *Physician's Desk Reference*, she would have seen her error. There are other drugs that maintain the stabilization of mood swings while the person is coming down off Lithium. Haldol is one. She should have used it. It's an oral medication that carries on the effects of Lithium for patients that require prolonged treatment. Sammy just lost all grip on reality."

Gabe listened intently and tried to speak, but Dr. Gandmeten interrupted him. "And two similar drugs can also have an overdose effect. The Lithium and Thorazine together probably over-sedated him and made the withdrawal crash much worse. When Dr. Loar withheld the Thorazine and Lithium, his mood swings were so wide that the Haldol couldn't have stabilized them even if Sammy had been taking it. He was not in control of his mood swings as much as Dr. Loar had thought when he stabbed Webster."

Gabe asked, "Did she get in trouble for that?"

Gandmeten shook his head. "No, doctors make mistakes all the time. She thought she was doing the right thing. Sometimes you can't know what drugs or dosages will work. Sometimes you have to experiment. Unfortunately, Webster paid the price for Dr. Loar's experimentation. She could never be held criminally liable for his death."

Gabe sat silently and didn't respond. Dr. Gandmeten continued, "Don't get me wrong, officer, I have no respect for Dr. Loar. I don't think she should be practicing psychiatry. She certainly shouldn't be prescribing drugs. It's just hard to get someone's medical license yanked. Psychiatry is not an exact science. You'd have to prove criminal intent or gross negligence to have her license revoked. Make no mistake. I did report her to the state board of psychiatric review. They didn't think there was enough evidence to suspend her license. It's amazing what a claim of ignorance and a simple apology will get you out of."

Gabe thought for a second, then asked, "So, Doctor, aren't there safeguards built into the system to prevent that? If Loar had prescribed drugs that shouldn't be taken simultaneously, wouldn't the pharmacist catch that and refuse to fill the script?"

He shook his head. "Not necessarily. If the scripts were filled at different pharmacies, neither pharmacist would know that there was another script being filled for a similar drug somewhere else. The pharmacies aren't computer linked yet. If Dr. Loar instructed Mrs. Pritchard to fill the scripts at different pharmacies, that might have raised a red flag with her. But if Dr. Loar wanted to avoid suspicion, she could give Mrs. Pritchard one script to be filled wherever she wanted, then give another patient the second script. When that script was filled, the patient could have brought the drug back to Dr. Loar, and she could have given it to Sammy's mother and instructed her to administer it to him. Sammy's mother could have thought the medication was a free sample. Extremely devious, I know, but since we're thinking dirty, there is a way to pull it off. The only way you could catch her doing that would be to have her medical records and scripts audited."

Gabe stared at Dr. Gandmeten in silence, then asked, "Even if Sammy's medications were numbing his senses and distorting his judgment, where did he get the idea to stab Webster in the first place? Who put the idea in his head? He didn't know Webster. They'd never had an altercation. What made him stab Webster out of the clear blue?"

Dr. Gandmeten shook his head slowly. "Can't tell you, officer. I don't think Sammy even knew. His mind was so detached from his body that I don't think he even knew where the thought came from. He probably didn't even realize that he'd stabbed Webster. I'm positive he can't remember at this late date. I've completely taken him off the Thorazine and Lithium. His moods are easily controlled with less radical drugs and he's doing fine. Sorry, I can't help you."

Gabe nodded as he stood. He couldn't think of any more questions. He thanked Dr. Gandmeten as he shook his hand. "Thanks, Doctor, I appreciate your time. Can I call on you if I have any more questions?"

"Sure, anytime."

The next night, Gabe reduced his interview with Dr. Gandmeten to a report and taped it to the bottom of Webster's data sheet. The notion that a highly respected psychiatrist like Dr. Loar could make such an elementary mistake haunted him.

He kept rolling the scenario around in his head. Was it an accident or intentional? If it were intentional, what motive could she have for wanting Sammy to stab Webster?

6

LEN SHELLEY SAT in a dark field across from the industrial park. A van drove up to the computer supply warehouse with its lights off. The tip from the burglary unit's snitch was good. The suspects were pulling up right on time. Shelley picked up the mike and said over the scrambled radio channel, "Give them time. Wait till they get inside. Sit tight."

Angus Blauw, Victor Lyzett and Arvid Hallos all sat quietly behind the Baptist church three blocks away. They sat in a straight line with their engines running, like horses at the starting gate.

Through his binoculars, Shelley watched the thugs enter the metal fire door with no force. The door was unlocked, indicating an inside job. Three entered the business while the fourth backed the van up to the door to facilitate the easy loading of merchandise. Shelley said, "Now!"

In the distance, Shelley heard the roar of the engines. As the three sped past, he joined the rear of the procession. They quickly converged on the van and put the driver at gunpoint. Once he'd been brutally slammed face-down on the pavement and handcuffed, the officers rushed into the building.

The burglars were caught completely off-guard. They dropped their armloads of merchandise and threw their hands up. After they were cuffed, Angus walked up to the three and removed their ski masks. When he removed the third man's mask, his eyes lit up and he smiled from ear to ear. In his gravely voice he yelled, "Val Machka! Well it's about time! How long have we been after you, Val?"

Val smiled at Blauw. "Angus, my boy, too many years to count. You old tumor, you finally got lucky."

Angus turned Val around forcefully and frisked him as he talked. "Yep, too many years, Val. Hell, it's been so many years since I heard anything out of you that I thought you'd gone straight. Nice to know I'm still a good judge of character. I was about to lose faith in myself."

Val grunted from the pain as Angus kicked his legs apart. "Well, Angus, you should lose faith in yourself in spite of me. You're a pathetic example of a human being. I hope aliens never come to Earth and see you first. I hate to see the whole human race judged by a specimen like you."

Angus growled. "Well, Val, that doesn't speak very highly of you. I may be pathetic, but I caught you."

Lyzett looked over at Angus and asked, "You know this mope?"

"Yep, sure do. Victor my boy, you're looking at the most successful, clever, slippery and elusive burglar in the history of mankind."

Machka turned quickly in shock at the glowing summation of his career. "Why, Angus, that's the nicest thing anyone's ever said about me." He then turned to Lyzett and said, "Yes, officer, and this man is the most underhanded, corrupt and devious police officer in the history of American law enforcement. It's a real honor to be arrested by him."

Lyzett and Shelley looked at each other in disgust. Shelley interrupted the exchange and said, "Okay! If you two love birds are though blowing smoke up each other's ass, let's get these guys to jail."

Gabe pondered the brick wall that he'd run into at Beacon South. Aside from an innocent mistake in medication, there was no reason for Pritchard to kill Webster. He decided to investigate the other side of the equation and talk to Mrs. Webster. She'd been a teacher in the same school district as her deceased husband.

128

Mrs. Webster wouldn't meet Gabe at her house. She was uncomfortable around men. Her grief had not diminished and she wanted to meet at the police station.

To avoid embarrassment and difficult questions about his accommodations, Gabe interviewed Mrs. Webster in the detective unit. He met her at the rear of the station and escorted her upstairs. He accounted for the lack of personnel in the unit by telling her that he worked nights.

Once comfortably seated in Ben's office, Gabe eased into the interview and tried not to repeat the mistakes that he'd made with Dr. Gandmeten. Mrs. Webster rambled for the first few minutes and Gabe was content to let her talk. Again, he had no idea what he was looking for, so Mrs. Webster's rambling was welcomed.

After several minutes of Mrs. Webster bragging on the qualities of Bruce, Gabe pinned her down to the point of the interview. "Mrs. Webster, do you have any idea why Sammy stabbed Bruce?"

Mrs. Webster shook her head in disappointment. "No, officer, I don't. I've wracked my brain since Bruce died, trying to figure that out, but I don't have a clue. Bruce usually told me about the kids that he'd had problems with, but he never mentioned Pritchard. I was told that his medications were distorting his judgment and the stabbing was random. Do you know anything other than that?"

Gabe stared at the floor and shook his head. "No. No, Mrs. Webster, I don't. I guess I was hoping that you could shed some light on that for me. Did Bruce know Sammy's parents or anyone else that Sammy might have known?"

Mrs. Webster again shook her head. "Other than the students and staff at school, no. Bruce didn't know any of Pritchard's family. There was no reason for the attack. I think Pritchard just decided to stab a teacher and Bruce was the first teacher he came across."

Gabe thought out loud, "That just doesn't make sense. He'd passed several teachers before reaching Bruce. He even asked for him specifically at the counter. There has to be a connection somewhere."

Mrs. Webster made small talk for a while, then sat quietly. Gabe stood and extended his hand. "Well, Mrs. Webster, sorry to have wasted your time. I guess I could have done this over the phone and saved you a trip."

"No, that's okay. I didn't mind at all."

Gabe escorted her to the door and studied her as she walked to her car. As she drove out of the lot, he thought sarcastically, *Boy, that was productive. Why am I wasting my time on this? I don't even know what questions to ask. Sure wish I could get Ben interested in this again.*

Gabe inserted *The Searchers* in the VCR and waited for one of the midnight crew to pick him up for lunch. As the movie played, he grew more frustrated. He now knew how Ben and Angus must have felt when they were in his place. He glanced periodically at the data sheets while the movie played.

When the movie was over, he hit the *Rewind* button and put on his coat. He usually met his lunch partner in the squad room. He tried to be a little early so he could visit with the dispatchers and jailers.

On the way out the door, he glanced once again at the data sheets. Suddenly, another common thread leaped out at him. Bruce Webster was a faculty member killed by Pritchard in 1995. The data sheet next to it was that of Howard Wilcox. He'd been the president of the school board and was shot in the head behind the health club two years earlier. Both worked for the school district.

As he waited for Sgt. Shelley to pick him up, he identified his next interview. It had to be Mrs. Wilcox. Maybe the school district was the common thread.

Angus met Shelley and Gabe at the diner. The three ordered, then Angus and Shelley exchanged friendly barbs until the food arrived. Gabe had forgotten how much he enjoyed the officers' company until they'd met for lunch. The barbs and slams humored him.

Angus was the funniest, but Shelley wasn't far behind. His rank afforded him no refuge. He was fair game and thoroughly enjoyed the sparring. Shelley could slug it out with the best of them in a war of words.

130

After lunch, Gabe couldn't sleep. He was thinking about interviewing Mrs. Wilcox. He pulled her address and phone number out of her husband's case file and called her at eight.

She was not the cheerful lady that Mrs. Pritchard and Mrs. Webster had been. She was still angry and felt robbed by the death of her husband. She reluctantly agreed to a meeting and allowed Gabe to come to her house.

The tone of Mrs. Wilcox's voice intimidated Gabe. If he didn't come up with some structure to the interview, she might become suspicious. He didn't want her to call the chief to verify the authorization for interview.

Mrs. Wilcox seemed a little more congenial when he arrived. She escorted him to Mr. Wilcox's den and sat on a sofa across from him. Gabe masked his apprehension and began. "So, Mrs. Wilcox, how have you been these last couple of years?"

She seemed pleased that Gabe cared. "Fine, I guess. It's been very hard for me. I miss Howard a lot."

Gabe didn't have to pretend. He was sincerely sorry for her loss. "I can only imagine how you feel. You must feel cheated."

Mrs. Wilcox nodded her head adamantly. "Yes, I do. Howard and I had been very close our whole lives. We'd worked very hard to get our kids raised and were looking forward to retirement. Just when we could see our retirement years coming into view, he was killed. It was so senseless."

This was the opening that Gabe had been looking for. "Yes, I know. I've been assigned to the cold case unit. I've been reviewing some of our old cases to see if I can make some sense of them. The detectives who investigated your husband's killing never developed a suspect. He was apparently well liked and had no enemies that they could find. Have you developed any theories that might help us at this late date?"

"No, I haven't. I'm just as baffled as ever. Howard had made some people mad over some of his decisions on the school board, but nothing that would have made someone want to kill him."

"Mrs. Wilcox, why was Mr. Wilcox at the fitness center?"

"When the weather was too cold to run outside, Howard would sometimes use the indoor jogging track at the fitness center. Running helped him deal with stress. I wasn't aware that he was going to the fitness center that night, but he frequently didn't tell me when he was going there. His runs took about twenty minutes and he would sometimes stop there on his way home."

Gabe stared at Mrs. Wilcox as she talked. He then stared at the floor, trying to imagine what Ben might ask if he were here. "Mrs. Wilcox, do you have any idea who would want to kill Mr. Wilcox?"

Tears swelled up in her eyes. She took a deep breath and said, "No, I don't. There hasn't been a day since Howard died that I haven't asked myself that question. No one hated him enough to kill him. It had to have been a random act. Someone must have shot him for fun. Believe me. I'd love to find out who killed him. I'm a Christian woman, but I don't think I could contain myself. I think I'd hunt him down and kill him like he killed Howard."

She got angrier as she continued. Gabe had to stop her before she went to pieces. "I understand how you feel, ma'am. Is there anything I can do for you?"

She caught herself and regained her composure. "No, officer, I'm okay. I just get mad when I think about what that person took from me."

Gabe stood to leave and shook Mrs. Wilcox's hand. "I know how you feel. I'd like to find him myself."

As they walked to the door, Gabe turned and asked Mrs. Wilcox if she or Mr. Wilcox knew Bruce Webster. Mrs. Wilcox replied, "Oh sure, Bruce and Cheryl were good friends of ours. Howard got Bruce his job with the school district."

Gabe stopped at the door and turned back toward Mrs. Wilcox in surprise. She continued, "Bruce's death was another tragedy. He was such a good man. He was destroyed when Howard died. Howard was like a father to him. Howard even saved his career for him when he had that affair on Cheryl."

By now Gabe had stepped out onto the porch. He stopped and turned again. "Affair?"

She replied, "Yes, a one-time mistake. They were having problems and Bruce was seeing another woman. Howard went to him and told him that the matter might come before the school board. He told Bruce that he could face disciplinary action and may lose his job and marriage if the affair went public. Howard was instrumental in making him terminate the affair and save his job and marriage. I've never told anyone about it because I didn't want to hurt Bruce or Cheryl, but I guess it's okay now. Bruce is gone and Cheryl will never know about it now."

Gabe thought quietly for a few seconds, then thanked Mrs. Wilcox for her time. He walked down the steps toward his car. Mrs. Wilcox finished with one closing bombshell. "The other woman was a psychiatrist here in town, Dr. Loar."

He froze in shock, but Mrs. Wilcox failed to pick up on the nerve that she'd just struck. She closed the door, but Gabe stood at the bottom of her steps unable to move. He wanted to turn back to her, but he couldn't. He had to remind himself to breathe and grabbed the railing to steady himself.

In one short sentence, Mrs. Wilcox had suddenly revealed the motive and common thread that Gabe and Ben had been looking for. Bruce Webster's and Howard Wilcox's murders suddenly made perfect sense. Sammy Pritchard was Dr. Loar's patient, and her miscalculation of his medications was no accident. Gabe now knew who had put the idea of stabbing Webster in Sammy's head.

Wilcox died for interfering in the relationship between Webster and Loar. Webster died for dumping Loar, and Sammy was the tool. That accounted for Webster, but Sammy couldn't have killed Wilcox. He didn't have access to a gun, transportation to the fitness center or the brainpower to plan Wilcox's death. Who was Loar's tool for that killing?

Gabe raced back to his office and dug around on his desk. He found Dr. Gandmeten's number and dialed it hurriedly. When Dr. Gandmeten answered the phone, Gabe quickly identified himself and said, "Doctor! I'm sorry to bother you so soon, but I have a question."

"Sure, Gabe, shoot."

He took a deep breath and organized his thoughts. "I found out that Dr. Loar was having an affair with Webster, and Wilcox was the school board president who made Webster stop seeing her. That explains why she would manipulate Sammy's medication to destabilize his mood swings and numb his senses, but how did she plant the idea in his head?"

There was a long silence as Dr. Gandmeten contemplated if he should continue the conversation. He finally said, "I hate to speculate about another colleague, but you may have something here. I guess if I were to think the worst about Dr. Loar, as you do, I'd have to say hypnosis."

Gabe gasped as the obvious hit home. Why hadn't he thought of that? "My God, you're right! Sammy would have been susceptible to the suggestion, wouldn't he?"

Dr. Gandmeten replied, "While under the influence of sedation, he would have been extremely susceptible to her powers of suggestion while under hypnosis. She could have sedated him right there in the office just before the hypnosis session began. She wouldn't have to write a script for that, and his parents would never know that she was using hypnosis on him. She could sedate him and plant the idea in his head while his mood swings were under control, then yank his Lithium and Thorazine. When he turned violent and uncontrollable, the deep, subconscious hatred for Webster would surface. Webster would be his likely target. We also don't know what other leverage she might have had over him. If he was dependant on her for other things such as emotional support, or if he was infatuated with her, he might have done anything she suggested just to please her. He might not have killed Webster out of hatred. He might have killed him out of fear of losing Loar's affection. Have you ever met Dr. Loar, Gabe?"

He quickly responded, "No, I haven't had the pleasure."

"When you do, you'll see why her patients could be infatuated with her. She's the most striking woman that I've ever seen."

The entire picture now became clear. Dr. Gandmeten was only speculating, but Gabe took it as fact. Dr. Gandmeten continued, "I want to help you, Gabe, but you have to understand something. I could get in big trouble for making false accusations about another psychiatrist. I'm not accusing her of anything. I'm only offering you speculation. I'll deny that we ever had this conversation."

Gabe assured him, "Don't worry, Doctor, no one will ever know that we've talked, but let me ask you one more question. How could I prove any of this? I suppose her prescriptions would provide a paper trail of the scripts that she'd written, but how about the hypnosis?"

"That's right. Her scripts could be audited, but you would have to see her medical records to find out the rest. Frankly, that would probably be futile. Her records would only contain what she'd written in them. If she left out the medication manipulation, hypnosis sessions and made no mention of Sammy's emotional dependency on her or her suggestion to kill Webster, you'd be up a creek. Frankly, she's too smart to leave any incriminating documentation that could be discovered in an audit or found with a search warrant. You'd never be able to use Sammy against her. He's incapable of testifying in court with any degree of credibility. A defense attorney would tie him in knots under cross-examination. And frankly, I doubt that he remembers anything that took place during his conversations with Loar. I'm sorry, Gabe, but if this is true, you'll have to find another way to prove it."

Gabe sat quietly as Dr. Gandmeten burst his bubble. His heart sank as he said, "Yeah, maybe you're right. Okay, Doctor, thanks for your help. We never talked."

As Dr. Gandmeten hung up the phone, Gabe wondered where to go from here. He slowly hung up the phone and slumped down in his chair. He stared hard at the data sheets and thought, *Ben! He'd know what to do. Not yet, though. Soon.*

Val Machka was facing many years in prison. His extensive criminal record had long ago thrust him out of candidacy for probation in the sentencing phase of his upcoming trial. Since he'd been caught red-handed, he knew a conviction was eminent and was eager to do anything to avoid prison short of flipping on a friend.

The informant who'd given Machka to the burglary unit had recently died in a head-on crash on I-5 between his motorcycle and a trash truck. The crash took place two weeks before Machka's trial.

Arvid Hallos was first to roll up on the crash and called Reaves in to investigate the crash since he was an expert accident reconstructionist. When he described the vehicles involved and their direction of travel, it was apparent to every officer listening that it would be a bloody mess. Even though they weren't dispatched, they all drove by to satisfy their morbid curiosity.

Shelley had long ago discouraged his officers from leaving their districts unprotected and driving by calls that they weren't dispatched just to sightsee. He did this by dragging them in the call and assigning them tasks that usually required a written report and a possible court appearance. Since most policemen try to avoid writing as many reports as possible, the tactic usually worked. This time, however, Arvid's description of the carnage was too much to resist.

Shelley and Blauw arrived simultaneously. Since Angus had no district to protect, his presence was tolerated more than the others. He parked the wagon well out of the way of the fire apparatus and strolled up to the edge of the crash scene with his hands in his pockets. He laughed quietly at Shelley who was squeamishly tiptoeing around the blood and body parts.

Angus stayed well back so he would not be asked to assist. When the coroner's team pulled the mangled body out of the grill of the truck, Angus eased closer for a good look. Shelley heard him cursing loudly as he stormed off the scene.

At dinner, Shelley asked Angus what his problem was at the crash scene. "What's the matter, Angus, the gore getting to you after all these years? You see something nastier than that every morning when you look in the mirror."

Angus stubbornly refused to admit that he needed reading glasses, so he held the menu far away from his face and squinted hard as he replied, "Listen here, fat boy, I ain't the one who was tippy-toeing around the blood puddles like some tight-ass, light-footed ballet boy."

His gravelly voice resonated throughout the diner and embarrassed Shelley to the core. He motioned for Angus to keep his voice down. "Watch your voice, you old fool, there's decent folks in here and you're going to get a complaint filed on both of us. If you don't quit that cussing, you're going to get us both fired."

Angus looked around to see who'd heard his comment. His curiosity was satisfied when he saw every disapproving eye in the restaurant focused on him. Completely unfazed, he looked back at Shelley and said, "Let's spend our suspension days at the lake, Len. We might as well get some good fishing in."

Shelley's face was buried in the menu. He'd hoped to avoid being identified, but quickly realized that his size and skin color would betray his anonymity. He lowered the menu in defeat and said, "Okay, loud mouth, now that you've got us both suspended, what was your problem at the crash scene?"

"That guy having sex with the truck? The one whose brains you were walking through? That was our snitch, the one who ratted on Val Machka. Since he's not going to be around to testify, that fucking thief will skate again."

"How do you know that, Angus? His face was gone."

"I heard Reaves read his name off the driver's license that he'd removed from the guy's wallet."

Shelley bowed his head in frustration. "Shit, we're never going to put that asshole away. He's the luckiest bastard I ever saw. Anyway, why do you hate him so much? He's just a burglar."

"Ah, the sneaky fucker took a shot at me once. I swore I'd return the favor someday."

Shelly perked up and leaned angrily into Angus. "Hell, Angus, I didn't know that! For God's sake, pal, when did this happen? Where was I and the other guys? If we'd known that, we'd have gunned his ass down for you right there on the spot!"

Angus leaned back and yawned, then said, "I don't know where you guys were. I was off duty. Machka walked in his apartment and caught me banging his old lady. When I grabbed my clothes and climbed out the window, he popped a cap at me as I was climbing down the fire escape."

Shelley stared at Angus in disbelief for a few seconds, then lowered his head in disgust. He leaned back and glared at Angus, then said, "Well hell, Angus, I can't say as I blame him. He should have hit you in the head, then none of us would have to put up with you now. What were you doing screwing Machka's girlfriend anyway? You know he never has any decent women. He only runs with meth-whores, and they'd screw anyone if they thought it would benefit them somehow."

"Yeah, I know. I didn't have any choice. I had to take her to bed. She'd walked in and caught me burglarizing his apartment. I was looking for some stolen jewelry that he's taken from an old lady in my district. I convinced her that I had a search warrant and that she was going to jail. She thought she was screwing her way

137

out of a criminal charge. You know me, Len, always willing to take one for the team."

Shelley cringed and said, "Don't tell me this, Angus. You're confessing to a felony, for God's sake. I'm supposed to write your ass up and suspend you when I hear things like this. You're putting me in a bad position. And listen, old man, you're going to get your senile ass killed or indicted someday if you don't quit this sneaky shit."

"Ah, Len, if I ever get killed, you know you'll bawl your eyes out. There aren't many wholesome role models like me left in the world."

Shelley picked up his menu and started to read. He mumbled, "Role model, my ass. You're a good policeman, but you're just in the wrong country. You'd fit right in if you were in Russia."

Angus smiled as Shelley lectured him. Shelley looked over the top of his menu and said, "I never know when you're pulling my chain. You're just lucky that I don't believe a word you say. You're going to push me too far someday, old man. Anyway, it looks like Machka will walk this time."

Angus read the menu and casually said, "Maybe for now, but his luck will run out. Someone will kill his snobby ass someday. He's pissed off some pretty influential people in town. Besides, we don't need the snitch to prosecute him. The prosecutor can claim that the information was anonymous. We still caught him in the act."

"I don't know, Angus. You're asking the prosecutor to lie. He's already got a statement from our dead informant. That statement is part of the case file that the defense attorney can get through discovery. He's not going to jeopardize his career just to put one thief in jail."

Hoping the prosecutor would go along, Angus told him that the state's informant had been killed. It should have been a minor obstacle, but the prosecutor owed Machka's attorney a personal favor.

He told Angus that he was going to dismiss the charges against Machka because the case was fatally flawed when the police interviewed Machka and his co-conspirators without giving

138

them the Miranda Warning. Although it had been given at the station, admissions were obtained at the scene before Miranda was read.

Even with the confessions thrown out, the fact that they were caught in the act would salvage the case, but that argument fell on deaf ears. The owner of the business also lost his desire to prosecute. Angus suspected that that was a result of a substantial bribe paid by Machka through his attorney.

Knowing that the charge was going to be dropped, Angus decided to salvage what he could from the case. Machka would never know the identity of the snitch unless the case went to trial. He therefore would not know that the snitch was dead.

Angus convinced the prosecutor to hold off dismissing the charge until he'd talked to Machka. He spoke with Machka in the county jail and got him to agree to act as his informant.

Without knowing when or where Angus would call in the marker, Machka reluctantly agreed. It went against everything that he'd ever believed in, but so did prison. He only hoped that Angus would never ask him to give up someone that he liked.

Machka left the county jail indebted to Angus. He believed that Angus had gotten the charges dropped. He had no clue that the charges were going to be dismissed anyway.

Angus knew that Machka would probably back out of their deal after talking to his attorney, but he hoped that Machka's quirky obsession with keeping his word would bind him to their agreement.

Gabe attacked his job with a renewed sense of purpose. He was no longer an inexperienced boob killing time in the cold case unit. He planned out his leads like an experienced detective. He was determined to add Dr. Maura Loar's name to every data sheet.

Every case had two key players: the killer and the victim. He pulled the oldest data sheet from the wall and worked his way to the most recent.

A phone call to Paul Siles's wife revealed that Siles had been seeing Dr. Loar for treatment of manic depression. The question that remained was why Siles had targeted Jared Cutchall. What had Cutchall done to anger Loar? Maybe Mrs. Cutchall could help.

Gabe located Mrs. Cutchall in another town. A phone call to her mother revealed that she'd remarried and moved to Massachusetts. Her new name was Deagal.

He waited until he got off the next morning to call. Mrs. Deagal was shocked to hear from him. With specific questions in mind, the interview took little time.

Mrs. Deagal said that Dr. Loar had treated her the year before her husband's murder. She said her husband had refused to pay the bill because he'd felt that Dr. Loar was overcharging them. Dr. Loar's hourly rate was high, but not more than the going rate for psychiatrists.

Dr. Loar had submitted bills to the Cutchalls' insurance company for office visits that had never occurred. The arguments between Dr. Loar and Jared Cutchall had gotten heated, but Dr. Loar adjusted her fees and settled for less rather than send it to a collection agency and prolong the matter. She only did that after Mr. Cutchall threatened to hire an attorney to sue Dr. Loar and make a formal complaint against her with the state board of psychiatric review. The threat of an insurance fraud investigation greased the wheel for Mr. Cutchall.

Cutchall also beat Siles out in a promotional exam for supervisor. Siles had already been hostile toward Cutchall long before Dr. Loar had planted the idea of killing Cutchall in his mind. The murder would be an easy seed for the doctor to plant.

The attorney that the Cutchalls had used to send the threatening letter to the doctor was Jonathan Lynch, the attorney that Tommy Ryan had killed. Lynch was killed eleven years later, which only confirmed one thing in Gabe's mind. Dr. Loar carries a grudge for a long time.

Siles killed himself three months after killing Cutchall. It took the good doctor eleven years to find the right person to kill Lynch.

The next data sheet was that of Dr. Albert Sabre. Dr. Sabre was not married and his only surviving heir was a son in China Spring, Texas. A personal visit would be out of the question, so Gabe called him on the phone.

Quinn Sabre had not been close to his father after his parents divorced. His mother had moved him to Texas where she could be close to her family. Dr. Sabre and Quinn had only seen each other on holidays.

Dr. Sabre had never discussed his business affairs with Quinn, and Quinn had never heard of Dr. Loar. A deeper search of Dr. Sabre's case file revealed that the secretary who had found Dr. Sabre dying after Nat Benson had left the office was Phyllis Hayes. She'd retired shortly after closing down the doctor's office and moved to Arizona where she could enjoy her grandkids and the warmer climate.

Phyllis was surprised to hear from Gabe and was eager to cooperate. Although she never admitted it, and Gabe didn't have the nerve to ask, it was clear by her words and tone that she had served Dr. Sabre as more than a secretary. She was a wealth of information. Her intimacy with the doctor had made her privy to his most personal matters.

Dr. Sabre had been Dr. Loar's most outspoken critic. He'd treated many of Dr. Loar's patients who hadn't responded to her unorthodox methodology. He'd made numerous complaints against her to the state board of psychiatric review. He'd also publicly criticized her and challenged her to a public debate. The challenge was made in anger. No respectable psychiatrist would air his dirty laundry publicly, but the fact that the challenge had been made at all embarrassed Dr. Loar.

As Gabe reduced this interview to a report, he thought how manipulative Dr. Loar must be. She must have treated hundreds of patients in her career. If only one percent of her patients could be manipulated with drugs, hypnosis and seduction, there could be dozens of homicides around the state attributable to her. He leaned back in his chair and thought, *What will happen if I make her mad? Surely she wouldn't go after a cop, would she?*

Nat Benson was the second half of the Sabre investigation. She was found dead in an alley a few weeks later. A quick phone call to Benson's father revealed that Nat had indeed been a patient of Dr. Loar's at the time of the Sabre murder.

Nat was a paranoid schizophrenic and homosexual. Mr. Benson said that she not only had wide mood swings and was impulsive and violent, but also had severe self-esteem problems because of the internal war that she'd been fighting between her homosexuality and her strict Christian upbringing. She had also taken a lot of ridicule from the other kids in her school.

Nat was found in an alley wrapped in a towel. She'd apparently just stepped out of the shower when she was killed. Gabe knew now that Benson and Moesen had been killed to keep them quiet. They were killed by the lateral vascular neck restraint just like Dutch Windsor. Tommy Ryan would have been killed the same way, but he'd saved Dr. Loar the trouble by shooting himself.

Since the LVNR was such a rare technique, Gabe was certain that the same person had killed them all. Since no suspect was ever located, he was also sure that the killer's identity lay buried in Dr. Loar's medical records.

The surveillance videotape from the garage where Windsor had been killed showed an unidentified woman leaving the garage shortly after Windsor was killed. Ben had discounted the notion that she'd killed Windsor. He didn't think a woman was capable of killing a man with that technique. Gabe disagreed.

The Tim Allis investigation had also been a brick wall. Mrs. Allis had never heard of Roger Moesen, and Tim had never discussed with her any of his dealings with Dr. Loar. It would take someone inside the D.A.'s office to clear up any questions about the relationship between Allis and Loar.

A phone call to Moesen's mother confirmed Gabe's suspicions. Roger had been a patient of Dr. Loar's. He was psychotic, paranoid and delusional. He was also madly in love with Dr. Loar. Mrs. Moesen said he couldn't wait to see her and talked about her incessantly.

She didn't know why Moesen had killed Tim Allis. To the best of her knowledge, Roger had never known him. Gabe knew though. Allis had angered Loar somehow. The answer to that question had gone to the grave with Allis.

Roger Moesen was found dead in his apartment by detectives who went to question him about Tim Allis. They'd gotten his name from an anonymous tip. The LVNR had been used to cut off the blood supply to his brain.

Gabe laid Moesen's data sheet on top of Tim Allis's. Ben would see the relationship and draw the same conclusion as Gabe.

If they found Benson's killer in Loar's medical files, they would clear Moesen and Windsor's murders, too.

He spent the next week trying to link the deaths of the three elderly ladies to Dr. Loar. They'd been raped, strangled and posed. None of their family members could shed any light on the killings. The ladies hadn't known each other and none of them had known Dr. Loar. Apparently, these three murders were committed by a serial killer and were unrelated to Dr. Loar.

The drug dealer, Lucian Green, was the next data sheet in the pile. A review of his case file and interviews with family members revealed no relationship between him and Dr. Loar. He was a known trafficker in illegal drugs. If there was a common thread between him and Dr. Loar, it was very thin and obscure.

Mickey Clearey was another story. He had been a patient of Dr. Loar, but he'd been strangled with clothesline cord. It was left embedded in his neck. He was the only Loar patient who hadn't been killed with the LVNR. He hadn't killed anyone, but that didn't put Gabe's suspicions to rest. Maybe he was killed because he wouldn't kill for her or was going to tell others about her manipulation and suggestions while under hypnosis.

An interview of Mickey's mother revealed that Mickey had been treated for depression. He was doing well under Dr. Loar's care and he liked her very much. She said he looked forward to his visits with Loar and spoke fondly of her. Gabe read between the lines and speculated that Dr. Loar had tried to use Mickey's sexual attraction for her as leverage.

Howard Wilcox and Bruce Webster had already been linked to Loar through Sammy Pritchard. Gabe put his interview reports with their data sheets, then put them in chronological order with the rest.

Jonathan Lynch was already linked to Loar through Jared Cutchall, Paul Siles and Tommy Ryan.

Dutch Windsor was the next puzzle. Mrs. Windsor was open about her relationship with her husband. He'd been emotionally abusive, arrogant and condescending toward her. She knew he'd been involved with several women, but she'd kept the marriage together for the sake of the kids and financial security.

Gabe pressed her to search her memory for a link to Dr. Loar. Mrs. Windsor remembered that Dutch had been present at a dinner party where Dr. Sabre had gone into a tirade about Dr. Loar.

Dr. Sabre had been inebriated with his favorite bourbon. Windsor tried to facilitate the public debate and use his radio show as the forum. When Dr. Sabre came to his senses, he wisely declined.

Windsor wasn't content with Dr. Sabre's retreat. He invited Dr. Loar to come on his show and discuss psychiatry. When she declined, she became the target of Windsor's attacks on psychiatry as a fraudulent, money-making scam. Dr. Loar became his poster-child for phony psychiatry.

Being a woman also didn't help Dr. Loar's standing with Windsor. His blatant contempt for women subjected her to added ridicule. She was the brunt of several on-air sex and psychiatry jokes.

As Gabe reduced Mrs. Windsor's interview to a report, he knew that Windsor had found himself on Dr. Loar's hit list and had suffered the consequences. Again, his murder would be cleared when they found out who'd killed Moesen and Benson.

Gabe contacted Linda Boreman at her house late one evening. She was torn between the grief of Swede's death and the relief of being out from under his abuse. She was in good spirits and appeared as a woman recovering from a long mental illness. Cruel as it seemed, Swede's death had been a blessing for her.

No suspect had been developed, but Linda admitted that she'd been a patient of Dr. Loar. Gabe had to be careful. He didn't want to alert Dr. Loar that he was investigating her. He played down the significance of Mrs. Boreman's treatment, hoping she wouldn't mention his visit to Loar.

Linda had been part of a group therapy project for abused spouses, which met once a week. Gabe wished he could get a list of the group members. Swede's killer was probably one of the members who'd sympathized with Linda and had succumbed to Dr. Loar's powers of suggestion and medication manipulation.

Ben had cleared Linda. She and her son were having supper with her parents at the Boreman residence at the time of Swede's death. The patrons of the bar also said that Linda didn't fit the description of the woman that Swede had hustled away.

144

Again, there was the Dr. Loar connection, but who shot Swede? The answer had to be in Dr. Loar's patient files.

7

GABE WAS WRAPPING up his interview reports when he heard pounding on his door. When he opened it, he saw Ramón and Angus standing outside. Ramón asked, "Hey, where you been lately, man? You never come to lunch with us anymore?"

He motioned for them to come in. Angus didn't give Gabe time to reply and attached his own assessment of Gabe's conspicuous absence. In his raspy growl, he told Ramón, "Hell, you stupid Cuban, can't you see? Kinnett here prefers the company of these rats to his old buddies."

Ramón laughed and agreed. "Yeah, man, I think you're right. He must be losing it, man. He's been in this cellar too long."

Gabe shook his head and let the two have their fun. When they'd finished, he said, "Yeah, you're right. It's not that I prefer their company, it's just that I get more intelligent conversation out of them."

Being the nosiest policeman on the department, Angus couldn't restrain himself. He walked over to Gabe's desk and picked up his interview reports. He asked, "What's this, Kinnett? You deviant, you ain't got no work to do down here."

Gabe snatched the files out of Angus's hand before he could read the first sentence and laid them back on his desk. He replied, "It's something you wouldn't understand, Angus, it's police work."

Ramón broke into laughter as Angus tried to look offended, but it was a thin façade. Nothing was so demeaning that Angus would take offense. He was impervious to insult. He said, "Oh that hurts, especially coming from two snot-nosed butt-wipes like you two."

Ramón stopped laughing and looked genuinely hurt. Angus laughed and put his arm around Ramón's shoulder. "Oh, you greasy, little fucker, I'm just kidding. Stick with me for the next twenty years and you might learn a tenth of what I know about police work."

Gabe shook his head as he chuckled at Angus. He didn't want to spur him on, so he wisely chose to remain quiet. He couldn't win with Angus. He could only remain quiet and hope that Angus would shut up on his own.

Ben was on vacation up in Astoria, so Gabe had to wait a week to see him. He grew impatient and couldn't wait for Ben to see the interview reports. He dropped by Ben's house the night before Ben was to return to work.

When Ben opened the door, he greeted Gabe cheerfully and invited him in. "Hey, Gabe, come on in. Pull up a chair and take a load off your feet." Gabe sat down and laid the files on Ben's kitchen table. Ben looked at the files as he poured himself a cup of coffee. He smiled and shook his head. "Bound and determined to be a detective, aren't you? Just couldn't let those dead files rest in peace, could you?" Ben sat down and read.

The first report was about the Cutchall killing. Gabe could tell when Ben got to the part about Siles being a patient of Dr. Loar. His patronizing smile faded into a look of concern. When he read about Cutchall's threats of legal action against Loar, his mouth dropped open in shock. When he read that Cutchall had used Jonathan Lynch to write Loar the threatening letter, he unconsciously rose to his feet. When he read that Tommy Ryan had been a patient of Loar, he looked at Gabe in total shock. Gabe smiled and said, "Interesting reading ain't it?"

Ben put his coffee down and quickly shuffled the pages until he came to the report on Howard Wilcox. When he read that Wilcox had warned Webster to stop the affair with Loar, and that

Sammy Pritchard was Loar's patient, he collapsed back down in his chair.

Gabe was pleased that Ben was impressed. He reached over and found a report for Ben. "Here! Here, Ben, read this interview with the doctor from Beacon South. See how Loar manipulated her patients to kill for her."

Ben read Dr. Gandmeten's hypothesis about Loar's manipulation of her patients' medications and emotions through hypnosis. He laid the files on the table and stared into space as he sank deep into thought. He looked back at Gabe in shock and said, "You little shit. How did you come up with this? I've racked my brain for ten years trying to make sense of this mess. I can't believe I missed all this. How did you find it?"

Gabe smiled proudly. "I just went back and interviewed the family members and came up with the connection to Loar. It didn't hit home until Mrs. Wilcox mentioned that Webster had been having an affair with Loar and that her husband convinced him to break up with her. I then talked to Sammy's doctor at Beacon South and found out that he'd been Loar's patient. Then it was easy. I just went through all the cases and looked for the Loar connection. She turned up in every case file somewhere. Everyone except the drug dealer and the old ladies had a connection to Loar. All the others were either her patients or someone who'd pissed her off. Pretty good, huh, Ben?"

Ben stared at the smug kid smiling back at him. He looked back at the files and thought for a second. He was at a loss for words. He stood and walked over to the coffeepot to warm his cup. He didn't turn around, but said softly, "Yeah, Gabe, that's some fantastic work, but you don't know what you've done. You've stirred up a political nightmare. Do you know who Dr. Loar is?"

Gabe was confused. "No, Ben, I don't, but does it really matter? If she's killing people, let's nail her."

Ben waited until he sat down to explain. "Yeah, I agree with you, but that won't be easy. Loar is the most respected psychiatrist in the northwest. She's a celebrity. She's the driving force behind a lot of the civic programs in town. She's a personal friend of every high-ranking official in the city, county and state. She's a personal friend of Garrison and the D.A. She's a friend to all the judges, councilmen and county board members. She's

149

active in all the Lions and Kiwanis clubs. She's a personal friend of the Governor and his wife. She knows every legislator in the state and was instrumental in writing Oregon's domestic violence law. She performs all the psychological profiles for our police applicants, negotiators and S.W.A.T. team members. She gives all the departments around the state a discount on counseling for officers who've been involved in critical incidents. She teaches at the university and teaches psychiatry at the medical school. This is the most powerful woman in Oregon, bar none. She's Jesus Christ in a skirt."

Gabe leaned into Ben and pleaded, "Hey, Ben, come on, we're the cops. We aren't supposed to care how powerful someone is. Let's go after her. She's a killer and it's our job to put her in jail."

Ben shook his head in frustration. "You don't understand, kid, I agree with you. All I'm saying is that it's going to be tough. Let me read this. Give me a few days to absorb it and develop a plan. I'll get back with you." Gabe left the file with Ben. He felt uneasy as he walked home. He hoped Ben wouldn't lose his nerve.

Gabe didn't hear from Ben the rest of the week. He hoped Ben wasn't running with the ball and leaving him on the bench after all his hard work. He'd been asleep on his sofa and awoke to a gentle knock on his door. He stumbled to the door and looked out the peephole. To his surprise, he saw Ben waiting outside.

As the door opened, Ben stepped in quickly and greeted him. "Hey, Gabe, sorry to wake you. Got time to talk?" Gabe nodded sluggishly and motioned for him to sit on the sofa.

"Listen, kid, we've got problems with the Loar case. We're going to have to work her under the table for a while."

"What do you mean, Ben? What's the problem?"

"First of all, she's good friends with Garrison and the D.A., Baumgartan. I've snooped around and found out that Garrison has dated her in the past. I don't know who dumped who, but he still sniffs around her every chance he gets. He wants back in her pants so bad that he'd burn our asses in a heartbeat to protect her. If he gets wind of this investigation, he'll kill the whole thing and find some way to charge us with professional misconduct."

150

Gabe sighed in frustration. "So, let's go around him. Will the sheriff or attorney general take it?"

"I don't know. The sheriff won't because he's too close to Loar. We can't get the thing filed in this county because Loar has been in bed with Baumgartan. No, I think we're going to have to work it ourselves till we get enough to file, then go to the D.A. If he plants his heels on us, we'll have to go public and generate so much bad press that he'll have to file charges."

Gabe rubbed his eyes and asked, "So where do we go from here?"

"I don't know, but we need help. I have a friend in the D.A.'s office, Beck Eisman. We'll meet you here about five."

"Sure, Ben, sure, see you then." Ben let himself out and Gabe laid back down. He couldn't sleep or stop thinking about what Ben had said. He finally gave up and dressed.

About 5:30, Ben knocked on the door. When Gabe opened it, he was surprised to see a stunning woman enter with Ben. She was lean, tanned and well proportioned. She had short blonde hair and was wearing a business suit. Ben introduced her as he entered. "Gabe Kinnett, meet Beck Eisman."

Gabe was surprised as Beck extended her hand and said, "Nice to meet you."

He shook her hand and asked, "D.A.'s office?"

"Yes, assistant D.A. I'm part of the homicide trial team."

"When Ben said Beck, I was expecting a man."

Beck smiled. "Yes, the name throws a lot of people. It's short for Rebecca."

Everybody settled on Gabe's only piece of furniture. Beck cleared the air. "Okay, Gabe, I've got to get some things straight before we begin. I'll tell you what I've told Ben. I'm not here. We're not having this conversation, understand? If Baumgartan finds out that I'm sneaking over here, my career is over. I can't afford to get fired at this early stage of my career. Baumgartan has a non-negotiable policy, no secret investigations, no freelancing. I'll consult on this case only because I owe Ben a favor. If you guys burn me or compromise my job, I'm out of here. If anyone gets wind that I'm even talking to you, I'll pull the plug and wash

151

my hands of you both. If there are any questions or comments, get them on the table now."

Gabe looked at Ben and shrugged his shoulders. Ben said, "She's taking a big chance here, Gabe. We can't burn her."

"You got it, boss. No one will ever find out from me."

Beck smiled and said, "Yes, that's what I hear. It's that ability to keep your mouth shut that got you your plush office with a view."

"Lucky me. So what happens now?"

She continued, "Don't call me. We'll meet here. We can meet at the P.D., but it will have to be late. There are too many people leaving the building at five. Gabe, you go to work at 11:00 p.m.? I'll meet you here in the evenings if we need to talk."

Gabe reached over to the orange crate and retrieved copies of his apartment and office keys. He handed them to Beck. "I thought we might have to use this place as a war room, so I had these made. Here are my office and apartment keys. Let yourself in if I'm not here."

With the formalities over, Ben began. "Okay, let's get started. I spoke with Beck briefly, but let's go over the cases. First of all, Beck, we've got some circumstantial evidence, but nothing strong enough to support a charge yet."

"I understand. Run it down for me."

Ben picked up Gabe's files and began. "In 1985, Jared Cutchall was shot in the face by Paul Siles. Cutchall had threatened to sue Loar and make a formal complaint against her. Siles was Loar's patient and was being treated for manic depression. The attorney that Cutchall used to mail the threatening letter to Loar was Jonathan Lynch, who was shot to death by another Loar patient, Tommy Ryan, in 1996. Probably revenge for helping the Cutchalls. Siles committed suicide before going to trial. Tommy Ryan committed suicide immediately after killing Lynch. In 1986, Dr. Albert Sabre was stabbed to death in his office by Loar's patient, Nat Benson. Loar was treating Benson for paranoid schizophrenia. Sabre was Loar's most outspoken critic and had lodged formal complaints against her with the state board of psychiatric review. Loar persuaded Benson to kill Sabre out of revenge. Benson was murdered later to keep her from talking. In 1987, assistant D.A., Tim Allis, was shot by Roger Moesen. Loar

152

was treating Moesen for paranoid schizophrenia. He was found murdered in his apartment before he could be arrested. He was killed to keep him quiet, but we don't know why he'd targeted Allis. Allis must have been investigating Loar and posed a threat to her somehow. In 1987 and 1988, we had three elderly ladies killed. They were raped, strangled and posed. They don't appear to be connected to Loar. The killings stopped, so the killer must have left town or died. In 1988, a doper, Lucian Green, was beat to death in an alley. No apparent connection to Loar. In 1990, Mickey Clearey was strangled in his room. He was strangled with a piece of clothesline cord. He'd been a patient of Loar's, but didn't kill anyone. He was probably killed because he wouldn't kill for her or to keep him from telling anyone about Loar's manipulation of him. In 1993, the school board president, Howard Wilcox, was shot in the head at the fitness center. He'd found out that Bruce Webster was having an affair with Loar and persuaded him to break it off. No suspect was ever identified, but Webster was killed in 1995. He was stabbed to death by another of Loar's patients, Sammy Pritchard. He was probably killed for dumping Loar. In 1996, Dutch Windsor was killed. No suspect, but he'd bashed Loar many times on his radio show. In 1996, Swede Boreman was shot to death. No suspect, but his wife had been attending Loar's group therapy sessions for abused women. Windsor, Benson and Moesen were all killed in a unique manner. They had the blood supply to their brains cut off by the use of a lateral vascular neck restraint. Has to be the same killer. That's a very rare method of killing and it takes someone with a lot of expertise to pull it off. Since Moesen and Benson were Loar's patients and Windsor was making life rough for her, she's got to be involved some how. She probably has another patient who does her strangling for her."

Beck was writing frantically to keep up. When finished, she looked at her notes for a few seconds. "Interesting, Ben, but you're right. There's nothing concrete. She might be involved, but we're a long way from tying her to any of these killings. She sees hundreds of patients a year. Any psychiatrist is going to have a predictable failure rate. Hers may not be higher than the norm. Even if she's made some mistakes, they can be chalked up to errors in judgment, a lack of cooperation by the patient or

153

incompetence at the most. We're going to have our work cut out for us proving that she manipulated these people to kill for her. This is going to be a tough case. Any viable witnesses?"

Ben shook his head. "Nope, not one. All of the people that she used to do her dirty work were killed to keep them quiet. The only one left is the retarded kid who killed Webster. He's at Beacon South. He doesn't even remember the killing according to his doctor there. He'd be a lousy witness. He wasn't competent to stand trial, so I'm sure he couldn't hold up under cross examination."

"That's not good enough. We have to have someone who can sit on the witness stand and testify with some degree of credibility that Loar encouraged them to commit murder. Anyone like that?" Ben shook his head.

She asked, "Is there any physical evidence at all to link Loar to these killings?" Ben again shook his head. Beck sat quietly and thought.

Gabe asked angrily, "So we're dead in the water? She just gets away with this and keeps on using other people to kill for her?"

Beck looked sternly at him. "Looks that way for now. Don't get me wrong. I agree that there's too much coincidence here for her to not be involved, but understand this. When and if we ever go public with this, heads are going to roll. Ours will be the first if we're wrong. We've got to be right. That's my job. I play the devil's advocate here. If I don't do that, we won't see the holes in our case. There's too much at stake here for us to go off half-cocked. You're going to get tired of me shooting holes in your theories, but don't bark at me. I'm on your side. I'm just trying to cover our butts." Ben understood and didn't interrupt. The chastising was for Gabe.

She continued, "Okay, Ben, let's set up a conference call with a credible psychiatrist. I want to know what we're dealing with here. We're also going to need some expert assistance if we ever get our hands on her medical files. I know a couple of psychiatrists that we've used from time to time, but they're tight with Loar. We need someone out of the area who doesn't know her. Know anyone?"

Gabe spoke up, "Yeah, I do, Dr. Gandmeten at Beacon South. He's out of the area and has no allegiance to Loar. He knows she's dirty and will talk to us. I'll set it up."

Beck asked, "What about the assistant D.A.? That intrigues me. He was before my time."

Ben said, "Don't know, Beck, I was about to ask you. Allis must have been collecting evidence against Loar and was killed for it. It's going to take someone inside the D.A.'s office to snoop around and find that out. You game?"

Beck thought for a second and shrugged her shoulders. "I'll see. I don't know who I can trust there. I can't let Baumgartan know that I'm snooping. Let me play with the idea for a while."

Ben pointed out one thing for Beck to consider. "Listen, Beck, you have to consider the possibility that Baumgartan found out that Allis was collecting evidence on Loar and tipped her off. Baumgartan is pretty tight with her. I wouldn't want you to end up like Allis."

She looked surprised for a second, then said, "I'll keep that in mind."

Gabe sat quietly for the most part. He finally spoke up. "Listen, Beck, we'll know more after we talk to Dr. Gandmeten, but we'll eventually have to get a search warrant for Loar's medical records. I think the identity of her strangler is somewhere in those files. I also think one of her patients killed the Clearey kid and shot Boreman and Wilcox. We can clear up all of these cases except the drug dealer and the three old ladies. We just need those files."

Beck thought for a second, then agreed, "Maybe, maybe not. Her files will contain only what she's written in them. If she's left that out, the files will do us no good. But before we can get a search warrant or a subpoena for her records, there has to be some factual basis for the request or the judge will throw it out. We can't subpoena her records based on mere speculation. We have to link her to at least one killing. Remember, she's connected. Baumgartan will kill the whole thing if he gets wind of it. The judge will call Baumgartan as soon as he sees the search warrant affidavit. Baumgartan will recall the warrant and call the chief of police. We've got some significant hurtles here, guys. We're not going to strap her on without a fight."

Gabe shook his head and tried to speak, but Beck held up her hand and cut him off. "No! Don't give me that crap! I told you we have to play by the rules here. I didn't make the rules or choose the teams. You asked me to help and I will, but don't make me out to be the bad guy here. I know this woman. She's got more clout than Jesus Christ himself. She's slept with every power broker in the state. She'll have the best legal counsel and it'll be free. She'll have the judge and D.A. in her pocket right out of the starting gate. She'll be calling in every marker she holds. Baumgartan will prosecute the case personally, if we can force him to prosecute at all. He'll conspire with the Judge to look for any reason to have the case thrown out. He'll screw it up on purpose to keep her from spilling her guts about his relationship with her. She'll walk away laughing, and we'll be out on the street looking for jobs. We're only going to get one shot at this woman. It has to be our best effort, and I'm not going to be butting heads with you every time things don't go your way. You're a rookie cop. I'm a prosecutor who's graduated from law school with honors. I know all the rules of evidence and what it takes to win in court, you don't. Don't bust my chops anymore about the injustice of the system. Now! Do you want me here or not? If not, I'll walk and you can shop around for another D.A. Good luck finding one who'll put their ass on the line like I'm doing."

Gabe listened in disbelief throughout Beck's tirade. He was shocked. He threw his hands up in defeat and said, "Okay, sorry, we'll do it your way."

Beck continued, "Ben, those interview reports are no good. They're in narrative form. When the time comes, go back to those witnesses and take formal statements. They can always claim that they never told Gabe anything in those reports. Lock them into their story with a question and answer format. Get their signatures on them and have them witnessed so they can't change their stories later. I'll be in touch with you, Gabe. Give me your home number. I'll call you here." He wrote it down and gave it to her.

She stood to leave and turned to Gabe. "Get on that conference call with your psychiatrist friend. I'll call a friend of mine at the junior college. They have a room set up for conference calls. We'll do it there. I don't want to get caught talking to this guy at the P.D. or my office." With that final instruction, Beck showed herself out.

Gabe stared at the floor. Ben laid the files on the orange crate and stood. He patted Gabe on the back and said, "Welcome to the real word, kid. She's a little hard-nosed, but she's what we need for this case. She's the only one in the D.A.'s office with the balls to do the right thing. We need her in our corner, so don't piss her off."

The message was clear. Gabe said, "Oh well, I'm used to getting my ass kicked by women. She's no worse than my ex-wife." Ben left and closed the door behind him. Tomorrow Gabe would call Dr. Gandmeten.

Dr. Gandmeten was not eager to get involved. He agreed to the conference call, but refused to be a witness against Dr. Loar. He didn't want to be branded a character assassin and he feared the wrath of Dr. Loar if prosecution was not successful.

Gabe awoke to a knock on his door about noon. He stumbled to the door in his underwear and peeked out the peephole. He panicked when he saw Beck Eisman standing outside. He yelled, "Just a minute!" He hurried to put on his sweat pants. He didn't want to leave Beck in the hall for long. It was a rough neighborhood.

As he jerked the door open, Beck smiled affectionately as if they had been close for years. She stepped in uninvited and looked around at Gabe's meager existence. Even though she'd seen the apartment before, Gabe was embarrassed. He explained, "You'll have to excuse my place. I don't have much. My wife left and took---"

Beck turned abruptly and held her hand up. "Stop, you don't have to explain. Ben told me about your divorce. I didn't come here to embarrass you. I just wanted to apologize for jumping down your throat the other night. I know the system is frustrating and you weren't directing your criticism at me."

Gabe was self-conscious about his bare torso and looked around for a shirt. Beck wasn't at all embarrassed. She was impressed with his physique. His months of weight workouts were paying off.

He put on a T-shirt and invited her to sit on the sofa. She sat and looked around at the apartment. She said, "Looks familiar, like my old apartment."

He sat at a safe distance on the other end of the sofa. "You used to live in a dump like this?"

"Yep, sure did. I didn't have a decent apartment until I got out of law school and got a job."

Gabe wanted to get to the purpose of the visit. "You didn't have to come here to apologize. I had the ass-chewing coming. You ought to hear old Sergeant Shelley when he gets wound up. You're nothing compared to him."

She smiled. "Thanks, I'll take that as a compliment. I did come here to apologize, but I also wanted to tell you that I have the conference room reserved for Thursday night. Can you set that up with Dr. Gandmeten?"

"That shouldn't be a problem. He's a little spooked though. He'll talk to us, but he won't be a witness. I think he's afraid of Loar. He knows what she did to Dr. Sabre and doesn't want to end up the same way."

"Can't say as I blame him. I'm a little spooked myself. Without knowing who her strangler is, we could all be in jeopardy when we file the charges."

"Do you really think that will happen?"

Beck shrugged her shoulders. "I don't know at this point. I've been thinking about this a lot. We're going to have to tie her to a killing before we can get the Judge to give us a subpoena for her medical files. We're going to have to get her medical files to link her to a killing and find out who's killing for her. I really don't know what's going to happen at this point, but coincidence and speculation won't cut it. We'll just have to give it our best shot."

Gabe asked, "Is there anyone that we can get to help us if we run into a brick wall?"

"Yes, we'll have to see if the U.S. attorney and FBI will help. No one in this state will go against her. The problem is that the case has to meet certain criteria before the feds will jump on board. They'll consult, but we'll have to prove corruption at the state and local level before they'll intervene in a state murder case."

After a clumsy period of silence, Beck stood and walked to the door. Gabe jumped to his feet and rushed to open the door for her. She said, "Well, I guess I'd better go."

"Thanks for coming by. I enjoyed talking to you. I don't get much company here."

She smiled. "I'll drop by again. We're going to use your apartment to meet. It's too risky anywhere else." He agreed and closed the door behind her.

He flopped back down on his sofa. Beck wasn't the man-hating ball-buster that he'd initially thought she was. She was actually pretty decent for a female. He laughed as he envisioned a discussion about male domination of females between Beck Eisman and Ramón Carlos.

Gabe met Beck and Ben at the junior college conference room. They dialed Dr. Gandmeten who was waiting at Beacon South. The video link was clear and everyone could talk face to face.

Dr. Gandmeten had a stack of journals in front of him. He listened to Beck's questions about depression and paranoid schizophrenia, then finally said, "Listen, I've prepared some notes on the topic. Let me go through them and maybe that will answer your questions." Everyone settled back for the doctor's lecture.

The doctor began. "First of all, paranoid schizophrenia has a variety of symptoms. These symptoms are visible in people who go untreated or don't respond to their medications. These symptoms cause some degree of social or occupational dysfunction. The symptoms can be delusions, hallucinations, grossly disorganized or catatonic behavior, disorganized speech and negative symptoms or a demeanor devoid of emotion. A delusion is a mistaken belief or misinterpretation of reality. The delusion might be grandiose such as, 'I am God or I am the President of the United States.' It might be religious such as, 'God has instructed me to do something.' It might be referential like, 'the television or telephone is sending me a message,' or it might be somatic, 'my skin is decaying.' It might be persecutory, 'someone is trying to kill me.' Delusions can range in scope from mild like, 'everyone is out to get me', to extreme like, 'aliens are conspiring with the C.I.A. to kill me.' Hallucinations can be associated with any of the five senses. The most common hallucination though is auditory. They hear voices. Those voices are not their own. They're usually insulting, condemning and threatening."

He took a drink of water and continued. "There are several types of schizophrenia. The paranoid type frequently has delusions or auditory hallucinations. Paranoid schizophrenics are commonly coherent and their delusions usually focus on a specific preoccupation. These people are usually nervous, hostile, aloof and argumentative. They frequently have heightened perceptions of themselves and are arrogant and condescending to others. These people are dangerous. They may have false perceptions of themselves or their obsessions, but their behavior is generally organized and calculating. They are capable of premeditation and careful planning in order to accomplish their goals. If their goal is to kill someone, they can be extremely calculating and dangerous. The onset of schizophrenia typically occurs in the late teens to early thirties. Men are likely to display symptoms earlier. There is evidence that genetics plays some part in schizophrenia. Evidence also shows that this is a biological illness and many of the available treatments are antipsychotic medications."

Beck interrupted Dr. Gandmeten and asked, "So, Doctor, these patients are time bombs anyway. Dr. Loar could have a rational explanation for her failure rate?"

Dr. Gandmeten replied, "Absolutely. She could claim that their delusions and hallucinations prompted an unwillingness to take their medications or that they didn't respond satisfactorily to the medications at all. Psychiatry is not an exact science and relies on the cooperation of the patient. Some patients stabilize very well with outpatient therapy. Others may need placement in a group home or institutionalization."

Ben tried to ask a question, but was stopped. Dr. Gandmeten said, "Let me finish. Because of their paranoia, these people believe that they are in peril and distrust everyone. They are capable of extreme violence to protect themselves or someone that they have become dependent on. Now, if Dr. Loar has keyed in on the fear of some of her patients and has convinced them that she is the only person in the world who can manage their fear, they might see her destruction as their own. Through hypnosis, the idea could be planted that Dr. Loar was being threatened, and the patient would defend her as they would themselves. Even though these people are suspicious of everyone, they can quickly develop a chemical dependency on their medication and an emotional dependency on their psychiatrist. They can develop an almost fatal obsession with their therapist. To avoid this unhealthy dependency, it's a good idea to introduce another therapist into the treatment program so the patient can see that there are other people who care and can help. This also prevents the feeling of abandonment if the therapist can no longer treat the patient for some reason. Patients who feel abandoned often feel betrayed by the system and lose faith in the psychiatry profession and the medications that are stabilizing their mood swings. They can feel hopeless and helpless, and turn suicidal or violent toward others."

Ben asked, "Like Nat Benson stabbing Dr. Sabre? Dr. Loar could have convinced her that Dr. Sabre was going to cause Loar to lose her license and could no longer treat her. If Benson thought she was going to lose Dr. Loar, she could have killed Dr. Sabre to save Dr. Loar and ultimately herself?"

Dr. Gandmeten replied, "Yes, that's possible. If she'd developed an emotional dependency on Dr. Loar, she may have been the only person in the world who Benson trusted. Losing Dr. Loar would have been tantamount to dying. With mild manipulation of her medications, subtle reinforcement of Benson's mission to kill Sabre, and a failure to bring Benson back into socially acceptable parameters of behavior, Dr. Loar could have allowed a monster to grow rather than do the ethical thing and try to keep Benson in check and seek a nonviolent solution. Loar would be completely out of line by introducing her personal conflicts into her patients' treatment programs."

Gabe said, "Yeah, like Roger Moesen killing the assistant D.A. If he'd thought the D.A. was going to put Loar in jail, he could have targeted Allis to save Loar. And Sammy Pritchard could have stabbed Webster thinking that Webster was hurting Loar."

Dr. Gandmeten nodded and said, "Yes, all that is possible. I'm not saying it's true. I'm just speaking hypothetically. Also, keep in mind that Dr. Loar is a magnificent looking woman. Her patients could very easily develop a deep romantic attraction to

161

her. The threatened loss of affection could also offer substantial leverage in their manipulation."

Gabe sat quietly as Beck and Ben thought. Beck then said, "That's going to be tough to prove."

"Very tough. Like I told Officer Kinnett, Dr. Loar's patient files will contain only what she's written in them. Without credible witnesses or documentation, you have nothing. I can guarantee you with absolute certainty that if your suspicions about Dr. Loar are true, there won't be a single notation confirming any misconduct in any of her files."

Everybody remained quiet for a minute. Dr. Gandmeten gathered up his notes and prepared to terminate the interview. Beck asked, "Thanks, doctor, any other advice?"

Dr. Gandmeten thought, then said, "Possibly, a lot of serial killers want to relive the thrill of the kill at a later time. If Dr. Loar is the killer that you think she is, she's nothing more than a serial killer who uses psychiatry patients as her weapons, like another psychopath would use a gun or knife. She may keep souvenirs of her killings; something that she can pull out occasionally and help her relive the crime. Even though she wasn't present at the actual killing, she may get some gratification from fondling a souvenir. I don't know what her souvenirs would be. They could be something as innocent as her patient files. She may keep them in her head and you'll never find them. Sorry I can't tell you more."

As Dr. Gandmeten stood, he knelt in front of the camera and said, "Also, keep something else in mind. Dr. Loar may herself be a paranoid schizophrenic. She's aloof, organized and possibly capable of extreme violence. She may be lucid enough to recognize the onset of paranoid schizophrenic symptoms and may be medicating herself. To avoid getting caught medicating herself, she may be writing scripts to a patient who turns the medication back over to her. Many possibilities exist, and I wouldn't count on an examination by another therapist to accurately diagnose her. I know Dr. Loar. She wrote the book on psychoanalysis. It'll be impossible to get inside her head unless she wants you there. Before that happens, she may have to self-destruct first."

Beck responded with a quick question. "Doctor, would there be any outward signs that she's medicating herself?"

"The most common antipsychotic medications can produce side affects that might give her away if you know what to look for. If she is self-medicating, she might exhibit side effects like involuntary movements of the tongue, jaw, trunk and extremities. Don't be surprised if those side affects aren't apparent. There are other medications that could control them. If she wants to hide those side affects from people who would recognize them, such as other psychiatrists, she would secure those medications the same way that she gets the anti-psychotics, through another patient."

Ben asked, "Would you suggest that we get the F.B.I.'s behavioral science unit involved in this? Maybe they could give us a psychological profile that matches Dr. Loar."

Dr. Gandmeten shook his head adamantly. "No, not at all. It's your investigation, officer. Do what you want, but that would be futile. This is like no other murder case that I've ever heard of. They might be able to give you a profile of the killer, but Dr. Loar isn't the actual killer. She's effectively insulated herself by having someone else kill for her. The FBI's profile might match Pritchard, Moesen, Ryan or Benson, but it would never match Loar. She probably planted the idea in their minds, then left it up to the patient to work out the details of the killing. Since everyone is an individual, none of the killings would be identical and certainly not traceable to Loar. Good luck, folks. Call if I can help and above all, be careful. You may not realize it, but you're in extreme danger. If Loar is the monster that you think she is, she gets extreme pleasure from killing. Serial killers are like big game hunters. The bigger and more challenging the game, the more thrilling the kill. Cops and prosecutors would be big game for her."

With no additional questions, Dr. Gandmeten disconnected the video link. Gabe, Ben and Beck sat quietly. Ben finally shook his head and asked, "What next? Want me to go back and get formal statements from the family members that Gabe interviewed? Want me to start a case file?"

Beck said. "No, not now. We can't alert Loar. The more smoke we stir up, the greater the chance that one of them will tip her off. She'll just drop her pants for the D.A., chief of police or the judge and get the investigation buried. Let's let her sleep for now."

Gabe asked, "Where do we go from here?"

She stood and put on her coat. "I haven't got a clue. You guys owe me a cup of coffee though. Coffee first, then we'll see what our options are."

Gabe had finished his weight workout and was preparing to jump rope when he heard pounding on his door and a barrage of swearing on the other side. He smiled as he thought, *Blauw.*

When he opened the door, Angus and Shelley were glaring at him. Shelley stepped in forcefully and demanded an explanation. "Okay, boy, you've been making yourself scarce lately. What's going on? You're either going nuts or you think you're too good to associate with us night crawlers, which is it?"

Gabe laughed and replied, "Well, I've certainly gone nuts, but that only makes me more compatible with you two. I haven't been ignoring you. I've just been busy."

Angus said, "Busy! You fool, you ain't got nothing to do down here. How can you be busy?"

Gabe thought for a second and realized that he was coming dangerously close to leaking information about the Loar investigation. He looked at Angus and Shelley and decided that they were safe. He decided to let them in on the case. "Well, Angus, I've been looking into some of the dead files. You won't believe what we've found. Most of these killings were committed by psych-patients. They were all patients of Dr. Loar. All their victims had pissed Loar off at one time or another. She's been manipulating her patients to kill for her."

Shelley looked at Gabe in shock, then looked at Angus. Angus pointed his finger at him and growled, "Didn't I tell you that years ago?"

Gabe asked Angus, "You mean you figured this out when you were down here?"

"Yeah, I figured it out, but everyone thought I was nuts. I told my old buddy, Shelley, here and he laughed at me. I had to let it go. I forgot about it because I didn't want to get my time in this hole extended."

Shelley said, "Kinnett, you said we. Who else are you working with on this? You know Garrison will cut your nuts off if he finds out that you're stirring up a scandal about Dr. Loar."

"I showed it to Ben Hire. He's helping me. We're keeping it quiet, so don't tell anyone."

"Well, okay, I guess you're doing it right. Ben's the best. If he's your backup, I won't worry about you. You just be careful. That bitch is powerful. She can flush your career down the toilet with one phone call and have your shiny ass killed even quicker."

Angus was shaking his head in disgust as he chastised Shelley. "You big asshole, when I told you the same thing years ago, you told me to shut up and keep my nose out of those files. You didn't give a shit if I got killed. Why the change of heart all of a sudden?"

Shelley shrugged. "Hell, Angus, I knew no one would ever believe a delusional old drunk like you. You're crazier and more psychotic than the people you were accusing. Kinnett here has got some brains. People will believe him. Besides, I don't want Kinnett here to get killed. I like him. I didn't care what happened to you. Besides, no one would have tried to kill you. Anyone who looks at you thinks you're dead already."

Gabe laughed at the barbs that Angus and Shelley were hurling at each other. He grabbed his coat and said, "Come on, boys, lunch is on me tonight. I finally got enough money to buy for once."

At the diner, the three were joined by a couple more officers, so Angus couldn't talk freely to Gabe. On the way to the wagon afterwards, he leaned into Gabe and said, "Listen, son, if you run into any hurdles that you can't clear, call me. I might be able to help."

Gabe wasn't sure what Angus meant. Knowing his wide ethical parameters, he was afraid to ask. He thanked Angus and climbed in the wagon.

8

A WEEK PASSED, and Gabe hadn't heard from Ben or Beck. He didn't want to pry, but he didn't want to be left out of the investigation. He was afraid they were proceeding without him.

After his noon nap, he called Ben. "Hey, Ben, Gabe. Sorry to bother you, but I haven't heard anything about Loar. Have you and Beck made any progress?"

Ben put Gabe's fears to rest. "No, not yet. We won't do anything without you." Gabe gave a sigh of relief. Ben continued, "I am glad you called though. Beck wants to talk to us. Is your place at seven tonight okay?"

Gabe eagerly replied, "Sure! I'll spring for dinner. What do you want?"

"Oh, surprise us. See you then."

Beck and Ben tapped on Gabe's door at seven. He quickly opened it, hoping no one would see the two enter. He had pizza and paper plates on top of the stove for his guests. After flipping the tabs on cans of soda and dishing up the pizza, everyone sat on Gabe's sofa and dug in.

Beck made small talk while eating. Gabe was impressed at how down to earth and congenial she was. When she was not working, you wouldn't know that she was an assistant D.A.

He couldn't keep his eyes off her. She was beautifully proportioned and wore tight blue jeans that accentuated her figure.

When everyone had eaten their fill, Gabe collected the paper plates and cans and put them in a trash bag in the kitchen. He hurried back to the sofa so he wouldn't miss any of the conversation.

Beck pulled some notes out of her bag and started down the outline. "Okay, here's where we are at this point. There's no need to explain the relationships between Dr. Loar, her patients and the murder victims. I think we all have a clear picture of that. I've researched some case law on our ability to subpoena medical records. First of all, in the affidavit we have to be very specific on the exact medical records that we want, and we have to articulate the probable cause that supports the request. For example, we can ask for the records on Pritchard, Moesen or Benson. We can ask for the records of Mrs. Boreman and any other patient tied to one of our killings if we can support the request with ample probable cause that the records contain evidence of value in a criminal trial. In order to get the affidavit past the judge, we have to list some evidence of causality. We can't request all of her records as merely a fishing expedition. There has to be a reasonable suspicion that those specific records will contain evidence that will assist in prosecution. At this point, we don't have a thread of evidence linking Dr. Loar to any of the killings. All we have is speculation based on coincidence. I frankly think it would be an exercise in futility even if we could get the affidavit past the judge. She's not stupid enough to document her manipulation of patients in their medical records. If anything, she's documented a textbook treatment program to cover her butt in case her records are ever audited."

Ben asked, "So, how about sitting her ass down in front of a grand jury? Let's ask her about all these relationships and see how she squirms out of it. She's not entitled to an attorney while sitting in front of the grand jury. Maybe she'll incriminate herself."

Beck shook her head, "No way! There's not enough evidence to classify her as a suspect. Even if I subpoena her as a witness, all she has to do is plead ignorance about the killings. She'll be well coached before she testifies. We'd look like fools if we went to the grand jury with no more than we have now.

Besides, these are all dead cases. Baumgartan approves all the cases that go to the grand jury's docket. He'd never let these cases through. They'd have to be approved by Garrison before they ever got to Baumgartan. If Garrison refuses to allow his designee, meaning you, Gabe, to present these to the D.A., the D.A. certainly isn't going to put them before the grand jury. The grand jury is a good sounding board to see if we would have a decent case in court. At this point, there's not a grand jury in the world that would indict Loar."

Gabe's frustration boiled, but he didn't want to anger Beck again. He sat quietly, then chose his words carefully. "So, even if we can't charge her, maybe we could find out who her strangler is if we got her records. If we could get him to break down, maybe we could go after Loar through him."

"Yes, maybe in a normal case, but remember, as soon as Loar gets wind that we're after her, she'll have us shut down before we get to first base. We can't get her files. Forget that angle. Even if I wanted to go out on that limb, Baumgartan, Garrison and the judge would saw it off behind me. Forget her medical records."

Ben rubbed his face. "Well, looks like we're through. We're going to have to wait till one of her patients kills again and hope we can get to him before Loar does. Nothing we do at this point will get a charge filed, and we'll only send her underground if we tip our hand now. Maybe if she doesn't know that we're investigating her, she'll get careless."

Beck said, "I agree. That's the best approach at this point. Sorry, guys, I know it's a tough pill to swallow."

She put her notes back in her bag. Gabe thought out loud, "Too bad we're cops. If we could burglarize her office, we'd find out who her strangler is."

Ben closed his eyes and cringed. That was the wrong thing to say in front of Beck. She turned promptly to Gabe and glared at him as she began her lecture. "Yes, maybe you could, and maybe you couldn't, but remember one thing. You're cops, and make no mistake. If you do something stupid like that, you'll get caught and Garrison will fire you in a heartbeat. He'll prepare a case file and present it to Baumgartan. He'll file charges on you and ask for the maximum penalty. You'll go to prison, lose your career and won't contribute one ounce to Loar's downfall. The evidence would be obtained illegally and would be inadmissible in court, and it would be my luck that Baumgartan would assign your case to me and I'd have to prosecute you. I like you too much to do that, so don't put me in that position. The consequences of something like that are so terrible that I'm going to pretend that I didn't hear it."

She stood to leave. Gabe hurried to the door and wished her a good night as she left. When he sat back down, he said, "Boy, that wasn't the smartest thing I've ever said."

Ben agreed. "Oh the foolishness of the young tongue."

"Yeah, but it made sense to me. Why do we have to be hamstrung while the criminals have no rules to play by?"

"Because that's the way the legal system was built. It was built by attorneys for attorneys to get rich in, and it's not ever going to change. Take my advice. Just survive it and grow old enough to draw your pension. Then you can wash your hands of it and live out your years knowing that you had more integrity in your little finger than all these attorneys put together."

"That's not much consolation, Ben, I want Loar."

"I know, Gabe, but it's not going to happen. Loar is untouchable now. Be patient. She'll screw up someday."

"What about the people who'll die before then? How many murders will occur before she grows a conscience and stops? You know that's never going to happen."

"Maybe not, Gabe, but the really important thing here is to not become one of her casualties. You can't save the world. People die every day. It won't be our fault if she kills again. We'll get her someday, but we have to survive the system to do it. Keep your nose clean and do your time. Get back on the road and go on with your career. If I ever get a shot at Loar, I'll let you in on it."

Gabe went back to his old routine in the dungeon. He lifted weights, jumped rope and watched movies. He thought by now that he would be adjusted to midnights and wouldn't need naps, but he wasn't. Dr. Maura Loar was in his every waking thought. She haunted him and robbed him of sleep.

Beck Eisman was also in his thoughts. He felt a strong attraction to her, but couldn't think of a graceful way to contact her. With the investigation stalled, any attempts to strike up a relationship would be awkward. Besides, he thought she was out of his league.

Weeks passed, and winter was beginning to surrender its grip on the city. Gabe wanted to talk to Angus alone, but they always had lunch with other officers.

One night, Gabe heard pounding on his door and a barrage of swearing outside. He opened the door and to his surprise, Angus was alone. He growled, "Come on, you little deviant, let's eat."

Gabe quickly grabbed his coat and followed Angus to his wagon. Once in the truck, Gabe asked, "How have you been, Angus?"

"Ah, okay I guess. My diabetes and arthritis are acting up, but my stomach is feeling better. I guess the doctor finally found the right medicine for me."

"Sorry to hear it, Angus. Old age is no fun."

"No fun! Hell, boy, it's an ever-loving bitch, then it has puppies. I hate it! My mind is as young as ever, but my body is falling apart. I remember when I was twenty years old. Seems like a few weeks ago. I swear I don't know where the years have gone. Life is just so short."

Gabe sympathized with Angus. He was well into his sixties and trying to do a young man's job. He could have retired years ago, but the job was all he had to live for. He was struggling to stay one step ahead of a medical retirement. He asked, "So, Angus, you old germ, where's Shelley tonight?"

"Ah, the fat fucker strained a hernia the other day. He's home praying that he doesn't have to have surgery."

"Oh, that's too bad. He's a good guy to have around when things go to hell."

"Yeah he is, and by the way, when are you coming back on the road?"

"Ain't got a clue, Angus. I was hoping that Garrison would forget about me before now, but I guess I've pissed him off more than I thought."

"Well, don't worry. It'll happen someday."

Gabe sat quietly, then decided that he'd better talk to Angus before they got to the diner. Other officers might meet them there. "Listen, Angus, I've got a problem and I need some advice."

171

Angus puffed up with pride. "Hell, boy, I'm your man. People don't ask me for advice much anymore and that's unfortunate because I'm a wealth of information. Shoot."

"This Loar mess has got me bothered. We tied her to all those murders, but we can't touch her. I'd like to see her patient files, but we can't substantiate enough probable cause to get a search warrant. There aren't any witnesses left to testify against her, so we're at a dead end. We think she's got some souvenirs from the killings, but I need to get in her office to look for them. I'm not even sure I'd know what to look for. I wish there was some way to circumvent the search warrant process without jeopardizing my career."

Angus listened intently as he thought. He finally said, "Well, son, there's not. That's one of the cold, cruel realities of this job. We have strict rules to play by, and if you break them, the rats upstairs will fire you. The courts will put you in jail, and society will put you in a lower class than the scumbags that you're breaking the rules to catch."

"So what's the answer, Angus?" Do I burglarize Loar's office or sit quietly by and protect this sacred system that we operate in while she kills someone else?"

Angus replied, "Now, Gabe, you're getting cynical. You ain't been here long enough to get an attitude." Gabe didn't respond. After a few seconds of silence, Angus said, "Well, since you asked, I'll tell you what I'd do. I'd burglarize the bitch's office and make sure I didn't get caught. Whatever you find won't be admissible, but you might find out who she's using to kill for her. You could then surveil them and maybe hang some charges on them. If you could do that, maybe you could pressure them to break down on Loar. If you could hang serious enough charges on them that they'd be facing a long prison sentence, they might give her up to get a shorter sentence. All they'd have to do is wear a wire during one of their counseling sessions when she tried to talk them into killing for her. If she confessed to any of the murders, that'd be enough to get a search warrant. It would be a long shot, but it's better than sitting on your ass and waiting for her to kill again."

Gabe wasn't surprised to hear that from Angus. "I thought you might say that. I just don't think my ethics would let me do that."

Angus glared at Gabe and growled, "Why you little shit, you saying I ain't got no ethics?"

Gabe quickly retracted his words. "No! No, Angus, it's just that I don't see how you can justify that, being a cop. How would you live with yourself?"

"Listen, boy, I'm going to give you a lesson on ethics according to a true expert in human nature, Angus Blauw. First of all, we're the only ones in this whole fucked-up system who get hog-tied by ethics. The lawyers and judges ain't got none. Look at old Judge Niles. That sleazy bastard sits on his bench, preaches honesty and ethics in his courtroom and throws up this façade that he's protecting the integrity of the criminal justice system. I've seen him take on cases in his private practice where he's lied his ass off. He knew before the trial ever began that his client was guilty because he tried to broker a plea bargain with the prosecutor. When the pleas didn't materialize, he fabricated alternative scenarios to confuse the jury. While he's sitting there lying his ass off, he's screaming bloody murder if he thinks the police officer is lying. These attorneys are nothing but professional liars. That law degree gives them license to be as devious as they want."

"Yeah, but you can't prove it."

"Hell, boy, you only have to prove it if you're in a court of law. We don't have to prove it to know it in our hearts. Listen, here's how the system works. These asshole lawyers wrote the laws in their favor. They're full of loopholes that tilt the scales in the defense's favor. A defense attorney has the right to file a motion for discovery before a trial. The prosecutor has to disclose every document and piece of evidence that he intends to use in his prosecution. The defense attorney then sits down with his scumbag client and helps him fabricate a lie to account for the evidence. He then hires some professional prostitute to come in and give expert testimony that refutes the prosecution's experts. It's all a lie, but because he's got a title and degree after his name, his lie goes into the record as expert testimony. A trial isn't an exercise in justice. It's a contest to see which side can most effectively sway the jury.

It's a salesmanship contest. The truth has nothing to do with it. Now, the police and prosecutors have to tell the truth, but the defense doesn't. These judges know damn good and well that these defense attorneys are lying their asses off to get their clients acquitted, and they let them get away with it. Did you ever hear a judge tell a defense attorney in open court, 'You're lying your ass off, counselor'? Hell no, and you never will. They're all in bed together. They scratch each other's back. When Judge Niles defends a case in Judge Peterson's court, he lies his ass off. Peterson doesn't say a word because he knows he'll be lying his ass off in Niles's court the next week. That's called professional courtesy, kid, and then the hypocrites have the nerve to sit there in their black robes, look down their self-righteous noses at us and threaten us with a contempt citation if we lie. Well, I learned long ago how to beat them at their own game. I just out-lie them. It's all in how you write your reports, boy. I know what lies they're going to fabricate and what accusations they're going to throw at me. They're all the same. They're going to say that I didn't read their poor, defenseless client the Miranda Warning. They're going to say that I lied about what their client said and that he never confessed to me. They're going to claim that I planted evidence and falsified my reports. They're going to claim that I used excessive force and intimidated their client into confessing to something that they didn't really do. They're going to claim that I violated some minor rule that entitles their client to a free walk. I know all the bullshit that they're going to throw at me and I'm ready for them. I just write my reports to cover all those possibilities."

Angus pulled into the parking lot of the diner and put the truck in park. They sat in the lot while Angus finished his ethics lesson. "Listen, kid, you're still young. They pounded ethics up your ass at the academy, and you haven't been around long enough to see the world as it really is. You're still too idealistic."

"You think that'll change?"

"I don't know. You may not, but if you don't, you'll never be able to deal with the hypocrisy of the criminal justice system. It'll eat you alive. You'll certainly never catch Loar. She'll never be caught by conventional methods. Listen, kid, ethics are not pillars of steel set in concrete. They're not unbendable and rigid.

174

Ethics are flexible and fluid. They're relative and can shift with your values and the circumstances at the time. You're not a stagnant creature. Your values will change over time, and every set of circumstances is different. I would never dream of burglarizing the office of a man who was cheating on his taxes or running a fencing operation. The stakes aren't high enough for my conscience to allow me to live with myself if I did that. But my conscience wouldn't bother me a bit for burglarizing Loar's office. She's killing innocent people. The consequences of her actions are severe enough that we're justified in bending the rules to catch her. Now, those hypocritical fuckers upstairs and in the courts don't see it that way, but it happens, and don't kid yourself into thinking it doesn't. Those pricks upstairs have pulled stunts ten times more devious than anything I've ever done. Let me give you an example. Our government wouldn't dream of publicly condoning murder for any reason. It wouldn't be politically correct. Hell, they execute murderers all the time in this country. But look throughout history at how many foreign governments that we've overthrown. We'll never know how many murders our government has been responsible for, simply because there was no other way to rid the world of some godless, yank-hating asshole. Our own government recognizes that there are times when the system doesn't work. If you want a good example of corruption at work, look at Washington. Sometimes you have to step outside the box to catch the hard ones. Listen, boy, Loar doesn't operate inside the box. She doesn't play by our rules. No one in the criminal justice system has to play by the rules but us. She's the kind of asshole that calls for a creative approach. Would I feel guilty about breaking into her office to stop her from murdering someone else? Hell no! And don't look at me like I'm some crooked bastard. If the stakes are high enough and nothing else works, your ethics will bend. Everyone's does. Just think for a second. What if you knew that Loar's next victim was going to be your mom or dad, maybe even your only child. What would you do? Would you sit back, cross your arms and say, 'Oh well, I can't stop her because I'd have to break the rules?' Hell no you wouldn't! I know you. You're the same kind of goon that I am. You'd hunt the bitch down and blow her foxy ass off before she could get to your kid. So what makes your kid anymore precious than someone else's

175

family member? The people we serve love their families as much as we love ours. What difference does it make who we break the rules for? Was Webster, Wilcox or Sabre any less valuable? Did their families love them less than we love ours? What would their family members have done if they'd been able to look into the future and see that Loar was going to kill their loved ones? Hell, boy, they'd have done the same thing. They certainly couldn't have come to the police and said they think Loar was going to kill their family member. We couldn't do anything till after the crime was committed. We could try to prove a conspiracy charge, but we'd have to find her killer first. We could stake out Loar, but she'd just lay low and kill them when we gave up."

Gabe sat quietly and looked straight ahead as Angus raved. As hard as he tried, he couldn't think of a rebuttal. He was afraid to admit it openly, but he agreed with everything that Angus said. He sighed. "So how would I live with myself if I broke the rules? How do you live with yourself?"

"You couldn't. You're still too idealistic and straight-laced. You've got this bullshit image of yourself as being a knight in shining armor. You believe that bullshit that they packed up your ass in the academy, that the good guys always win. Just follow the rules and trust the system. Trust your chief and the courts. We're all in this together. You'd do something stupid like confess to Garrison just to clear your conscience. Me on the other hand, I'd live with myself just fine. My ethics are extremely flexible. If I'm after a dirty fucker, I play the game the same way they and their shithead attorneys do, and I win. They're in prison where they belong, justice is served and society is much better off because of it. Hell, boy, I'm a real-life hero. They make movies about guys like me."

"I don't know if I'll ever get to that point, Angus. I was always taught that right and wrong never change. Ethics aren't situational. The determining factor of what's right isn't whether we can get away with it or what the consequences are if we do get caught. Just because we rationalize it away in our own minds doesn't mean it's justified before God. There's a price to pay for consciously breaking the law, if not in this life, certainly in the next."

176

Angus sighed and replied, "Yeah, you're right, Gabe. God never changes. He's the same now as He was when the earth was created and He'll be the same a million years from now. But we're not God. We're not capable of living our lives without breaking His rules. He knew that when He sent His son to die on the cross for us. But I believe that He overlooks lies if it serves a greater purpose. If a person lies to protect a greater underlying principle, I think God overlooks it. Breaking into Loar's office isn't legal, but if it'll save the lives of innocent people, I think He'll overlook it."

Gabe's mouth dropped open in shock. He stared at Angus and said, "No, not you! Angus Blauw, you phony old goat, don't sit there and tell me that you believe in God! No one that cusses as much as you do can believe in God!"

Angus frowned at him and growled, "Kinnett, you dumb bastard, just because I don't act the way I should doesn't mean I don't believe in Him. I'll straighten up some day. I'm working on it. Cussing is a hard fucking habit to kick. Give me a break here, I've got a conscience, too, you know."

Gabe laughed and patted Angus on the shoulder. "Angus, you old dog, I misjudged you. I guess there's hope for you yet." He turned serious and continued, "I still don't know if I can be a crook without letting my conscience eat me alive."

Angus barked back, "Kinnett, you hard-headed little prick, did you rat on me when I beat the shit out of that phony preacher?"

Gabe looked down at the floor and shook his head. He knew where Angus was going. Angus reached over, patted him on the shoulder and said, "See? You're closer than you think. Remember, Gabe, ethics are relative. Every human being in the world lies at one time or another. Under the right circumstances, everyone is capable of stealing or killing someone or breaking the rules of their particular profession. Ain't no human being ever lived that didn't do something contrary to their conscience at one time or another. You're only human, don't beat yourself up over it. And listen to me, stupid, if you go into Loar's office, make sure you practice my philosophy in life."

Gabe rolled his eyes and hesitated to ask, but he knew Angus was going to tell him anyway. "And what would that be, Angus, as if I didn't know?"

Angus smiled big and said proudly, "Make sure you don't get caught. Never admit to anything. If they accuse you, lie your ass off and swear it wasn't you. If they have witnesses, swear that their witnesses are lying or confused. If they ain't got pictures, they ain't got shit. If they have pictures, you have a twin that looks just like you. And never, never, never let the bastards see you sweat! Fear and anxiety is a sure sign of guilt. Got that, boy?"

Gabe shook his head and laughed. "Good philosophy, Angus. Is that part of your commitment to change your ways?"

Angus shrugged his shoulders and replied smugly, "It's hard to argue with success. It's worked for me."

"Well it doesn't work for me. Look where it's got me so far."

Angus opened his door and said, "That's because you're just an amateur, Kinnett. It takes a law degree or years of practice to be an expert liar like me. If you do it long enough, you'll get good at it. Come on, you self-righteous little asshole, buy me a cheeseburger. And don't preach at me no more. All this philosophizing has made me hungry. I'm not used to working my brain so hard."

He was through being serious and nothing would change that now. A straight answer would be impossible from this point forward. Gabe shook his head in frustration and opened the door. He followed Angus into the diner and smiled at his gate.

Angus hobbled along in front of him like a quivering, arthritic old Chihuahua. It was obvious that he was in constant pain. Gabe saw through his facade. He was really a deeply compassionate man with a strong sense of justice. With all of Angus's faults and wide ethical parameters, Gabe thought he was one of the wisest men that he'd ever met. He saw now why Angus was loved by so few and hated by so many. He counted himself lucky to be one of the few.

Gabe spent the next few weeks thinking about Maura Loar. His frustration gradually brought him more in line with Blauw's philosophy. Sometimes the end does justify any means.

He'd expected another homicide at any time. He'd also been obsessing over Beck Eisman, but couldn't think of an excuse to call her. He wasn't sure he was ready for a relationship anyway.

His anger over Loar's invincibility festered. He caught himself obsessing over her as well. He wondered if he needed therapy himself. Once again, he found himself losing sleep. This time, it wasn't because of his divorce or job assignment.

He'd begun to unconsciously distance himself from the other officers. He'd become bitter and confrontational. He looked at himself in the mirror when he got up each evening and saw a different person now, and he didn't like him.

With no leads jumping out at him, Gabe spent time at the fitness center where Howard Wilcox had been killed. He didn't know what he hoped to learn there, but it made him feel like he was doing something productive.

The dues were $600.00 a year, which put a membership out of his reach. He spoke with the manager who allowed him to pay month to month since he didn't know how long he would be coming.

The fitness center was posh. It had a well-stocked free-weight room and a strength training circuit encircled by a carpeted 1/8th mile jogging track. It had two aerobic rooms, racquetball courts, an Olympic-sized pool, whirlpool and sauna.

Gabe lifted weights and watched people. He thought the exercise would be good for his morale and he might meet someone who'd known Wilcox. He tried to be subtle about his inquiries.

He made a point to be friendly to the manager. After a few casual conversations, he'd learned that the manager remembered Wilcox. He'd also learned that Loar had been a member of the club at the time of the Wilcox murder and had dropped her membership shortly afterwards.

For several weeks, he went to the club in the early afternoons. He liked the free-weights and began feeling improvement in his strength. As his physique improved, so did his self-esteem. The diverse equipment of the club allowed him to work all muscle groups and was a vast improvement over the dumbbells that he was restricted to at work.

He noticed a group of body-builders who used the free-weights about the same time every afternoon that he did. They were cliquish and stayed to themselves. One woman in particular caught his eye. She was overdeveloped, had reddish blonde hair and was six feet tall. She was in her late 40s and her skin was scarred and wrinkled from too many hours in the tanning bed. He had no physical attraction to her, but she was an imposing figure. He couldn't keep his eyes off her, and occasionally she caught him staring at her.

One afternoon, Gabe was finishing his last set of reps on the bench press when the burn drained his strength. He knew one more press would leave the bar on his chest without the strength to lift it off.

As he struggled to get the bar in the rack, a hand grabbed the middle of the bar between his hands. The extra lift was sufficient to get the bar in the cradle. He quit straining and opened his eyes, but all he could see was a woman's crotch standing over his face. He looked farther, but only saw two breasts blocking the woman's face.

As the bar came to rest in the rack, she stepped back. Gabe saw the hardened face of the woman that he'd been watching with awe from afar.

He sat up quickly and thanked her for the help. Her voice was deep and raspy from too many years of steroids and male hormones. Gabe said, "Thanks for the help. I shouldn't work out alone I guess."

The woman smiled and agreed, "That's right, but you're probably safe here. There's always someone around who'll help if you yell. It's embarrassing to have to ask a woman to pick the bar up off your throat though."

He nodded and extended his hand. "Gabe Kinnett."

The woman gripped his hand firmly and answered, "Jenna. Jenna Kerse. Would you like to join us?"

He looked her up and down and shook his head. "Nah, I'd just slow you down. You're out of my league."

"I don't think so. I've been watching you. You're coming along quite well. You look like a serious lifter."

"Thanks, but I'm not. I'm trying to stay in shape, but I don't have the time to devote to it that you do. You're huge."

Jenna let the compliment slide. She wiped the sweat from her face with the towel that hung around her neck. "Thanks, but I've been bigger. In my competitive years, I had a lower body fat content. I just lift for fun now."

He shook his head as he allowed his eyes to wander down Jenna's torso. "Well, you look pretty good to me. How big are your arms?"

Jenna replied arrogantly, "Eighteen inches. I'm six feet tall and weigh two hundred pounds. I bench press three hundred and leg-press five hundred. Not bad for a forty-eight year-old woman."

Gabe smiled and patronized her. "Glad you told me. I'll know not to wrestle you."

"If you do, just a warning, I teach karate and self defense classes and I don't fight fair."

When the conversation stalled, Jenna excused herself and walked to the women's locker room. From the rear, she looked like a well-developed man in a wig. Gabe finished his workout and showered for work.

As he exited the club, Gabe saw Jenna leaning against his car. She asked, "Got time for a bite to eat?"

He threw his bag in the car. "I'd sure like to, but I've got to get to work. I work midnights and my shift starts in twenty minutes."

He didn't know what Jenna wanted, but he hoped it wasn't romance. The thought of going to bed with a woman with such masculine traits and mannerisms repulsed him.

The next two weeks produced several passing conversations with Jenna at the club. Gabe also met other casual lifters who weren't allowed access into Jenna's clique. When he could shift the conversation to her without raising suspicion, he asked about her. From what he'd learned, she was a confirmed lesbian with a hatred for men.

She taught self-defense classes and, on numerous occasions, had punched out men who'd made derogatory comments about her or challenged her masculinity. Her scarred face wasn't entirely a result of age and tanning beds. She sported several trophies from knock-down, drag-out fights with men and other lesbians at the bars that she'd frequented. Gabe quickly decided that Jenna was not someone that he wanted to be involved with.

When Gabe got to work, he was thrilled to see a phone message from Beck Eisman taped to his door. Since it was after hours, she'd left her home number, which thrilled him even more. He rushed into his office to return her call. When she answered, he tried not to sound over-anxious. "Madam Prosecutor? Officer Kinnett."

Beck returned the professional courtesy. "Officer Kinnett, how's the exciting world of law enforcement?"

"Oh, you know, a thrill a minute. Exercise, naps and television really tax my abilities."

There was a short silence, so Beck took the lead. "I thought you would at least have stayed in touch even though Loar's investigation has stalled. I hope you don't blame me."

Gabe's light-hearted demeanor turned serious. "No, Beck, I don't blame you. I just can't accept the fact that she's getting away with murder. It makes me furious."

She listened patiently as Gabe revealed what she already knew. After he had vented, she said, "Listen, I'm going out tonight. Can I stop by your office?"

"Sure, I think I can take a few minutes out of my hectic schedule for you."

Len Shelley awoke from his evening nap to pounding on his front door and a barrage of swearing. As he lowered the footrest on his recliner, he shook his head in disgust. Only one person in the world swore like that. He opened the door and chastised Blauw. "Angus, you old fool, keep your voice down. I got neighbors, you know."

Angus said as he stepped in, "Hell, boy, they're used to it, having a pervert like you in the neighborhood. Just wait till they go to sell their houses to get away from your black ass. They'll really be pissed when they see how much you've depreciated their property values."

Shelley opened the refrigerator to get a beer for Angus. He didn't get one for himself since he had to work in two hours. He shook his head in frustration as he twisted the top off the bottle and handed it to Angus. "Angus, you irreverent old psycho, ain't you got no compassion for anyone? You ain't supposed to talk to us black folks like that. It's not politically correct. We got feelings, too, you know."

Angus took a long draw from the beer and smiled as he swallowed. "Ah, Len, you ain't fooling anyone. You ain't got no feelings. Besides, the only people who depreciate property values more than you black folks are some of us white trash. I'd rather live next to you than most whites I know."

Shelley sat back down and accepted Angus's back-door compliment. "Well, thanks, Angus, I guess that's as much of a compliment as I'm ever going to get out of you."

Angus looked sternly at Shelley and replied, "Compliment! Hell, boy, that wasn't no compliment. I only said I'd live next to you because you keep my brand of beer in your refrigerator. It ain't because I like you."

Len's wife, Jackie, came downstairs and hurried over to Angus. She put her arm around his shoulders and gave him a hug. Angus put his arm around her waist and hugged her back. She said, "Hello, Angus, where you been keeping yourself lately?"

Angus's demeanor instantly changed. As crude as he was toward Len, he was the consummate gentleman around Jackie and the other officers' wives. He politely said, "Hello, Jackie. I've just been busy lately. You know how we international playboys are. By the way, you're looking exceptionally hot tonight. Have you lost weight?"

Jackie giggled with glee as she soaked up Angus's compliments. She walked into the kitchen to fix Len a snack before he went to work. Len shook his head and said quietly, "Angus, you old phony, if you treated everyone like you treat her, you'd be president of the United States by now."

Angus took another draw from his beer. "I keep telling you, Len. I treat people the way they deserve. I can't help it if you deserve to be treated like shit."

Shelley realized once again that it was useless to spar with Angus. He thought for a minute, then said, "Listen, Angus, I'm glad you came by. I've been meaning to ask you, what's happened to Kinnett? That kid's been avoiding me lately. I think his attitude has gone down the toilet."

Angus nodded in agreement. "Yeah, you're right, Len, I've noticed it, too. Just be patient with him. I had a talk with him a while back. He's going through a lot right now. His job is eating at him. He's frustrated with the system. He's pissed that we can't go after Loar. I've talked to Ben and there's nothing anyone can do to her right now."

"I can certainly understand that. I remember when I was a kid and got on the department. I had this idealistic notion that I was going to save the world. I guess we all change when we mature and realize that we're never going to change anything."

Angus took another draw and said, "We've got to keep an eye on him, Len. He's going through some heavy-duty burnout. He's developing a real nasty attitude. I don't want to lose him. He talked to me a few weeks ago about Loar. I think he's going to get himself in trouble over her."

Len cringed and shook his head. "Oh no, whatever you do, stay close to him. Don't let him ruin his career over that psychotic bitch. She'll trip herself up someday. Tell that knucklehead to set back and wait."

After a lengthy conversation, Jackie brought Len's tray of food and placed it on his lap. Angus put his empty beer bottle on the table and stood to leave, but Jackie interrupted him. "You don't have to leave, Angus. You want something to eat?"

"No, Jackie, I better go. You're going to start harping on me about being single. You're going to try to hitch me up with one of your friends, so it's time for me to get out of here."

Len chuckled softly as he took his first bite. Angus opened the door as Jackie said, "You need a woman to mellow you out, Angus Blauw. You're not as tough as you pretend. I've got a nice girl in mind for you. She's just right for you and she's wanted to meet you for over a year." Jackie was still talking when Angus closed the door.

As Angus walked to his car, depression set in. Jackie was right. He should swallow his pride and give it a chance. The years of loneliness had taken a heavy toll. He especially hated being alone on his days off and during the holidays.

Beck knocked on the metal fire door. Gabe opened it and invited her in. Once inside, he took her coat and offered her his chair.

When she sat down, he couldn't help but notice how beautiful she was. In the dim light, her blue eyes glowed and her skin looked dark and tight. Her clothes accentuated her firm body. He looked away before she caught him staring. "So, Beck, how have you been? You here on business or pleasure?"

She sensed a hint of sarcasm in his tone and shrugged her shoulders. She hadn't expected him to be so direct. "Both, I guess. I haven't heard from you for a while and wondered if you were still alive."

Gabe realized that he was turning her off with his hostile attitude, so he softened his tone. "That's nice. I'm glad someone cares."

"Oh, you've got lots of friends. You've probably got lots of girlfriends, too. You're just playing hard to get."

"Yeah, that's it. I'm doing a pretty good job of it so far. I'm just afraid that you women want me for my money and millionaire lifestyle."

She smiled and encouraged him, "It won't last forever. You'll dig yourself out. It just takes time."

With that bit of encouragement, Gabe shifted the conversation to Loar. "So, Beck, any more ideas how we can bag Loar?"

Beck shifted in the chair and leaned forward. "I've been thinking about her. We still need a witness who can testify that she put them up to murder. Even with that, we'd need some corroborating evidence to back up their story. We're going to have to get one of her patients to cooperate with us. To do that, we're going to have to find out who her patients are. I'm thinking we should talk to some of the other psychiatrists in the area. Maybe they've treated some of the patients that she couldn't help or couldn't talk into killing for her."

Gabe thought for a few seconds, then suggested a more direct approach. "I don't know, Beck, I've been thinking about going straight to her and asking her about her relationship with Webster and Wilcox. I know that would tip our hand, but word is going to get back to her anyway when we start talking to other psychiatrists."

"Maybe, but you know what's going to happen as soon as she knows that we're investigating her, don't you? She'll go straight to Garrison and Baumgartan. I'll be out of a job and Garrison will transfer you out of here."

"Good, he can't do anything worse to me."

"Listen, Gabe, don't con yourself. It could always be worse. He could put you in property or records. How would you like to come to work ever night and count fired pistol brass or work in records and shuffle reports and citations every night? You'd go nuts for sure. A transfer doesn't necessarily mean back to patrol. As much as you hate it here, it could always be worse."

He thought for a second. "I guess you're right. I just can't sit by and do nothing any longer. This thing is eating me up. I wish I were more like Angus and Shelley. Even old Ben has all the patience in the world. They're content to sit back and wait for her to kill again. I can't do that."

Beck didn't like what she was hearing. She crossed her arms and looked sternly at him. "Gabe, you're worrying me. I've got this sick feeling that you're about to do something to get us all in trouble. Please tell me that you aren't thinking what I think you're thinking."

He sat quietly and stared at the floor. He took a deep breath and said, "Oh, I don't know what I'm going to do. I just need to get away from the whole mess for a while."

Beck smiled. "I'm glad to hear you say that. I've got an idea. My dad has a cabin at Upper Klamath Lake. Let's go down there this weekend. It'll do us both good."

The shock was written across his face. Beck laughed at his expression and said, "Relax. No strings attached. You'll have your own bedroom."

He realized that his inexperience was showing. He thought, *My own bedroom! Man, did I just blow it.* He knew he couldn't sleep under the same roof with Beck and not try to manipulate her into bed. Rather than make a fool of himself, he declined.

She stood to leave. "If you change your mind, the offer stands. But just remember, don't do anything stupid. If you get me fired for going behind Baumgartan's back, I'll be ten times worse to deal with than Loar."

Beck stopped at the door. "I really came here tonight because I'm worried about you. I checked into what Tim Allis was up to just before he was killed. One of the secretaries was typing

186

his files for him. He'd approached Loar about some of her patients two weeks before Roger Moesen shot him. That's why I don't want you to approach her. You'll be sealing your own death warrant if she knows you're investigating her."

He thought quietly for a second, then asked, "Any proof of that?"

"None. Someone destroyed all his files on Loar. The secretary was so scared that she kept her mouth shut. The only person who could have destroyed those files is Baumgartan. He's been wrapped around her little finger for years. He either wants to get her in bed or she's got something very damaging on him. Either way, he's in her corner." Gabe didn't know what to say. Beck turned and closed the door behind her.

He rubbed his eyes and thought what a fool he'd been. He'd just blown the best proposition of his whole life. A weekend alone with Beck Eisman would be any man's dream. Enough about Beck, what about Maura Loar?

9

GABE OPENED HIS apartment door and stepped into the hall. He locked the deadbolt with his key, then turned toward the stairs. To his surprise, a man that he hadn't seen was leaning against the wall. He jumped, then realized it was Angus Blauw waiting for him in full uniform.

"Damn it, Angus, you scared me to death. What are you doing lurking around out here like some senile old child molester?"

Angus showed no emotions. "Just trying to show you how easy it is for someone to take you out if they want to. None of us are Superman, kid. If some asshole wants you bad enough, you'll be spending the night in the coroner's cooler."

Gabe walked past him and asked, "So what's your point?"

Angus grabbed him by the arm and spun him around. He pinned Gabe against the wall and got in his face. "Listen, you little shit, you might fool the rest of the world, but you ain't fooling me one bit! I know what you're up to! You're going to burglarize Loar's office! You're going to try something that you know nothing about, and you're going to get your dumb ass caught, sure as hell!"

Gabe glared angrily at Angus, then realized that he was being lectured by a friend. When Angus had finished, Gabe relaxed his tightened muscles and said, "Yeah. Yeah, Angus, you're right. I am going to burglarize her office. You're also right that I don't know what I'm doing, but I have to do something. You don't understand. Everything we need is right there. It's not right that we can't go in and get it. You know I'm right. That's exactly what you'd do. You said so yourself."

Angus released Gabe's arm. He stepped back and said, "Come on, kid, I'll give you a ride." Once in Angus's wagon, Gabe braced for the lecture. "Look, Gabe, everyone has seen a change in your personality. You're not the good-natured kid that you used to be. When you get withdrawn and quiet like this, people stop trusting you. That's how the rat-bastards upstairs act."

Gabe didn't respond. Angus said, "I know you don't think anyone understands how you feel, but you've got to remember something. We were all in your shoes once, me, Shelley, Ben, all of us. One of the hardest lessons that you've got to learn is that the good guys don't always win. There are hundreds of murders around the country each year that are never solved. In most cases, the detectives know in their hearts who the killers are, but they can't make a case on them legally. The key to success is not to become a crook, but to become a better detective. It's okay to bend the rules a little once in a while, but you can't destroy yourself in the process. You mark my words, boy, if you go in her office without a search warrant, you'll get caught. Nothing you find will ever be admissible in court. Once you seize it illegally, it's fruit of the poisonous tree and can never be used against her. You'll go to jail and she'll be no closer to prison than she is right now. You know what happens to cops in prison? When those cons get through raping your young ass, they'll bend you over and use your asshole for a basketball hoop."

Gabe looked straight ahead and replied, "I know that, Angus. I have no illusions of getting her convicted. I just want to know who her strangler is. I just want to know who she's manipulating to kill her next victim. Is that so bad? Is it wrong to gain an advantage by bending the rules a little so we can know who to hang charges on and force them to work for us as an informant? I don't think so, and neither do you. I remember what you said about doing what you had to do to catch a crook. I'm only doing the same thing that you'd do."

190

Angus shook his head in frustration. "Gabe, you don't get it. When I said I'd burglarize her office, that wasn't advice for you. What works for me won't work for you. We're different people. Look at you, just the thought of doing something wrong is eating you up. Your conscience won't allow you to do the things that I do. You can't even look at yourself in the mirror anymore. You're too honest to do this. Give it up. Old Ben Hire will catch her. Just get your head screwed on straight again and forget that bitch. Get your life in order."

Gabe thought how wise Angus was. He had figured out what was going on in Gabe's head weeks ago. "How do you know so much about me, Angus? How do you know what I'm thinking? What makes you so smart?"

He suddenly realized the foolishness of his questions. Angus knew what he was going through because he'd gone through it himself many years ago. Angus finally said, "Listen, kid, you're not the first cop to wonder about his own ethics. We all go through it. The survivors decide to outlast the system. They last long enough to draw their pension, retire and tell the world to kiss their ass. The fools throw it all away over some misguided sense of justice that doesn't exist anywhere else in the world except in their own minds. The whole world is corrupt, boy. We all like you, but we're not going to let you take any of us down with you. If you're going to piss away your career, we're going to wash our hands of you. If you care about us, don't do this. You're just a young snot-drip. You don't know what you're doing."

Angus pulled into the underground garage of the police station and stopped at Gabe's door. As Gabe stepped out, Angus exited the driver's door and walked to the front of the wagon. Gabe stopped and stared straight ahead. He finally said, "I don't think I can stop this, Angus. As soon as Loar hears that I'm sniffing around, she'll come after me. She killed Tim Allis for doing the same thing."

Angus growled, "Okay, Gabe, that's different. If the bitch comes after you, you can smoke her Barbie-doll ass righteously and it'll be self-defense. Hell, we'll all help you."

"That could take years, Angus, if ever. How many people would we have to sit by and watch her murder before we'd get a shot at her? Besides, she's too smart to come after me head-on.

She'd get me when I least expect it. She'll use some psychotic basket case that I don't even know to get me when I'm least prepared. How do you defend yourself against that?"

Angus didn't reply. Gabe broke the silence and asked, "Help me, Angus? You've been through this before. You wouldn't back off just because someone was going to kill you. You're not afraid of anything. Help me with this."

Angus heart melted as Gabe wrestled with his conscience. He saw himself forty years ago. "You'll get caught, Gabe. She's got an apartment behind her office. If you go in, she'll know you're there. She'll come home while you're there and sense your presence. That bitch is the devil incarnate. She can smell your body odor. If you wash your body and clothes in unscented soap and give off no odor, she'll smell your fear. If you're the least bit nervous, she'll hear your heart pounding. She'll smell your breath. She'll hear you breathing. If you move one item out of place, she'll know it. There's no way you can enter her home and not leave some sign that she'll detect. The bitch is supernatural. Hell, she scares me and I ain't scared of nothing."

Gabe looked in total shock at Angus. Angus slowly looked into his eyes. Gabe yelled, "Angus! Angus, you old fossil, you've been in her apartment! You broke into her apartment yourself! You broke into her apartment when you were stuck in the cold case unit years ago! You old son-of-a-bitch, you did exactly what you're telling me not to do!"

Angus looked around to make sure no one was watching. "Yeah, and I almost got caught. Take my word for it, Gabe, you can't get away with it. You could break into anyone else's office and probably get away with it, but not Loar's. She can look in your eyes and read your mind like a book. She listens to your words and knows every secret in your soul. She's got powers that I can't explain. I did everything perfect and she still knew that I'd been in her apartment. She confronted me about it and knew my every move. She told me how I broke in, what path I took and what items I'd touched. She even told me what I'd eaten four hours earlier by the smell of my breath. She couldn't prove that I was there, so she didn't go to Garrison, not officially anyway, but she knew I did it. If I'd gone back, she'd have been waiting for me. I wouldn't be here now if I had. That woman can get inside a person's head like no one I've ever seen. She gets these people to kill for her because she can somehow crawl inside their heads and drive them like a remote controlled car. Listen, kid, Garrison and Baumgartan aren't weak people. They didn't get where they are by allowing people to manipulate them. They're both strong, dynamic people, but Loar manipulates them like silly putty. She does that to everyone she meets. She strokes the governor like a lap dog. He'd do back-flips and set fire to his hair if he thought it would get half a smile out of the stone-faced bitch."

Angus sighed and stared at the ground. "Gabe, we're both out of our league tangling with that bitch. We're just simple street cops, Gabe. She's a demon in the truest sense of the word. I'm not a sci-fi believer, but if I've ever met a person with supernatural powers, it's her. There are actually demons walking the Earth and occupying peoples' bodies, and she's one of the worst. Someone better than us is going to have to catch her. Maybe it'll be one of those weird shrinks that the feds have stashed away in a secret research facility somewhere. It'll probably take some wild-eyed, Bella Lugosi-looking fucker to outsmart her."

Gabe leaned against the side of Blauw's wagon. He fumbled for his keys and said, "There's got to be a way, Angus. I've got to try. Is there anyone who can help me?"

Angus sighed deeply as he realized that he had not detoured Gabe one bit. He shook his head and decided that if he couldn't stop Gabe, he wanted to give him all the help he could. "Maybe, kid, but if you're bound and determined to throw your career away, remember one rule. If you do anything illegal, never talk to anyone about it. They'll use it against you someday when they're mad at you or hold you hostage with it for the rest of your life. You sit tight for a while. Let me think about this. I busted a burglar a few months ago. I thought he was going to go to prison, but he got off. Let me see if I can get some pointers about Loar's office. If anyone can help, it's him."

Gabe waited for several days, but Angus didn't call. His curiosity got the best of him. He had to meet Loar and thought an innocent office visit couldn't hurt. He called her receptionist and scheduled an appointment.

Loar's receptionist was a consummate professional. She was friendly and helpful when she asked him to fill out the insurance forms. After a half-hour wait, she showed him into Dr. Loar's office.

Gabe grew angry with himself. His heart was pounding and he knew his fear was smeared across his face. If Angus was right, Loar would know why he was there within the first minute of their conversation.

Maura Loar entered from her apartment and walked to her desk without looking at Gabe. She glided as though she was on a cushion of air. Her hair looked like black silk, and her tight skirt accentuated her perfect figure. Her makeup was flawless, and Gabe thought she was one of the most beautiful women that he'd ever seen. But why was he surprised? Some of the deadliest animals on Earth are beautiful.

He now saw why her patients were so infatuated with her. Her beauty was hypnotizing and her scent was intoxicating. He tried not to stare, but she was magnificent.

She wore a low-cut business suit. As she slid her chair under her, Gabe could see the veins stand out in her arms, neck and chest. She didn't look at Gabe until she was fully seated and comfortable. She then slowly raised her eyes and looked deep into his soul without the slightest facial expression.

The uncomfortable silence convinced Gabe that he was losing the mind game. Loar finally let him off the hook. She spoke in a deep, soft voice. "Officer Gabriel Thomas Kinnett, it's so nice to finally meet you."

Gabe was taken by surprise. "Do you know me?"

"Robert Garrison has told me all about you."

He looked at the floor and reasoned that if Dr. Loar knew Garrison well enough to call him by his first name, he'd probably given her everything in his personnel jacket. He said, "Well, I'll bet he said wonderful things about me."

Loar studied him carefully and said, "There's no need for sarcasm, dear Gabriel. He actually spoke quite highly of you. He said that your assignment was unfortunate and he hopes to be able to reassign you back to patrol soon."

Gabe looked into her eyes. He knew he had to play hardball with her. "Dr. Loar, you're lying to me. I was hoping that we could have a more honest relationship than this."

He watched intently to gauge Loar's reaction. To his surprise, she was completely unshaken. Without the slightest facial expression, she looked deep into his eyes and said, "Dear Gabriel, I don't lie. I'll prove it to you. Let me dial Robert for you. He's in his office right now. We can speak with him on the speaker-phone."

Without taking her eyes off him, she leaned over and punched the speed-dial button with the chief's number on it. As soon as Garrison's phone rang, Gabe began to fall apart. Panic radiated from his face. He desperately didn't want Garrison to know that he was talking to Loar. His mind raced for an excuse for being in Loar's office. To make matters worse, Loar was locked into his eyes watching every nerve in his body unravel.

When Garrison answered the phone, Loar continued to stare deep into Gabe's eyes as she identified herself. "Robert, this is Maura. Sorry to bother you, dear, but Gabriel Kinnett is in my office. There seems to be some doubt about our conversation a while ago. We're on the speakerphone. Would you please assure him that our conversation about him was strictly complimentary?"

Garrison's tone changed when he heard Gabe's name. He yelled, "Kinnett? What are you doing in Dr. Loar's office?"

Gabe tried desperately to compose himself. He tried to look away from Dr. Loar's stare, but her eyes were hypnotic. He said, "Well, sir, I've been depressed about my assignment and thought Dr. Loar could help. She is the department's psychiatrist, isn't she?"

"Yes, she is, but I didn't see a request from you to see her! I want to see you in my office right now!"

Dr. Loar stepped in and saved Gabe. "Now, now, Robert, Gabriel is my patient. I can't help him if he doesn't trust me. Let's not add to his anxiety by chastising him for seeking treatment. Thank you for your assistance, Robert." Loar dismissed Garrison without the slightest regard for his position.

Throughout the session, Loar never withdrew her hypnotic stare from Gabe's eyes. He realized that he'd made a terrible mistake. Loar was out of his league. There was no chance that he could manipulate her into incriminating herself. He had to make a graceful retreat. "I'm sorry, Doctor, this was a mistake. I shouldn't have come here. I've only hurt my career by talking to you."

With no facial expression, Dr. Loar looked at Gabe through her lazy eyes and replied, "Nonsense, Gabriel, I'm here to help you. I just want you to trust me. Dear Robert is just angry that you bypassed the chain of command and came here without clearing it through him. He doesn't dislike you personally. I won't let him harm you. I'll protect you."

He was shocked at the power and control that Loar apparently held over Garrison. Garrison had always been an intimidating figure, and Gabe thought no one could ever dominate him. He stood and said, "Maybe some other time, Doctor. I need to think about this. I've got a lot to lose. Garrison can make my life more miserable than it already is. Thank you for your time."

Dr. Loar sat quietly as he made his awkward retreat. As he walked home, he was furious with his embarrassing performance. Angus was right. Loar was no one to screw with. He had failed miserably at his first mental chess match with her. He wished he'd listened to Angus, Ben and Beck.

Gabe spent that evening licking his wounds. He went to the fitness center to work out and hurried though the circuit so he could get to work on time. He didn't trust Garrison. He might be waiting at the office.

He showered quickly and hurried to the parking lot. To his surprise, a large, imposing woman was sitting on his car hood. He instantly recognized Jenna Kerse. She slid off the hood as he approached. "Hi, Gabe, how was your workout?"

Gabe was uneasy around Jenna, but he tried to hide his nervousness. "Fair, I guess. How was yours?"

"Okay. I thought you might like to go for a ride."

His stress level was still high from his miserable performance in Loar's office. He wasn't in the mood to play head games with Jenna. "I'd like to, Jenna, but I'm late for work. My boss will probably be checking up on me tonight. I really need to be there on time. Maybe later this week would work."

Jenna stood by as Gabe threw his bag in the back seat of his car. When he slammed the door, she said, "Well, if we're going to get together, I'd like to do it soon."

He was puzzled and asked, "What's the hurry?"

"You've been asking questions about me. I'm anxious to find out why you're interested in me." He stopped and stared at her. He thought he'd been more discrete. She continued, "I know you're a cop. I just want to know if your interest is personal or professional. If it's personal, we might see what happens. If it's professional, tell me what you want."

He slowly walked up to her and looked her in the eye. They were the same height, so they were almost nose-to-nose. Jenna stood her ground and waited for him to make the first move. He was confused and said, "Excuse me for asking, but I thought you were a lesbian."

Jenna's stone face cracked slightly with a smile. "Well, there are more tactful ways to put it, but yes, I do prefer women. I don't like men as a general rule. I have a lady who I've been in love with for several years, but I've found myself strangely attracted to you. If I ever were to have a man on the side, it would have to be someone much younger than me; someone who won't try to dominate me."

Gabe stood in shock as Jenna revealed her life style with total candor. She continued, "I'm not saying it's a slam-dunk. Maybe we wouldn't hit it off. Maybe there isn't any chemistry between us, but maybe there is. All I'm saying is that I'm open to some recreational sex with the right man, as long as it doesn't compromise my relationship with my soul mate. I'd die to protect what I have with her."

He contemplated Jenna's proposal and didn't want to say the wrong thing. He felt no attraction for her, but she was well connected in the club. Maybe he could get close to Wilcox's killer through her. He certainly didn't want her to realize that he was using her. The last thing he wanted was to deal with her when she was angry.

He wondered how long it would take her to realize that he was using her. "Well! Jenna, I don't know what to say. I'm flattered, I guess, but why me? Haven't you ever met men that you were attracted to before?"

Jenna looked around the parking lot suspiciously and replied, "Yeah, sure, a few. Nothing ever materialized though. Most men are afraid to go to bed with a woman who can lift more than they can. They don't like to roll in the sheets with a woman who is bigger and harder than they are. I guess it makes them feel like they're in bed with another man. How about you, Gabe? You got a problem with that? You afraid that I'm more masculine than you are? Afraid that I'll overpower you in bed?"

Gabe stepped back. He unconsciously looked Jenna up and down. His mood hadn't been good lately and he wasn't in the mood for a testosterone contest. It would probably end up in a slugfest. He was confident that he could take her, but he didn't need the grief of a citizen's complaint. He chose discretion at this point. "No, Jenna, you don't intimidate me. It might be fun. Let me think about it." She showed no emotion and walked back toward the club while Gabe hurried off to work.

Gabe raced into the underground garage and screeched to a halt in a parking space. He hurried to his office and fumbled for his keys. As he trotted past the last row of cars, he saw a man leaning against a car. He recognized the man as Chief Robert Garrison. He'd been right. Garrison was checking up on him.

He stopped in his tracks as Garrison approached. He waited and let Garrison take the lead. "Evening, Gabe, how's life treating you?"

He saw through Garrison's facade and responded, "Like crap, but of course you know that. You didn't come here to give me a big fuzzy hug and a few words of encouragement. What do you want?"

Garrison smiled. "Gabe, Gabe, you're so hostile. That's what got you in this predicament in the first place, that and following the wrong role models. I think I've been too hard on you. Maybe it's time to transfer you back to patrol. I just want to see what your attitude is like."

Gabe desperately wanted to go back to patrol, but he had some loose ends to tie up first. He knew he couldn't work on Loar while in patrol. "I don't know, Chief, I liked you better when you called me Einstein and tried to intimidate me. This nice-guy routine doesn't fit your personality. Besides, I like it here. I don't know if I want to go back to patrol."

Garrison's pretentious smile faded and rage swept over his face. He quickly checked his anger and forced himself to be civil. "You know, Gabe, you'll work where I put you. I just made the suggestion because Dr. Loar likes you. I don't care if you ever get back in patrol. Just don't think that you can manipulate me through her. You may think that you're going to take her to bed, but let me assure you, she's way out of your league. I don't mind if you cry on her shoulder about your hopeless, pathetic existence, but get sex out of your head. If I find out that you're trying to use your screwed-up life as a sympathy ploy to get her in bed, I'll bury you."

Gabe's anger rose by the second. He no longer felt the fear that he had the first time that he'd tangled with Garrison, but he could not hand himself to Garrison on a silver platter. He forced himself to be civil. "Yeah, I guess you're right, Chief, she's out of my league."

Garrison stepped back and smiled sincerely. He relished a hostile confrontation when he had the upper hand. "That's good, Kinnett, I like that. I'm glad to see that you've finally grown a brain."

He laughed as he backed toward his car. He was laughing loudly as he slammed the door and drove away. Gabe remained in the garage for a minute thinking about Garrison. He shook his head and thought, *You idiot! What have you done? Why didn't you stroke Garrison? You could have stroked him into a transfer back to patrol!*

He shook his head in disgust as he walked to his office. When he inserted his key, he saw a note taped to the door. It was a handwritten note with just a phone number. He studied the number for a few seconds and realized that he had no idea who it belonged to. He flopped down in his chair and dialed the number.

A very articulate and personable man answered the phone. "Hello, how may I help you?" Gabe didn't want to disclose his identity, so he said, "Hi, I got a note to call this number. Who am I speaking with?"

The man relaxed into a chair and began. "You must be Angus Blauw's friend. He wouldn't tell me who you are, but asked if I could help you. I owe him a favor. You don't know me, but my name is Val Machka."

Gabe put his feet up on his desk and said, "Oh yeah, Angus told me about you. You're the burglar that he busted a few months ago."

"Sir, please, don't call me a burglar. That implies that I'm just a common sneak-thief. I'm far more professional than that. I'll admit that I break into other people's homes and businesses, but I choose to refer to myself as a rare commodities agent. If you want something unusual, I can get it for you for the right price."

Gabe chuckled at Machka's ingenuity. "That's good, I like that. Why would you help me? Acquisition agents don't usually rub elbows with the police."

"You're absolutely right, my boy. I normally wouldn't urinate down a policeman's throat if his intestines were on fire, but Blauw blackmailed me into informing on someone. I won't give up a friend, but I've got a score to settle with Loar. I don't mind using the police to exact my revenge."

His interest peaked. "Oh? Tell me about it."

"Blauw didn't catch me by his brilliant intellect and cunning stealth. He'd received a tip from a lady that I'd been romantically involved with. She'd gotten herself in trouble for trafficking in illegal drugs and sold me out to the drug task force to stay out of jail. She used her ex-boyfriend to relay the tip. I found out later that he'd been killed in a motorcycle accident, but it was too late. I'd already made the deal with Blauw and I always keep my word. I should have known better than to get involved with her. Before I'd begun seeing her, she'd been involved with another associate of mine. His name was Bishop Aqui. I believe you've heard of him. Some of your cowboys blew him in half during a liquor store robbery. She sold him out the same way that she did me."

Gabe sat up in his chair and responded, "Aqui? Sure, I knew him. I was on the stakeout team when he got shot."

"Oh, so you're one of those cowboys."

He quickly defended himself. "No! I was there, but I didn't drop the hammer on him. I was hiding in the cooler."

Machka didn't care anyway. He didn't like Aqui. "Oh, that's okay, it didn't break my heart to hear about him being separated from his posterior. He was far too prehistoric for my liking. Anyway, as I was saying, I've got a bone to pick with Loar. She talked my lady friend into selling me out. Loar had been counseling her for depression and meth addiction. She convinced her that I was the root of all her problems. Loar's a devious witch, and I'd like to see her take a fall."

Gabe agreed. "Yeah, me, too. She's killed a lot of people."

"Yes, she also had another acquaintance of mine killed a few years ago. A good friend, Lucian Green. He was Loar's cocaine, meth and steroid supplier. She got unreasonable when he couldn't deliver a promised shipment. It was totally out of his control, but she had him killed anyway. He told me the night before he was killed that Loar was going to have one of her psychotic goons eliminate him."

Gabe came out of his chair when he heard the name Lucian Green. He jerked his head toward the fact sheets taped to the wall. As he stared at Green's synopsis, he remembered that Green was the drug dealer that had been beaten to death in the alley. He hadn't been able to link Green to Loar until now. "Val! Are you sure?"

Machka sighed in frustration. "Sure? Certainly I'm sure. Everyone in town knew that she'd had him killed; everyone but the police. You people are always the last to know."

Gabe sat back down in shock and rubbed his eyes. He then asked, "Okay, Val, here's what I need. I'm not going to tell you who I am because I don't want this to come back to haunt me later, but all the information that we need to link Loar to a number of murders is in the medical files in her office. She's also solicited someone to kill for her, but we haven't identified him yet. Without some evidence to link her to the crimes, we can't get a search warrant. We want to get a look at her medical files so we can see who we have to target for investigation. We need to see who we can approach to work for us. We need someone who'll get her on tape soliciting a murder. It has to be someone who'll testify with some degree of credibility. Without a search warrant, we're going to have to break in. Now, I don't suppose I could talk you into doing it for us, could I?"

Val laughed, "Sorry, lad, not on your life for two reasons. First of all, I don't trust you. One more pinch, and I'm going to prison for a long time. Secondly, I don't want that devil after me. One of your officers burglarized her office years ago. I don't know who it was, but if she'd figured it out, he'd be dead by now. I won't do it for you, but I'll help you if I can."

Gabe knew he was referring to Blauw's attempt. He thought for a minute, then said, "Hell, I don't even know where to start. How would I go about it?"

Machka grumbled in disgust, "Oh, son, this job would take all the expertise that I could muster, and then I'm not sure I'd be up to it. I'd probably call in some pros that I know to help me. You're picking a dangerous target to cut your teeth on. If you're going to try this yourself, you ought to rehearse somewhere first. Blauw told me what he said to you about Loar. I promise you, lad, his assessment of Loar was completely accurate. That woman has psychic powers that this world hasn't even heard of yet."

Gabe interrupted him, "I know, Val, he told me all about her. Spare me the sermon. Where do I start?"

"Okay, it's your funeral. First of all, her apartment is in the rear of her office. It's posh, man. You name it, she's got it. It takes a key to get you in the building. I know one of the night security officers. I got a key to the building from him years ago. Now, once you get inside, you've got to dodge the security officer. He'll stay on the ground floor. He never goes up to Loar's floor unless he's called. Use the stairs and avoid the elevators. They make too much noise."

Gabe interrupted him, "Val! You mean to tell me that you've burglarized her apartment yourself?"

Machka replied, "Well, I'm not going to say anything incriminating, but let's just say that she used to own some custom jewelry pieces that a client of mine envied."

"I figured as much."

Machka continued. "Now, make sure you wear latex gloves. Cover your head with a ski mask. Pull it over your face once you get inside. Loar won't be able to find your fingerprints, but if she thinks that you've been in her apartment, she'll call that chief of yours that she's so chummy with. He'll send out a team of evidence techs and they'll pick up your prints. The ski mask will keep you from dropping head hair on her carpet. Also, when she realized that your predecessor had entered her apartment, she upgraded her security system. She's got a motion sensor that activates a high-grade video camera. If you're caught on tape, the ski mask will prevent you from being identified. Wash yourself and all of your clothes in unscented soap and don't wear cologne. Sleep in clean sheets washed in unscented soap the night before you go in. Brush your teeth and don't eat anything for eight hours before you go in. She has an uncanny sense of smell. Now, you'll need the code to her security system. I have a friend who works at the alarm company that monitors her system. I'll get her security code for you. Her system is fairly old. Once you get in her office, you'll have thirty seconds to punch in her code and push the *OFF* button. That turns the system off. When you leave, you have to punch in the same code and push the *ON* button. You'll then have thirty seconds to close and lock the door. That'll activate the system again after you leave. Don't forget to turn the system back on or she'll know you've been there. She'll then change her security code. You'll punch in the wrong code the next time you go in. That'll signal the guard downstairs and summon the police. Even if you elude the guard, you'll have your fellow officers to deal with once you get outside."

"I don't need that grief."

"No, you certainly don't. You're looking for medical records. She maintains hard copies, but she also keeps them stored on the hard drive of her computer and backs them up on disc in case her hard drive crashes. Her hard copies are kept under lock and key. I can't get you into them, so you'll have to go after her computer files. You'll never be able to access her computer with her there. It makes too much noise. You won't be able to tell if she's home from outside her office. You'll have to enter her office, then go straight to her apartment door and listen to see if she's home. She likes to listen to soft music, so if you hear the music, get your posterior out of there. If she's leaving her music on to make an intruder think she's home, you're out of luck. Just accept your defeat and save yourself. Don't try to pull this thing off with her in the apartment. I guarantee you that she'll know you're there."

Gabe said, "Don't worry. I'd never try something like that."

"That's wise. Now, if you get lucky and get in when she's not there, turn her computer on and access her patient folders.

Take a blank 3.5-inch disc and shove it into the disc drive. She uses a Windows program, so it should be easy to copy her files. The last time I was in her computer, she had her patient files listed by last name. I guess she's never felt the need to code them because she's never suspected that someone like you would be sneaking in and copying them. Now, it'll take you forever to open each file and copy it, so here's what you have to do. When the computer is booting up, you'll see an icon called *My Computer*. Double click the left mouse button on the icon. That'll open up another window listing all the drives available. Click again on the *C* drive. That will list every file on the hard drive. Double click on each file to open it. Once open, click on *File* and go down to *Save As*. That'll open up a menu that will let you select 3.5 inch disc drive. Then hit *Save As*. Once saved, go back to *File*. Go down the menu and hit *Close*. That will close that patient file and allow you to repeat the process till you've copied every patient file. That's the slow way to do it. If you want to do it faster, after you open the *C* drive and see the list of patient files, just push the *Control* and letter *A* buttons at the same time. That will highlight all the files at the same time. Then save them all simultaneously to the disc and close down her computer. Now, if she's hidden her files under a password, you're out of luck. I doubt if she has since she has a secretary working on them. She's probably not worried about someone getting her files anyway. But if she found out that I'd been snooping around in her computer, she may have hidden everything under a password. These files aren't going to help you anyway. She's not stupid enough to put anything incriminating in them for her secretary or police burglars to read."

Gabe was furiously scribbling notes. He finished writing down Val's last instruction, then asked, "Okay, anything else?"

"Yes, there's another way that you can get caught. When Loar's receptionist opens up the medical files the next morning, that particular Windows program will list the last five files that were opened the night before at the bottom of the option menu. If she's sharp, she'll see the files that you've copied and realize that she didn't open them the previous day. If she asks Loar if she'd opened them and Loar says no, she'll know that you were there that night and copied her files. To cover your tracks, you have to do one thing. Before you do anything in the computer, open the

Word program, click on *File* and wait for the option menu to drop down. At the bottom of the option menu will appear a list of the last five files that the receptionist had worked on the day before. Write those file names down on a piece of paper and pay attention to what drive they're on. It'll most likely be the *C* drive. After you're through copying all the medical files, pull up those five files starting with the bottom file on the list, then close them. Open and close the file at the top of the list last. That'll recreate the original recall list of the most recently opened files. The receptionist will never know that you were there. Remember, when you go in, you have to leave everything exactly as you found it. Before you sit down in the chair at her computer, remember the exact position of that chair. When you get up, put the chair exactly where it was before you sat down. If you open a drawer, put it back in the same position when you leave. If you look through any of her papers or files, make sure everything is in its original position when you leave. Leave her computer files exactly as they were. Be sure to take a small pen light with you. She's installed a motion detector just inside the office door. When you enter, if you turn your attention to the security system panel before looking for the motion detector box, you'll trip the video camera and alarm. Look for a small box with a laser light on the wall by the floor. You'll have to step over the light beam. She used to have one motion detector. Don't count on that now. Before you start walking around, check the walls high and low for motion sensors. Now listen, this is important. I can tell that you're a hardhead and won't listen to anyone. Blauw tried to talk you out of this, but you're determined to go through with it. You're going to get caught, so do yourself a favor. Make sure you go in there unarmed. Leave your gun at home. I know you cops can't defecate without your precious security blanket, but that gun will be your downfall. The state law calls for a mandatory ten-year prison sentence for anyone caught carrying a firearm during the commission of a felony. Anyone else would get probation for their first burglary conviction, but you're a cop. You'll get a couple of years as a lesson to the rest of law enforcement. You can probably survive a couple of years in a minimum-security prison, especially if they move you out of state where no one would recognize you. If you have your gun with you, you'll do a solid ten years just for packing the gun. The new minimum sentencing mandate that they have in federal court will leave the judge no discretion. He'll have to give you the full ten years. And this new *Truth In Sentencing* law will leave the judge no choice. He'll have to give you ten years and you'll serve every day with no hope of early release for good behavior. I know it's a risk. If Loar catches you in her apartment, she'll kill you for sure. When you're staring down the barrel of her pistol, you'll wish that you had yours with you. That's the risk that you're going to have to take. Any questions?"

Gabe was listening intently. He said, "I'm not worried about federal court. I don't think they'd charge me in federal court when burglary is a state charge. They'd probably put me through magistrate court, but point well taken. I'm sure the sentence would be more severe for carrying the gun no matter which court I would go through. I can't think of anything else right now. Can I call you again if something comes up?"

"Sure. One last piece of advice."

"What's that?"

Val put an urgent tone in his voice. "Give this up! You're not good enough to pull it off! I've been doing this for years and I'm not good enough!"

Gabe thought for a second, then said, "Thanks, Val, I'll be in touch."

10

ANGUS FLOORED THE accelerator of his prisoner transport wagon and sped toward the domestic disturbance that Ramón Carlos, Deloris Gapky and Victor Lyzett had become involved in. The call had gone sour and they'd put out a call for assistance.

The three alert tones over the radio signaled that officers were in peril. Caution was thrown to the wind. Everyone dropped what they were doing and raced to the aid of their fellow officers. Their personal relationship with the officers meant nothing. They might dislike them immensely, but the fact they were wearing blue and were being assaulted was all that mattered.

Angus didn't like Deloris Gapky, but she was a cop. He disliked anyone who would assault a cop even more. Ramón and Victor were different. He was very fond of them and would head-butt a cruise missile to save them.

He screeched the wagon to a halt in front of the residence just as Len Shelley charged up the sidewalk with his collapsible baton extended. Reaves and Smith skidded their cruisers to a halt beside the wagon and the officers charged after Shelley.

Angus was shoulder to shoulder with the youngsters at the street, but his age had long ago caught up with him. They quickly outran him and leaped onto the porch after Shelley.

The cold, misty night was alive with sirens and red lights. The rest of the shift arrived and raced to the house. Everyone's mindset was the same. Negotiation was not an option. It was the long-standing and unwritten policy of the nightshift that if you put your hands on a policeman, you automatically earned yourself a trip to the emergency room. If you tried to kill a policeman, your stop at the emergency room was only long enough for the E.R. physician to pronounce you dead. You were then off to the coroner's office, where you would spend a restful night on a shiny, stainless-steel autopsy table in a modern, state of the art cooler at no charge.

Shelley didn't wait for the cavalry to arrive. He lowered his shoulder and hit the door at a full sprint. The door and frame stood no chance of repelling 320 pounds at a full charge. The exploding door was like the opening of floodgates. A torrent of blue poured through the door and engulfed the entire room.

Ernie Flagg was a fifty year-old grocery-sacker, who'd long ago lost his battle with alcoholism. He'd been arrested many times for alcohol related offenses, but he'd never scared his wife like tonight. With the frustrations of life closing in, he'd finally endured all he could stand. Intoxication hadn't made him any more receptive to the intervention of the police into his personal affairs.

Things had been going fine up to a point. Victor Lyzett had dealt with Ernie before and had established a tenuous rapport upon arrival. Ernie was volatile, but was at least listening to reason.

Deloris Gapky entered the house without one ounce of objectivity or compassion for Ernie. As soon as the dispatcher had informed the three responding units that the call involved an intoxicated male, her mind was set. Her hatred for men was written all over her face.

Victor and Ramón had been standing safely between her and Ernie, so Deloris felt safe expounding her perception of Ernie's worth as a human being. That was all it took to ignite Ernie like a Roman candle.

He charged through the feeble arm tackles of Ramón and Victor and expounded his perception of Deloris's value as peace officer. She was completely unprepared for his opinion.

Shelley stopped briefly inside the door to assess the situation. Deloris was unconscious in the corner of the room, where she'd slid to a stop after her alligator mouth had set in motion a series of events that her hummingbird ass wasn't prepared to deal with. Mrs. Flagg was cowering in another corner, trying to avoid the fracas.

Ramón and Victor were involved in a toe-to-toe slugfest with the bruiser. They were battered and bloody, but were holding their own. The air was filled with the smell of Ernie's supper, kraut and brats, mingled with the smells of whiskey, sweat, blood and O.C. spray.

Len Shelley's eyes widened in rage the second he saw the fracas, but he moved too slowly. The two young goons who had outrun Angus lowered their shoulders, hit Shelley in the back simultaneously and sent him face first to the floor with a loud crash that vibrated the whole house.

From inside the house, Angus heard the screams, breaking glass and crashing furniture. As he jumped up on the porch, he could feel the whole house vibrate under his feet as the massive weight of Ernie and the officers bounced off the walls and floor. Not wanting to miss out on the fray, he hurried through the splintered doorway.

Shelley was doing a push-up, trying to get his feet under him. There was a mountain of blue in the corner with Ernie Flagg on the bottom having seriously doubts about the wisdom of his earlier actions. The feel of his knuckles against Gapsy's chin felt so good at the time, but the gratification now seemed so short-lived and insignificant.

Angus's eyes widened as he inhaled the aromas of chaos. The odor of cat urine-soaked carpet and furniture combined with the kraut, whiskey, sweat, blood and OC made an intoxicating cocktail that Angus had long ago became addicted to. He charged in and jumped on top of the mountain. He looked for an opening, but found none. He was battered, punched, kicked, head-butted and knocked off his feet by the flailing bodies and batons.

Realizing that he had no chance of carrying out any part of the nightshift's policy, Angus wisely decided to spare himself any further injury and crawled away from the fray. What he didn't realize was that as he'd charged the mountain, he'd inadvertently stepped in the center of Shelley's back, driving Shelley's face back down into the feline-stained carpet. He'd used Shelley as a springboard to launch himself into the storm.

As Angus crawled from the mass of flailing fists and batons, he looked up to see Len Shelley again struggling to his feet. Shelley's nose was bleeding and rage shot from his eyes. He was looking to inflict serious injury upon anyone who got in his way, friend or foe.

Angus quickly jumped to his feet and ran to the corner where Mrs. Flagg was cowering. He controlled his laughter long enough to ask her if she was injured. When she shook her head, he ran past her and exited the back door to escape Shelley.

He stumbled around the side of the house, laughing uncontrollably. He made his way back to the street where he opened the rear doors of his wagon for Ernie.

While order was restored inside the house, Angus stood beside his wagon, laughing hysterically. As tears poured from his eyes, he kept his face pressed against the side of the truck so the neighbors wouldn't think he was being insensitive.

One by one, the officers exited the house. Each walked by Angus and looked at him curiously. Unable to talk, Angus motioned for them to continue on to their cars. Victor finally emerged with Ernie in tow and helped him into the back of the wagon.

As soon as Angus slammed and locked the doors, he quickly climbed behind the wheel. A quick check through the viewing window revealed that Ernie was seated and securely belted in. Angus wiped the tears from his eyes sufficiently to see and raced to the emergency room.

Ernie was unable to go to jail. He'd sustained a broken arm and numerous head injuries. The E.R. doctor felt it prudent to keep him overnight for observation. Angus returned to the station to hose the blood out of the back of the wagon. As he walked into the squad room, most of the nightshift was freshening up from the brawl.

As Angus strolled up and chastised the youngsters for knocking him away from the brawl, Len Shelley burst into the room. He'd left his gun-belt in his office and stormed into the squad room with his waistband partially opened and wearing his white T-shirt. There were drops of blood on the front of his T-shirt and wads of Kleenex tissue protruding from each nostril. The room quickly grew silent as the raging giant stormed in.

Shelley held up his uniform shirt by the corners and displayed the perfect form of a dirty shoe print between the shoulders. He roared, "Alright! Which of you rotten fuckers knocked me down and trampled my ass back at Flagg's house?"

As if on cue, the entire squad room erupted in hysterical laughter. Not wanting to suffer Shelley wrath, everyone bolted for the door. Angus tried to get out first, but the youngsters were too fast. Again the combined weight of the crowd knocked him back. He had to wait until the herd had squeezed through the door, then hurry out at the tail end.

As the room emptied, Shelley yelled, "I haven't dismissed any of you yet! Get your shiny asses back here and let me see your shoes! That's an order!" Of course no one heeded his order. Everyone ran to their cars and left Shelley holding his trampled shirt.

Shelley turned and walked back to his office, laughing softly. As angry as he was, the mental image of being trampled made even him chuckle. If it had happened to anyone else, he would have been laughing as hard as his officers.

As he was removing his badge and collar brass from the dirty shirt, Gabe walked in. Shelley said, "Hey, boy, haven't seen you for a while. Where've you been?"

Gabe flopped down in a chair. "Oh, nowhere, just keeping a close eye on those dead files. Wouldn't want anyone to break in and steal them. They're pretty valuable you know."

Shelley smiled as he removed the Kleenex from his nostrils and threw it in the trash. "That's good, kid. You're doing a bang-up job. I don't care what everyone else says."

Gabe asked, "So, sarge, I heard the call come out. Did Flagg lower the boom on you or was it one of your own men?"

Shelley stretched and tried to pull a cramp out of his shoulder. "Ah, it was one of mine. Everyone gets in such an all-fired hurry to get a piece of the action that we wind up hurting each other as much as we hurt the suspect. Kind of funny, I guess. It would be funnier if I hadn't been the guy that got mowed down. It felt like I got ran over by a tow truck."

Gabe smiled. "Yep, I remember those days. I learned a long time ago that too many cooks spoil the soup. When there's enough officers to do the job, stay out of their way or you'll take a few whacks yourself."

Shelley grimaced as he opened his locker and removed a clean shirt. "Yeah, I did, too. I just didn't move quick enough this time. Oh well, I'd rather have a shift of guys who are too enthusiastic than a bunch of deadbeats that you have to kick in the ass to get them to do anything. Enough about my bloody nose, tell me what you've been up to. I never see you anymore since you got all uppity on us and locked yourself in your hole."

Gabe looked around the office to see if any one was close enough to hear. "Oh, not much, sarge. My attitude has been pretty bad lately. I've been avoiding people to keep from pissing everyone off. I've not been fit company for anyone. I've royally pissed Garrison off again. Looks like I'll never get back to patrol. Every time I hear a hot call go out over the radio, I get the itch to jump in a car and race to it. I miss the rumbles."

Shelley glared at Gabe and growled, "What did you do to Garrison, boy?"

He shrugged his shoulders. "Oh, he tried to dangle a transfer back to patrol in front of my nose to get me to stop seeing Dr. Loar."

Shelley interrupted Gabe and yelled, "Loar! What are you doing messing around with that bitch? Boy, are you crazy? Don't you know you could wind up dead?"

Gabe leaned his head back and stared at the ceiling. "Yeah, I know, sarge. I just thought I could get close to her and manipulate her a little. I thought if she believed that I was depressed, she might try to recruit me like she did the others. Stupid idea. She saw through me like a clean window."

Shelley sat down and leaned across his desk as he lectured. "Listen to me, boy, I know you've been depressed over this whole mess. Angus and I were talking about you the other night. Frankly, I've been worried about you. You can't afford a bad attitude right now. If Garrison wants to transfer you, make it easy for him. Don't keep pissing him off. Secondly, keep your dumb ass away from Loar. You don't know what that ball-busting bitch is capable of. She scares me and I'm meaner than you are. She can't be manipulated. You may think that you're crying on her shoulder and baiting her into recruiting you to kill for her. Just when you think you're getting enough evidence to go to the D.A., she'll be giving you enough rope to hang yourself. Soon as she hears enough to conclude that your depression renders you unsuitable for police service, she'll beat you to the punch and type a *Psychological Fitness Report* to Garrison, reporting that you're psychologically unfit for duty. Boom! Garrison's got you. You'll be out on the street and Loar will be laughing her ass off at you."

Gabe opened his eyes in surprise. "Boy, sarge, I guess I never thought of that. I'll watch myself around her."

Shelley shook his head vigorously. "No, kid, you don't get me! Don't just watch yourself around her! Keep your young, shiny white ass completely away from her! What the hell's the matter with you, you trying to dick her? Do you need a piece of ass so bad that you're willing to throw your career away? Hell, boy, if you need it that bad, we'll set you up with some!"

Gabe shook his head and squirmed uncomfortably in his chair. "No, sarge! No, that's not it. I don't know why I wanted to see her. Curiosity, I guess. I'm not going back to her office anymore. At least not while she's there."

He suddenly realized that he'd slipped. Shelley's eyes opened wide with rage as he slid his chair back. He glared deep into Gabe's eyes as he stood and slowly walked around his desk. He sat in the chair beside Gabe, reached up and gripped the back of Gabe's neck with his huge hand.

Fear gripped Gabe's throat. He could no longer maintain eye contact and dropped his eyes to the floor. Shelley squeezed Gabe's neck and shook him as he chewed. "Son, son, son, I don't believe what I just heard! Don't you never talk like that! There ain't nothing in this whole world worth throwing your life away! You think this dumb old black man ain't smart enough to know what you're up to? You think I'm too stupid to figure you out? Well, genius, let me tell you something. I was going through this same shit back when you were still hanging on your mama's tit. Boy, we all go through a period when we think the system sucks bad enough to justify breaking the rules, but we're never justified in doing that. Every cop fudges a little now and then, even the good ones. That's different from out-right breaking the law. If you think you're going to do anyone any good by turning crooked, you're wrong. If you do that, you're not the man I thought you were. If you break the law, I'll slap the cuffs on you myself and haul your white ass off to jail. I'll be crying my eyes out while I'm doing it, but I'll do it. I love you like my own kin. It'd kill me to see you rotting away in some prison somewhere. I've only got a couple of years till I can retire, so don't do that to me."

Gabe hung his head in shame. Shelley released the grip on his neck and leaned back in the chair, waiting for a response. Gabe finally nodded his head. "I know, sarge. You're right. I don't know what I want anymore. I just know that I hate that bitch with a passion. Not because she's a murderer, but because she's using this phony criminal justice system and her political power as a shield. Then she's got the nerve to flaunt it in our faces. I don't like people who beat us at our own game. The rules are supposed to give us the advantage, not the crooks."

Shelley let Gabe vent. When he'd finished, Shelley said, "You want perfection, Gabe? Wait till you get to Heaven. You'll have it there. This is the real world, boy. There's nothing perfect about this world. You've been around long enough that it's time for you to lose that idealistic fantasy. Grow up and get real. This is the world we live in. We can't change it. We're stuck with it. All we can do is survive it. You've got to learn to stroll through this world and let the injustices of life roll off your back. Grab what pleasures you can and throw the rest in the trash. Life will be a lot better when you learn to let the good things in and put up a wall to keep the bad things out."

Gabe stood and slowly turned to the door. He looked down at Shelley and said, "Thanks for understanding. You must be right. Everyone is telling me the same thing. I've got to let go of this bitterness. It's eating me up inside. Blauw's right. She'll self-destruct without my help."

Shelley jumped to his feet and slapped Gabe on the back. "That's what I want to hear, boy! You're going to be fine! You just go up there and give Garrison a great big, sloppy kiss on his big, ugly, white ass. Get that transfer back here to the goon squad. You'll see, life will be a blast again. I'll even buy you some mouth wash to get the taste out of your mouth."

Gabe leaned back and laughed. He'd forgotten how good it felt to laugh. He truly missed Shelley and the goons. Half way across the squad room, he turned back to Shelley. "Hey sarge, I never had a dad. He wanted nothing to do with me. I'd give anything if I could have had a dad like you. Your boys are lucky kids."

Gabe awoke to knocking on his door. This time was different. There wasn't the pounding and swearing typical of a visit from Angus Blauw. He stumbled to the peephole and looked out. He panicked when he saw Beck standing outside.

He wanted to jerk the door open and not leave her standing in the dingy hallway any longer than necessary, but he wasn't dressed. He quickly ran to the sofa and grabbed his sweatpants. He pulled them up to his waist as he opened the door. "Beck! How are you? Sorry to make you wait so long. I was---"

Beck smiled and held her hand up to stop his apology. She patted his bare chest as she walked by. "Relax, Tarzan, I'm a big girl. It's okay, I can take care of myself."

She moved Gabe's blanket and sat down. He put on a sweatshirt and sat beside her. "So! What brings you out slumming? Are you on duty?"

"Yes, I'm on my lunch break. I can't stay long. I wanted to talk to you about Loar. I tested the waters with Baumgartan yesterday. I was right. He wouldn't sanction an investigation of her for any reason. I didn't use her name. I referred to her as a prominent physician. We'd have to have some very credible witnesses and evidence before he'd take her to the grand jury. Good news though, I talked to an expert witness that we use sometimes when we need a psychiatrist. He gave me some good advice. He said if we can get any of her patients to swear that she'd suggested that they harm anyone, he'd help us draft a complaint to the state board of psychiatric review. He's got some pull there and would give our complaint an extra push. He said even if we only had hearsay or anonymous information, the board could investigate her. If they find any wrong-doing at all, they could take action. They could force her to produce her medical records. I know she's self-medicating and falsifying scripts. They have less of a burden of proof than we would have in court. They could at least get a piece of her and maybe get her license yanked for a while. That's more than we can do right now."

Gabe shook his head. That wasn't good enough. He wanted Loar to bleed. "That's not a permanent solution, Beck. She'll just get her license back and be up to her old tricks again. And if we take a cheap shot like that, she'll be after us for the rest of our lives."

"I know, Gabe, but it's a start. I just wanted to tell you this so you wouldn't do something stupid."

He didn't look at Beck. His guilty appearance suddenly hit home with her. She squared up to him and asked, "You haven't, have you?"

He leaned back and stared at the ceiling. "Yeah, I did something stupid. I went to see her. I thought I could gain her sympathy and get her to think I was dependant on her like Pritchard and her other patients. I hoped that if she thought she could manipulate me, she might try to enlist me to kill for her. Bad idea. She saw through me right away. I didn't get to first base. All I did was make a fool of myself and get Garrison pissed at me."

Beck put her face in her hands, then rubbed her eyes. She swallowed her anger, then calmly said, "Look, Gabe, Ben and I told you a long time ago that you'd have to be patient. You can't go off half-cocked and be your own little mercenary. You don't have the experience for that. The tough homicides are only cleared by good, solid police work and a strong team effort. Loar is going to be one of the toughest. We may never get her, but if we do, we can't have all of our evidence thrown out because you broke the rules. Her attorney will insist on a suppression hearing to get our evidence excluded. He'll have a hay-day if we've seized it illegally. It may very well come down to a credibility contest in front of the jury. They'll be confused enough when the defense's expert witnesses dispute the opinions of our experts. They might go with the team that they like the best. If we lose our credibility with them, they'll side with her for sure. She's got a lot of jury appeal. It'll take every bit of charisma that we can muster to stay on a level playing field with her. She's charming as hell."

He stared at the ceiling throughout Beck's lecture. She said, "I'm sorry, Gabe. I don't mean to chew you out. You don't work for me, but I don't want you to get us all in trouble."

"Oh, that's okay. I've been getting lectured a lot lately. I deserve it. It was a stupid thing to do." There was an uncomfortable silence for a few seconds. Beck stood to leave and Gabe asked, "So, what's our timetable? When can we make a complaint with the board?"

"I don't know. I want to talk to Ben first. I want to make sure this thing can't come back and bite us in the butt. We'll need more than the speculation that we have now."

He stood and walked her to the door. He said, "I'm not going to wait long, Beck. Even if the board suspends her license, she still has someone out there killing for her. I want that person as bad as I want Loar."

He opened the door for her as she said angrily, "Just wait! We're only going to get one shot at her! We have to have our guns loaded when we strap her on! She'll have the best attorney that money can buy, and he'll ram it down our throats if we're not prepared! You can go on with your career after a beating like that, but those are the kinds of black eyes that end prosecutors' careers! Dr. Loar is not going to be my downfall, and neither are you!"

"I got the hint, but I'm curious about something. You didn't have to come here to tell me this. You could have told me this over the phone. Why did you really come here?"

Beck's anger dissipated. She put her hand up to Gabe's face and turned his head so she could look deep into his eyes. She took a deep breath and sighed. "I want Loar as much as you do, but I want you safe even more. Loar kills anyone who gets close to her. I don't want you ---"

Gabe rudely slammed the door before she could finish. Beck jumped and looked at him in shock. He encircled her waist with his arm and jerked her close. She dropped her purse and jumped toward him at the same time. She threw her arms around his neck and grabbed him by the back of the head. They clung tight to each other and kissed deeply for what seemed like several minutes. All thoughts of his ex-wife were long gone. All that mattered now was how much he wanted Beck.

He found himself pushing her toward the sofa. She broke their kiss and put her hands against his chest. He realized what he was doing and brought himself back to reality. Not wanting to offend her, he stopped at her first protest.

She breathed deeply and tried to slow her pounding heart. She patted his chest one last time and forced herself to step back. She picked up her purse, opened the door and walked out.

He stood in shock, trying to figure out what had just happened. He had no idea what made him do something so out of character. He walked slowly to the sofa, flopped down in frustration and pulled the blanket up to his chin. He was unaware that Beck was leaning against his door in the hallway, fighting the urge to come back in and spend the afternoon with him.

Ben Hire had not been inactive the past few weeks. He'd secretly typed all of Gabe's reports and put them in the format that the D.A.'s offices preferred. He did this in anticipation that something would break and they could take Loar to the grand jury. With Gabe's reports done, there would be less to do if the D.A. gave him the green light.

He was putting in more hours to complete the Loar file. He had to work after five so the other detectives and office staff wouldn't see him compiling the file. Frequently, he would be leaving when Gabe was coming into work.

Ben was walking to his car when Gabe jogged into the parking lot. He hadn't talked to Gabe since he and Beck had met two weeks ago. He wanted to bring Gabe up to speed on the case. He yelled for him to wait. Gabe opened his door and waited for him to jog across the garage. "Hi, Ben, come on in."

He held the door open and offered Ben the chair. "I can't stay, Gabe, the wife's holding supper for me. I just wanted to get you up to speed on Loar."

"I appreciate that, Ben, but Beck came by the other day. I guess she's got a connection with the board of psychiatric review who can help us push a complaint through, right?"

"That's right. She's content to let the board take action, but I don't think that'll solve our problem. I didn't tell her this because I didn't want to worry her, but Loar won't take a complaint lying down. She'll go after whoever files the complaint. She had Allis killed for inquiring into her affairs. She'll do the same to you, me, Beck or our contact on the board. We're going to have to get her some significant prison time to get her off our asses."

Gabe lit up with delight. "Yes! Good! Finally, someone agrees with me! Everyone in the world has been telling me to back off and let her hang herself! Finally, someone sees things my way!"

Ben held up his hands. "Hold on, kid. Beck told me what you're thinking. I don't agree with Beck, but I don't agree with you either. I only have a few years till I can retire and I have no intention of being your cellmate during my golden years."

Gabe slumped back down in his chair in disappointment. "So what, Ben? What are we going to do?"

"We aren't going to do anything, Gabe. There ain't no we. You've got to understand something. You're not a detective. These are my cases. You're just a poor nightshift goon who pissed off the chief and got himself pigeon-holed in the cold case unit. Now, I'm sorry to be so blunt with you, and I deeply appreciate your help. I'll give you credit, you're a smart kid. You tied this whole thing together for me, but they're my cases, and I'm not going to let you piss them away because you want to go too fast. I was beating my head against a wall over these cases years before you ever came along. Besides, I like you and I'm not going to let you throw your career away."

Gabe looked at him in shock. His candor was brutal. Gabe realized that he and Ben were not the partners that he'd thought they were. He shifted his eyes to the floor and said, "I'm sorry, Ben, I thought you wanted my help."

Ben's heart melted as he saw the wind go out of Gabe's sails. He sat on the edge of the desk and tried to comfort him. "I do, Gabe, I do. And when we make the case on her, I'll let you in on it, I promise. You can be the one to slap the cuffs on her and haul her ass off to the county jail. You can put on your suit and get your picture on television leading her to the courthouse for arraignment. When the newspapers interview me, I'll tell them that you're the one who broke the case. I'll give you all the credit, but we just have to do this my way. You've got to understand that. I'm not going to let you ruin your career just to get someone that we're going to get anyway by honest means. It'll happen, kid. I'm also not going to let you destroy me and Eisman. We've got too much to lose. If I didn't care about you, I'd let you stumble on your merry way and get yourself in trouble, but I like you too much to

219

let that happen. And in case you haven't figured it out, Eisman likes you, too. She's just as worried about you as I am."

"I understand, Ben. You're right, and I got the hint that Beck cares. She's not very subtle. I just want to ask you one question. Even if we get the evidence on Loar, how are we going to find out who her strangler is? You know she'll never confess or give up her accomplice. She'd never give us anyone who could testify against her."

Ben stared off into space as he thought. He finally acknowledged, "That's going to be tough, Gabe, but there are ways. Tips will come in. We've launched a real aggressive media blitz. We're asking for any information leading to the arrest and conviction of the person who strangled Windsor, Clearey and Benson. We're also trying to use the same blitz to buy tips on who shot Boreman and Wilcox. If that doesn't work, we'll try something else. If nothing works, we'll just have to wait till we get lucky. Time is on our side, Gabe. We're dealing with psych patients here. They all unravel sooner or later, and if we can hang a solid charge on her, she'll give up her accomplice. She'd sell her own mother to the devil to avoid jail time."

Gabe stood as Ben walked toward the door and asked, "Ben, what if there was a way to get Loar's medical records so we could target her accomplice? What if we could find out who her patients are without seizing any evidence that could be thrown out later? We could work on her patients and maybe find one who'd roll over on her. What if we could do that without getting ourselves in trouble?"

Ben stopped at the door and turned to Gabe. He looked at him for a long time before he answered. "Listen, kid, I know what you're getting at. I'm going to share something with you that I've never told anyone else before. You're talking about becoming a crook to catch a crook; trying to right one wrong by committing another. I know it sounds appealing, and if you con yourself long enough, it'll even start to make sense. You can even put enough candy coating on it to make it taste better to your conscience. But in the end, your palate may be able to tolerate it, but your stomach will know the difference. You might fool your mind, but your conscience will know better. I tried that once. Years ago, I wanted to hang a charge on Lenny Belknap. He was an arrogant little prick who was raping women in the projects. I'd convinced myself that I was going to save future rape victims the trauma of being raped. I'd even convinced myself that I was going to save lives. I staked out the little bastard on my off-duty time. When I saw him leave, I broke into his house and found a bunch of photos and underwear that he'd kept from the crime scenes as souvenirs. I falsified a report saying they were given to me by an anonymous informant who'd taken them from Lenny's house. I used that information in a search warrant affidavit and got a search warrant. We found all the evidence that we needed to put his little ass in prison for the rest of his life. I thought I was pretty slick, kid. No one ever found out what I'd done. But one person knew and he's haunted me ever since. Every day, he reminds me of what I did and robs me of sleep and my self-esteem. To this day, I can't look the son-of-a-bitch in the eye. He's always throwing it up in my face that I broke the law. I don't want you to go through that, Gabe."

Gabe knew the rat had to be Lumas or someone like him. He stared at Ben in shock and said, "Oh, Ben, I don't think a bit less of you. Who's the asshole who keeps rubbing it in your face?"

Ben watched Gabe grow indignant. He calmly said, "He doesn't have a name, Gabe. He's the man in the mirror. I see him every day. I can't shake him. I can't lose him. I can't hide anything from him or con him. It doesn't do any good to lie to him because he knows everything that I'm thinking. I just have to live with him. I don't ever want you to do anything that'll cause you to hate him. You have to look at him every day of your life, so it's important that you like each other."

Gabe was left without words. With nothing else to say, Ben patted him on the back and closed the door as he left. Gabe finally gave up. After everyone close to him had chewed him out for thinking of breaking into Loar's apartment, he decided that they were right. He gave up the notion and decided to trust Ben and Sergeant Shelley's advice.

Gabe contacted the chief's secretary and made an appointment to see the chief. He sat nervously in the waiting room rehearsing his speech.

The secretary motioned for him to enter the chief's office. He walked in fully prepared to eat crow. He didn't like the idea of

Garrison thinking that he could intimidate him, but he was going to do anything to get back in patrol.

Garrison shot him a sinister smile as he walked in. Ecstatic over the opportunity to extract another pound of flesh, Garrison leaned back in his chair, interlaced his fingers and said, "Well, well, well, if it isn't my favorite little sewer rat. Feeling tough today?"

Gabe's anger immediately boiled. He fought the urge to grab Garrison by his windpipe. He forced a smile and said, "No, sir, that's not why I'm here. I was out of line the other night. I owe you an apology."

Garrison's sinister smile faded to confusion. This was not at all what he'd expected. He looked at Gabe with deep mistrust. "What do you mean?"

"I mean that I may not agree with your decisions. We may have our personality conflicts, but you're the chief. I have to respect the position even if I disagree with the person in it. You approached me with a gesture of kindness and I got nasty with you. I owe you an apology and I'm here to deliver it."

Garrison stared at him through a suspicious squint. Gabe saw that he'd totally baffled Garrison and wanted to make a tactical retreat before Garrison could push his anger button again. He quickly said, "So! I apologize, and if you ever think it's in the best interest of the department to put me back in patrol, I won't disappoint you. Thanks for your time."

He turned and walked out, grumbling as he walked down the stairs. The taste of crow didn't agree with him and he vowed to never again put himself in the position of having to apologize to Garrison. From now on, he would beat Garrison at his own game. No more displays of anger.

Gabe took the night off with some comp-time. He needed some time away from work to sort out the many issues that were clouding his judgment. He stopped by the market and picked up two pounds of large shrimp, a bag of boiling spices and a half-gallon of expensive ice cream. He hadn't treated himself this good in years.

The evening began well. After he'd washed the bitter taste of Garrison's ass from his mouth with a beer, he was surprised at how good he felt.

With the shrimp boiled, the cocktail sauce made and a cold beer, he settled down on his sofa and savored his meal. When the shrimp was gone, he started on the ice cream. With only a fifth of the container left, he dropped the spoon in and sat it on the orange crate. He took a deep breath as he looked at his distended stomach and loosened his belt. He was totally unashamed of his momentary hedonism.

He was relieved at his decision to forget about Loar. All he could think about was Beck Eisman. He relived their kiss over and over in his mind. She'd become a welcome distraction from his problems.

When his thoughts drifted back to Loar, he caught himself rationalizing again. If he didn't seize any evidence, why was it wrong? Sure it was illegal to break into another person's residence, but the state statute said it was only a burglary if he broke into the inhabitable structure of another with the intent to commit a crime. If he didn't take anything, he wasn't committing a burglary.

If he only downloaded Loar's medical records and didn't steal any hardcopies, he could learn the identity of her patients without taking the files. Reading them wasn't the same as stealing them. It would be trespassing, but that was a small price to pay to save lives.

Gabe put himself in an honest person's shoes. He wouldn't mind if a stranger read his medical files if it would save another person's life. Surely the man in the mirror would forgive him for that.

The night grew late and he dozed off on the sofa. He was awakened by a gentle knock on his door. It was the same soft knock that he'd heard when Beck surprised him a few days ago.

He quickly awoke and sat straight up. His excitement shot through the roof at the prospect of taking his passion for her to the next level. He jumped off of the sofa and sprinted to the door. He didn't look out the peephole, but turned the deadbolt and jerked the door open. He almost fell backward in shock when he looked into the hallway. He was speechless when he saw Jenna Kerse smiling at him.

Jenna conspicuously lowered her gaze to Gabe's crotch. She slowly stepped into his apartment and looked around. He wanted to tell her that she couldn't come in, but he couldn't think of an excuse. She walked around the edge of the room, nodding her head. "Dated, gloomy, Spartan, crying for a female's touch, but I can do this."

Gabe looked up and down the hall, hoping that no one had seen her come in. He closed the door and tried to act composed. "Like it?"

Jenna stopped and turned abruptly. She shot him an evil smile. "I didn't say I liked it. I said I could do it. Besides, I didn't come here for the décor."

He got the hint, but ignored it. Jenna's visit annoyed him. Police officers like to think of their home as a sanctuary. Although it's not hard to find out where an officer lives, they like to think that they are detached from the job while in the sanctity of their home. Jenna was not someone that he wanted in his apartment. He asked, "How did you find out where I live?"

She sensed his annoyance, but didn't care. She had been in many violent confrontations, and this young kid posed no threat. She outweighed him, could lift more and could out-fight him. He didn't intimidate her and she showed him no respect. "You think you cops are the only ones who can find someone? I just watched you walk home from work the other morning and followed you. When I saw you come into this apartment building, I checked the names on the mailboxes downstairs."

"And you don't believe in phone calls before dropping in?"

Jenna shook her head casually. "Nope, I wanted to see who you're screwing. Thought I could catch you in the sack and see who my competition is."

She peeled her jacket off, revealing a sheer white body suit. Gabe's eyes drifted uncontrollably downward and saw every minute feature of her anatomy through the shear suit. White made her tan skin look even darker. A pair of black exercise pants covered her legs. She stepped toward him and sized up his reaction. She cocked her head and asked, "Is there any unfinished business that you and I need to discuss or are we ready to go to bed?" She slid her thumbs inside the waistband of her pants and slid them over her hips.

Gabe didn't want Jenna in bed. Her bulk, leathery skin and masculine mannerisms did not appeal to him. If she were nude, he wouldn't be able to dress her if she didn't want to leave. Not wanting this encounter to turn into a wrestling match, he quickly seized her waistband and pulled her pants back up over her hips. He smiled and said, "As a matter of fact, there is some unfinished business that we need to discuss. Why don't we go out for coffee?"

Anger swept over Jenna's face. Her nostrils flared and rage shot from her eyes. She stepped back and growled in her deep voice, "You don't want me?" She stepped up to Gabe and poked him in the chest with her finger. "You know something, little boy? I can't count the number of men over the years who've wanted me in bed, but I wasn't interested. They were too macho, too stuck-up, too queer, too fat, too skinny, too ugly or all of the above. I haven't wanted a man since I was a teenager. I thought I would be happy with women for the rest of my life. I finally found a woman that I love, and I thought I'd never need to feel a man inside me again. Then you came along. I found feelings that I thought didn't exist anymore. Having you as my second lover would make my life complete. You're not going to reject me like I'm some old street-whore. I've worked too hard to become what I am. When I make up my mind to get something, I get it. You hear me?"

Jenna grew angrier as she spoke. Her volatility took Gabe by surprise. He now saw clearly how she'd gotten in so many fights. She'd stepped into him nose to nose, clenching her fists and flexing her arms. He either had to get off the first punch or defuse her somehow.

He wanted to establish his dominance without alienating her. He needed her, so he forced a pretentious smile and spoke in a calm voice. "Boy, you sure know how to charm a guy. I'll bet you worked on that pickup line all night. Do you think the sex will be good if you get me there by intimidation? My arms don't twist. I'm not saying no, I'm just saying I'm not ready yet. You may bully your girlfriend into bed, but you won't do that to me."

Jenna stood her ground and refused to step away. She'd made it clear that she was going to dominate him. She finally realized that it was going to take some compromise to get Gabe to participate. "Okay, so what do you suggest?"

He shrugged his shoulders. "Well, I would say let's go to dinner, but I just ate and I'm stuffed. Maybe we could go for a drive."

She relaxed her fists. "Okay, I'll let you off the hook this time. I'll drive." Gabe stepped around her to put on his shoes and get his gun and jacket. She had mixed feelings as she watched him put on his shoulder holster. She hated him and lusted for him at the same time.

Jenna had successfully forced her will on women in the past, but they were smaller and weaker. Gabe was different. He would be much harder to dominate. He could not be forced to have sex if he didn't want to. Her mind was set, though. He would be hers and she would leave him no choice. If she couldn't have him, she would hurt him so badly that no one would.

She was still angry about being hustled out of Gabe's apartment and talked little as they drove. Gabe finally directed the conversation to Wilcox. He tried to stroke her. "You know, Jenna, one thing that I admire about you is your unpretentious, straightforward personality. I respect that, so I'm going to be straight with you. I'm curious about a guy that was killed a few years ago. He was the president of the school board, Howard Wilcox. He was shot in the parking lot behind the club. You were a member of the club at that time. Do you remember anything about him?"

Jenna had not cooled down from the power struggle in Gabe's apartment. She certainly wasn't in the mood to be interrogated. "Wilcox? Sure, I knew him, but why are you asking me?"

Gabe replied casually, "I read his file at the office and saw that it had never been cleared. I thought the killer might have been a member and that you might have heard talk around the club. You're pretty well connected."

She didn't respond. He knew that he'd struck a nerve. He finally asked, "Did I say something that hit close to home?"

She looked straight ahead and replied, "There was talk. Wilcox was a chauvinistic asshole. He deserved what he got."

226

Gabe was shocked by her response. "What do you know about him?"

She shrugged her shoulders, "I knew all I needed to know. He was a conservative, condescending prude who didn't like gays or lesbians. If he hadn't gotten killed, I would have beaten the crap out of him myself."

Gabe had stumbled onto something. Jenna knew more than she was telling. She might even know the killer. "I didn't mean to scratch the scab off an old wound. I'd just like to know who killed him."

"If I knew, I wouldn't tell you. You may be my toy, but you're still a cop. I'm going to enjoy screwing your young ass off, but make no mistake. That's as far as it'll go. I won't be your snitch. Just use me for the pleasure that I can give you and leave your job out of it. We're lovers, that's all. Don't mix business and pleasure with me if you know what's good for you."

Jenna's threat annoyed him. His anger rose as he thought of a blistering retort. He looked around and realized that he was too far from home to walk, but he could walk to a payphone and call Angus for a ride.

He sat quietly until he could formulate his thoughts. He had always admired Blauw's ability to butcher people with words. He wondered what Angus would say in this situation, then emulated his personality. He finally took a nervous, deep breath and said, "We're not lovers yet, Jenna. You're going to have to accept a cold, hard fact of life. If we have sex, I'll be the boss. I'm not some limp-wristed liberal who's uncertain about his sexuality. I like women, not men. If you want me, you're going to have to lose that Butch act and quit trying to be more masculine than me. Knock off this macho, dyke bullshit. I can whip your ass in a fight and in bed, so that makes me the best man. If you want to kick my ass, you're going to have to pack on another fifty pounds of muscle and grow a set of balls. You don't have to help me, but you better lose that hostile attitude with me or I'll trash your phony ass and find me a real woman."

As Gabe spoke his last word, he knew the party was over. Jenna slammed on the brakes and skidded to a stop. Being Angus worked well for Angus, but it didn't always work for Gabe. Maybe it was his youth and soft, tenor voice, but he'd never been able to pull off the Blauw persona as effectively as Blauw.

Jenna raged inside and no longer cared about sex. She was ready for a fight. As the car screeched to a halt, she threw open her door without a word and stepped out. Gabe mistakenly said, "I can let myself out."

He searched for the door latch, but Jenna had no intention of being a gentleman. Before he could step out, she reached back inside the car and grabbed him by his jacket. She'd never let a man get away with talking to her like that, and this punk-kid wasn't going to be the first. Sex or no sex, this asshole was going to learn who the boss was.

With one hand, she pulled Gabe over the console and out the driver's door. He felt like he was in the grip of a pro linebacker and his fear shot through the roof. As soon as she got him out of the car, the games began.

Gabe had been frustrated over his job for months and was ready for anything that Jenna dished out, but she was an intimidating figure. He would never let her know it, but he was intimidated by her physique. A good fight would vent his frustrations, but he was scared. He'd always fought harder when he was scared. The man in the mirror didn't protest the thought of punching out Jenna. She was as masculine as any man.

She'd pulled him out the driver's door and had grabbed his jacket with both hands. She lifted him to his toes and slammed him against the roof of the car. The drip-rail hit him across his shoulder blades and shot pain up his neck. The pain helped fuel his survival instinct.

He drove his arms vertically between Jenna's arms and broke her hold. He thrust his palm under her chin and snapped her head backward with sufficient force to knock her to the ground.

Completely undeterred, Jenna bounced to her feet as though she'd landed on a springboard. She grabbed him by the collar of his coat and cocked her fist. He prepared to block her punch, but it didn't come. She froze and glared into his eyes. With her overpowering strength, she threw him to the ground, got back in her car and drove away.

Gabe watched her speed away. He rubbed the back of his neck to reduce the pain. He breathed a sigh of relief that the fight had gone no further. He wondered if this was the end of Jenna. Since she wasn't going to help him, he hoped it was.

He walked a couple of miles to a payphone at an all-night convenience store and called Angus. He was on his night off, but was too drunk to drive. Another call to the station found Len Shelley in his office. He was out of the city limits, but Len picked him up and gave him a ride home.

11

GABE REPORTED TO work late. He'd been fighting a flu bug over his days off. He was going to stay home sick, but decided at the last minute that he wanted to visit the guys on nights. He didn't feel good, but knew he would feel bad whether he was at home or work.

As he walked into the underground garage, he noticed an envelope on the ground in front of his door. He picked it up and opened it. Inside were a key and a slip of paper that simply said, *1218-OFF, then 1218-ON*. He knew instantly that the key was to Loar's office building and the numbers were her security code. Val Machka had delivered on his promise.

He hurried inside with renewed enthusiasm and began making arrangements for his first entry. Several nights earlier, he'd assembled the items that he would need to enter Loar's office. He committed the code to memory, then burned the paper. He couldn't wait to begin. Knowing that he wasn't going to steal anything, the man in the mirror seemed content with his decision.

Gabe walked to Loar's building. He thought he should look the building over and see which door would offer him the most concealment during his entry and exit. The building sat on 10th street and had an alley running beside it. All the exterior doors were apparently keyed the same. The key that Machka had given him worked perfectly.

He had no intention of entering this night, but when the door opened so effortlessly, he couldn't resist the temptation to look inside. The building appeared vacant. He didn't see a security guard and felt confident stepping inside. He felt an eerie twinge of conviction, as if crossing over the threshold had somehow changed him forever.

He turned to lock the door, but if he had to flee the building, he didn't want to have to stop to unlock it. He decided it was wise to leave it unlocked. He approached the doorway that led to the stairwell. As instructed by Machka, he avoided the elevator.

There was music coming from around the corner. Curiosity got the best of him, so he walked to the corner of the stairwell and peeked around. In the center of the lobby was the guard desk. The guard was seated with his feet up on the counter, watching the late movie.

At each floor, Gabe stuck his head out of the stairwell and looked at the display case hanging on the wall opposite the stairs. The cases were black with white letters and listed the offices on that floor. As he peered out of the stairwell on the 12th floor, he found what he was looking for. Dr. Loar was in office 18. Twelfth floor, office 18, he now knew how Loar had come up with her security code.

Loar's office was ideally situated. It was the end office next to an adjoining hallway. The short distance to the adjoining hallway made a perfect escape path should someone step off the elevator while Gabe was entering or exiting Loar's office. There was sufficient echo in the stairwell for him to hear someone ascending the stairs.

When he'd decided to approach the building that night, he had no intention of going this far. He marveled at how composed he was. As he approached Loar's office, he looked through the vertical window next to the door. Seeing no movement, he decided to go in.

He turned the doorknob and found it locked. He inserted the exterior door key, but it wouldn't turn. Machka had forgotten to give him the key to Loar's door. With no alternative, he turned to leave.

He made his way quietly to the ground floor. He opened the stairwell door slightly and peered out, looking for the guard. Still hearing the music, he smirked and eased to the corner of the stairwell. The guard was still seated with his feet up.

Gabe walked unconcerned toward the alley door. He grabbed the knob, but bounced off the door when the knob didn't turn. It was locked.

Shock overwhelmed him as he realized that in the time that it had taken him to go to the 12th floor, the guard had made rounds on the first floor and had found the door unlocked. Thinking that he'd forgotten to lock it earlier, he locked it again.

Gabe panicked. He hoped the guard hadn't heard the thump. He quickly reached in his pocket and retrieved the key. He nervously fumbled with it and managed to get it in the lock. He turned the key, let himself out and locked the door behind him. He then sprinted conspicuously down the alley.

He regained his composure at the end of the alley and thought how suspicious he must look, running through an alley at that time of night. He slowed to a jog and returned to his office.

When his nerves had settled, he called Val Machka. Val laughed when Gabe described his first bungle. Val assured him that he would have the key to Loar's office at the foot of Gabe's door the next night.

Len Shelley called for Angus to meet him at the park. Angus dropped Reaves' arrest off at the jail and headed for Shelley's favorite hiding spot.

The weather had warmed considerably, and Shelley was eating gizzards and admiring the stars. Angus parked beside him and asked, "What's up, fat boy?"

Shelley glared at him. "Fat boy! I ain't fat, you senile old wad of phlegm. You think anyone that ain't some emaciated old cadaver like you is fat. I'm just fleshy."

Angus laughed and slapped Shelley's leg. "Well, fleshy, you can fool yourself if you want, but you can't fool me. What did you drag me out here in the boonies for? You know I'm scared of the dark."

Shelley finished grinding up the gizzard in his mouth and swallowed hard so he could speak. "I'm worried about Kinnett. I

233

want you to stay close to him and make sure he doesn't do anything stupid. I had a heart to heart talk with him the other night, but I don't think I got through. He called me the other night to go out of the city to give him a ride home. He wouldn't tell me what he'd been up to, but I could tell that someone had dumped him out there. He wouldn't discuss it, but I'm afraid he's up to no good. I think he's trying to bang that psychotic bitch, Loar. She's probably the one who dumped him out there."

Angus frowned. "Yeah? Strange. Okay, I'll watch him. I don't think he's banging Loar though. He hates her something fierce."

Shelley said, "There's a fine line between love and hate, Angus. You know as well as I do that a stiff dick ain't got no conscience. That lad could set his hatred aside long enough to pound her ripe, little ass through the mattress. He's gotten pretty calloused lately. He'd poke her for fun and throw her away. That would put his pasty ass on her hit-list. He thinks he's a tough guy, but he's just a drippy-nosed kid. He's not ready to step up to her league yet."

Angus couldn't resist the opportunity to insult Shelley. "And what do you know about chasing pussy, Len? You're so straight that you ain't never got a strange piece of ass in your whole life. If you even thought about it, Jackie would slit your bag and run your leg through it."

Shelley glared at him. "Yeah? That may be, but I've seen what a miserable old broke-dick that you've turned into, and I don't want that kid to wind up like you. Besides, you ain't had a piece of ass since your wedding night."

Angus protested loudly. "The hell I ain't! I have sex four times a week, regular as clockwork! I'd do it more often, but it scares me."

Shelley was confused until Angus delivered the punch line. "Yeah, it scares me cause it's always dark and I'm all alone."

Shelley bounced as he and Angus laughed hard. Angus feigned ignorance, but knew what Gabe had been doing. He'd pressured Val Machka to help Gabe get into Loar's office.

Shelley was the last person that Gabe needed snooping around. As he drove away, Angus vowed to keep an eye on Loar's

234

office building in case Gabe needed help. He also vowed to stay sober on his nights off so he would be available.

Gabe stopped going to the fitness center. He knew Jenna would be there and wanted to avoid another altercation. He knew she would not pull her punches next time. Once she punched him, he would do everything in his power to tear her head off.

It was obvious by the scars on her face that she had a high pain threshold. He would have to hurt her badly to win. He would also likely suffer considerable injury in the process.

He hadn't learned much during his short career, but one thing that he had learned was that when he fought, he fought to win, whether his opponent was male, female or both.

The Oregon weather had turned warm. Gabe resumed running on the street and lifting his dumbbells at work. He'd changed his jogging route to include a tour around Dr. Loar's office building. The more familiar he was with it and the surrounding terrain, the easier he could escape if he were discovered.

He had just concluded a run and noticed lights on upstairs in the detective unit. He knew Ben occasionally worked late, so he dropped in. When he walked into the unit, he stopped in shock. Ben was there, but he wasn't alone. Ben motioned for him to come in. Beck smiled enthusiastically. She was genuinely happy to see him. Ben said, "Sit down, Gabe, let me get you up to speed."

Ben handed him a nicely bound file titled *Dr. Maura Loar.* When he opened it, he saw a table of contents that listed not only the original case files of the unsolved murders, but typed statements of the people that Gabe had interviewed. He smiled and nodded. Ben had kept his word and not left him out of the loop.

Beck asked, "What do you think?"

He was impressed. "Well, I'm not a detective, but it looks good to me."

Beck looked at Ben, who looked away, not wanting to get in the middle of this discussion. Beck said, "When I said that, I just meant that you're not a detective by title. You've done a good job of doing the work."

Gabe laid the file on Ben's desk. He held his hand up to stop Beck's apology. "That's okay. You were right. The truth hurts sometimes."

Ben sat down and said, "I've been putting the file together in case we ever go to the grand jury. This is the format that Baumgartan likes. Beck helped me with it."

Gabe asked, "What do you mean, if we ever go to the grand jury? You mean when, don't you?"

Beck sat down and shrugged her shoulders. "We mean if, Gabe. I'm going to start a synopsis of our case file for the state board of psychiatric review. I've got someone who will submit it to the board for us. We could lose our jobs if we get caught circumventing our departments' policies."

He didn't respond, but Ben said, "Yes, and we don't want to get on Loar's hit-list. If she doesn't go to jail, she'll be on the street. We'll be her next targets."

Gabe stared at the floor. Beck said, "Gabe, I know that look and I don't like what I see. What are you up to?"

He looked up and shot her a pretentious smile. "Oh, nothing. I don't think that's going to solve our problem. I know we can't use any evidence obtained illegally, but there's a way to obtain what we need without shooting ourselves in the foot."

Ben crossed his arms and glared suspiciously at him. "Okay, kid, what are you up to now?"

Gabe shrugged his shoulders. "I'm just saying that we can get our witness against Loar if we flush him out. Give him a target and nab him when he tries to make the kill."

Ben said, "That sounds all well and good, but who's going to be the target? How are we going to do surveillance around the clock without Garrison finding out? If we miss and our target gets killed, who's going to take the flack for that?" Gabe simply smiled.

Beck stood up and protested loudly. Ben leaned over his desk and chastised Gabe, but he held his hand up. "Stop! I've taken all the ass-chewing that I'm going to take. You two want to do this legally, and you're right, but you both admit that we might never get enough evidence to put Loar in jail. So this is the only solution. We've got to catch her killer in the act, then get him to roll over on Loar. There's no other way."

Ben froze in place as Gabe explained. Beck leaned over him. "Good idea, bad choice. I don't want you killed."

He shook his head and explained, "Listen, guys, all of Loar's victims were killed because they never saw it coming. Wilcox was surprised and never saw the gun. He took the round in the side of the head. Windsor was caught off-guard. He never would have let the strangler near him if he'd been prepared. Benson was killed by someone that she trusted. I'm not going to be caught off-guard."

He lifted the left side of his jacket and revealed the butt of the Colt Commander .45 that hung under his arm. "Hell, I'm a policeman and I've got a big gun. Ain't no one more competent to catch a crook than a policeman."

Beck looked at Ben for support, but he didn't respond. She grabbed her purse and stormed toward the door. When she stopped and turned, her eyes watered as her anger flared. "Okay, you idiot, I can't stop you! I've tried to be nice about this, but I've had a gut-full of your stubbornness! I'm washing my hands of this whole mess! Don't call me! Don't ask for my advice! If you want to get yourself killed or fired, go ahead! I don't care anymore!"

As Beck stormed out of the unit, Ben glared at him. He finally said, "We can't do this without her, Gabe. Baumgartan will trash this case in a heartbeat. We need someone in the D.A.'s office to ram this through when we get enough evidence."

Gabe nodded in agreement. "I know, Ben, but what else can we do? You know we need bait. We just can't wait for another murder and hope to be close enough to catch the killer before he gets away. Besides, I've screwed around and pissed off one of Loar's acquaintances. It's entirely likely that Loar will find out that I've been asking about her anyway. I've been to her office and made a complete fool of myself. She'll know my visit wasn't for depression. As soon as her acquaintance tells her that I've been asking questions about the Wilcox murder, she'll put two and two together. She's probably going to send her killer after me anyway. Let's make the most of it. I'll be careful. We'll arrest the scumbag when he tries to take me out."

Ben was curious. "Who did you piss off?"

"Jenna Kerse. She's a leathery old muscle-dyke at the fitness center where Wilcox was killed."

Ben sat straight up in his chair and yelled, "Jenna Kerse! Do you know who she is?" Gabe shook his head. "She's only the meanest bitch on two legs. She's the worst man-hater in the world. She loves to beat the hell out of men and does it on a regular basis. She's been before the court a dozen times for assault. What did you do to her?"

Gabe smiled and said proudly, "Well, Ben, you're looking at the only man in thirty years that she's wanted to go to bed with. She insisted on wearing the pants and lost the power struggle."

Ben was disgusted. "You weren't seriously going to bang that beast were you? She's got more testosterone than both of us put together. She's sickening."

"Nah, I just let her think I would. I thought she might remember the Wilcox murder. She did, but wouldn't discuss it. She thought he deserved to be killed. I'm sure she knows Loar. She knows everyone who's been a member since she's been there. She'll probably tip Loar off just to get even with me."

Ben leaned back in his chair. "You're not going to do this my way, are you?"

Gabe said, "You said you didn't want the evidence thrown out, Ben. I'm not going to do anything to cause you to lose your evidence in a suppression hearing, but I'm also not going to sit back for the next several years, hoping someone rolls over on Loar. These are your cases, but they're mine, too. You investigate them your way, but I'm going to do what I can to speed up the process. I'm single. I don't have anything to lose, and I sure ain't going to get myself killed."

"You'd better not. Now! We still need Beck Eisman. Even if we catch Loar's killer and get him to roll over on her, we've still got to have someone in the D.A.'s office who isn't in bed with Loar." Ben leaned over his desk and growled at Gabe. "So! You get your ass out there and get her back! We need her!"

Gabe walked home from the corner market with two sacks of groceries. It was dark and drizzling rain. As he walked up the steps to his apartment building, he looked down the street and saw a familiar car in the line of parked cars. He recognized the car as the one that Jenna Kerse had pulled him out of a couple of weeks ago.

He ran upstairs and dropped off his groceries, then ran back downstairs and out the back door. He ran down the alley far enough that he could come out on the street behind Jenna. She had the seat reclined, so she was looking barely over the dash at Gabe's apartment building.

Gabe slipped up beside her door and yelled as he stuck his face in the window. Jenna jumped and yelled, "Damn! You scared the shit out of me! Don't sneak up on me like that! You're lucky I didn't knock your ass out!"

Gabe shook his head. "You're lucky you didn't try. Besides, if you don't want to be startled, quit staking out my apartment. What are you doing here anyway?"

"Just seeing what times you come and go, and seeing who you're running with. Trying to decide how I'm going to get inside your apartment so I can snoop around when you're not home. You know, the same thing that you cops do to other people."

Surprised by Jenna's lack of respect, he said, "Boy, I'll give you credit for one thing, you've got balls. Don't you know what I'd do to you if I caught you in my apartment?"

With a total lack of fear, Jenna replied, "I know what you'd try to do." She shook her head angrily at Gabe's stubbornness. "You know, I guess you're just going to have to learn the hard way who the boss is. I was hoping that you'd come around and accept the fact that I'm a better man than you are, but I guess I'm going to have to kick your ass up between your shoulder blades to convince you."

Gabe was hesitant to push Jenna's anger button. He knew what she was capable of. He wanted to back away gracefully, but she wouldn't let him. His ego also wouldn't let him be intimidated. "Yeah, I guess that's just what you're going to have to do. So! How are you going to do it? You going to wait till I'm not looking? You going to wait till a car hits me, then jump on when I'm down? You going to get some goons to hold me down for you? What's it going to be? You've got to have a plan of some kind. I know you won't take me on man to man. That's not your style. That's how you whipped every man you ever fought. You surprised them and they underestimated you. You couldn't fight your way through a spider web without some help."

He studied Jenna to gauge her reaction. He fully expected her to climb out of her car and take him on right there under the street light. The more he thought about it, the more convinced he was that Jenna knew who had killed Wilcox. The sooner he could get her to assault him, the sooner he could arrest her and try to pressure her into rolling over on the killer.

Jenna wouldn't bite. He was impressed with her restraint. She was not as volatile as the night that she'd pulled him out of the car. She sat quietly with no response. She was also completely without fear. Gabe tried one last prod. "I didn't think so. I thought you were all talk."

She glared at him fearlessly. "Oh, I'm not all talk. I'm still trying to finesse you into bed, but make no mistake, if you don't come to your senses, I'll give up on sex. When that happens, you're going to find out just how much talk I really am. I've decided that you're either going to be my toy or you're going to be a little girl for the rest of your life. When I'm done with you, you won't ever be able to please another woman."

Gabe wondered if he'd pushed her too far. She was not just a man-hating lesbian trying to establish her masculinity. She was a vicious, evil malignancy that would not go away. She was capable of anything including murder.

He asked, "So, tell me something. Do you go through life terrorizing everyone into doing what you want? Don't you know how to walk away from something and let go of the bitterness?"

"No, I'll never let anyone use me and get away with it. You used me. You made me think that you wanted me. You let me know that you were available, then screwed with my mind when I made the first move. Now you're going to pay for it. You don't know me. I'm not like anyone that you've ever met. When I make my mind up to get even with someone, nothing in the world can stop me. I'm not afraid of your tin badge. I'm not afraid of your little popgun. I'm not afraid of jail. Nothing you can do is going to scare me off. I'm going to watch you like a hawk. I'm going to bust up your girlfriends so they'll never come near you again. I'm going to ruin your life, and you'll never ever get rid of me. So, it doesn't matter if you get lucky and whip my ass the first time. There'll be a next time. If I can't handle you in a fair fight, I'll knock your ass out with a club. I'll knock you out and cut your nuts off while you're sleeping. You've screwed up, little boy. You've got me obsessed with either having you for my toy or ruining your life. The choice is yours, and frankly, I'm just pissed enough that I don't care which."

She sat her seat up straight and started her car. She put it in drive and looked Gabe in the eye. "I'm yours, lover, for better or worse. Take the better. You won't survive the worse."

Gabe stood on the curb and stared as Jenna drove away. What had he done? He now realized that he had incurred the wrath of the worst stalker that he'd ever heard of. He knew he would soon have to kill her. He'd never killed anyone before, but he would somehow find the courage to do it. She was not going to put him in the morgue.

That night, Gabe decided that it was time to make another visit to Dr. Loar's office. He had to time his visits perfectly. The midnight officers were accustomed to him jogging around town after he got to work. They knew he did his weight workout after that. They also expected him to go to lunch with them about three. Loar would likely be in her apartment every night before three, so he had to get in between 9:30 and 10:30.

He gave himself one more advantage. He ran Loar though the computer and accessed her vehicle registration information through the state department of revenue. If he found her car in the underground parking garage of her office building, he would know she was home.

He intentionally delayed his run this night until after lunch with Angus and Sgt. Shelley. He began his run about 4:00 and ran directly to Dr. Loar's office building. He ran to the garage and ducked under the automatic barrier. He jogged up and down the rows of cars. When he came to the reserved parking spaces, he found what he was looking for. A space with a sign that read *Reserved for Dr. Loar* and a white BMW parked in it. The mission this night was scrubbed.

The next night, Gabe tried another entry. Machka had delivered an office-door key, and Gabe was ready to download Loar's medical files. He again jogged to Dr. Loar's office building and through the garage. He was in luck. Loar's car was not in its reserved parking space. He checked his watch and saw that it was 9:15. Dr. Loar was still out for the evening.

He walked to the door, hoping that his earlier assessment that all exterior doors were keyed the same was correct. It was. The key worked flawlessly.

He stopped at the ground floor and looked for the guard. He heard the television, but the guard wasn't in sight. He was making rounds.

He closed the stairwell door and leaned against the wall. Should he go on up to the 12th floor or wait till the guard returned. He didn't want to meet the guard in the stairwell, but he hated to wait till the guard had finished his rounds. He didn't know how long it would take the guard to check every door in the building. He pulled his ski mask down over his face.

As risky as it was, he stepped quietly, relying on the echo effect in the stairwell to alert him if the guard approached. He stepped out of the stairwell on the 12th floor and breathed a sigh of relief. He listened for a minute to make sure the guard wasn't on the 12th floor. Machka said the guard never leaves the ground floor, but Gabe wasn't taking any chances.

He peered through the vertical window beside Dr. Loar's office door and saw no movement. It was safe to go inside. The office-door key worked perfectly.

There was only a thirty second delay in the alarm system, so he planned his movements carefully. He noted the position of the sweep second hand on his watch and opened the door. Before stepping inside, he shined his light along the walls to find the motion detectors. He saw only one. It was located close to the door, and he couldn't approach the security panel without tripping the motion detector unless he closed the door first.

Gabe opened the door just far enough to squeeze in. He closed it and hugged the wall to make sure that he didn't break the beam. He closed the door and quickly looked behind it to the alarm panel.

He quickly punched 1218 on the keypad and pushed the *Off* button. The activation lights immediately went out, indicating that the system was off. He checked his watch. Ten seconds to spare.

He shined his light along the walls high and low all the way to Loar's apartment door. He saw no more motion detectors, so he hurried to her apartment door and listened. No music. He was in luck. He didn't think she was home since her car was gone, but he wasn't taking anything for granted.

Not knowing when Dr. Loar would return, he quickly grew nervous. He hurried to her computer and immediately examined the chair where the receptionist worked. He memorized its position and sat down.

After turning on the computer, he opened the *Word* program and clicked on *File*. As promised by Machka, there was the list of most recently opened files at the bottom of the option menu.

Disappointment hit. He suddenly realized that he'd forgotten to bring a pen and paper to copy down the recall list. He looked around and found a note pad used by the receptionist. On her desk was a cup of pens used by patients to fill out medical forms. He grabbed one and carefully wrote down the list. He put the pen back in the cup and went to work.

He closed out the *Word* program, clicked on the *My Computer* icon and opened the *C* drive. There he found a long list of patients' names. He inserted his disc in the disc drive and pushed *Control* and *A*. When all the patient files highlighted, he saved them to the disc. He closed them, then opened the *Word* program and looked at his notes. He accessed the *C* drive and began opening and closing the files on his list until he'd reached the top file. With the recall list restored, he shut down the computer and put the disc in his pocket.

He couldn't resist the temptation to take a look at Loar's living quarters. He approached the door and listened. He turned the knob and found the door open. He shined his light around the walls, searching for motion detectors. Finding none, he stepped in and found the opulence of a royal palace.

He walked slowly around the edge of the living room, shaking his head at the leather furniture, plush carpet and expensive art on the walls. He thought of his own apartment and chuckled at the contrast.

Loar's bedroom was even more luxurious. There was a marble and gold headboard and mirrors on the ceiling. He again

243

smiled and wondered who the lucky man was who watched himself perform in those mirrors.

Loar's large, walk-in closet was immaculate, as was the rest of the apartment. Every suit of clothes hung on wooden hangers. Shoes were lined up neatly on a shelf below. The shelf above contained other accessories.

At the end of the closet was a metal locker. Gabe opened it and saw shelves of videotapes and large manila envelopes. He opened one of the envelopes and gasped. It contained autopsy and crime scene photos of the Dutch Windsor murder.

He quickly put them back and opened another envelope. It contained autopsy and crime scene photos of the Tim Allis murder. He recognized both sets of photos because he'd seen the same photos in the dead files. They even had the department's evidence stamp on the back.

He stepped back in shock. He looked at the videotapes and wondered what they contained. He would not rest until he'd viewed them. Time was running out though. An internal alarm rang loudly in his ear. Loar could come home at any minute and he'd be trapped. He wanted to grab the tapes and run, but Loar would miss them immediately. Machka's words rang loud in his head. *Leave everything exactly as you found it.*

Gabe knew he had to find a way to remove the tapes, copy them and return them without alerting Loar. The only way was to replace the tapes with blank tapes that had the same labels, and hope that Loar wouldn't view them before he could return the originals.

He removed one of the tapes and examined the label carefully. The tapes were 3M with 3M labels. The labels were marked with a thin, black, felt-tipped marker. He committed the label to memory, closed the cabinet door and made a hasty retreat.

On the way out of the office area, Gabe surveyed the receptionist's desk one more time to make sure that he hadn't forgotten anything. Satisfied that everything was exactly as he'd found it, he hurried to the door.

He stopped suddenly as something caught his eye. It was Dr. Loar's appointment book. He opened it and thumbed through the pages. He stopped at the Monday after next. The entry read, *Dr. Loar-Vacation-Caribbean*. Beside the entry were a confirmation number and the phone number of the hotel where she would be staying.

Gabe was elated to find a line drawn through the entire week indicating that Dr. Loar would be in the Caribbean all that week. That would be the perfect time to copy her tapes. Five nights of free access to her apartment was more than he had hoped for. His only worry now was the security guard, but he wasn't much of a threat.

Cautiously, he hurried toward the door, but stopped in his tracks. He backed up to the receptionist's desk and ripped the top sheet from the note pad where he'd written the computer's recall list. He put the list in the pocket with the disc and moved toward the door.

Once he'd punched 1218, then *On,* he opened the door wide enough to squeeze out and locked the door. Just as he turned the key, he heard a loud ping. He spun toward the elevator and saw the number 12 glowing in the dark. He raced to the stairwell door and jerked it open. He jumped though just as the elevator door slid open.

Gabe watched through the cracked door to see who exited the elevator. Stark fear overwhelmed him as Dr. Loar exited and walked toward her door. His heart pounded so hard in his chest that he was sure she would hear it.

Loar stepped off the elevator with her fur coat over her arm. She stepped casually to her door and inserted her key. She stopped before going in and turned back toward the elevator. She stood silently for a few seconds, then turned toward the stairwell door. She sensed a presence.

There was an abnormal air movement in the hall, like someone had moved quickly down the hall. The air was always still on the 12th floor at this time of night, and the night security officer never came up to this floor.

Sensing that he was about to be caught, Gabe quickly descended the stairs to the ground floor. He peered in the lobby and saw no guard. He exited the stairwell door, looked around the corner and saw the guard watching television. He walked quietly to the alley door and unlocked it with the key. Once outside, he locked the door and jogged back to the police station.

Dr. Loar stepped softly to the stairwell and quietly opened the door. She stuck her head in and listened. The echo effect in the stairwell intensified every sound.

A couple of floors down, she heard the rustling of fabric. Someone was rapidly descending the stairs. It could be the guard, but she discounted that possibility. He was fat and out of shape. He never got in a hurry to go anywhere.

She stepped back from the stairwell and inhaled a deep breath. She closed her eyes as she analyzed the scent. She slowly walked to her door, pondering the possibilities. As she reached her door, she broke her stoic stone face with a subtle smiled and stepped inside.

Gabe slammed his office door behind him and leaned against it to catch his breath. He'd set his pace too fast on the return run and had lost his rhythm.

He removed the disc, keys and recall list from his pocket and shed his jacket. He collapsed in his chair and nervously ran his fingers through his hair. He'd almost gotten caught.

His hands trembled and his mouth was like cotton. Machka's words echoed in his head. *You're going to get caught. You're not good enough.*

He curled dumbbells for a half-hour to settle his nerves. He then plugged the disc into his computer and opened Dr. Loar's patient files. Tonight's close call had scared the hell out of him, but there was incriminating evidence in Dr. Loar's hidden cabinet. The photos themselves may not be incriminating, but God only knew what the videotapes would reveal.

Gabe stared at the first file, but he couldn't concentrate. His mind kept replaying his close call. He reconsidered his earlier decision. He had a week and a half to think about it. Maybe his courage would return when Loar was in the Caribbean.

Beck Eisman shoved her files into her brief case. The last minute decision of the defendant to take his attorney's advice and accept Beck's plea offer brought a quick closure to the trial. The defendant glared at her as she stepped away from the prosecutor's table. She ignored the glare and walked quickly to the door at the rear of the courtroom.

246

The defendant's family lined the aisle as she walked through the gauntlet of derogatory comments. She put her shoulder into the door and glanced to her right. The defendant's father was waiting.

She threw her weight into the door and hurried outside. Herb Winn followed. As Beck hurried toward the stairs, Winn asked, "You happy now, you little slut?"

Beck ignored Winn and kept walking. Winn hurried to catch up with her and grabbed her arm. He spun her around violently and said, "You ain't walking away from me, you little bitch! I asked you a question!"

Beck turned abruptly and glared at Winn. She jerked her arm free and tried to mask her fear. "I heard you, Winn! I don't owe you an answer! Your son got off easy, and no, I'm not happy! I'm never happy when a child molester gets off with anything less than the maximum sentence! Get your hands off me! I'm an assistant district attorney! I'll have you in front of the judge for this!"

Winn grabbed Beck's arm again and squeezed it harder as he pulled her close to him. He pushed his unshaven face to her nose and gritted his stained teeth. He'd taken a deep breath to spit out another threat when the lights went out.

Gabe couldn't get his mind off Beck and their kiss in his apartment. Ben's direct order to regain her cooperation was the only excuse he needed to contact her. He was hoping to catch her before she left court.

When he topped the stairs, he saw Beck struggling to free her arm from Winn's grip. Winn was a big man and outweighed Gabe by at least seventy pounds. That didn't matter. One of the first things that he'd learned from the old-timers on the department was that there's nothing in a cop's tool chest more useful than a good sucker-punch.

Winn was so focused on Beck that he never saw Gabe ease up beside him. Gabe drew his fist back and planted a hard slobber-knocker directly below Winn's ear. The blow sent Winn's saliva and false teeth flying across the lobby. His toupee flew straight up in the air and landed on the floor three feet away. He collapsed on his feet as if a switch in his brain had been turned off.

Gabe looked at his fist and smiled with pride. He turned to Beck and asked, "What's wrong, lady? You two couldn't agree on a price?"

Beck tried to regain control of her nerves. She wiped the tears from her eyes and shook the cramp out of her arm as she said, "I wouldn't sell it to anyone that repulsive for any price. It's pigs like him that make girls turn lesbian."

The courtroom doors opened as Winn's family poured out. Gabe said, "We better get out of here, Beck. Let me pick up my trash and we'll go. He reached behind his back and removed the handcuffs from his belt. He rolled Winn over and cuffed his hands behind his back.

Winn was waking up, so Gabe used a wristlock to generate enough pain to get Winn to jumped to his feet. Gabe escorted him down the stairs while the family followed and yelled obscenities. At the bottom of the stairs, the security officers held the family back while Gabe called an on-duty officer to transport Winn to the jail.

The disturbance dissipated after the arrest of two more family members. Gabe escorted Beck to the underground garage where her car was parked. She was still shaken from her altercation, but Gabe asked, "Listen, I know you're mad at me, but I'd appreciate it if you'd have dinner with me tonight. I really want to talk to you."

Beck sighed. "You just saved me a trip to the emergency room. I guess it's the least I can do."

He smiled and squeezed her hand. "I'm sorry he scared you. You need to start carrying a gun. A bullet through Winn's belly-button would have ended the matter."

"Oh, that'd be precious, a prosecutor gunning down a defendant's father right outside the courtroom."

"No more precious that a prosecutor getting herself killed by the defendant's father right outside the courtroom because there was no one around to help her and she couldn't defend herself."

Beck stared at Gabe for a few seconds, then conceded. "I know. Everyone else in the office has one handy. I have one, but I've convinced myself that we live in a civilized society."

"We do, Beck, but what do you think keeps it civilized? It's the nagging fear in the back of the minds of the assholes of the world that they might get their asses shot off that keeps them at bay. Peace never comes without the threat of force."

"I know. My dad tells me the same thing. He's an old Marine and barely survived Iwo Jima. I don't feel like a lecture tonight." Her anger had not dissipated, so Gabe dropped the matter. She asked, "Where to?"

He took a mental assessment of his finances. "How about pizza? I can't eat much. Maybe we could split a small."

Beck chuckled and shook her head in amazement. "Don't you ever eat anything besides garbage? You're worse than some old stray dog."

Gabe was surprised by her accusation. He stuttered as he mounted a feeble defense. "Well, yeah, sometimes."

Beck smiled at his boyish clumsiness. "Relax. It's a free country. You can eat crap if you want, but tonight we're going to eat right. How's Italian sound? I'll buy."

She had just spoken the magic words. He perked up and said, "Well, okay then, nothing but the best for my girl!" She couldn't stay mad at him long. Her heart melted as they drove out of the parking lot.

Beck and Gabe sat in a booth at the back of the restaurant. He spoke little as he inhaled his meal. She watched in amazement and said, "I like to watch a man enjoy his meal, but I don't think you had time to enjoy anything. It was in your stomach before you had a chance to taste it."

With his cheeks full of food, he looked up and mumbled, "Sorry, I don't get to eat like this very often. I love this stuff."

"It's okay. I remember those days. I was lucky that I had an understanding mother who let me drop in for Sunday dinner."

Gabe stared at her as she talked. Her bright blue eyes mesmerized him. She caught him staring and looked down at her plate. She decided to get to the point. "So! You're going to offer yourself to Loar as a sacrificial lamb."

He straightened up and snapped back to reality. He looked around to see if anyone was close enough to hear. "I wouldn't put it that way."

She leaned over the table and glared at him. "Oh yeah? Well just how would you put it, Gabe? Offering yourself as a target is insane. What good will it do for you to find out who Loar's killer is if you get killed in the process? What are you going to do, scribble us out a note on the sidewalk before you die?"

Gabe again found himself at a disadvantage trying to argue with Beck. He said, "Look, Beck, I can't deny that it's dangerous. I'm not saying that I'm going to throw caution to the wind. I'm just saying that I've tipped my hand to someone who knows Loar. I'm sure she or her strangler will come after me soon."

He leaned over the table. "Look, you said yourself that Loar will be one of the toughest killers to catch. We're not going to do it without some risk. If this were a joint effort between the police department and prosecutor's office, we'd have a task force working on her. We'd have plenty of help and none of us would be at risk. That's not going to happen. We're as much at risk from our bosses as we are from Loar. Now, I don't challenge your expertise in the courtroom. You have to show me the same respect. I know more than you about personal safety. Trust me. I can take care of myself."

Beck continued to stare at him long after he'd stopped talking. When he broke his serious expression with a mischievous, child-like grin, she gave up. She leaned back in her chair and shook her head in frustration.

She realized now just what it was about him that she liked so much. He was a boy trying to do a man's job. He was tough when he had to be, but his boyish charm was impossible to resist. The dramatic contrast in his personalities fascinated her. She said, "Okay, I can't stop you anyway. I suppose Ben Hire sent you to get me back on board?" She studied his face carefully, hoping he wanted to see her for more than that.

"Yeah, he did, but I really wanted to see you again. I haven't forgotten your last visit. I hope that kiss meant something to you. It did to me."

"It did, Gabe, but I want you to understand something. I have to keep my personal life separate from my professional life. That was personal. As much as I like you, I'm not going to throw my career away for you. If I mean anything to you, don't put me in that position."

"I won't. Listen, you can't come to my apartment anymore. I've pissed off one of the local psychos, Jenna Kerse."

"I've heard of her. We've had her in court for assault on numerous occasions. She's bad news."

"I know. I found that out too late. I was leading her along, trying to find out who killed Wilcox, but I wound up getting in a testosterone contest with her. She's made a project out of me. She's watching my apartment and swears that she's going to ruin my life. I wouldn't want her to know that I'm seeing you. I don't want her after you, too."

"Neither would I. She frightens me, Gabe. She's capable of anything. The older she gets, the more violent she becomes. I think it's time to dig my pistol out of my underwear drawer. She'd go through me like a buzz saw."

Gabe felt bad about alarming Beck. "Sorry, I didn't realize that she was so nuts when I began sparring with her. I hope this doesn't mean that you're going to avoid me."

"I don't think I'll do that. We'll just have to be careful. Let's just not let her see us together. And listen, you need to start documenting your encounters with her. If we can show a pattern of harassment and intimidation, we might be able to hang a stalking charge on her. We can at least get a restraining order against her. That might not be a deterrent to her, but we need to try."

After a half-hour of small talk, Beck paid the bill and drove Gabe home. She stopped a block from his apartment building in case Jenna Kerse was watching. She pulled to the curb, put the car in park and turned off the lights.

A bone-chilling drizzle shrouded the city in mist and fog. In a few seconds, the windshield was covered with water. Both figures inside were obscured beyond recognition.

Gabe knew he should simply thank Beck for dinner and leave, but he wanted more. He sighed deeply. "I should go, but I don't want to. I don't suppose I could talk you into taking me to your apartment."

Beck looked down and replied, "I'd like that, but it's too soon. I got in a hurry once a long time ago and it was a disaster. I swore that I'd take these things slow from then on. It's not you. I don't want to make any more mistakes like that one."

He patted her on the leg. "Same here, slow is fine with me." He reached to open his door when Beck trapped his hand on her leg. She leaned over and encircled his neck with her hand to

251

pull him close. He fell into her and put his arm around her waist. He pulled her close as they kissed deeply. His memories of their first kiss came rushing back as he savored every sensation.

Again, their passion consumed them. Within seconds, they were grinding their torsos against each other. The windows quickly fogged up and their view of the outside world was completely obscured. To them, the rest of the world ceased to exist and they were the only two people alive.

She climbed over the console and straddled Gabe's lap. She fought the temptation to tell him that she'd fallen in love with him. She didn't want him to have that much power over her yet.

As they kissed harder, he found his hands uncontrollably probing the openings in her clothing. His hand found its way under her shirt. He lost all touch with reality when he found her breasts. She put her hand over his and pressed it hard against her breast, encouraging him onward.

He broke their kiss and looked up at the roof of the car as she hungrily sucked on his neck. He pulled his hand out of her shirt and said, "Beck, listen, we can't do this here."

After a long period of heavy breathing, she regained her composure and pulled her shirt down. She climbed back over the console and adjusted her clothes. He hoped she would start the engine and drive him to her apartment.

He sighed with relief when she started the engine. He thought what a wonderful night this was going to be. She said, "Thanks for stopping, Gabe. I respect you for that. Have a nice night and call me?"

Gabe looked at her in disbelief for a second, then nodded his head. Not wanting to embarrass himself, he acted as though he'd planned it this way. "Sure, I want it to be right for both of us."

He opened the door and stepped out. She drove off after he'd closed the door. He walked toward his apartment, hoping he didn't pass anyone. He was sure his arousal was conspicuous from any angle.

Gabe spent most of the night staring at the ceiling, listening to the rain and thinking about Beck. She was a welcomed relief. He hoped she would never find out about his entry into Loar's office. He didn't want to lose her respect. He certainly didn't want to be prosecuted by her. She was tough. The thought of being prosecuted by Beck Eisman scared him to death. His close call with Loar should be a learning experience. There should be no more late night burglaries.

He stuffed a pillow between his legs, rolled over and reminisced about Beck's body. He wondered what had ever attracted him to his ex-wife. He couldn't remember ever feeling this way about her. He wondered if he ever really loved her at all.

12

JIMMY CLOSSAN GLARED hatefully at the jailer who was shoving his personal property through the slot in the protective screen. His one-year sentence in the Marion County Jail had concluded and he was receiving the property that he'd deposited the first day.

The jailer checked each piece off of the property report as he pushed it through the slot. When he'd finished, he shoved the property report through the slot and said, "Sign here, Clossan."

Clossan glared at him as he scooped up his property and turned to leave without signing. He stepped to the exit door and waited for the jailer to push the electronic lock button to unlock the door. He stood quietly for a minute, then looked back to the jailer. The jailer was shaking his head. "No signature, no release."

Clossan turned in frustration and stormed back to the screen. He put his property down and picked up the pen. He scribbled something unintelligible on the paper, gathered up his property and walked back to the door. When the electric lock released, he barged through and resumed his place in society. His first order of business was to see Dr. Loar. His second was to see the person responsible for putting him in jail.

Maura Loar was dictating notes when her secretary rushed in. Dr. Loar showed no emotion as she asked, "Yes, Beth, what is it, dear?"

Beth was frightened as she approached Dr. Loar's desk. "Dr. Loar, I'm so sorry to bother you, but there's a man at the desk who insists on seeing you. He's angry and won't make an appointment. His name is Jimmy Clossan."

Dr. Loar laid her microphone down and turned the Dictaphone machine off. She stared out the window for a few seconds and never looked at Beth. She said calmly, "Show him in, Beth. Please close the door behind you."

Beth nodded and returned to her desk. A few seconds later, she returned with Clossan. He glared at Beth as she made a hasty retreat and closed the door.

Dr. Loar walked up to Clossan and looked deep into his eyes. His rage was apparent and he had a twitch in his left eye. Without the slightest facial expression, Dr. Loar put her arms around Clossan's neck and pulled him close. Clossan dropped his bag and wrapped his arms around her waist. He buried his face in her hair and inhaled her intoxicating scent. Dr. Loar said, "Oh, James, I've missed you so much. My life has been so empty without you."

Clossan broke into tears and clung tightly to her. He finally regained his composure and said, "I've missed you, too, Maura. I'm in bad shape. Those damned guards wouldn't give me my medications. They kept telling me that you hadn't written the scripts, but I knew they were lying. I knew you wouldn't leave me in jail without my meds."

Dr. Loar broke their embrace and led Clossan by the hand to a chair. "Sit down, James." She pulled a chair up directly across from him and sat. "Now, James, we'll start your sessions right away. I'll write you a script for some Lithium. We'll get your mood swings stabilized and you'll be as good as new."

Clossan wiped the tears from his eyes and nodded. "I've been so pissed off this last year. I've tried to control myself so I wouldn't get any more charges filed against me that would prolong my sentence, but I've had a gut-full of this system. I especially hate that asshole cop who put me in jail. He lied his ass off in court and cost me a year of my life."

Dr. Loar still showed no emotion as she said, "Yes, I know, James. How tragic. You should never have been incarcerated. You should have been placed in a hospital. This whole unfortunate incident wasn't your fault. I tried to convince the court that you shouldn't be incarcerated, but they wouldn't listen."

Clossan nodded adamantly. "I knew it! I knew it! They said you never spoke to the judge, but I knew better! They all lied! They're all against me! I'll kill them all!"

Dr. Loar calmly studied Clossan as he raged. When he'd stopped, she seized the opportunity to direct Clossan's rage toward the officer. "So tell me, dear James, which one of Robert Garrison's finest was it that told all those horrible lies about you?"

Clossan again turned red with anger as he spit out the name through gritted teeth. "It was that asshole, Blauw! Angus Blauw! I'll never forget him! I've made a point to stay in good shape this last year. He's a broken-down old man. I'll catch him when he least expects it and send him to hell where he belongs!"

He then looked at Dr. Loar with inquiring eyes. "Am I right to hate Blauw, Maura? Should I go after him or let him get away with ruining my life? I want to kill him so bad, but I don't want to lose you again. What should I do?"

Dr. Loar studied Clossan's eyes. She then replied in a soft voice, "James, my darling, I don't ever want to be separated from you again either. Just the other day, Robert was telling me what an evil person Blauw is. He's the most corrupt officer on the department. He's still working his evil devices on other innocent people, just as he did to you. He should be stopped, James, but I can't in good faith recommend you do anything that will cause you any further harm. I only wish I could do more. He's been a terrible problem for me, too."

Clossan perked up and glared at Dr. Loar. He interrupted her, "Problem? What problem?"

Dr. Loar shook her head. "No, James, I can't burden you with my problems. You've been through so much already. I'll work it out."

Clossan stood and towered over Loar. He firmly seized her by her arms and lifted her to her feet. He looked into her eyes and ordered, "Tell me! What has he done?"

Dr. Loar feigned fear. "Well, I'm sorry to have to tell you this, James, but he's been stalking me. He's been trying to coerce me into bed. I've refused because I'm frightened of him and I've been waiting for you to come back to me. As a matter of fact, he told me that if I didn't go to bed with him, he would falsify charges against me, just as he did against you. He says that he's going to put me in jail. I'm afraid that might happen very soon. I may not have time to see you or start you on the medications that you need."

Dr. Loar gauged Clossan's response then continued. "I don't know what has obsessed him about me, James. I suspect that he broke into my office a few years ago, but I could never prove it. I think he wanted to rape me, but I wasn't home. He must have decided to falsify charges against you to get you out of my life. Once you were in jail, he then felt safe taking me away from you. I'm so sorry, James. I wish people like him didn't exist. I wish there was some way to simply make them disappear."

Clossan quivered with anger. He slowly released Loar and stepped to her window. He stared into the rain as he pondered his options. He slowly turned and growled, "There is! He'll never do anything to you again!"

Dr. Loar again feigned relief. She sighed and smiled. "Thank you, James. I don't want you to get in trouble, but I feel safer knowing that you're here. You do what you think is best. I know you'll do the right thing. I only hope we have enough time to renew our love for each other."

Clossan rushed to her and seized her shoulders. "Maura, I've got to have you! I've thought of nothing else for the last year! Reliving our lovemaking sessions was the only thing that kept me alive!"

She put her hands on his chest to stop his advance, then said apathetically, "Oh, James, I live for that, too, but Beth is in the next room. You know I could never make love to you quietly. She'll know what we're doing. We simply can't right now. You must go home to your mother, and I'll schedule an appointment to start your sessions. I promise you, dear, we'll be lovers again very soon. As soon as that awful policeman is out of our lives, we'll both be able to relax and enjoy each other."

Dr. Loar circled her arms around his neck and kissed him deeply. He had no self-control and forced her to break the kiss before he became unmanageable. He growled, "I hate that woman. I know she's my mother, but I hate her. That was the only good thing about prison. I got to be away from her. Can't I stay with you, Maura? Please?"

Dr. Loar simply shook her head as she led him to the door. She instructed Beth, "Beth, dear, please schedule James an appointment next week. We're going to start sessions at once." Without looking at Clossan, she turned and dismissed him. "So good to see you, James. I look forward to seeing you again."

She gently closed the door and walked back to her desk. Unconcerned about Clossan, she picked up her microphone, turned on the Dictaphone machine and resumed dictation.

Beth entered Dr. Loar's office after Clossan had left. She approached nervously and asked, "Dr. Loar, I'm so sorry to bother you again, but did you want to start Mr. Clossan on medication right away? He seems very angry today."

Dr. Loar stopped and stared into the rain as she thought. In a detached tone, she replied, "No, dear, not just yet. Poor Mr. Clossan has a mission to accomplish first. He'll need every ounce of anger that he can muster to accomplish it. We'll deal with his medical needs later."

Dr. Loar sensed Beth's confusion in her conspicuous silence. "You don't agree, dear. Trust me. Poor Mr. Clossan has some issues to resolve before I can help him."

"I couldn't help overhearing your conversation with him, Doctor. He seems to have a great deal of animosity toward Officer Blauw. Did Officer Blauw really falsify charges against him?"

Dr. Loar stood and walked slowly to Beth. "No, dear, he didn't. Mr. Clossan is delusional. Part of his problem is his inability to accept responsibility for his own actions. He's a paranoid schizophrenic with manic-depression, obsessive-compulsive disorder and an inability to make rational decisions. He's impulsive and volatile. He all too frequently reacts out of emotion rather than a rational thought process. We might be able to stabilize his mood swings later, but let's see how he deals with his dilemma with Officer Blauw. I can't determine the appropriate medication and dosage without knowing the depths and frequency of his mood swings. I also have to evaluate his emotional response to conflict and his propensity for violence."

Beth again looked puzzled. "But, Doctor, aren't you afraid one of them might get hurt? Shouldn't you warn Chief Garrison about Mr. Clossan's threats?"

Loar slid her fingers through Beth's hair and caressed the back of her head. "No, not at this point, dear. Officer Blauw is a trained professional. I'm sure he's entirely capable of dealing with Mr. Clossan. Mr. Clossan might succeed in getting himself arrested, but I don't believe anyone will get hurt, not seriously anyway."

"You don't care for Officer Blauw, do you, Doctor?"

Loar thought for a second, then answered without emotion, "I must admit, dear, Officer Blauw is a crude, abrasive man. My dealings with him have been most unpleasant and I find him to be foul-mouthed, completely unscrupulous and violently offensive. And yes, I do believe he entered this office illegally a few years ago, but I don't wish him any harm. Please don't concern yourself with Officer Blauw's safety. If I thought Mr. Clossan was capable of injuring him, I would call Robert immediately. Keep in mind, dear, my hands are tied in this matter. I do have a doctor-patient confidentiality to maintain. I can't help Mr. Clossan if he believes that I've violated the trust that he's put in me."

Loar then pulled Beth's face to hers. She gently kissed her on the lips. Beth responded by encircling Loar's waist with her arms and returned the affection. Loar broke the kiss and turned Beth around. She escorted Beth back to the door and said, "By the way, dear, I've noticed how wonderfully that you've responded to your medications. You seem much better. The depths of your depression seem much shallower than before."

Beth nodded. "Yes, I feel much better since my divorce. My life has been less stressful since I got out from under my husband's thumb. Working for you has also been a pleasure. It does me so much good to be near you each day."

Dr. Loar patted Beth on the back and asked, "I'm glad, dear. Your ex was so abusive. He and I will have a heart to heart talk someday when the opportunity presents itself. One last thing, Beth, have you been paying attention to the recall list on the computer when you shut it down each night?"

"Why no, Doctor, I haven't. Should I?"

"Yes, dear, please make a mental note of the last files that you work on each night. When you boot-up the computer the next day, make sure those are the files listed on the recall list. I suspect that someone else has attempted entry into our office. I want to make sure that our patient files aren't tampered with."

Beth nodded and turned for one last question. "Forgive me, Doctor, but I have to ask you something. Were you really romantically involved with Mr. Clossan? He's so disgusting and you're so beautiful. You could have done so much better than him if you'd been interested in a man. It'd bother me to think of you in bed with anyone but me, but it would especially upset me to think that you were giving yourself to someone as repulsive as Mr. Clossan. That would be such a waste of a beautiful woman."

Loar approached her and put her hand against Beth's face. She looked deep into Beth's eyes and softly whispered, "No, Beth, I'm not interested in Mr. Clossan. You're absolutely right. He is repulsive. I could never have with him what I have with you. But you have to understand something, dear. Everyone has different needs. In order to help the diverse personalities that I deal with, I have to be many things to many people. That forces me to assume many different roles. The colors of my personality have to change like a chameleon. That's what makes me so successful. My patients feel a deep attachment to me because they identify with me. I help people who no one else can reach. Psychiatry is as much about meeting a patient's emotional needs as their psychological ones. Often times the two are intertwined. But rest assured, dear Beth. I cherish the love that we have for each other. I melt when you work your magic on me."

Beth smiled as Dr. Loar put her mind at ease. Her eyes watered and she became overwhelmed with affection for Loar. She kissed Loar, turned her around and led her by the arm to the sofa. She gently sat Loar down and pushed her back to a reclining position. She knelt beside her and said, "I'm so glad, Doctor. I'll get back to work in a minute, but first, I want to please you. Just relax and enjoy me."

Gabe downloaded Dr. Loar's patient files onto the hard drive of his computer and kept the disc as a backup. As he read

261

each file, he tried to keep a killer's profile in mind, hoping that someone would stand out.

As he closed each file and opened another, he grew more frustrated. The files contained nothing of value. They all read the same, merely documenting the patient's identifying information, their complaints and Dr. Loar's assessment of their condition. There were notes throughout the files containing prescription information, but nothing incriminating. It would take someone with more expertise than him to identify any wrongdoing.

He gave up in frustration after reading only a few files. His attention span grew increasingly shorter as the lack of sleep took its toll. He assessed the cause of his sleeplessness and determined that it was his obsession with Dr. Loar. She was again robbing him of sleep.

After long deliberation, he reconsidered his decision to refrain from entering Loar's apartment. As time wore on, the shock of almost being caught had diminished. The stress of his decision was compounded by the fact that he had no one to bounce the idea off of. He couldn't let any one know what he was thinking.

He studied the calendar. Five more days until Loar would leave for the Caribbean. He recalled the success of his last entry, aside from almost being caught by Loar. If his timing were better, another entry should be a breeze. He desperately wanted to see her crime scene photos again. He had to make another entry in spite of all the warnings from people around him.

Blauw, Schumacher, Ellis and Carlos screeched to a halt in front of the bar. Flying beer bottles and mugs had shattered the front window and the thunder of crashing furniture emanated from inside. Reaves turned his car sideways in the street to block traffic until order could be restored.

Schumacher grabbed Ramón and Angus as they hurried inside and said, "Remember, guys, let's stir the pot a little here. Old Shelley hasn't been thumped in months." Everyone laughed and nodded in agreement as they stormed though the door.

Reinforcements arrived as the fray spilled out into the street. Order was restored, but there were more arrests than handcuffs. The participants who were not handcuffed were frisked, seated on the curb and ordered to keep their hands on their heads.

With calm restored, Angus and Ramón paced in front of the brawlers. They explained that it was the custom of the midnight sergeant to kick everyone in the testicles before placing them in the wagon. Angus explained that the sergeant hated white people and felt that it made everyone more docile during the booking process.

The sell wasn't too difficult considering the level of intoxication and the collective brain cells seated on the curb. Three of the thugs were brothers who had grown up on a dairy farm outside of town. They were products of generations of indiscriminant breeding within the immediate family, and their gene pool had the depth of a dinner plate.

Assisting officers began to handcuff the remaining brawlers, but Angus stopped them. He pulled them aside and briefed them on the plan. Shelley arrived completely unaware of the plot.

Shelley saw that order had been restored and strolled up to the officers totally unconcerned for his personal safety. After a brief explanation of the circumstances, he casually walked up to the seated suspects to see if he recognized any of them.

As if on cue, the three brothers and two friends leaped from the curb and attacked Shelley like a pack of dogs. They overpowered him with their collective body weight and rode him to the ground.

The only part of Shelley's body visible from outside the pile was his feet. Fists were flying fast and furious and their impacts on Shelley's body sounded like a stampede of horse's hoofs.

The night crew was laughing hysterically as they pulled the suspects off of Shelley. They rendered the mob semi-conscious with batons and metal flashlights, then threw them into a pile at the curb.

Shelley staggered to his feet ready to carry on the fight. His uniform was destroyed and his eyes were open wide with rage. He heaved like an angry bull and roared at Angus, "What the hell brought that on?"

Angus wiped the laughter from his face and feigned concern for Shelley's welfare. "Sorry, Len, I don't have a clue. The crazy, inbred bastards just went nuts. I don't know why they jumped you like that. We didn't have any trouble with them. Must be something about your personality that pisses people off. Maybe you ought to go through some of that sensitivity and cultural diversity training that they're teaching out at the academy."

Shelley roared back at Angus, "Fuck you, Angus! You had something to do with this and I'm going to get to the bottom of it!" Shelley turned and glared at the rest of the officers who were choking back their laughter. They immediately began grabbing prisoners and throwing them into the wagon to avoid Shelley.

Upon arrival at the station, Shelley retired to the locker room to shower and put on a clean uniform. Ramón bounced in and opened his locker to get his shoe brush. As he brushed the dirt from his immaculately shined shoes, Shelley asked, "Okay, you shit-stirring little Cuban, who put the idea in those assholes' heads to jump me?"

Ramón broke into laughter and said, "Ah, sarge, we wouldn't screw with you if we didn't like you so much. We knew you wouldn't get hurt. We just wanted to see the surprise on your face. You were priceless, man."

Shelley tried to intimidate Ramón, but he imagined his face when he immerged from under the pile. He broke into a smile, then chuckled. "I guess I did look pretty surprised. I was just pissed that I couldn't get a good punch in on someone."

Ramón approached Shelley with a serious tone. "Listen, sarge, I want to warn you about something. I talked to one of the guards at the county jail the other day. An asshole that Blauw sent to prison just got out. He made some threats, and I wouldn't want old Angus to get hurt. I told him about it, but the senile old derelict just laughed it off. He's too stupid to be afraid. I think he's got a death wish, man."

Shelley was concerned. "Yeah, I know, son. He's got this fear of dying in a nursing home with no friends. He wants to be killed on duty rather than die of old age. I'll keep an eye on him. Thanks, and by the way, you greasy little communist, if you ever set me up like that again, I'm going to stuff your scrawny ass in a bottle and float you back to your home island."

Ramón laughed hysterically. "That's okay, sarge, just take good care of my sister and mother."

Gabe suited up for his run. He gathered his mask and gloves for another entry. He timed his arrival at Dr. Loar's office earlier than last time. He ducked under the security barrier and glanced toward Dr. Loar's parking space. Her car was gone. Surely a beautiful, single woman of her status would be occupied later than ten on a Friday night.

The stairwell door was locked. Machka's key again opened the door and Gabe made his way to the 12th floor. A quick peek through the vertical window revealed that no one was in. He repeated the delicate entry ritual and found himself alone in Loar's office.

He eased up to Dr Loar's apartment door and quietly opened it. He heard no music, so he went in. To make sure it was safe, he shined his light high and low along the walls. He wanted to make sure that there had been no new motion detectors installed since his last visit.

Finding none, he made his way to Loar's cabinet in her bedroom closet. He browsed through her crime scene photos and wrote down the case numbers on the back to compare with the dead files in his office.

Loar's videotapes intrigued him. He wanted to play one on her VCR, but he didn't want it playing if Loar came home unexpectedly. She would hear the ejection mechanism of the VCR for sure.

He carefully examined the labels. Dr. Loar's week in the Caribbean would be the ideal opportunity to copy the tapes.

He decided to leave early. His nerves were getting the best of him and he didn't want to risk another close call. He carefully replaced the photos and closed the cabinet door. He walked to the apartment door and prepared to enter the office area when he heard a sound that made his heart skip a beat.

Dr. Loar inserted her key in the door and turned it. She opened the door and did not pause this time. She sensed no unusual air movements that would alert her to an intruder. She quickly turned to the security system control panel and noticed that it was off.

Gabe frantically made his way back through Loar's apartment, desperately seeking a hiding place. With every step, he found himself moving deeper into her lair. Before he realized it, he had trapped himself in her bedroom.

With no other place to hide, he found himself at the end of Dr. Loar's walk-in closet. Panic set in as he realized that he was trapped with no escape route. He turned and stared at the entrance of the closet frozen in shock. Blauw's words screamed in his head.

He searched frantically for a place to hide. Like a trapped animal, he paced desperately. He didn't want to make any noise, but he knew he had to become invisible before Loar stepped into the closet. The door was only ten feet away. Once inside, she had only to look right and he would be face to face with her.

Paralyzing fear overwhelmed Gabe as he examined her clothes that hung on the rack. He compressed them and made room to step in. He flattened himself against the wall and pulled the suits in front of him as much as possible without creating a conspicuous protrusion in the line of perfectly hung clothes. He pulled his ski mask over his face and hoped for the best. If she sensed his presence, he would be forced to bolt from her apartment and hope that he could dodge the guard on the first floor.

Gabe pressed his left arm against his side and agonized over the conspicuous absence of his Commander .45. The anxiety was unbearable. He vowed never again to be without his .45, regardless of the mandatory jail sentence for carrying a firearm while committing a felony.

Loar opened the coat closet by the front door and carefully hung her fur on a hanger. She took the coat of her guest and hung it up also. She then escorted her guest to the bedroom where she kicked off her shoes. She backed up to her friend and raised her long hair so her guest could unzip her dress.

When her dress fell to the floor, Loar removed her slip and underwear. She pulled down the comforter and sheet on her bed, then slid in. Her guest soon joined her.

Gabe pressed himself flat against the wall and tried to slow his breathing and heartbeat. Blauw's words haunted him. His description of Loar's keen senses convinced Gabe that she could hear every breath and beat of his heart.

He was breathing too hard to breathe quietly though his nostrils and hoped Loar would not smell his breath. He thought he must be too paranoid. No one could smell that well. However, Blauw's words still haunted him and his imagination ran wild. He closed his eyes tightly and prayed frantically.

When Loar and her guest entered the bedroom, Gabe heard voices. He couldn't understand their conversation, but recognized Loar's soft, whispery voice. The man's voice, however, was not immediately recognizable. He was talking too quietly.

Gabe heard the rustling of the comforter as it fell to the floor, then heard the bodies falling on the bed. He quietly exhaled a deep sigh of relief and looked Heavenward as he thanked God. Had Loar or her gentleman friend stepped into the closet to hang up their clothing, he would have been discovered. He thanked God for the overactive hormones and impatience of Loar and her guest.

Almost immediately, he heard the sounds of foreplay. He heard kisses being exchanged and gentle moans of pleasure. This was the perfect opportunity to escape. He stepped out from between the suits and quietly rolled from heel to toe as he eased toward the doorway.

When he reached the doorway, he saw something that made his heart sink. Dr. Loar had not turned out the lights. He'd hoped the darkness would conceal his escape once the two lovers became too engrossed in each other to notice. He thought, *Why would she turn out the lights? What good are all those mirrors if it's too dark to see?*

He stood quietly and considered his options. There were none. He had no choice but to wait till Loar and her lover were so engrossed in their lovemaking that they wouldn't notice him crawl past on the floor. He had to stay low if he were going to avoid detection. He didn't know who the man was, but he didn't want to fight him. He prayed that it wasn't Chief Garrison.

As the minutes passed, Gabe mustered the courage to peek around the corner to see what position the lovers were in. He hoped Loar would be looking to the other side of the room and that her lover's face would be buried in the pillow.

Loar was on her back with her arms over her head. As frightened as Gabe was, he couldn't help but notice an obvious birthmark on the left side of her left breast. It was shaped like a small heart and was the only blemish on her perfect bronze body.

Her legs were spread wide with only a sheet covering her from the waist down. Under the sheet was the large bulk of her lover. His legs were extended off the foot of the bed and his head was between Loar's thighs. As he hungrily savored her, she closed her eyes tightly and tossed her head from side to side with pleasure.

Gabe had never seen emotion on Loar's face before. Seeing her nude convinced him that she was one of the most perfectly proportioned women that he'd ever seen. If he weren't so scared, it might have excited him.

He waited nervously, hoping the man would crawl out from under the sheet and lay with Loar. That would offer him the best opportunity to belly-crawl out. The man reached both hands over his head and caressed Loar's breasts. Gabe was impressed with his obvious size and power. Veins stood up on his hands and arms.

Within seconds, Gabe was stunned beyond belief. As the man crawled from under the sheet and covered Loar, he recognized the hulk. It wasn't a man at all. It was Jenna Kerse.

He stepped away from the doorway to catch his breath. Loar was the woman that Jenna had mentioned in their previous conversations; the woman that she was so fiercely protective of.

He again tried to slow his breathing. The heavy breathing in the next room drowned out his own, but he didn't want to take any chances. He again peered around the corner and saw the two women trading places.

Loar was now on top of Jenna. She interlaced her fingers with Jenna's and pushed her arms over her head. With Jenna's hands pinned to the bed, Loar hovered over her face while she stared into Jenna's eyes. She then lowered her breast to Jenna's mouth and moaned.

Gabe didn't know how long the session would last. His greatest fear was that once finished, Loar would sense his presence. He had to make his move before then.

His first instinct was to make a mad dash for the door. He would certainly be discovered, but he was sure he could make it out the door before Jenna would realize what was going on. Surely she wouldn't pursue him down to the lobby in the nude.

He reconsidered that option. He wouldn't make it to the alley door before the security officer would be alerted. Even if he got past the security officer, he might run into one of his friends on the midnight shift in the alley. As much as he wanted to throw caution to the wind, he had to rely on stealth.

Dropping to his knees, he eased to the doorway. When Jenna released Loar's hands, she pulled Loar down on top of her and began a long passionate kiss. It was now or never. He eased out of the closet and crawled to the foot of the bed.

He glanced up to see if there was any shift in positions. Seeing none, he crawled to the doorway. Without stopping to see if he'd been seen, he crawled into the living room. He stood and eased back to the doorway to see if he had been discovered. The doctor's therapy session continued uninterrupted.

Gabe quickly exited Loar's apartment and approached the security system control panel. He entered 1218 and pushed the *On* button. He breathed easier as he made his way down the stairwell to the first floor.

Once in the alley, he removed his mask and gloves and jogged back to his office. He had barely gotten seated at his desk when there was a knock on his door. Thinking it was Shelley or Blauw, he jerked the door open. To his surprise Ezard Lumas stood there smiling at him. "Evening, Kinnett. How's things going for you?"

Ezard casually stepped toward the door as if Gabe would fade to the side. Gabe stood his ground and blocked Lumas's entry. "Fine, Detective Lumas, what can I do for internal affairs tonight?"

Lumas stopped, surprised by Gabe's hostility. He glared angrily and said, "I've received another complaint on you. A mister Herbert Winn has filed a formal complaint against you alleging excessive force. It appears that you broke his jaw in the hall outside of court the other day while making an arrest."

Gabe replied, "He was man-handling one of the assistant D.A.'s. I arrested him for assault. Beck Eisman will verify---"

Lumas held his hand up and stopped Gabe in mid-sentence. "I don't care what Eisman says. I don't work for her, and neither do you. She doesn't dictate the police department's arrest policy. You weren't wearing a uniform. You didn't identify yourself as a police officer or warn him to release her before you blind-sided him. You took a cheap-shot on him just for the joy of it. It's excessive force to use more force than necessary to affect an arrest. At the time, you didn't know that he wouldn't have released Eisman had you only identified yourself and warned him not to resist arrest. But of course, you didn't want him to release her. If he had, you wouldn't have gotten the opportunity to blast him. See you in my office tomorrow at eleven for a statement." Lumas turned and walked back to his car.

Gabe fumed as he closed his door and stormed to his desk. Once again, Lumas had scheduled the interview in the middle of Gabe's night. Once again, he would be numb from lack of sleep. He wondered what Blauw would do in a situation like this.

He called the dispatcher and found that Angus was on duty. He asked the dispatcher to have Angus call him. Fifteen minutes later, Angus's gravely voice was swearing at him over the phone. As usual, he had an answer. It wasn't the answer that would satisfy Lumas or Garrison, but Gabe decided to try it.

He pounded out a textbook narrative statement on his computer and said that if Lumas had any further questions, he could contact Gabe at his office during his assigned hours. He went upstairs and slid the statement under Lumas's door. When he went home that morning, he turned off his phone so Garrison couldn't interrupt his sleep again.

Angus had finished hosing out the prisoner transport wagon and was letting it air out when the dispatcher called. When he responded, the dispatcher instructed him to call for information rather than put it out over a monitored frequency.

He was told that an anonymous informant wanted to give him some information about an armed robbery that was going to occur soon. He told the dispatcher to send a district officer, but was told that the informant refused to speak to anyone but him.

His suspicion peaked. It was not uncommon for officers to be set up for ambush by convicts that they'd put in jail. After a few minutes of deliberation, he decided to go since he'd recently

270

cultivated Machka as an informant, and his information would be valuable.

Shelley pulled into the lot as Angus was leaving. He pulled along side Angus and asked, "Where you going, grandpa?"

Angus shrugged his shoulders apathetically. "Oh, I gotta go meet a snitch. He wants to meet me behind the paper mill. He wouldn't give the dispatcher his name. Probably wants to rat on his poor old mother who's responsible for his life of crime."

Shelley recalled his recent conversation with Ramón. This had to be the convict who had made threats against Angus in front of the jail guard. "Listen, Angus, I wouldn't dismiss this too lightly. You might be driving into a set of crosshairs. I'm coming with you."

Angus shook his head in frustration. "Nah, you got things to do, Len. Besides, if things go sour, you'll just start screaming like a little girl and I'll have to save your big ass again. I'll be better off if I only have to worry about myself."

Shelley roared back in righteous indignation, "Why, you old drunk! How would you like this screaming little girl to drag your broken down old carcass through that window and stuff you up that exhaust pipe?"

Gabe had finished his nightly run and jogged into the lot just as Shelley was finishing his tirade. Angus was laughing loudly at how easily he'd pushed Shelley's buttons. Gabe ran between the vehicles and interrupted the chaos. "What's going on, sarge? Angus is responding to disciplinary counseling in his normal fashion, I see."

Angus continued to laugh as Shelley said, "Yeah, the old corpse thinks he's invincible. He's going to meet a snitch, and I'm going to go with him to make sure he doesn't get spanked."

Gabe perked up and asked, "Hey, sarge, mind if I ride along?" Shelley motioned for him to climb in. "Nah, kid, come on. The way Angus lets his mouth overload his ass, it'll take both of us to get him out of this alive." Gabe raced to his office and retrieved his shoulder rig and .45. He hurried back and jumped in the passenger seat of Shelley's car.

Angus turned off his lights and pulled over two blocks away from the mill entrance. Shelley did the same. Angus stepped

271

out of his wagon and walked back to Shelley. "Listen, Len, I'll drive straight in, but why don't you go around to the back entrance and come in behind that row of pallets. I'll stay close to my truck and make him come to me. If it is a set-up, he won't try anything as long as he's out in the open and I've got my truck for cover." Shelley agreed and drove around to the rear entrance.

Angus waited a few minutes to give Shelley and Kinnett time to get in position. He then notified the dispatcher that they were going in and asked her to keep the air clear of all non-emergency radio traffic in case they needed help. The request for radio silence caught the interest of the rest of the midnight crew. They quietly moved toward the mill to see what Angus was up to.

Angus drove in slowly and stuck close to a stack of logs waiting to be sawed. He sat quietly for a few minutes while he watched Shelley and Kinnett move closer, using the pallets for concealment.

Five minutes passed before he saw a shadowy figure step out from behind a trash dumpster. He walked slowly toward Angus, looking around to make sure they were alone. Angus picked up the mike and whispered, "One male walking toward me from your left. Stay low." Shelley and Gabe crouched as they ran to avoid being seen.

Jimmy Clossan burned with hatred as he walked toward Angus. He'd seen Angus step out of his wagon and psyched himself up for the confrontation. Angus was too street-savvy to catch off-guard. Clossan would have to lure him into his confidence. That wouldn't be easy. Angus was like a senile old dog. He growled at everyone and would bite you if you accidentally walked too close.

Clossan pasted on his most pretentious smile. He walked up with his hands extended out to his sides so Angus could see that he wasn't armed. He was focused on Angus and never saw Shelley and Kinnett ease up close enough behind him to overhear the conversation. He greeted Angus. "Officer Blauw, Jimmy Clossan! Nice to see you, sir, remember me?"

Angus stepped toward Clossan and snarled, "Clossan? Hell yes. How could I forget a sleazy little queer like you? When did they let your sorry ass out of jail? You finally suck enough dicks to buy your way out?"

Shelley cringed as he closed his eyes and shook his head in anger. He whispered to Gabe, "Well, so much for tact and diplomacy. If he was going to give us a tip, he sure as hell won't now."

Seeing that the civility of the conversation had dissipated like smoke, Shelley unholstered his pistol. Gabe quietly reached under his left arm and removed his .45 from its shoulder holster. His memory then kicked in. He hadn't read all of Loar's patient files, but he'd read a few.

Clossan began with C and was close to the top of Loar's alphabetical files. He'd read about Clossan. This had to be Loar's revenge for Angus breaking into her apartment. He grabbed Shelley by the arm. He leaned into Shelley's ear and whispered, "Clossan! Sarge! Jimmy Clossan was one of Dr. Loar's patients! This is a hit on Angus!"

Shelley panicked as Gabe's prompting sparked his own memory. He hadn't known that Clossan was Loar's patient, but he remembered Clossan. Knowing his capacity for violence, Shelley broke into a hard sprint to get around the end of the pallets so he could get a clear shot. Gabe was close behind, looking for a gap in the stacks of pallets to shoot through.

Clossan's smile vanished as he realized that no facade could mask his hatred. He could see in Angus's lazy eyes that the hatred was mutual. Their cards were on the table.

Angus knew that Clossan had no information for him. As they stared into each other's eyes, it became clear to both men that the whole matter would only be resolved by a contest of reflexes. Both men simultaneously went for their guns.

Shelley rounded the end of the row of pallets and saw both men drawing their weapons. He yelled, "Angus, take cover!" Shelley began firing his high capacity Beretta as he ran. Gabe found a gap in the pallets to extend his Colt through. He didn't wait to see who had the quicker reflexes. He stabilized his sight picture on Clossan's back and squeezed the trigger.

Although Angus had already broken open the thumb-snap on his holster to gain an edge, Clossan was younger and faster. Angus had barely cleared leather when Clossan jerked a nine millimeter from the back of his waistband and fired. Angus took three quick rounds in the chest.

273

The rounds knocked Angus backward and his feet left the ground. His arms extended out in front of him as he crashed to the ground with a loud grunt. He landed on the back of his head and shoulders.

Gabe began emptying the magazine in his Colt. Shelley was charging full-speed, firing his pistol and yelling at Angus. Gabe's first shot hit Clossan in the back of his left shoulder and spun him around violently.

Clossan jerked around facing Shelley. He hadn't seen Gabe concealed behind the pallets and assumed that Shelley had implanted the horrendous pain in his back. He screamed as he raised his pistol and fired at Shelley in rapid succession.

Shelley continued to fire, but his stride made it impossible to acquire a steady sight picture. As Clossan's rounds screamed past his ear, Shelley dove to a prone position and slid to a stop in the sawdust as he continued to empty his high capacity magazine.

Gabe remained calm, exercising discipline and fire control. He'd focused on his front sight and was scoring hits. Not every round hit solid, but the ones that had were taking a heavy toll. Each 230-grain hollow point from the big .45 staggered Clossan backward and raised small dust-clouds from his dingy, denim jacket. He tried to resist the blows and struggled to stay on his feet.

When Gabe's slide locked open, he was already reaching for a loaded magazine so he could continue the fight. He suddenly realized that they needed Clossan alive to testify against Loar. After dropping the empty magazine, he shoved a loaded one into the magazine well. He hit the slide release lever and the slide slammed into battery, ramming a live round into the chamber. He yelled at Shelley, "Sarge! No! We need him alive!" Shelley couldn't hear Gabe and continued to fire.

Angus regained consciousness and sat straight up. He smiled sadistically as he raised his Beretta. Gabe stared at him in disbelief and yelled to no avail, "Angus! No, don't kill him!"

Unable to hear, Angus took a sight picture on the back of Clossan's head and gave the trigger a gentle press. His .40 caliber roared, and Clossan dropped as if he'd been struck by lightening. He instantly went limp and crashed to the ground in a lifeless heap.

Gabe ran around the row of pallets and passed Shelley who was struggling to his feet. The night came alive with the distant sirens. Gabe and Shelley raced to Angus who was sitting upright. Angus laid back down on the ground and yelled as loud as he could, "Yeeeeee haaaaaah! Is this a great fucking job or what?"

Gabe tried to kneel beside Angus, but was knocked away by Shelley. He had dropped to his knees and slid to a stop at Angus's side. With tears in his eyes, he gripped Angus's uniform shirt with both hands and ripped it open like a paper sack.

Gabe leaned over Shelley's shoulder as he straightened up and sighed with relief. Angus's vest had trapped all three bullets. Aside from severely bruised ribs, Angus would live to offend again.

Infuriated by Angus's celebration, Shelley stood and walked away to regain his composure. He wiped the tears from his eyes, then turned and stormed back to Angus.

Angus was breathing deeply and wallowing in the exhilaration of the battle. "Can you believe it, Len? All this fun and we get a paycheck, too. Ain't this better than the best sex you ever had?"

Shelley bent down, grabbed Angus by the shirt and jerked him to a seated position. Angus groaned loudly and grabbed his chest. Realizing that he was hurt, Shelley released him. He knelt beside him and yelled through watery eyes and gritted teeth. "Angus, you hard-headed old son-of-a-bitch, you scared me to death! Why didn't you take cover when I told you to? Are you trying to get your dumb ass killed?"

Angus looked up at Shelley with a smile and replied calmly, "Ain't dying of old age, Len. Ain't no better way to go than in a good ass-kicking contest."

Shelley stared at him and once again realized that there was no way to best him. He shook his head and yelled, "Angus, you're going to be the death of me yet! For my sake, would you please not get yourself killed on my shift? Taking that asshole on face to face was the dumbest thing I ever saw! Wait till I'm not around if you're going to commit suicide!"

Shelley ripped open the Velcro straps that held Angus's vest in place. He then removed the front panel and saw the massive bruising around Angus's heart. He immediately grabbed his portable radio and yelled for the dispatcher to send an ambulance.

As the cavalry screeched to a halt around Angus's wagon, Gabe walked over to look at Clossan. He grabbed Clossan's shoulder and laid him out straight. His body was riddled with bullet holes, but amazingly, he was breathing. Gabe knelt beside him in disbelief and rolled him onto his side to see where Angus's round had entered his head.

Apparently Angus had been sufficiently stunned by Clossan's well-placed shots that his aim had been unstable when he'd fired. He'd aimed for Clossan's head, but had missed. The bullet had entered Clossan's neck just below the ear and slightly off-center, grazing the spinal cord.

Gabe's excitement shot though the roof. He compressed the bleeding wounds in Clossan's neck and chest. The paramedics arrived quickly and took over the first aid efforts.

Angus spent two days in the hospital. He, Shelley and Gabe were placed on routine administrative leave pending the outcome of a shooting review board. Fortunately for them, Ben Hire chaired the board, which was composed of representatives from outside agencies for the sake of objectivity.

Gabe avoided the police station during the day so he wouldn't run into Lumas. Ben anticipated that the shooting board would take three days, so Gabe had to sneak into his office late at night to read Loar's patient files.

He pulled up Jenna's file and read it carefully. She fit the classic profile of an organized serial killer. She was paranoid schizophrenic and manic depressive. Gabe had learned of her violent tendencies and anti-social personality first hand.

Realizing how protective she was of Dr. Loar, he made the obvious connection. Jenna had to be the woman who'd killed Dutch Windsor and walked in front of the parking garage security camera. She was a self-defense instructor. She was physically capable of properly applying the lateral vascular neck restraint and she had a motive.

Windsor had ridiculed Loar on the air. Jenna had the temperament and propensity for violence and was a confirmed man hater. She had all the tools and motivation to kill Windsor.

Gabe wondered how long she had stalked Windsor before she'd found the opportunity to kill him. He wondered how long it would take her to make a move on him.

If Jenna had killed Windsor, then logically, she had to have killed Nat Benson and Roger Moesen. They were all killed the same way. The connection wasn't hard to make. Benson had been a patient of Loar's. After Benson had killed Dr. Sabre, Jenna had obviously killed Benson to keep her from implicating Loar. Jenna had also killed Moesen to keep him quiet about Loar's plot to kill Tim Allis.

With each encounter, Jenna Kerse had become more frightening. Gabe had seriously underestimated her earlier. She was a serious psychopath, and he had to be very careful. For the first time, he seriously doubted his ability to handle her.

Ben called Gabe in for his interview. Unlike Ezard Lumas, Ben had scheduled the interview at Gabe's convenience. Gabe wasn't at all nervous. He trusted Ben implicitly. After he'd given his statement, he visited with Ben about the Loar case.

The theory about Kerse seemed plausible to Ben. When asked how he'd learned of the relationship between Kerse and Loar, Gabe shrugged his shoulders and chalked it up to good police-work. He couldn't confide to Ben that he'd witnessed their affection for each other first hand.

Ben didn't want to pry. The less he knew about Gabe's activities, the better he felt. He agreed that they needed to hang a charge on Kerse as soon as possible to flip her. Both agreed that that would probably be fruitless. She wasn't afraid of jail and certainly wouldn't betray Loar over a simple city-ordinance violation or even a misdemeanor.

A search warrant for Jenna's apartment seemed the next logical step. There were fibers from the killer's coat under Windsor's fingernails. If those fibers matched a coat in Jenna's apartment, they might have grounds for an arrest.

A conviction would be a stretch, however. Putting Jenna's coat at the scene wouldn't put Jenna in the coat. It would only be one circumstantial nail in her coffin.

The most promising news was that Angus's bullet had missed Clossan's brain stem. The bullet had ricocheted off Clossan's spinal cord and had paralyzed him from the neck down.

The doctors were keeping him in a drug-induced coma for a while. He was critical, but they thought he would survive long enough to talk if they could stave off infection.

Ben stayed abreast of Clossan's condition. He would interview him at the first opportunity. He was sure that Loar had put Clossan up to killing Angus and hoped Clossan would roll over on her.

If Clossan were to live long enough to implicate Loar, it was imperative that all the bases were covered. He spoke with Clossan's doctor and the director of security. Knowing that Loar would not allow Clossan to implicate her in the attack, Ben was sure that she would kill Clossan to save herself.

He normally would have tried the conventional means of catching a killer by staking Clossan out and arresting Loar when she made her move on him, but Loar was not conventional. She would have someone else kill him. Without knowing who that person was, a stakeout would be too time consuming and probably fruitless. Loar would simply wait until the stakeout crew gave up, then kill Clossan when he was unprotected.

Clossan's doctor left explicit orders that no one was to visit Clossan without his personal approval. The nurses had direct orders to call security immediately as soon as anyone asked to see him. They kept him in a secluded room and moved him periodically. His name was omitted from the patient registry at the information desk.

The shooting review board wrapped up their investigation and made their recommendation to the chief. All three officers were exonerated in the shooting of Clossan.

Shelley had re-injured his hernia when he proned out on the ground to avoid Clossan's gunfire, but went back to work. Angus remained on injury leave a few more days. His bruises had healed, but he enjoyed the time off. The shooting was a perfect opportunity to milk workman's comp for more injury days.

Gabe was met by Lumas in the parking lot his first night back. Lumas simply handed him a letter and walked away. The letter was a direct order to report to Garrison's office the next morning.

He waited an hour outside Garrison's office. When the secretary told him to go in, he found Garrison and Major Richey waiting. Garrison's patience was wearing thin. He no longer erected a façade of congeniality. "Don't bother to sit down, Kinnett. What's this I hear that you won't cooperate with the internal affairs investigation of the Winn complaint?"

Gabe tried to explain, but Garrison held his hand up. "Don't want to hear it, Kinnett. Don't care. Give me your commission card and badge. I'm suspending your police powers pending the outcome of the investigation. You're also ordered to remain in your hole and stay out of those squad cars. I don't want you on the street again. You had no business at the Clossan shooting."

Gabe didn't speak. He removed his badge and commission card from his wallet. He laid them on Garrison's desk and turned to leave. Garrison stopped him and said, "Kinnett! I can't suspend you without pay yet, but don't push your luck. Stay in your office. You're not a cop now. Don't be trying to use your arrest powers. You don't have any. Now! Stop off at Lumas's office and give him that statement that he asked for."

Gabe left Lumas's office thoroughly humiliated. He'd given a textbook statement, but Lumas's bias and condescending demeanor was more than he could stomach. He went back to his apartment and vented.

He walked up to the window and stared out across the city. As he pondered his future, he caught sight of a familiar car. Jenna was parked on the street down the block. She was watching his apartment again.

Anger burned in his gut. He wanted to go down and drag her out of her car, but knew that would only generate another excessive force complaint. He was no longer a policeman and couldn't even carry his pistol legally. It didn't matter though. He would be a criminal, but he would not be without his .45.

Jenna had a boring day. Gabe laid on his sofa and pulled his blanket over his chest. He took his mind off of his anger by reminiscing about his last meeting with Beck Eisman. He decided to sleep for a couple of hours, then call her when she got off work.

Beck wasn't home, so Gabe left a message. He felt awkward, but he wanted to see her again. He hoped she would call soon.

The weekend passed slowly. Gabe wanted to see Beck, but knew he wouldn't be good company. He wanted to call her again, but chose to avoid her rather than risk alienating her with his attitude.

He ran in the evenings with Jenna Kerse following at a distance. He pretended not to see her. He knew she would only get pleasure from stalking him if she thought he was annoyed. He wasn't going to give her that pleasure.

Gabe arrived home late Sunday afternoon from the market. He looked down the street and saw Jenna's car. He wanted to confront her, but thought it unwise in his current emotional state. He didn't want Jenna to know that she was getting under his skin, but she was. He wisely chose to ignore her and went up to his apartment.

As he topped the stairs, he stopped in shock. Jenna was sitting against his door, resting her head on her knees. Gabe burned as he asked, "Your car not comfortable enough?"

She stood and brushed the dust from her seat. "My car is fine. I just wanted you to know that I'm still around."

Gabe nodded as he fumbled for his keys. "Yeah, I know. You're like a bad venereal disease, just when you think you're rid of it, it shows up again."

He was trying to annoy Jenna as she had annoyed him, but she wouldn't bite. He was amazed at her restraint considering her volatile nature. "Clever analogy, junior, but I'm a lot worse than V.D. V.D. won't kill you."

Gabe stared her in the eye and replied, "Is that a threat? Because if it is, climb your ass on. If you want me so bad, quit playing these cowardly games. Quit sneaking around in the shadows like a gutless coward. You're not going to surprise me like you've done your past victims."

Jenna could no longer mask her anger. She gritted her teeth and growled, "Oh I want you, Kinnett, I want you bad, and I'll

280

take you in my own good time. You think you're bad, but you're not. And don't count on my affection for you to save you. I don't care about you anymore. I wouldn't go to bed with you if you were the last man on Earth."

"Well, if you're not going to jump, then we have nothing to talk about. I guess I'll see you when you grow a set of balls."

Gabe opened his door and stepped inside. Jenna couldn't resist one more exchange. "Homosexuals really frighten you, don't they? You're so insecure about your own sexuality that you can't stand those of us who aren't. It's really funny to watch you macho, straight guys cringe in fear when you meet someone like me. I'm glad you're afraid of me. It's going to make it more fun when I show you how queer you really are."

Gabe sat the groceries down inside his door. He turned back toward Jenna and laughed. He shook his head in disgust and said, "You know, you queers are the frightened ones. You're so afraid to admit the truth about your moral degeneracy that you'll do anything to find legitimacy. You throw up all kinds of facades. You form all kinds of support groups and go on all the talk shows. You applaud each other for your courage and try to convince the world that you're just one more poor, oppressed minority, but you're not. You're just a bunch of perverts. Your position isn't defensible, so you attack straight people personally. Let me educate you about this. Straight people aren't afraid of homosexuals. We're just disgusted. There's a difference between homophobia and homonausea. You don't scare us; you make us sick. We react to you as we do to anything that makes us sick. That emotion you queers mistakenly call fear is really repulsion. No, Jenna, I'm not afraid of you. You're just disgusting and revolting. This isn't fear that I'm feeling. It's the same disgust I have for all deviants. I look at rapists and child molesters the same way, so don't flatter yourself. You don't scare me one bit. Now! Unless you're ready to make me scream like a girl, you'd better leave. You may not be ready to show your balls, but I am. If you're not ready to dance, you better leave the stage."

Jenna burned with hatred as she contemplated her choices. She was now committed more than ever to killing Gabe. She wanted more than anything to take him to the mat right there, but she wasn't sure she should yet. She wanted to talk to Maura one more time. She growled as she backed toward the stairs, "Soon! Soon!"

Gabe was putting away his groceries when the phone rang. He hurried to pick it up, hoping it was Beck. He tried to act calm, but he was still burning from his exchange with Kerse. Beck was cool and detached, which was discouraging to Gabe. "Hi, Gabe, sorry I didn't get you called back right away."

"Oh, that's okay. I really didn't expect you to call me back anyway."

"Why do you say that?"

"I get the feeling that things are going too fast."

"Maybe a little. I'd still like to get together."

He was encouraged, then remembered his shadow waiting on the street. "I'd like to Beck, but Kerse is watching my apartment. Maybe I can slip out the back door."

"Come over if you can, but be careful. I don't want her to know we're seeing each other. She's much more than I can handle."

Gabe slipped out the back door of his building and made his way to the alley. He peered around the corner and saw the back of Jenna's car. He hadn't been seen, so he hurried to Beck's apartment.

The night with Beck began slow, dinner and casual conversation at first, then an escalation of the passion from their last meeting. When they'd gone as far as they could without going to bed, she halted the tailspin just short of consummation. She sat up, breathed deeply for a few seconds, then instructed Gabe to dress and go home. He complied without protest.

As he approached the front of his apartment building, he made sure Jenna saw him. He stepped up on the landing, stretched his arms and yawned as though exhausted from a fun-filled evening. It humored him immensely to imagine Jenna's frustration when she realized that she'd wasted the evening watching an empty apartment.

13

MONDAY MORNING ROLLED around, and Gabe awoke early from the anticipation of another entry into Loar's apartment. This was the Monday that she was to leave for the Caribbean. He had to see what was on her videotapes.

He left a message for Ben to call when he returned to his office. Ben returned the call shortly after lunch. "Hey, kid, you called?"

"Yeah, Ben, do you mind if I use your video recording equipment tonight? I've got some tapes I need to copy."

Ben sighed deeply as his suspicion peaked. "Yeah, I guess. What are you---? No, never mind. I don't want to know. Just don't let Garrison catch you. The VCRs and TV are on a stand with rollers. Roll it into my office and shut the door. Leave the lights off and put things back just the way you found them."

Gabe dressed and hurried to the mall. He needed additional supplies tonight. He would soon know what was on Loar's videotapes.

Gabe jogged to the alley door of Loar's office building. He used Machka's key to enter. It was dark, as usual, and the guard was not in sight. He quickly made his way to the stairwell and ascended to the twelfth floor. He performed the entry ritual flawlessly and hurried to Loar's bedroom closet.

As he opened the cabinet, memories of his close calls haunted him. His fear rose and his heart pounded. He didn't want to go through another close call like the last one. He squeezed his left arm against his shoulder holster to calm his nerves. Feeling the bulge of his old friend under his arm was reassuring.

From his bag he removed four videotapes identical to Loar's. He'd placed the labels on the tapes at the office. He removed a black felt marker from his pocket and held his small flashlight in his mouth as he wrote.

He examined each tape carefully and reproduced the label as closely as possible to Loar's handwriting. The tapes were blank, but he would have the originals back before Loar returned. They were only a prop to fool anyone who might be checking the apartment while she was gone. Jenna Kerse immediately came to mind.

When he'd finished, he glanced around for anything interesting, but his nerves were pushing him to leave. He closed the cabinet and hurried out of Loar's apartment. As he passed the receptionist's desk, he glanced at the calendar to make sure he had a full week to review the tapes. Loar would be back in town next Saturday.

He hurried out of the building and ran back to his office. He removed his mask and gloves and went to Ben's office. He rolled the video equipment into Ben's office and began.

Gabe placed the first tape in the player and put a blank in the other VCR, which recorded from the TV. He pushed the *Play* button of one VCR and the *Record* button of the other, then sat back to enjoy the show.

The tapes were clearly recorded in Loar's apartment. He knew instantly by the background that Loar had cameras throughout the apartment. He suddenly realized that if her cameras had been rolling the night that he'd crawled out of her closet, he, too would be on tape. He was glad that he'd taken Machka's advice and worn a mask.

The first tape was video of Loar having sex with several different men. Gabe recognized one as District Attorney Baumgartan. He looked so out of place. She was so lean and striking, while Baumgartan was fat, pale and unattractive.

It was clear that this tape was blackmail material to be used when Loar needed power over politically influential people. It was obvious by the blank expression on her face that it was strictly business. She'd derived no pleasure from it at all.

Gabe didn't recognize the other men, but he was sure that Ben would. He wasn't sure how he would explain the tapes to Ben. As the first tape concluded, he wondered why Loar had not videotaped her session with Jenna Kerse. Perhaps Jenna needed no blackmailing. Perhaps Jenna's love for her and a chemical dependency was enough leverage.

He checked his watch, then inserted the second tape and another blank. The first episode shocked Gabe instantly. He watched his arch nemeses, Robert Garrison, step from the bathroom totally nude. He shook his head as he wondered why he was surprised. Loar had leverage over Garrison. Videotape of him having sex with her was a good as anything.

He waited in repulsion for Loar to enter the room and repeat her business-like ritual with Garrison. To his total shock, another girl entered and got in bed with Garrison. The girl was small and thin with reddish-blond hair. She couldn't have been older than thirteen or fourteen. She was clearly under the legal age of consent.

Gabe watched in shock as the girl nervously performed oral sex on Garrison. He rose to his feet slowly as he realized that Garrison was a pedophile. He got his thrills from having sex with very young girls.

He stood silently as Garrison laid the child on her back and opened her legs wide. He then covered her small body with his large, fat one. Gabe could no longer see the girl. With only her arms and legs sticking out from under Garrison's body, he began violent intercourse.

After about two minutes, Garrison rolled off of the girl. She climbed out of the bed and walked to the bathroom. Her face revealed no emotion. It was clear that she was a willing participant.

Garrison remained on the bed, trying to catch his breath. When the session was over, Gabe hit the *Pause* button to collect his thoughts. He had to find the girl and interview her. She had to be one of Loar's patients. Surely her identity was buried in Loar's patient files. If she were indeed as young as she appeared, he now had complete power over Garrison. Joe Rand's reminder to get ahead any way he could immediately flashed through his head.

Loar's next production interested Gabe. Her previous lovers had been unremarkable, but this man was incredibly cut. He was lean and had obviously spent some time under a weight-bar.

The man was about thirty, around six feet tall, and his bulk was magnificent. Jenna Kerse had to know this man. His most remarkable feature was not his physique, but the scars on his body. He was tattooed and pierced extensively and had scar tissue on virtually every area of his body that he could reach. The scars were evidence of his propensity for self-mutilation. His pain threshold had to be incredible. It was clear why he was a patient of Dr. Loar.

Gabe watched as Loar enjoyed herself immensely. This was only the second time that he'd ever seen genuine emotion on her face. The first was with Jenna Kerse.

This session took about thirty minutes. Loar repeatedly stopped the man just before he climaxed to prolong the pleasure. He had an evil persona, but Loar clearly directed the session. She had power over him, but Gabe could only speculate what that power was. Aside from his physical attraction for her, perhaps medication manipulation added to her power.

He wasn't the politically influential type. Gabe wondered why Loar needed to blackmail this thug. Maybe she wasn't blackmailing him at all. Maybe this videotape was just a souvenir of good sex.

The next production was particularly unnerving. The segment opened with Loar's camera filming an empty shower. It was the one next to Loar's bedroom.

A young girl stepped into the shower and soaped herself up. It appeared from her reddened face, mussed hair and sweaty skin that she had just crawled out of bed. Gabe assumed that she'd been in bed with Loar. He instantly recognized her as Nat Benson from her autopsy photos.

As Benson rinsed off, the door behind her opened. To his shock, Jenna Kerse stepped in behind Benson and encircled her waist. Jenna was nude also and pulled Benson against her. Benson had not been expecting Jenna.

It was clear by her lack of concern when the door initially opened that she had expected Loar to shower with her. When Benson realized that Jenna was her shower mate, she jumped in fright. She struggled to pull away, but Jenna easily overpowered her. Gabe surmised that Loar had had sex with Benson, then allowed Jenna to surprise her in the shower.

Jenna tried to calm Benson by stroking her hair and massaging her shoulders. Benson was clearly frightened, but stopped struggling. For a while, it appeared that she was going to respond to Jenna's manipulation.

Jenna continued to stroke and reassure Benson with a calm voice. She finally moved her massage to Benson's breasts. Benson cringed and resisted. She gently tried to remove Jenna's hands from her breasts, but Jenna would not be deterred.

When Benson became more forceful, Jenna lost her patience. She released Benson's breasts and grabbed her by the hair on the back of her head. She jerked Benson's head back and yelled at her. It was clear that Jenna was going to take what she wanted with or without Benson's consent.

Benson was unable to remain calm after Jenna's display of force. She panicked and struggled desperately to get away. She yelled for Loar, but Loar never appeared. In one fluid motion, Jenna encircled Benson's neck with her arm and applied a lateral vascular neck restraint. She applied bone-breaking pressure until Benson blacked out. She continued the pressure until Benson was dead.

Gabe watched in horror as he realized that he was watching Benson's murder. This video had to have been filmed after Benson had killed Dr. Sabre and before she went to trial. He realized now that this was how Dutch Windsor and Roger Moesen had been killed. If Loar needed blackmail material against Jenna, this was it.

Jenna eventually released Benson. She checked her pulse and determined that Benson was dead. She stood and breathed heavily as she savored the exhilaration of the kill. It was clear that she had derived immense sexual stimulation by the strangling.

She hovered over Benson's body for a minute, then opened the shower door and wrapped Benson in a towel. She picked her up and carried her out of the camera's view. Gabe was sure that

Jenna immediately carried Benson out of Loar's apartment and dumped her in the alley. When found, Benson's body was still covered with ice from the shower in Loar's apartment.

Gabe had pushed his luck as far as he dared. He would review the two remaining tapes tomorrow night. He removed the tapes and put the video equipment back where he'd gotten it. He returned to his dungeon and began combing Loar's files for anyone matching the description of Loar's tattooed lover and Garrison's underage victim.

The next night, Gabe repeated the procedure and copied the remaining tapes. The third night, he returned to Loar's apartment and put her tapes back exactly as he'd found them. He put his decoy tapes back in his sack and left Loar's apartment undisturbed.

One of the interesting episodes on the fourth tape was the Lucian Green murder. Loar's tattooed lover was videotaped meeting Green in the alley where he'd been killed. Gabe assumed that Loar was the person operating the camera.

Green had approached tattoo man cautiously. He'd kept his distance and handed tattoo man a small bag. Gabe assumed it was narcotics. Tattoo man tried to walk away without paying, but Green grabbed his arm. Tattoo man spun quickly and backhanded Green hard in the face, knocking him to the ground. Loar's lover then picked up a pipe and beat Green in the head until he was dead. His face was unrecognizable.

The brutality of the killing was revolting, but Gabe was especially shocked by the look of pleasure on tattoo man's face. His eyes were open wide and he was breathing heavily. The adrenaline rush had sent him into an intoxicated euphoria. The video stopped as tattoo man approached the car. The camera operator obviously didn't want him to know that he was being filmed.

With the tapes safely returned, Gabe settled down to his case files and tried to put names to the faces on the tapes. He also wanted to find out how Loar had gotten copies of the crime scene photos of the other murders in the dead files.

Angus finally came back to work after milking his bruised ribs as long as possible. He was met with cheers as he walked into the squad room. Shelley allowed the brief celebration, then called the meeting to order.

After the district assignments were made, everyone made their way to the parking lot for vehicle inspection. Shelley hurried to catch up with Angus. He put his arm around Angus and said, "Glad you decided to join us again. I thought you were going to milk this thing into retirement."

Angus laughed and replied proudly, "Nope, I only milked it till I ran out of Seagram's. I had to come back to work to sober up."

Shelley shook his head and smiled. "With anyone else, I'd say they were kidding, but since it's you, I know that's the truth."

Angus nodded in agreement as he laid his brief case on the truck hood. Shelley continued, "Listen, Angus, Jackie must be losing her mind, but she wants you to come to dinner for some unknown reason. I told her that you eat shit sandwiches and howl at the moon, but she assured me that that wasn't true. She said she knows first hand that you don't like bread."

A puzzled look fell over Angus's face. "Yeah. Yeah that's right, I don't eat bread, but how did Jackie know that." Shelley laughed loudly at Angus's total oblivion to insult. Character assignation was impossible with Angus Blauw.

Shelley said, "Tomorrow night. Be there at six and don't be late. Jackie hates for dinner to get cold."

Angus nodded. "Okay, Len, but I don't trust you black folks. What's up?"

Len threw his hands up. "Don't know. I learned years ago not to ask. Maybe she's just concerned about you. Who knows? I told her she was nuts to worry about an old junkyard dog like you, but she's got this need to nurture."

Angus replied, "Oh well, she's probably just wanting to stay on my good side so I'll be there with waiting arms when you get your dumb ass killed. She'll be ready for a real man by then."

Shelley finally gave up. Once again, intelligent conversation with Angus was out of the question. "I give up. Open the back doors, you old cadaver."

Angus left the lot and drove straight to Gabe's apartment. He announced himself in the usual fashion. Gabe no longer cared about the opinion of his neighbors and casually walked to the door. Without looking, he unlocked the deadbolt and yelled, "Come on in!"

Angus strolled in like an old-west sheriff, beaming with arrogance and immortality. He looked around at Gabe's décor and said, "I like what you've done with the place. Looks like my place. The early American out-house theme suits your personality. So, Kinnett, what are you doing with all your time?"

"Nothing, Angus. You're going to have to teach me how to drink. I'm bored to tears."

Angus nodded arrogantly. "You came to the right man, son. Drinking can be fun if you learn from a pro like me. Most of these fools ruin their lives because they're not an expert like me. I'll teach you right."

Gabe smiled and sat down. Angus said, "Come on, kid, ride around with me."

"Can't, Angus. If Garrison catches me in a squad car again, he'll fire me. Thanks anyway."

Angus blurted out, "Fuck Garrison. That fat, useless waste of flesh ain't going to fire anyone. Besides, I won't let him catch us."

Gabe once again gained confidence from Blauw's bravado. "Okay, Angus, just don't let anyone see me." Once in the truck, Angus headed for the projects. Gabe asked, "Where are we headed?"

Angus calmly replied, "Oh, I gotta do a drug raid before lunch. I haven't raided the projects for a few weeks. It's about time to stir up the dopers."

Gabe looked at him in shock. "Drug raid! Angus, I thought we were going to keep a low profile!"

Angus frowned at him. "Relax, you big pussy, ain't no one going to be there but us."

Gabe panicked. "Us! Just us! You mean you and me are going to pull a drug raid without an entry team? Angus, are you crazy? We can't pull a drug raid by ourselves! We don't even have a search warrant! If we don't get our asses shot off, we'll sure as hell get fired!"

Angus looked at him and shook his head in frustration. He reached over, thumped Gabe in the chest with his fist and chastised

290

him. "Boy, when are you going to learn to go along and keep your mouth shut? How can I ever teach you anything if you're going to have a nervous breakdown every time we do something risky? Now just shut up and do what I do."

Angus pulled into the parking lot of the end building. He stepped out of the truck and said, "We'll start at this end and work our way to the other. Come on, boy."

Gabe nervously removed his Colt from its shoulder holster and cracked the slide open to make sure there was a round in the chamber. He checked his pocket to make sure his reserve magazine was there.

He shook his head in disbelief as he hurried to catch up with Angus, who was strolling casually with his hands in his pockets and his pistol secured in its holster. Gabe thought this had to be a bad joke. Surely this old fossil wasn't going to kick down doors without sufficient backup or a search warrant. But then, maybe he was. Angus's suicidal quick-draw contest with Clossan made Gabe wonder.

Angus entered the first building with Gabe close behind. Gabe covered the first door with his pistol as Angus approached. He casually pounded on the door with his fist and yelled, "Police! Open the door! He put his ear against the door and listened. From inside the apartment came the unmistakable sound of the toilet flushing.

He chuckled and stepped to the next apartment. He pounded on the door and yelled, "Police! Open the door! The toilet flushed right on cue. He then moved to the next apartment.

Gabe laughed as he shook his head and holstered his pistol. Angus had never intended to enter any of the apartments. Gabe moved to the doors on the opposite side of the hall and repeated Angus's instruction. Both officers made their way throughout each building, pounding on doors and yelling the same commands. With rare exception, the flushing of toilets signaled that all drugs in the apartment were disposed of.

Occasionally, an elderly person would open the door as ordered. Angus just thanked them for their trouble and informed them that he had the wrong apartment.

When finished, they returned to the wagon laughing about their raid. Without making a single arrest or writing a report, they had taken more drugs out of the complex than the entire department could have by raiding every apartment. Besides, search warrants for every apartment would have been impossible to obtain. Angus asked, "Well, boy, did you learn anything?"

Gabe replied, "Yeah, but what are you going to do when the residents call the chief complaining that we disturbed their peace by pounding on their doors with our phony drug raid?"

Angus shrugged his shoulders. "They can't prove anything. None of the dopers opened their doors. They can't identify us. Hell, those fools don't even know for sure that we were police officers. For all they know, we could have been a couple of drunks having fun or other dopers trying to rip them off. The honest folks aren't going to complain. They're glad to see us. We never advised the dispatcher that we were here. Who can hurt us?"

Gabe shook his head in disbelief. "Angus, you're amazing. Why do you do this stuff anyway?"

"Because, kid, the system doesn't work. I told you a long time ago, sometimes you have to bend the rules. The kids in this complex deserve a better chance in life than their lousy parents are giving them. These fuckers are shooting and smoking dope right in front of their kids, and we can't touch them because we don't have a search warrant. It won't do any good to knock on the door and ask for consent to search. They're too smart for that. The only way to shake them up is to make them think that we're going to kick their door down."

Gabe thought for a minute and asked, "Yeah, but don't they get wise after the first time?"

"Nah, the drug unit executes enough search warrants in here that the stupid bastards never know if it is a legitimate raid or not. This was a good night. Sometimes there isn't a lot of drug activity in the complex and we don't hear many toilets flush. But I don't care. Even if we get half of the assholes to flush their dope, we've made a significant impact on the quality of life for the kids who have to live here."

Gabe smiled as he thought through Angus's rationale. Again he marveled at the ingenuity of Angus Blauw. Angus broke Gabe's train of thought and said, "Listen, kid, the reason I wanted to talk to you tonight is because you need to lay low for awhile.

Garrison is planning something for you, and I don't know for sure what it is. He may be getting ready to transfer you to an assignment where you can't work on Loar. He might put you in records or somewhere where you're strapped to a desk with a sergeant watching over you. He might even put you back on the road. You need to be careful. Get all your case files out of that hole you work in and take them to your apartment. Don't leave anything in there that you don't want Garrison or Richey to find. You can't trust those fuckers. Richey will do anything to protect Garrison. He's not above putting a bullet in your head. Garrison promoted Richey when he wasn't qualified to supervise a rock. Richey knows if Garrison takes a fall, a new chief will find out how incompetent he is and run his ass out of the department. Garrison also has too much dirt on Richey. He'll do anything Garrison says to keep him from turning his files over to the DA."

Gabe listened in shock. "How do you know this, Angus?"

"I've got my sources. One of the secretaries upstairs is still in love with me from the days when I used to do the dirty thing with her."

Gabe was confused. "What's the dirty thing?"

Angus was amused at Gabe. "Hide the sausage, boy. Ain't you ever played hide the sausage? You've been playing it with that young assistant D.A., ain't you?"

Gabe laughed at Blauw's colorful description. "That's good, Angus, I've never heard it put that way before. And it's none of your business who I'm doing the dirty thing with." Gabe sat quietly for a few seconds. His eyes watered slightly as he pondered his feeling for Beck. He sighed and confessed, "I love her, Angus. I love her more than anyone I've ever known. I can't get her out of my head. I don't know what I'll do if it doesn't work out."

Angus smiled. "I'm glad, kid. Every man should feel that way about a woman at least once in his life. You're a good kid. You deserve her."

"Thanks for the warning, Angus. I'll move the files right away."

Jackie Shelley hurried to the door while drying her hands with a towel. She jerked it open and found Angus standing nervously outside. "Oh, Angus, come in!"

She threw her arms around his thin, feeble frame and hugged him tightly. Her show of affection made Angus uncomfortable. He patronized her by giving her a gentle pat on the back instead of a hug.

He stepped into the living room and found Len Shelley reclined in his chair and reading the paper. "Hey, Angus, you old goat, have a seat. The women are about ready to eat."

Angus froze as he bent over to sit down. He jerked his head toward Shelley and asked, "Women? Did you say women? You mean---"

Len laughed and nodded his head. "Yep, sure do. You're being set up tonight, Mister. How's it feel to be the one who's been conspired against for a change?"

Angus glared at Shelley as he slowly stood and tried to tiptoe back to the door. He wasn't quick enough. Jackie barged into the living room with another lady in tow. She said, "Angus! I want you to meet Millie. She's the friend that I told you about."

Angus squirmed in painful discomfort. He slowly turned to face the women and was pleasantly surprised to find that Millie was a beautiful, thin woman in her mid fifties with auburn hair. He was instantly smitten.

He clumsily approached Millie and stuck out his hand. Millie seized his hand and led him to the sofa as she talked. "Oh, Angus, I'm so thrilled to meet you! Jackie has told me so much about you. I feel like we've known each other for years."

Millie became concerned and asked, "And how are you, dear Angus, you poor man! Len told me how brave you were when that man shot you. That must have been a terrifying experience! You're so brave!"

Len and Jackie eased into the kitchen as Millie continued to embarrass Angus with her raving. Len's belly bounced as he struggled to keep from laughing out loud. Angus's discomfort amused him to no end.

Dinner was uncomfortable for Angus. He searched his memory for the table manners that he'd long ago forgotten. Len smiled throughout dinner as he relished Angus's discomfort.

After dinner, Len and Angus retired to the living room while the ladies cleaned the dishes. Angus leaned into Shelley and growled quietly, "You asshole, why didn't you tell me that Millie was going to be here? I'd have worn a nicer shirt."

Len laughed sarcastically. "Angus, you lying old fool, you would not. You wouldn't even have shown up. Besides, you ain't got a nicer shirt. You need to understand something. If you're ever going to impress a woman, you've got to quit rummaging through the Salvation Army trailers for your clothes. You dress like some destitute old attorney or used car salesman."

Angus took a quick assessment of his appearance and replied with righteous indignation, "What do you mean? These are good clothes. They got lots of wear left in them."

"See, that's what I mean. You'd wear an old potato sack as long as the seams weren't ripped out. Old man, you got to quit being so cheap. Go out and get you some modern clothes. Clothes make the man. You never see a black man dressing like that. If you expect to impress Millie, you've got to quit dressing like Fred Flintstone." Len lowered his voice and whispered, "And quit that cussing, you dirty old pervert, ladies don't like to hear that."

Jackie and Millie came into the living room after the dishes had been washed. Millie walked directly to the coat closet and retrieved hers and Angus's coats. She said, "Jackie, thanks so much for dinner and introducing me to this dear, sweet man. We're going to go for a drive and get better acquainted."

Angus perked up and panicked. He jerked his head toward Len, hoping to be rescued. Len recognized Angus's plea and stood as he eagerly betrayed him. "Good idea, Millie. You're going to like this dear, sweet man. He's so charming. He's a little bashful, as you can tell, but you kids run along and get better acquainted."

When Len looked at Angus, Angus was glaring at him. Len turned and walked into the kitchen so Millie wouldn't see him laugh. Angus put on his coat and walked out the door with Millie hanging on his arm. He looked nervously over his shoulder and saw Jackie waving enthusiastically. Nervous as he was, he was secretly thrilled to be in the company of a classy lady like Millie.

The dead files were too cumbersome to carry. Gabe drove his old car to work so he could haul the boxes home. He cleared out the files and videotapes. He also unhooked the computer that Todd Mullens had given him and took it to his apartment as well.

Once the car was unloaded, he walked back to the station and gathered up all the comforts that Ray Schneider and Todd Mullens had given him. If Angus was right, he didn't want Garrison to punish them for making his existence more tolerable.

Gabe contacted Mullens the next day and returned all the items that he'd borrowed, except the computer. He would return that in a few weeks. The cold case unit now looked as bleak and depressing as the day that he'd first set foot in it. The remaining dead files were lined up on their shelves waiting for another curious prisoner. All except the murder cases. They now resided with Gabe.

He continued to read the files, searching for the identity of tattoo man and the young girl who'd serviced Garrison. He had to occupy his time while Garrison decided what to do with him. He was sure the discipline for cold-cocking Herbert Winn would be severe.

Angus bounced into work after his days off, looking like a new man. He was clean-shaven and looked ten years younger with his usual two-day growth of beard gone. His uniform was pressed and his shoes and gunbelt were shined.

He hadn't noticed everyone in the room staring at him as he sat down for shift briefing. When he looked up at Shelley, he noticed that Shelley was staring at him as well. He then looked around and saw that everyone was focused on him. After a long silence, he snarled, "What are you staring at? Ain't you never seen a real policeman before?"

Shelley finally broke the silence. "Ladies and gentlemen, I do believe that crusty old Angus is in love." He then broke into song. "Angus and Millie sitting in a tree." The rest of the officers chimed in and finished the song in unison. "K-I-S-S-I-N-G."

Angus lowered his head in embarrassment and rubbed his face. Not wanting anyone to see him smile, he picked up his brief case and walked to the back lot. He would get the pass-on information later from the dispatcher. His pride would not allow him to admit that he was hopelessly in love with Millie.

For the first time in their young careers, the officers had seen Angus Blauw at a loss for words. They all applauded and cheered their victory as Angus walked out the door. As he exited the room, he put his hand up in the air and raised his middle finger in defiance.

This was Friday night. It was Gabe's last chance to enter Loar's apartment before she returned from the Caribbean. He wanted very much to locate Loar's cameras and look around for additional evidence. He especially wanted to see if she owned a pistol, particularly the one that had killed Swede Boreman, Tim Allis and Howard Wilcox. He knew she couldn't have loaned Tommy Ryan the gun that had killed Lynch. That one was recovered at the scene of the murder after Tommy had shot himself. It was secured in the evidence room.

It was a stretch, but finding the murder weapon would tie up a lot of loose ends. He just had to find a way to get it admitted into evidence through an anonymous source. Seizing it illegally during a burglary would render it totally useless in court.

He gathered his equipment one last time. He jogged to the alley door, let himself in and made his way to the stairwell. The entry into Loar's apartment was uneventful. He searched for anything that would connect Loar to other murders.

Knowing that most people keep their guns close to their bed, he searched Loar's bedroom. When he opened the drawer of her nightstand, he smiled. There lay her Colt .380 automatic. Remembering Machka's instructions to leave everything exactly as he'd found it, he memorized its exact location and picked it up.

He stared at the pistol and wondered how he would overcome the illegal seizure. He anguished over the dilemma, then decided that he couldn't take the chance. He removed his pen and notepad from his pocket, wrote down the serial number and returned the pistol to its original position.

He opened the box of ammunition beside the pistol and pocketed one round. He hoped Loar wouldn't notice one round missing. He wanted to compare the bullet to the ones found in Wilcox, Allis and Boreman.

Gabe then searched for Loar's video cameras. He located a small pinhole lens in Loar's shower. The camera was either behind the shower or linked with a fiber-optic cable. He searched for a hidden door, but felt uncomfortable taking so much time. Even though Loar was gone, it unnerved him being in her apartment.

He visualized the video of the bedroom scenes and quickly located the camera. He checked Loar's film cabinet and found no additional tapes. Maybe he'd gotten lucky when Loar was in bed with Jenna and had escaped her apartment without being recorded.

Gabe opened Loar's underwear drawer. The fragrance that rose from it was intoxicating. He fought the urge to handle her garments. He knew she would sense any disturbance of her personal items.

When he left, he repeated the alarm procedure and stepped toward the door. But as he opened the door, he lost his balance and stumbled one step backward. He jumped toward the door, hoping he had not tripped the motion detector beam. He looked at the alarm box and saw the blinking red light, indicating that the alarm had been tripped.

He panicked and jerked the door open. He quickly locked it behind him, then raced to the stairwell. He stopped just inside the stairwell door and wondered if the security guard would take the stairs or the elevator.

There was no choice. He had to calm himself and stay put until he knew where the guard was. He couldn't afford to meet the guard in the stairwell. The stress was unbearable. While he was waiting to see where the guard was, the alarm company was calling the police dispatcher. Gabe's friends on the midnight shift were likely enroute while he was playing hide and seek with the security guard.

The seconds seemed like hours. Finally, he heard the motors of the elevator and knew the guard was taking it to the twelfth floor. He raced down the stairs to the ground floor and charged through the door with no concern for the noise that he was making. He raced to the alley door and opened it. He immediately turned and locked the door with Machka's key.

He turned to flee the alley before the police arrived, but crashed into the grill of the prisoner wagon, which had its engine and lights off. His feet flew up behind him as he slammed face down on the hood and slid off onto the ground.

Knowing he was caught, he quickly jumped to his feet to see which of his friends had him at gunpoint. To his surprise, Angus Blauw was leaning against the fender with his arms crossed, shaking his head. He snarled, "Kinnett, you dumb son of a bitch, you tripped the alarm."

Gabe ran to Angus and pleaded as he tried to catch his breath, "Angus! You gotta help me! Everyone else will be here before I can get away! What am I going to do?"

Angus felt sorry for him as he saw the fear boiling up in his eyes. He growled, "Well, what did you expect? Do you have any idea what Shelley will do to you if he catches you here?" Gabe just lowered his head and nodded. Angus said, "Get your ass in the truck and lie down on the floor. Don't say a word."

Gabe quickly ran to the passenger door and jerked it open. He could hear the engines of the responding squad cars racing in the distance. He saw the reflection of the red lights on the business windows at the end of the alley. He dove into the truck and laid motionless on the floor. Angus climbed behind the wheel and drove to the end of the alley.

Before Angus could get out of the alley, Sergeant Shelley pulled in and eased up along side Angus's wagon. He rolled his window down and asked, "All secure, Angus?"

"Yeah, I checked the alley door. It's locked. The security guard probably tripped the alarm by accident. I'll go around the front and check the doors."

Shelley thought for a few seconds. "I don't know, Angus, that psychotic bitch, Loar, has her office in this building. Kinnett wanted to get a look at her patient files a while back. I talked to the security guard last week and he said he heard someone moving around on the twelfth floor over the building's intercom system. That's the floor that Loar's office is on. It sounds too coincidental to me. I think Kinnett is involved somehow. I had a heart to heart talk with him, but I don't think it sank in. Where is he now? Do you know?"

Angus sighed and feigned ignorance. "Nope, ain't seen the little fucker. See you later."

"Okay, I'm going back to the station and find out where Kinnett is. He's behind this somehow."

Angus quickly drove to the front of the building. He picked up the mike and told the dispatcher that the building was secure and that it was a false alarm. Gabe sat up in the seat as

299

Angus floored the accelerator and raced through the side streets to get ahead of Shelley.

Gabe said, "Boy, Angus, I didn't know there was an intercom system in the building. What are you doing?"

"I'm trying to get your dumb ass back to the station before Shelley gets there. You get you ass back in your office and play stupid when he asks you where you were tonight."

Angus screeched to a halt at the curb by the police station. Gabe bailed out and slammed the door as he sprinted to the building. He ran to the underground parking garage and entered his office just as Shelley pulled in the lot. He removed his mask and gloves and tried to slow his breathing. He quickly hid his mask and gloves and combed his hair as Shelley knocked on his door. He yelled, "Come in! It's open!"

Shelley walked in and found Gabe with his feet up on his desk. He looked around and asked, "What happened to your office, boy?"

Gabe replied casually, "Oh, I didn't want to get Mullens and Schneider in trouble. I was afraid Garrison or Richey would come snooping around, so I took back everything that they'd given me."

Shelley nodded as he studied Gabe suspiciously for a minute. He then leaned into Gabe and asked, "You been here all night, boy?"

Gabe yawned lazily and nodded his head. Satisfied, Shelley said, "Listen, boy, let's have lunch around three."

"Love to. Maybe we can get that tightwad, Blauw, to pay."

Shelley laughed. "Not likely, kid. He's spending all his money romancing the new woman in his life. You ought to see him. He shaves every day. He dressed nicer and smells like a French whore. She's even putting some weight on his scrawny ass. See you at three." He left and Gabe finished calming his nerves.

Gabe spent the next week combing through Loar's patient files. He was lost without the expertise to understand the terminology and medications. He hoped to find a patient who fit the description of tattoo man.

After a week of frustration, he decided to take a break. He hadn't seen Beck for several days. It was hard to concentrate on

300

the files while thinking about her. It was risky for him to go to her apartment with Jenna Kerse stalking him. He now realized that Jenna was a vicious killer who was just waiting to identity Beck as his love interest. She would kill Beck to hurt him.

The videotape was sufficient evidence to send Jenna to the gas chamber, but Gabe couldn't explain how he'd come into possession of it. Every piece of evidence that he'd collected was obtained illegally and would likely land him in prison.

He was about to set the files aside for a few days when he read something interesting. The file that he was immersed in belonged to a thirty year-old man, Lyman Ives. He was being treated for paranoid schizophrenia and manic depression, but the interesting thing about Loar's diagnosis was that Ives was acutely sadistic and masochistic.

She'd noted that he derived sexual gratification from inflicting pain on himself and greater pleasure from inflicting pain on others. Ives had a long history of abuse to animals and assaults on people. He'd regularly scarred himself and frequently inflicted wounds that required medical attention. He was antisocial and had to be home-schooled by his mother because he couldn't interact peacefully with other children. The last entry in Loar's file stated that Ives had been institutionalized in a private mental health care facility under a civil commitment order, which was signed by his mother.

Gabe stared into space as he thought. *He got too violent for his mother to handle, so she had to lock him away in a nut house before he killed her.* This had to be tattoo man. If he could only see a picture of him, he would know if Ives was the man in bed with Loar and in the alley with Lucian Green. He looked back in the file and found the address of Ives's mother. Perhaps a visit to her might shed some light on the matter.

Loar returned from the Caribbean and spent the next few days trying to figure out why she felt a strange presence in her apartment. She knew someone had been there while she was gone, but she couldn't put her finger on why she felt that way. Nothing was out of place, but her paranoia and keen senses would not let her rest.

She didn't want to take any chances. She suspected Gabe, but had no proof. She decided to speak to Garrison. A late dinner and an evening of entertainment would persuade him to look into the matter. She made the date.

She also needed a source close to Gabe who would report his activities to her. She decided to use a close personal friend of Gabe's who had desperately wanted to go to bed with her. He was an egotistical, young Cuban officer who could be manipulated quite easily. Perhaps this was the time to cultivate that relationship. She looked in her organizer and dialed the number. She used her most seductive voice when Ramón answered the phone.

Gabe was sitting in his office about 8:00 p.m. when he heard a knock on his door. He opened the door and was elated to see Ben. "Ben! Come in. How have you been?"

Ben entered, looked around at Gabe's dreary existence and replied, "Oh, fine, I just haven't heard from you in a while and was wondering what you've been up to."

"Why, Ben, I'm touched that you care."

Ben held his hand up and stopped Gabe from getting the wrong impression. "Don't be, kid. I'm not checking on you because I care. You're just like a little two year-old child. When things get quiet, that's when you have to go see what they're into. I'm just worried about what kind of trouble you've been getting into lately."

Gabe said, "Oh, Garrison is going to fire me for not cooperating with Lumas on the Winn affair, that's all."

Ben shook his head. "Nah, he won't do that. He can't make it stick. Beck Eisman stormed into his office and threatened him a couple of weeks ago. She told him the arrest was lawful and the force that you used was not excessive under the circumstances. She also told him that if he screwed with you in any way, she'd quit her job at the prosecutor's office and personally represent you in a civil suit against the department and him personally. He's just screwing with your mind."

Gabe was stunned. Ben laughed and snapped his fingers in Gabe's face to bring him back to reality. "The lady likes you, Gabe. Don't screw it up." Gabe could only nod his head. Ben continued, "That's not why I'm here. I know you haven't been patiently sitting back on your hands like I told you, so what's going on?"

"No, I haven't, Ben. I really can't tell you what I've been up to. I don't want to fight with you tonight, but just take it from me. Loar has been using her patients to kill for her. Jenna Kerse killed Nat Benson, Dutch Windsor and Roger Moesen. She's a self-defense instructor and knows the LVNR. I can't tell you how I know, but trust me, she's our strangler."

Ben shook his head and rubbed his face with both hands. "I knew I shouldn't have come down here. I knew I was going to hear something I didn't want to hear. How did you find this out?"

Gabe smiled and looked deep into Ben's eyes. "Illegally."

Ben cringed as he yelled, "Damn you! You're going to get us all thrown in prison! Just stop right there! I don't want to hear another word!"

Ben turned to leave, but Gabe stopped him. "Ben, don't go, please. Just listen to me for a minute. Loar's got copies of all our crime scene photos as souvenirs. I don't know how she got them, but she has them all in a cabinet in her apartment. She also has videotape of Kerse killing Benson and a tattooed man killing Lucian Green. Don't ask me how I know this, but I have it from a good source that this all exists."

Ben stopped and looked at Gabe without speaking for several seconds. He then asked, "And who's your source?"

Gabe looked down at the floor like a mischievous child who couldn't look his father in the eye. "Can't say."

Ben turned again to leave, but Gabe grabbed his arm to stop him. "Ben, please, help me with one thing."

Ben rolled his eyes. "What?"

"Ben, just help me with an interview. I think I know who the guy is that killed Green. He's a schizophrenic psycho named Lyman Ives. I need a picture of him. Go with me to his mother's house. Help me talk to her. Maybe she's got a picture of him on the wall somewhere. Maybe we can charge him with Green's murder."

A knot swelled up in Ben's stomach. He looked at Gabe long and hard, then said reluctantly, "Okay, kid, let's go."

"You mean right now?" Ben nodded and walked out the door. Gabe grabbed his coat and notepad and ran after him.

Ben stopped at the curb outside Mrs. Ives's house. It was an older home, but well cared for. He and Gabe walked up to the door. He said, "Let me do the talking." Gabe was so grateful for his assistance that he gladly agreed.

After Ben rang the doorbell, they waited for an answer. Finally, the door opened and a thin-framed woman of sixty years angrily asked, "What do you want?"

Ben pasted on his most congenial face and replied, "Mrs. Ives, I'm Detective Ben Hire. This is Detective Gabe Kinnett. We'd like to talk to you about your son, Lyman. May we come in?" Mrs. Ives reluctantly stepped aside and the officers entered.

They looked around and immediately noticed a conspicuous absence of family pictures. Ben said, "Mrs. Ives, we're going back through some of our old murder cases and trying to see if anything new has surfaced. Your son came up as an acquaintance of one of our victims. Is he---"

Mrs. Ives interrupted Ben and yelled, "I don't have a son! My precious baby turned against me when he grew up, and I sent him away! We haven't spoken for years!"

They sensed the bitterness in Mr. Ives's tone. Ben was caught off guard, but continued. "Sent him away? Where is he now?"

Mrs. Ives refused to answer. She just moved to the door and opened it for the officers. She growled angrily, "Don't know! Don't care! Like I said, I don't have a son! I don't have anyone! I can't help you!"

Ben looked at Gabe and both walked out the door. Mrs. Ives stepped out on the porch and glared at the officers like a watchdog protecting its territory. Ben turned to Mrs. Ives and said, "Thank you, Mrs. Ives, for your help."

When he turned back to speak to Gabe, his legs instantly locked and his feet froze in place. His mouth dropped open in shock and he grabbed Gabe's arm. Gabe looked at him and thought he was having a heart attack. He grabbed Ben by the chest and asked, "Ben! Are you okay?"

Ben stared straight ahead, then turned his stare slowly to Gabe. He whispered, "Look at her pose."

Gabe slowly looked over his shoulder. Mrs. Ives was standing under the dim porch light, leaning forward with her hands on her hips and an angry glare on her face. His mind was racing to recall where he'd seen that pose before. Just as his memory kicked in, Ben whispered, "That's the same way those three old ladies were posed after they'd been killed in the late eighties."

Gabe gasped in shock as his memory raced back to the crime scene photos of the murders. He turned back to the street so Mrs. Ives wouldn't hear him. "Yeah! It is! Grace Lindsey, Lois Andoever and Eleanor Rudder!"

Ben said, "They were posed just like that after they were raped and murdered."

Both men turned unconsciously and stared at Mrs. Ives. As their minds worked in unison, she growled, "What are you staring at?"

Neither officer replied. They turned simultaneously and walked to Ben's car. Once inside, they again could not restrain themselves. They looked hard at Mrs. Ives who was still posed exactly as the murdered women. Ben said, "That crazy son of hers killed those women. He wanted to kill his overbearing mother, but didn't have the guts. He killed those poor old women and pretended they were his mother."

Gabe agreed. "Yeah, no wonder he hated women so much. If I had to live with an evil, domineering witch like that, I'd hate women, too."

Mrs. Ives refused to back down. She stayed on the porch and stared the two officers down as they drove away. On the way back to the station, Ben told Gabe, "You find out where that asshole son of hers is. We'll go interview that prick."

"He's staying at the Perkins-Hays Institute under a civil commitment, Ben. Think he'll talk?"

"Nope, but I want him to know that we're on to him. I want him to sweat. I'll go through those cases again and see if there was any forensic evidence at the scenes that might link him to the crimes. If we can get a search warrant for hair and blood, we might be able to make a case on him. When we get back to the office, I'll get the case file."

305

Gabe said, "Ben, you better swing by my apartment first. Those files aren't in the cold case unit anymore. I moved them to be safe. I don't trust Garrison or Richey. I'm afraid they'll destroy them to keep me quiet."

Ben looked suspiciously at him. "I'll have to pick them up later. You're getting a little paranoid, aren't you?"

"Maybe, but my source thinks I have a good reason to be."

14

BECK OPENED HER door after checking the peephole and, once
again, Gabe had eluded Jenna Kerse. After dinner, the
conversation drifted to the investigation. Not wanting to incur
Beck's wrath, Gabe wisely chose to cut the conversation short.
Beck was being left out of the loop, but she knew she could count
on Ben Hire to bring her up to speed.

The kissing rapidly escalated to an all-out petting session,
stopping just short of consummation. Beck was falling in love with
Gabe, but couldn't commit until she knew the outcome of the Loar
investigation.

Tonight's passion drove them farther than before. They
found themselves in bed totally nude. They savored each other's
body until they could no longer restrain themselves. She wrapped
her legs around him and pulled him on top of her. He was delirious
with lust and was thrilled that Beck could no longer control
herself. He had wanted to make love to her for weeks.

As she opened herself wide for him, he assumed the best
position. She suddenly pushed him off, sat up and rubbed her face
with both hands. She got out of bed and walked to the bathroom
and washed her face with a cold washcloth. He rolled over on his
back in frustration and asked, "Did I do something wrong?"

Beck slowly exited the bathroom and put on her robe. She
sat on the edge of the bed and shook her head. "No, you didn't do

anything wrong. It's me. I can't jump in that deep with someone that I'm not sure will be around afterwards. It has nothing to do with how I feel about you."

Gabe thought for a few seconds, then asked, "Will you still feel the same way about me if I lose my job? Will you still care for me if I'm not a cop?"

She crawled on top of him and looked deep into his eyes. "Yes, I will. In fact, I wish you weren't one now. I know you love your job, but I'd feel safer if this whole Loar thing was over. Jenna Kerse scares me to death. I don't know what she looks like, but I'm sure I'm no match for her."

"I hope it'll be over soon. I don't know what Garrison is going to do to me. By the way, I can't thank you enough for threatening him for me. You shouldn't have done that. Baumgartan will have your ass if he finds out."

"Screw Baumgartan! I've had a gut full of him!"

"Boy, that's pretty tough talk from someone who only weighs a hundred and ten pounds. Anyway, I've got something that might help you with Baumgartan if you need it. He's been a bad boy, and I've got proof."

Beck rolled off of Gabe and glared at him. "What? What have you got?"

Realizing that he couldn't disclose any more information without revealing that he'd been in Loar's apartment, he said, "Never mind. I can't discuss it right now, but just remember, Baumgartan is toast if you need my help."

Ben quietly knocked on Gabe's door. Gabe rushed to open it and invited him in. "Hey, Ben. I've got those files for you."

He sat on Gabe's sofa and read. After a few minutes, he blurted out, "Here! Here it is! Ives left semen and hair samples at the scene of the Lindsey killing. Let's see about the Andoever scene."

He read for a few minutes, then said, "Here, too. Give me the Rudder case." Gabe handed him the Rudder file and he immediately flipped to the evidence sheet. "Yep, semen and hair at all three scenes. I'll go back and try to interview Mrs. Ives again. Maybe she'll talk if I put the pressure on her. I'll phony up an anonymous tip for a search warrant application, but we'll need more. After I talk to Mrs. Ives, let's take a drive over to the institute and talk to him. Maybe he'll verify something that'll add credibility to our anonymous tip."

Gabe was confused. "Like what, Ben?"

Ben closed the file and tucked it under his arm as he walked to the door. "Like a statement that he knew someone who lived close to the victims. Maybe he'll say that he was in the area of their houses to explain an anonymous tip that he was there. Who knows? You don't succeed if you don't try. We'll catch him off guard and blindside him. He'll say something we can use."

Gabe followed Ben nervously to the door and asked, "Where are you going to keep that file, Ben? If you put it back in the cold case unit, it'll disappear."

Ben thought for a second and replied, "I'll drop it off here when I'm done."

Gabe asked, "Listen, Ben, Ives is only there under a civil commitment. It's not very secure. If we show up there with a search warrant, he'll pack his bags and leave. Once he gets through the front gate and out into society, we'll never find him. What'll we do then?"

"Oh, no he won't. If we get a search warrant, we'll show up with the sheriff's transport team. We can hold him for twenty-four hours on investigation of murder. We'll take him into custody and transport him to the county jail. We'll collect his blood and hair there. I'll make sure the lab tech puts a rush on the analysis. We won't give him a chance to rabbit on us."

Gabe breathed easier as Ben left. He deeply admired Ben's savvy and expertise. He hoped he could survive Garrison and become a detective one day.

Gabe continued to report to the dungeon, but dreaded the nights without the creature comforts that he'd became accustomed to. Taped to the door one night was an order from Garrison to report to his office at eight in the morning. He could only imagine what Garrison had up his sleeve.

As he entered the bunker, He saw another note on the floor. It had been slid under the door. He didn't recognize the handwriting. It said, *Don't enter Loar's office again. She has changed her alarm code. You'll get caught.* He now had to call

Machka to see if he could get her new code from his contact at the alarm company.

Gabe decided to take the night off and get some sleep. No one would know. He hoped Garrison, Richey or Lumas didn't check on him. At eight the next morning, he was sitting in the secretary's area outside Garrison's office. She pleasantly said, "You can go in, Officer Kinnett. The chief will see you now."

As he walked into Garrison's office, he found Garrison smiling pleasantly and motioning for him to have a seat. When he looked at the chair beside his, he almost fainted. He saw Dr. Loar trying to feign a pretentious smile. Garrison said, "Good morning, Gabe. How have you been?"

He knew Garrison could care less how he was. He was putting on a show for Loar. He continued, "So, Gabe, let's get this internal affairs mess over with. I was really going to come down hard on you for using excessive force against Winn, but Dr. Loar has intervened on your behalf. She's convinced me that you may be having some personal problems that prompted you to attack Winn. Before I decide what to do with you, I'm going to ask Dr. Loar to perform a psychological evaluation on you. When I get her *Fitness For Duty* report, I'll make my decision."

Gabe was doing his best to slow his breathing. He knew Garrison could see his heart pounding under his shirt. He knew Loar could hear it. His mouth was like cotton and he couldn't collect his thoughts. While he sat quietly, Dr. Loar spoke up. "Gabe, dear, Robert has told me about your problems. We never got a chance to finish our conversation when you were in my office last time. I just want to help."

Gabe finally looked up at the ceiling to collect his thoughts. He tried to talk without his voice quivering. "I don't need a psychological evaluation, Chief. I didn't use excessive force against Winn and I don't have any personal problems. Do what you want about the Winn investigation."

Loar reached over and put her hand on Gabe's arm. "It's okay, Gabe, I can do you a lot of good here. Just trust me."

Gabe removed her hand. He knew Garrison wasn't going to do anything drastic after his ass-chewing from Beck Eisman. Garrison leaned over his desk and said, "That's not a request,

Kinnett, it's an order. Either be in her office Monday morning or turn in your equipment."

He studied Garrison for some sign that he was bluffing, but saw none. Maybe Beck's threat hadn't had the impact that he'd thought. He thought about the videotape of Garrison having sex with the underage girl, but this was not the time to play that ace. Seeing no choice, he stood and walked out.

Val Machka opened the car door for Monica. She was stunning in her evening gown. She was Brazilian, and the white dress accentuated her bronze skin. Val had never forgiven her for selling him out to the drug task force, but he was so enamored by her beauty and sexual prowess that he swallowed his pride.

Monica was stoned and semi-conscious. Val held her up with one arm as he opened the door. He poured her into the passenger seat and closed the door to keep her from falling out. Monica lost consciousness as soon as the car door closed.

Val thought as he walked around to the driver's door, *I've got to dump this lady. She'll never go straight, and she's going to get me killed. Her crowd is just too rough.*

As Val slid into the driver's seat, he marveled at Monica's body. Her dress rode up over her hips and she was wearing nothing under it. If he could just get her to her apartment and awake enough to perform, the nightcap would be memorable.

He inserted the key in the ignition and started the car. Out of his peripheral vision, he saw movement in the rear view mirror. He initially thought it was a car approaching from the rear with its light off. He glanced up just as a piano wire encircled his neck.

The movement in the rear view mirror became instantly clear. It wasn't a car. It was someone in the back seat. The wire tightened enough that Val couldn't force his fingers under the wire to get some breathing room. He clawed at his neck trying to get his fingers under the wire, but it was too tight. The lady in the back seat leaned close to him and said calmly, "Relax. Put your hands on the wheel where I can see them."

Val had no choice. He forced himself to comply. The lady continued, "You and I have missed each other on several occasions, dear. I'd hoped we could meet like this long before now, but you're very illusive."

The wire loosened slightly as Val complied. He took a deep breath, then looked in the rear view mirror and into the lifeless eyes of Maura Loar. Fear instantly gripped him as he tried to think of something to say. He didn't have to think long. Loar continued, "You know, dear Val, I make a point to get even with everyone who ever crosses me. You stole something very valuable from me years ago, but I couldn't prove it sufficiently to go to the police. You're a very accomplished thief. You don't leave much evidence. But fortunately, I don't have to prove something to know it in my heart. I've always known it was you. You would have been better off dealing with the courts. The judge would have shown you far more leniency than I will."

Val coughed and gagged as he tried to talk. He hoped his gagging would prompt Loar to loosen the wire so he could talk. He just needed one more chance to get his fingers under the wire. Loar said, "No need to talk, dear Val. You won't change my mind. Your contact at the alarm company finally broke down and told me that she'd given you my alarm code. That's how you defeated my alarm system. I'll deal with her later. You've also corrupted that dear, sweet officer, Gabriel Kinnett. You gave him my code so he could sneak in and spy on me. You fool! Your arrogance has doomed him to the same fate."

Realizing that Loar wasn't going to loosen the wire, Val made one last effort. He dug his fingernails deeply into his neck and tried to get them under the wire. Loar tightened the wire and said, "Nice try, dear boy. Maybe we'll see each other on the other side. We'll talk, maybe have a bite of lunch and laugh about tonight. We'll be good friends in the next life. Don't worry about Monica. I'll tuck her in for you."

Val panicked. This was the end. He arched his back and jerked violently to get free. His foot jammed the accelerator to the floor and the engine raced. Loar had the wire tied to wooden handles and crossed in the back.

She pulled her arms apart and pressed her face into the back of Val's head. She inhaled his fear and moaned in ecstasy as she savored every moment of his torture. The smells of fear and blood rekindled the same primitive impulses that she'd felt when she sat on Mickey Clearey's back and strangled him with a clothesline cord.

Val's agony aroused her sexually and her body responded as the wire cut into his neck. She breathed heavily as the wire cut through the soft tissue and stopped at Val's spinal cord. With the soft tissue and arteries severed, blood poured out and ran down his front. It pooled in his lap and splattered on the dash and windshield as he convulsed. He finally relaxed and floated into eternity.

Loar released the handles and left the wire embedded in Machka's neck. She leaned back and relaxed as she tried to slow her breathing. She ran her fingers through her hair and shuttered as one final spasm rushed though her pelvis.

Minutes passed. Loar wiped the blood spatters from her face and carefully studied Monica, who was still unconscious and splattered with Val's blood. Loar slid behind her and leaned over the seat. She buried her face in Monica's hair and inhaled her scent.

She encircled Monica with her arms and slid her hands down the front of Monica's low-cut dress. She inhaled Monica's scent as she massaged her breasts. She then wondered how she would get Monica home. Monica was larger than her, and Loar didn't want to get caught dragging her home.

Loar looked back over at Machka's corpse and smiled. She thought how amusing it would be to let Monica awake and find Machka beside her with his head nearly severed. She removed her hands from the front of Monica's dress, reached over and turned off the ignition, then opened the door.

As she stepped out, she thought the whole scenario was poetic justice. Monica deserved every ounce of grief that she would receive. She, too, had betrayed Loar. She had been Loar's favorite lover until she'd stopped their therapy sessions out of fear of Jenna Kerse.

Jenna had beaten her mercilessly. Loar severely disciplined Jenna and tried to assure Monica that she could control Jenna, but Monica simply disappeared. Monica would someday meet the same fate as Machka, but she was easy to find. Loar could take her at any time. She quietly closed the door and walked into the darkness.

The early morning sun illuminated Machka's car in the alley. One of the nightshift officers spotted it just before he got off

313

duty. Monica was hysterical when she awoke and saw Machka's body. Ben hire was the first call made by the sergeant.

Ben called the crime lab and made sure the scene was photographed and processed by the numbers. He then called Gabe and told him to get to the scene right away. He arrived thirty minutes later.

The coroner was removing Machka from the car as Gabe jogged up. He had never seen Machka before and was shocked when Ben broke the news to him. Ben asked, "Know him well?"

Gabe nodded slowly and turned away. Ben put his hand on Gabe's shoulder and said, "I thought you did. He was your source of information about what Loar has in her apartment, wasn't he?"

Gabe looked confused and wondered how Ben had drawn that conclusion. He then realized that Ben didn't know that he'd entered Loar's apartment. He nodded his head slowly. Ben said, "I thought so. Old Machka here has been working this city for years. If anyone could get into Loar's apartment, I knew it had to be him. He's the only person I know who's smart enough to pull off a job like that." Gabe looked at the ground and stared in silence. He couldn't tell Ben that there was another just as smart.

He turned and watched the paramedics try to calm Monica. Guilt overwhelmed him as he realized that Machka was killed for helping him break into Loar's apartment. For all he knew, Loar probably thought it was Machka who'd crawled out of her bedroom the night she had sex with Jenna Kerse. He'd worn a mask, and it would have been a logical assumption if Loar already suspected Machka of burglarizing her apartment earlier. Her video camera must have caught him crawling out of the closet.

The tow truck arrived and hooked up to Machka's car. Ben instructed the driver, "Take it to the garage. We'll go through it there. I doubt if there'll be any evidence inside, but we'll give it a try."

Gabe stared at Machka's car and said, "She killed him, Ben. That bitch killed him for helping me. We've got to get her ass."

"We will, kid, but don't get too upset over Machka. That asshole has had this coming for years. This is a case of one predator killing another. Society is better off."

Gabe didn't argue. He didn't want to arouse Ben's suspicions. He grabbed Ben's arm as he began to walk away. "Listen, Ben, Garrison has ordered me to go to Loar for a psychological evaluation to see if I'm fit for duty. What am I going to say?"

Ben's interest peaked. He leaned into Gabe and said quietly, "Nothing, Gabe, nothing. That bitch can sense everything you think. She can read a person's mind just by looking in their eyes. Just go in there and tell her that you don't want to talk, then leave. If you try to spar with her, she'll pick you apart. Garrison can order you to go to the session, but he can't make you talk once you get there. I'm telling you, he isn't going to fire you. Eisman put the fear of God in him. Trust me."

Gabe milled around while Ben cleaned up the final details of the scene. Ben motioned for him to come to his car. "Get in, kid, let's go get some breakfast."

Machka's murder had shaken Gabe to his very core. He hadn't known him, but Machka cared enough for him to try to talk him out of entering Loar's apartment. He owed him some loyalty. "Boy, Ben, I know Machka was a crook, but he didn't deserve this. He certainly didn't deserve this from Loar. She's a bigger scumbag than he ever was."

Ben nodded. "I know, but, that's what I've been trying to tell you. Loar is no one to screw with. This is why you have to avoid her. Show up at your evaluation and tell her you don't want to talk, then get your ass out of there. If she thinks you're hunting her, she'll target you. It might take a few years, but she'll get you if we can't get her first. We have to get some of her patients to turn on her. I'm hoping we can hang some murder charges on Ives and get him to flip on her. Maybe he'll sell her out to keep his ass off death row."

Gabe sat quietly, then said, "Ain't gonna work, Ben. An anonymous tip that he's the killer without corroborating evidence isn't enough to get a search warrant. Even I know that."

Ben nodded his head slowly, then said, "Well, since you mentioned it, I have to say you're right. I talked with the prosecutor yesterday afternoon. He won't even sign the affidavit unless we can put Ives at one of the scenes. We can subpoena the records of the institute and show that he was on the streets at the

315

time of the murders, but we have to link him to the three women somehow before we can get the courts consent to collect hair and blood. I'm still working on that."

Gabe shook his head in frustration. "It's going to take forever, Ben."

Ben frowned at him. "So, what's your hurry? You're young, be patient."

"Ben, let's just go confront him. Maybe he'll break down or something."

"No way, kid. Let me give you a piece of good advice. You never go into an interview without having your ducks in a row. If we go in there empty handed, he'll sense that we don't have anything to link him to the murders. We'll blow it. When I confront him, I want to beat him over the head with so much circumstantial evidence that he'll feel like he has to prove he's innocent rather than us prove he's guilty. If we can get him running in circles trying to create excuses for all the evidence that we have, he'll incriminate himself enough that we can get a search warrant. Once we get his hair and blood, the lab boys will nail his ass to the cross."

As Ben reached the end of the alley, Gabe asked him to stop the car. Ben stopped and looked at him to see what he was looking at. Gabe was fixed on the evidence tech in the crime scene van parked at the end of the alley. Ben asked, "Problem?"

Gabe said, "Ben, Loar has copies of the crime scene photos from all our murders. Who develops those photos?"

Ben looked at the van and said, "That guy there, Brent McHenry. He photographs and develops all of our crime scene photos." He rolled down his window and drove forward a few feet until he was beside the crime scene van. He yelled, "Hey, Brent, nice job."

Brent frowned and replied suspiciously, "Thanks, Ben, but you don't compliment me for no reason. What do you want?"

Ben laughed. "Brent! You cut me deep. Can't I compliment a good job?"

"Yeah, I guess, but I get the feeling that it's going to cost me something."

"Not this time, pal. Hey listen, how many copies of our homicide photos do you print?"

"Three, why?"

Ben was confused. "Three? One set goes in evidence. One set goes to the prosecutor with a copy of the case file. Who gets the third copy?"

Brent never looked up and kept writing as he answered, "Garrison. He always gets a copy. You know that."

Ben looked at Gabe in shock. He then looked back at Brent and said, "I didn't know that. What does he do with them?"

Brent shrugged his shoulders. "Now how would I know? He's the chief. He can wallpaper his house with them for all I care. I just do what I'm told."

Ben stared at Brent for a few seconds, then said, "Thanks, Brent, lunch is on you next time."

"I knew it! I knew you were up to no good!"

Ben didn't speak for a few blocks, then said, "Those are her trophies."

Gabe asked, "Trophies? What trophies?"

"Trophies, kid. Serial killers often keep trophies of their crimes. She keeps copies of our homicide photos as trophies. That asshole, Garrison, is supplying her with the trophies of her murders. Brent stamps the back of every photo with an inked evidence stamp that can't be erased. I'll bet if we could get into her apartment with a search warrant, we'd find that those photos have our evidence stamp on the back."

Gabe couldn't let Ben know that he'd personally seen Loar's photos, so he sat quietly. The evidence stamp was on the back of every photo that he'd seen in her apartment. Ben asked, "Did Machka say if he saw our stamp on the back?" Gabe sat quietly and shook his head.

Throughout breakfast, Gabe was quiet and picked at his food. Ben could see that he'd been shaken by Machka's murder. His years of reading human behavior told him that the man in the mirror was getting harder for Gabe to face.

Gabe agonized all weekend. He dreaded the meeting with Loar, but he was afraid that Beck's threat to Garrison hadn't had the chilling effect that he'd hoped. He passed the time searching Loar's patient files for the young girl with whom Garrison had made his acting debut.

When Monday morning rolled around, Gabe was sitting in Loar's waiting room as scheduled. Beth was her usual amiable self and offered him coffee.

Dr. Loar stepped out of her office and invited him in. She shocked him with her attire. She was wearing a sheer body suit with shorts. She turned to Beth and said, "Beth, dear, Gabriel and I are going to talk for a while. I don't want to be disturbed."

Beth, too, was surprised at Loar's attire. She nodded and looked suspiciously at the two as Loar took Gabe's arm and disappeared with him behind the office door. Once in the office, she opened the door to her apartment and said, "We'll be more comfortable in my apartment, Gabriel. Please make yourself comfortable."

He stopped abruptly. "I don't think that's appropriate, Doctor. People might get the wrong idea."

Loar pulled him by the arm into her apartment. "Maura, Gabe, please call me Maura."

He sat on the sofa and tried to create the perception that the interior of her apartment was foreign to him. As he looked at the furnishings, Loar sat uncomfortably close to him. Her sheer body suit revealed every detail of her breasts and would have made it difficult for him to focus, but he was too nervous to be aroused.

He had long ago decided to take Ben's advice. He nervously rubbed his hands together as he looked at the floor. He took a deep breath and said, "Doctor, I'm sorry that you've wasted your time, but I really don't want to be here. I have no need to talk, and I really don't care what Chief Garrison does."

Loar sat quietly and studied him. He nervously assessed his body language. He was sure that he was being videotaped. Loar's microscopic examination of his every movement soon angered him. He said, "You know, Doctor, there is one thing I'd like to say."

"Yes, Gabe."

"You really irritate me. I don't like being studied like some lab rat. If you have something to say, spit it out."

Loar was completely unfazed by his bravado. With a face completely devoid of expression, she asked in a soft voice, "Do I frighten you, Gabriel?"

318

He was now relaxed and ready to spar. He smiled and shook his head, "No, Doctor, not at all. Are you so arrogant to think that there's something intimidating about you?"

She shook her head as she studied Gabe's eyes intently. "No, Gabriel, I'm not, but I saw fear in your eyes when you walked in here and I just want to get through that wall. Now that you're ready to talk, why don't you and I make a commitment to each other?"

"Are you propositioning me?"

Loar's stone face almost cracked as she turned one corner of her mouth up in a pretentious smile. "No, dear boy, nothing like that. I'm talking about a commitment to be totally honest with each other. You're one of the few men that I've met who puts on no pretenses. You're refreshingly honest and genuine. With you, what you see is what you get. I feel a deep personal attraction to you. As you can tell, this isn't my usual business suit, and this isn't my usual counseling session. I would deeply cherish a personal friendship with you."

Gabe looked at her in shock, then looked down at the floor. He thought, *Boy, Ben wasn't kidding. This bitch is smooth.* He thought for a minute, then mustered a surge of self-confidence. He assured himself that he was capable of matching wits with anyone, including Loar. He shrugged his shoulders and said, "Sure, you first."

Loar studied him for a few seconds, then said, "Dear Gabriel, I know what happened to get you transferred to the cold case unit. Robert has kept me apprised of your problems. I also know that you've taken it upon yourself to single-handedly solve every murder committed in the city. You've been asking questions about me and you're convinced that I'm somehow responsible for a number of killings."

Gabe tried to mask any sign of shock, but he was stunned. She wasn't kidding about putting her cards on the table. He asked, "Aren't you? Surely you're not going to sit there and pretend that you've had absolutely nothing to do with some of them."

She feigned a look of disappointment and said, "Dear Gabriel, please? We can't be the close friends that I'd hoped to be if you're going to make such clumsy attempts to trick me into a confession. I wrote the book on psychoanalysis, dear boy. If you're going to be my friend, please respect me more than that."

He realized that she was right. It would take someone far more experienced at interviewing than him to squeeze a confession out of her. Even then, he didn't know if it were possible.

Loar again forced a pretentious smile in an attempt to restart the friendship. "Gabriel, I have sources all over town, very credible sources. I know that Valeri Machka gave you the code to my alarm system. My contact at the alarm company told me that she gave my code to him. I know that you've been entering my apartment when I'm not home. I know that you were in my closet the night that Jenna Kerse and I made love. You were in my apartment when Jenna and I arrived. I always turn my alarm system on when I leave. When we got here, the system was off. I knew you were hiding here as soon as I walked in the door. I turned it on immediately after we got inside. When you left, you thought you were turning the system back on so I wouldn't suspect that you'd been here. What you didn't know was that the alarm was already on when you left. You walked through my motion detector beam as you approached the door. That set off the alarm. You punched in my code and hit the *ON* button. You were obviously so preoccupied with getting away undetected that you failed to notice the alarm activation light indicating that the alarm was already on. You thought it was off, but the alarm was already on. By pushing the wrong button, the system ignored the command. You didn't have thirty seconds to open and close the door. Even if you'd had the presence of mind to step over the motion detector beam as you left, you certainly set off the alarm when you opened the door. You would have been caught by the guard, but I called him immediately and told him that I'd accidentally tripped the alarm. You also tripped the alarm when you left my apartment on another occasion, probably due to clumsiness."

Gabe sat in shock and didn't respond. He was stunned that Loar knew everything that he'd done. She knew he'd been in her apartment and had sex with Jenna anyway just to put on a show for him.

He pasted on his most stoic expression so he wouldn't give her any hint that she was right. He hoped she didn't bring up the crime scene photos and videotapes. His worst fear was realized when she continued, "You've also accessed my computer. You got into my patient files, and I have to assume that you've downloaded them onto a disc. You tried to cover your tracks by restoring the recall list of the last five files that my receptionist had accessed before she'd shut the computer down for the day. You wrote the list down on her note pad and took the list with you. Your mistake was that you have a heavy hand. You left the impression of the list on the sheet under the top page of Beth's note pad. I highlighted the impression lightly with a pencil. I compared the writing to your penmanship on the patient information form that you'd filled out when you came to me for counseling. The handwriting matched. Would you like to see for yourself?"

Gabe knew it was futile to spar with her. She would see through any facade that he tried to erect. She tried to comfort him, "It's okay, Gabriel, I'm not angry with you. You're a police officer. You're only doing what you've been conditioned to do. You're going about it the wrong way, but you're young and sincere. I understand. You haven't offended me. You see, Gabriel, I didn't ask Robert to order you here for your sake. I could have stood passively by and allowed him to crucify you over the Winn incident. I could have given him the sample of your handwriting on the notepad. I could have turned the pens in Beth's penholder over to him. You could explain your fingerprints on one of the pens because you used one of them to fill out your patient information form, but if your prints were on two of the pens, it would prove that you used one of them to write the recall list on the note pad the night you entered my office illegally. I don't want to hurt you. I don't want to hurt your career. I asked you here for both our sake. I would like to answer some of your questions and put your mind at ease. I can't stand to see us at odds with each other."

He could no longer maintain eye contact with Loar. He looked away as she continued. "You're also aware that Jenna is very infatuated with you. Even though she and I have been lovers for many years, there is room in our relationship for the right man. Jenna would like very much to have you for a lover. That wouldn't bother me. She needs that. If you and I can set our differences aside, I would like to welcome you into our bed. You can't know

321

how refreshing it would be to have a friend who doesn't have a psychological disorder. You would be a cherished confidant for me."

Many thoughts ran through his head. Should he ask her why she killed Machka? Should he ask her about her videotapes and crime scene photos? Should he ask her why she stood passively by and watched Nat Benson and Lucian Green murdered? Should he ask her about Lyman Ives?

He was relieved about one thing. She made no mention of the videotapes and crime scene photos. She apparently wasn't aware that he had copied the tapes. As he thought, he heard Ben Hire screaming in the back of his head. *You idiot! Get your ass out of there and keep your mouth shut!*

With no idea how to proceed, Gabe wisely decided to listen to Ben. He wished he had listened sooner and never gone to her office in the first place. He stood and said, "Well, thank you, Doctor. You've given me a lot to think about."

Loar stood and wrapped her arm around his waist as they walked to the door. She pressed her breast against him and said, "Gabriel, please, don't shut me out. You have nothing to fear from me. You don't have to run away."

Gabe stopped at the door and removed her arm from his waist. "Listen, Doctor, that respect that you spoke of has to be a two-way street. If you want me to show you respect, you have to show me some. You've got to quit trying to manipulate me. You can't push my buttons with feeble attempts to stroke my ego. You don't scare me, so stop acting like I'm some little schoolboy who runs from everything that frightens him. You might be able to manipulate Jenna and your other patients, but you can't stroke me."

Loar simply looked at him with her arms crossed as he walked out of her apartment. Her lifeless eyes masked the contempt in her heart. She turned and walked into her bedroom. She sat on the edge of the bed and crossed her legs as she contemplated her next course of action.

Jenna eased up behind Loar, encircled her neck with her arms and squeezed her gently. She kissed her on the back of the head and said, "Sorry, Maura, I told you he wasn't going to be easy. He's stubborn like that assistant D.A., Allis, and Webster, and all the other men that we've ever met. They only understand one thing."

Loar nodded. "Yes. Yes, Jenna dear, I know. If I could have maneuvered him into bed, we would have had him."

"I know, Maura. I was well hidden in the closet. It would have pleased me to no end to get a wire around his neck. Seeing him on top of you would have been added motivation. I can't stand the thought of anyone else touching you."

Loar was unmoved by Jenna's jealousy. She patted Jenna on the arm as she stood. "Yes, I know, Jenna dear. It wouldn't have gone that far, but you have to get over that."

Jenna jumped off the bed in a rage. She grabbed Loar by the hair and bent her head back. She gritted her teeth and growled, "No, Maura, I can't get over it! You don't know what it does to me to see you ---"

Although Loar was much smaller, she quickly grabbed Jenna's thumb and bent it back until the pain forced Jenna to release her hair. With no expression on her face, she spun around and backhanded Jenna hard across the face. She then released Jenna's thumb.

The blow had no physical affect on Jenna, but the emotional trauma was heartbreaking. She gritted her teeth and sobbed as Loar spoke softly without emotion, "Jenna, dear, I've cautioned you about this. I won't be manhandled. Please remember that. It hurts me so to have to discipline you."

Jenna looked at the floor as tears streamed down her face. Loar ran her fingers through Jenna's hair and caressed the back of her head. She pulled Jenna close, wrapped her arms around her and said, "Dear, sweet Jenna, I still love you, but you can't dominate me. You know that."

Jenna wiped her eyes and said, "You want me to sometimes. Sometimes you like me to hurt you. I'm not sure when you want it and when you don't."

Loar shook her head as she condescended to Jenna, "No, dear, you know. I give you clear and unmistakable direction when I want pain. You didn't receive that direction now, did you?"

Jenna simply shook her head and wrapped her arms around Loar. She couldn't stand for Loar to chastise her. As she hugged

Loar, she cried, "I'm never going to let him hurt you, Maura! Never! He's never going to take you away from me!"

Loar patted her on the back and said with an apathetic tone, "I know, dear, I know. If he persists, I'll turn you loose on him. The time isn't right yet."

The doctor broke their embrace and escorted Jenna to the door that exited to the rear of her apartment. Jenna would leave by the service elevator so Beth wouldn't see her.

She wiped her eyes again and faced Loar. She gently slid her finger under the shoulder strap of Loar's body suit, pulled it down over her shoulder and exposed her breast. She bent down and kissed Loar's breast and said, "I love you, Maura. Please let me show you?"

Loar opened the door and pulled her body suit back up. "I love you, too, dear, but some other time." She gently pushed Jenna out the door and returned to her sofa. Her facial muscles twitched as she contemplated Officer Kinnett's fate.

She wanted Gabe to disappear, and Jenna was the perfect tool. She was also growing tired of Jenna. She had served her purpose and was becoming a liability.

Loar had hoped to gain Gabe's affection and persuade him to eliminate Jenna. She was sure that she could prompt Jenna to try to kill Gabe, but what would the outcome be? The answer wasn't immediately clear.

One thing was clear though. With Jenna's propensity for violence and her love for Loar, she would certainly kill Gabe for having sex with Loar or trying to put her in prison. Gabe was just as likely to kill Jenna in a life or death altercation. One of them would die soon and half of her problem would be solved without having to lift a finger.

The next morning, Ben arrived at work to find Gabe waiting in his office. He was surprised to see Gabe and asked, "Kinnett, you sneaky little rat, what are you doing here?"

Gabe smiled. "Waiting for you, Ben. Don't be so jumpy, we've got a psycho to interview. Now don't tell me you're too busy. I've checked your calendar, and you have all morning free."

Ben laid his briefcase on the desk and examined his calendar to refresh his memory. "Yep, you got me there. Let's do it." Gabe jumped to his feet enthusiastically. He relished the opportunity to learn some good interview techniques from an expert.

They got in Ben's car and he asked, "Well, let's hear it. What happened with Loar?"

Gabe couldn't resist the opportunity to pimp Ben. He feigned a tone of regret and said, "Oh, Ben, I blew it. She had me figured out. She seemed to know everything that I've been up to, so I asked her about all the murders. I tried to get her to confess, but she was just too smart for me. I told her that we know about her tapes and crime scene photos, so they probably won't be there when we get our search warrant."

Ben looked at Gabe, totally unconcerned. "Funny. If I thought for one second that you'd said all that, I'd pull this car over and kick your ass all over the highway."

Gabe laughed and slapped his knee. He thought for a few minutes, then asked, "How are we going to crack this puke, Ben?"

"Don't know yet, kid. Maybe we won't. Some people are too smart to incriminate themselves. Let's start slow and work into it. This guy's smart. He won't say anything incriminating if we're too direct. Let's establish a rapport with him first. Nothing says we can't interview him several times. I'd rather be friendly with him at first. If we can establish enough circumstantial evidence through casual conversation to get a search warrant, we'll get down and dirty with him after the lab geeks match his hair and DNA with the samples found at the crime scenes. If we connect him to the murders, we'll crawl up his ass with a chainsaw and cut our way out. We'll break him down like a cheap toy."

Gabe boiled over with confidence as Ben talked. Although Loar had given him plenty to worry about, he rambled about the case as they drove. He was surprised at how enthusiastic he was, although he was watching his career disintegrate before his eyes. He couldn't hide his affection for Beck when she became the topic of conversation. Ben just let him ramble.

A guard manned the entrance of the Perkins-Hays Institute. Upon identifying themselves, Ben and Gabe were escorted to the director's office. She was a savvy, no-nonsense lady, Martha Rhinehart.

Dr. Rhinehart was a slow-moving lady in her late sixties, who had administered the institute for the last thirty years. She knew each patient intimately. She welcomed the detectives and began. "So! The guard informs me that you gentlemen want to talk to Lyman. He doesn't get many visitors."

Ben replied, "Doctor, you don't remember me, but we used you as an expert witness several years ago on a murder case."

She perked up and said, "Yes! Of course, I remember you now. How have you been?"

"Well, a little older and fatter, but I'm fine."

Dr. Rhinehart laughed and relaxed when she remembered Ben. After several minutes of casual conversation, the formality faded. "Okay, Ben, what can I do for you? You're here to haul Lyman off to prison, I hope."

"He's that big of a pain?"

"That he is. He's my biggest worry of the whole job. Each day when I come to work, I wonder if this is the day that he will kill someone. He doesn't belong in an institution like this, but he knows how to play the system."

"I sympathize with you, Doctor, but unfortunately, we aren't here to take him off your hands. I wish we could."

Dr. Rhinehart leaned back in her chair. "Okay then, proceed."

Ben said, "I assume that you'll keep our conversation confidential." Dr. Rhinehart simply nodded, and Ben continued. "In the late eighties, we had a series of murders. Three elderly women were raped and murdered. After they'd been killed, they were posed. The killer used duct tape to tape their hands on their hips and raise the corners of their eyes to make them look angry. We've received anonymous information that Lyman is our killer. When we interviewed his mother, we saw that same pose from her. We're speculating that he hated his mother and saw some resemblance between her and the three murder victims. We think he killed the women because they represented his mother. We also think he killed a drug dealer before he checked into this facility. He was being treated by Dr. Loar at the time. We have good reason to believe that Dr. Loar manipulated Lyman to kill the drug dealer for her."

Dr. Rhinehart sat quietly for a few seconds, then said, "That doesn't surprise me. I've suspected for years that Lyman has killed before. I've always thought that his mother created a monster, then put him in here when she could no longer control him. I've also known Dr. Loar for years. I felt at the time that she was helping Mrs. Ives put Lyman in here to hide him from the law. Lyman didn't want to be here initially. Dr. Loar has maintained close contact with him and was instrumental in persuading him to allow himself to be committed. He's under a civil commitment, and Mrs. Ives can take him out of here any time she wants. We can't stop her. If Lyman was killing before, he'll go right back to killing again. His mother will likely be his first victim. That's probably why she leaves him here. She won't even come and visit him. There's tremendous hatred between them."

Ben was encouraged by Dr. Rhinehart's assessment of Ives. "Good, Doctor, then you can appreciate the predicament that we're in. Here's the catch. Lyman murdered those women and left samples of his hair and semen at the scenes. Now, we can link him to these murders sufficiently to charge him if we can match his hair and DNA to the evidence left at the scenes. The problem is that we can't get samples of his hair and blood without a search warrant or consent. We both know that he'll never give consent. We can't get a search warrant without some credible evidence or witness testimony to link him to the victims. We have an anonymous tip that he's our killer, but that's not good enough. We have to support that with some corroborating evidence or testimony. That's why we're here. We're hoping that Lyman will say something that will link him to the victims."

Dr. Rhinehart nodded as she pondered the dilemma. She folded her hands and said, "I'll allow you to talk to Lyman, but I'm in a precarious position myself. I have to appoint a staff psychologist to sit in on the interview. We have to make sure that Lyman understands his rights and every question that you ask. Now, when the psychologist makes it clear to Lyman that he doesn't have to talk to you, he'll likely refuse to speak. Once he hears his Miranda rights, he'll know he has the right to remain silent. How are you going to get around that hurdle?"

Ben agreed with Dr. Rhinehart's assessment, except for one thing. "True, Doctor, but we're not obligated to give Ives the

Miranda warning. Miranda only applies to custodial interrogation. Since he's here under a civil commitment, he's not in official police custody for Miranda purposes. We just want to visit with him in a non-accusatory manner and see if he'll confirm enough information to link him to the victims. If he does, we'll get a search warrant for blood and hair, then transfer him to the county jail so he can't escape. When the lab matches his hair and blood samples to those at the murder scenes, we'll charge him and interview him in the county jail. Then we'll give him the Miranda warning and get accusatory with him."

Dr. Rhinehart stared at Ben for a few seconds, then said, "I see. So if Lyman doesn't suspect that you're trying to gather enough circumstantial evidence to obtain a search warrant, you have no intention of telling him. You're just going to humor him along in a casual conversation, hoping he'll say something to incriminate himself, right?"

Ben slowly nodded his head. "Yes, that's right."

She stared at Ben for a few seconds, then asked, "And that's ethical? It doesn't bother you to take advantage of a psych patient who may not understand what's going on?"

Ben pondered her question. He finally said, "No, it doesn't. First of all, crazy isn't the same as stupid. Secondly, Lyman may be your psych patient, but he's a calculating, cold-blooded killer hiding out here under the pretense that he's crazy. He really belongs on death row. We're not taking advantage of someone who doesn't understand what they're doing. We're merely using every advantage that the law permits. Lyman is smart, and we have to use every tool at our disposal. If he unknowingly admits to something that gets us over the probable cause hurdle with the search warrant, that's his misfortune and our good luck. That's not trickery. That's hardball in the big league. No, Doctor, I don't feel the least bit guilty. If you'd seen what he did to those ladies, you wouldn't either."

"That may be, but I have an obligation to protect him while he's in this institution, whether I like him or not. I'm sorry. I agree with your assessment of him personally, but professionally, I have a job to do."

The doctor sat quietly for a few seconds and twisted her wedding ring as she stared at Ben. She finally said, "I'll see if he's even willing to talk to you."

She picked up the phone and summoned an orderly. When the young lady entered, Dr. Rhinehart instructed her to ask Lyman if he would talk to the police. Ten minutes later, the orderly returned and said that Lyman laughed when asked if he would talk to the police. She thanked the orderly and said, "Sorry, gents, he's not going to take a chance of saying anything that might incriminate him. He's too smart."

Ben looked away in frustration and tried to think of another angle. He regretted being so open with Dr. Rhinehart. Gabe looked at the orderly and asked, "Listen, ma'am, would you please go back and tell Lyman that he and one of the detectives share a mutual friend, Dr. Loar?" Dr. Rhinehart squinted as she looked suspiciously at Gabe, then nodded at the orderly.

Ten minutes later, the orderly returned and said, "Ives said he'll see you." Gabe looked at Ben and smiled.

When the orderly left, Dr. Rhinehart gave the detectives one final instruction. "Listen, gentlemen, you have to be aware of something. Lyman is capable of incredible violence. He hates everyone and everything. He has only two passions. He loves pain and he loves Dr. Loar. She sends him love letters all the time, and he obsesses over her day and night. I've banned her from personal visits because he would become so unmanageable after she would leave. When he's taking his Haldol and has no personal contact with her, my staff can manage him without too much difficulty. When she visits, and he sets eyes on her and smells her perfume, he's an absolute monster. She's his one and only button. If you choose to push it, make sure you don't set him off. You can walk away, but we have to deal with him." Ben agreed and they left Dr. Rhinehart's office.

The orderly led the detectives to an interview room. They sat in front of a thick safety-glass screen with vent holes to permit voices to pass through. A couple of minutes later, Lyman Ives stepped through the door on the other side, followed by a staff psychologist. The door locked behind them and he sat in the chair opposite the detectives. The chair was bolted to the floor for safety.

Lyman sat motionless and sized up the detectives. He was an imposing figure and appeared as a rare, elusive specimen in a zoo. Gabe recognized him instantly as the man that he'd seen on Loar's tapes. He was the man in bed with Loar and the man who'd killed Green.

Ives was pierced and tattooed heavily. Scar tissue revealed his propensity for self-inflicted pain. Veins stood up in his arms, neck and chest.

Gabe wondered how he stayed in such good shape. He must have access to a weight room. He was cut and clearly stronger than hell. His black, slicked-back hair and pronounced facial bone structure made him look demonic.

Ives glared at the detectives through his steel blue eyes. He was the most intimidating man that Gabe had ever seen. Ben broke the ice with an introduction. "Morning, Lyman, I'm Detective Ben Hire and this is Gabe Kinnett. We'd like to visit with you for a few minutes."

Ives held up his hand to stop the interview. He glared at Ben and snarled through gritted teeth, "Shut the fuck up! You don't say shit to me, asshole! This is my house! I ask the questions here!"

Gabe was shocked by the hostility that Ives displayed right out of the blocks, but Ben was unfazed. He kept his cool as Ives asked, "Which one of you losers is Maura's friend?"

Gabe was almost afraid to answer, but he refused to be intimidated. He put on his Angus Blauw persona and spoke up with authority. "I am."

Ives turned his body slightly, focused on Gabe and refused to acknowledge Ben's presence. Ben waited patiently. He realized that the interview would not take place if not on Ives's terms.

Since this was a preliminary icebreaker, he was content to let Gabe take the lead. He kept his note-pad in his lap and jotted down notes, hoping to be inconspicuous. He subtly reached inside his coat pocket and made sure the *Record* button was depressed on his tape recorder.

Ives stared deep into Gabe's eyes. He was trying to assess Gabe's appeal to Loar and establish his dominance early in the interview. Gabe was younger and cleaner, but Ives had power and dominance that no other man could equal. Still, he wondered. He

330

squinted his bright blue eyes as he studied Gabe. Gabe decided to break the silence. "So, Lyman, tell me about yourself."

Ives shook his head and replied in a deep growl, "No, fuck you! You tell me about you! What's your relationship with Maura?"

This wasn't going to be easy. Ives was determined to dominate the interview. Gabe had to wrestle control away from him, so he planted his heels. "No, Lyman, you don't understand. You're not in charge here, we are."

Ives shook his head in defiance and smiled sadistically at Gabe. He extended his middle finger up to the glass and stood to leave. He snarled, "Interview over, asshole!"

He stopped at the door and waited for the psychologist to unlock it. Gabe didn't want to make Dr. Rhinehart's job any more difficult by pushing Ives's button, but he was desperate to sink the hook. He casually said, "Fine. I'll tell Maura you said hi when I see her tonight."

Ives tried to pretend that the thought of another man touching Loar didn't bother him, but he couldn't mask his rage. His whole body quivered and his muscles rippled. He could no longer stand the tension. He spun around and stomped back to the chair. As he sat down, he crossed his arms and glared at Gabe.

The cat was out of the bag. Gabe knew that thirty minutes after they left, Loar would know the context of the entire interview. He smiled and said, "Good. How long have you been here, Lyman?"

Ives shook his head again in defiance. "No way, answer my questions first."

Gabe said, "No, you'll get what you want, then walk away. Like I said, we're in charge, not you." Lyman simply glared at Gabe. After a few seconds, Gabe slid his chair back and stood. As he turned toward the door, he said, "Interview over, Lyman."

Ben took Gabe's cue and stood. As they reached the door, Ives growled softly, "Five years!" The bluff had worked. Both turned and sat down again.

Gabe didn't want to anger Ives any more than he already had, so he tried to soften his demeanor. "Five years, long time, Lyman. Any plans to leave?"

Ives shrugged his shoulders and mumbled. "Maybe, I can leave any time I want."

Ben asked, "I thought you were here under a civil commitment. Isn't your mother the only person who can get you out of here?"

Ives felt that he could still psych out the younger and less experienced detective. He knew from past experience that Detective Hire would not be intimidated or manipulated. He pretended that Ben did not exist. He continued to focus on Gabe's eyes.

Gabe looked at Ben to make sure that he wasn't imagining Lyman's contempt for Ben. He then realized that Ives would not answer Ben, so he repeated Ben's question. "Lyman, isn't your mother the only person who can get you out of here?"

Ives shot Gabe an evil smile. "My mother only put me here. It's up to me if I stay. This chicken coop can't hold me if I want to leave."

"Yeah, it's not the most secure facility in the world. I bet it's still hard to be in here. Tell me about your life before your mom put you in here."

Ives snarled, "What's there to tell? My mother and I hate each other, so she put me here! Pure and simple!"

Gabe wondered, *Is this a good time to bring Loar into the equation?* He decided to test the waters. "I understand that, Lyman, but what part did Dr. Loar have in that decision?"

He instantly knew that he'd struck a nerve. Ives leaned forward and glared at him as he enunciated every word. "Maura was my psychiatrist. She's still my woman. She thought it would be best for me to come here. Why the hell do you ask?"

Gabe shrugged his shoulders. "Just trying to get a feel for you, Lyman, that's all. No need to be so hostile. Ben and I aren't your enemies. We're just trying to establish a rapport with you. We need your help, but you can't help us if we can't trust you. We have to sell you to the prosecutor and we can't do that if we don't know you."

Ben was impressed with Gabe's quick thinking. Ives glared at Gabe suspiciously, then asked, "Sell me? Why the hell do you have to sell me to anyone? What do you want from me?"

Gabe smiled to lower Lyman's defenses. "Well, Lyman, we've been going through some of our old files, and it appears that you ran in some pretty rough circles. We were hoping that you might have known some of our victims or suspects. If it turns out that you knew some of them, you might be a good witness for us. We certainly can't use you if we can't sell your credibility to the prosecutor. We have to present you as a good guy, and frankly you're making it pretty hard to do that. What are you so mad about? We're not here to accuse you of anything. We just want to run some names by you."

Ives didn't buy Gabe's story for a second. He said, "Well, you'll have to excuse me if I'm a little suspicious of the police. If you knew what some of your asshole cops did to me when I was a kid, you'd be suspicious, too."

Gabe didn't respond. He was sure that Ives deserved every ounce of misery that he'd ever gotten. Ives continued, "So tell me, Kinnett. How's my old friend, Blauw, doing these days?"

When Gabe heard Blauw's name, he knew his work was cut out for him. Among the criminal element, Angus was the most hated officer on the department. "Oh, fine I guess. I don't talk to him. I don't really like him very much."

Ives shook his head in disgust and yelled, "Bullshit! You all sleep together! You cover each other's ass and lie through your teeth to protect each other!"

Gabe shrugged his shoulders and tried to calm Ives. "Well, Lyman, I can't change your mind, but I don't know how Blauw is."

Ben leaned over and whispered to Gabe, "Get me back in this."

Gabe looked at Lyman and said, "Okay, Lyman, here's the deal. We're in a position to help you. We need you, but if you ever want to get out of here legally without your mother, you need us, too. Ben and I are a team. You've got to deal with both of us. You're either going to talk to Ben or we're out of here. Our policy prohibits us from working informants alone. Either work with him or we're through. I know you're bitter, but get over it."

Ives thought for a minute, then glared at Ben. "Well, Detective Hire, looks like we're all one big happy family."

Ben asked, "How about we start slow? I'll run some names by you and you tell me if you know them."

Ives leaned back in his chair and shook his head. "Can't help you. I have a policy of my own. I never rat on anyone, and I never help the cops. Now, I might be willing to change my policy if you tell me what you're going to do for me."

Ben was completely unfazed. He calmly replied, "We can't make any promises, Lyman, but I just happen to be a personal friend of the judge who appointed your mother as your guardian and signed your commitment order. He might be persuaded to allow someone other than your mother to assume guardianship of you. If someone like Gabe or me were willing to take responsibility for you, maybe you could get out of here. I said maybe because if we assume responsibility for you, we have to be able to trust you. And right now, I wouldn't trust you as far as I could throw you. So I'm going to have to see a significant attitude change if we're even going to consider helping you."

Ben hoped his deception wasn't written across his face. He knew that no judge would ever appoint a police officer as guardian of a criminal. Lyman required strong supervision and tight control. Neither Ben nor Gabe could control him or devote the time it would take to supervise him. Even if they wanted to, the department would never allow it.

Ives stared Ben directly in the eye as he considered Ben's proposition. He looked up at the ceiling and sighed deeply. He asked, "So who do I have to sell down the river?"

Ben was pleased. Ives had no idea that he was their target. He had to be careful though. Ives would never give up Loar, so he had to work around her tactfully. He said, "I'm not sure yet, Lyman. You see, you were one of Dr. Loar's patients. She's had some pretty wild characters in her care. We think you might know some of them. Let's give it a shot. What do you say?"

"Sure, why not?"

Ben didn't want to alarm Ives so soon in the interview, so he avoided the names of Ives's four murder victims. He thought he could put him at ease by throwing out names that Ives had no information about. He began with the earliest murder. "How about Jared Cutchall, Lyman? Ever heard of him?"

"Yeah, I knew him."

Ben was surprised. Ives was going to claim to know more than he really did so he could have additional bargaining power. He tested Ives further, "How about Paul Siles, Lyman, ever heard of him?"

"Yeah, I knew him, too."

Ben looked up from his notes and stared at Ives for a few seconds. "Lyman, just to establish your credibility here, tell me about the Cutchall killing."

"I'm not sure I want to yet."

"Okay then, tell me about the Siles killing. Who killed him?"

"I'm not sure I want to tell you that either."

"Are you afraid to burn Siles's killer?"

"I'm not afraid of anything. I want to see what you're going to do for me before I give the guy up."

Gabe sat patiently as Ben tightened the noose. "So, Lyman, you're telling me that you know the two people who killed Cutchall and Siles, right?" Ives nodded his head. Ben continued, "How many people were involved?"

"Two."

Ben removed his glasses and rubbed his eyes. He glared at Ives and said, "You're lying your ass off, Lyman! You don't know anything about either of these two killings, do you?"

Ives glared at Ben with total hatred. Ben said, "There weren't two killers, Lyman, there was only one. Siles murdered Cutchall, then committed suicide before he went to trial. Now quit lying to me! You either play ball here or the whole deal is off! What's it going to be? Make up your mind!"

Ives looked at the floor and nodded as he replied, "Okay, I didn't know either of them, but give me another chance. Give me some more names."

Ben looked back at his notes and began again. "Albert Sabre?" Lyman shook his head.

"Nat Benson."

Lyman nodded his head. "Yeah, I knew her. She was a lesbian that Maura was counseling."

"How did she die?"

"Strangled."

"Who killed her?"

335

Lyman didn't like Benson's killer, so he gave her up without hesitation. "Another lesbian bitch, Jenna Kerse."

Gabe almost jumped out of his chair with excitement. He wanted to jump in and start asking questions, but Ben gently reached over and touched his arm, indicating that he should remain silent. Ben asked, "How do you know Kerse?"

"Everyone knows Kerse. She's a man-hating dyke who lives at the fitness center." Lyman patted himself on the chest and boasted proudly, "Jenna and I go way back. I'm the only man who ever scared her. She's terrified of me. I used to make her shake like a newborn pup when I'd get in her face. She thinks she's a badass, but she's nothing compared to me. If Maura hadn't stopped me, I'd have ----"

Lyman stopped himself in mid sentence. Ben and Gabe knew what the final words were going to be. Ben continued, "How do you know Kerse killed Benson?"

Lyman hesitated, then shook his head. "I just do. I'm not going to say anymore about it."

Gabe knew that Ives had seen Loar's videotape of Benson's murder in the shower. Ives clammed up because he didn't want to let them know that Loar had the tape. Ben continued, "Tim Allis." Ives nodded.

"Roger Moesen?"

Ives again nodded and said, "Allis was an assistant D.A. Moesen killed him. Kerse killed Moesen, too."

Both detectives knew that Lyman was being truthful. That was as far on the list as Ben could go without getting into the murders that Ives had committed. Anything after the Green murder would do no good because Ives was in the institute then. He would have no information on Clearey, Wilcox, Webster, Lynch, Windsor or Boreman.

Ben had to make a decision about pinning Ives down to his murders. He decided that this was the time to put them on the table since he had established his dominance and Ives was talking.

Ben glanced over at the psychologist, who up to this point had remained conspicuously silent. She had not done what Dr. Rhinehart said she should. She had not counseled Ives or explained any of the detectives' questions. Apparently, she knew Ives as well as Dr. Rhinehart. She knew Ives was fully capable of

336

understanding the questions and defending himself. Perhaps she, too, was hoping that Ives would say something that would secure his future in an institution other than Perkins-Hays.

Ben knew the next interview might involve another psychologist who might not be so passive. A more protective staff member might hinder the interview. He decided to push as far as he could while the momentum was in his favor. "Good, Lyman! Good! We're making some progress here. Let's go on. How about Eleanor Rudder? Ever heard of her?"

Lyman predictably sat quietly and shook his head. He repeated the same facade when Ben asked about Grace Lindsey, Lois Andoever and Lucian Green. At this point, Ben decided to try a bluff. "Oh, Lyman, we were doing so well. Now you're lying to me again. We know for a fact that you knew Lucian Green. This is your last warning, Lyman. Either quit lying to me or the interview is over."

Lyman sat quietly and glared at Ben. Ben calmly closed his folder and stood. Gabe stood also and both men walked to the door. This time Lyman didn't stop them.

They stopped outside the door and Gabe asked, "Should we go back in, Ben?"

"No, we've made good progress today. We'll let him sweat for a few days and try him again later."

"How will we know when he's ready to talk?"

He smiled and patted Gabe on the back as they walked down the hall. "We'll know he's ready when he calls. Make no mistake, he will call. He didn't get what he wanted. He didn't find out what your relationship with Loar is. As soon as he realizes that he let us go too soon, he'll be furious. When he settles down and swallows his pride, he'll call."

As they walked to the exit door, the psychologist from the interview yelled for them to wait. She hurried up to Gabe and slipped a business card in his hand. She said, "Call me," and walked away.

Gabe looked at the card and read the name out loud. "Lindsey Schaff. Wonder what she wants?"

"It can only be good, my boy. She wants to tell us something about Ives, but she doesn't want Dr. Rhinehart to know that she's talking to us. She could lose her job. Call her and see what she has to say."

15

GABE WAITED FOR Garrison's secretary to give him permission to see the chief. When she did, he walked in and sat down. Garrison was reading Gabe's file. He dropped it on his desk as he looked menacingly over the top of his glasses. "Morning, Gabe. How's life?"

He appeared to be making a genuine effort to be congenial. Gabe didn't want to anger him, so he answered politely, "Fine, sir. How are you?"

Garrison didn't answer, but took off his glasses. He laid them down and said, "You know, Gabe. I have to do something about you. We've been dragging this thing out for weeks and I've got to put some closure to it."

Gabe no longer feared Garrison. He could no longer look at Garrison as a chief. He only saw a nude child molester on top of an under-aged girl. He tried to hide his contempt. "Sorry, Chief, I'm afraid I can't help you. I'd like to convince you that I did nothing wrong, but I'm afraid that your personal dislike for me has clouded your objectivity."

Garrison feigned a pretentious smile. "No, Gabe, you're wrong. I don't dislike you. I can't have a loose cannon running around knocking the crap out of people. There are approved arrest procedures that have to be adhered to. You're going to get us sued. You're also a bad influence on the rest of the officers. I have to send the message that we won't tolerate excessive force."

He sat quietly while Garrison talked. He was amazed that he felt no intimidation. With Loar's videotape, Garrison was his any time he wanted. Garrison continued, "How did your counseling session with Dr. Loar go, Gabe?"

He shrugged his shoulders. "There was no counseling session. We talked, but Dr. Loar had no suggestions for me. We talked about personal things. She seemed concerned about me."

"Yes, she's voiced the same concern to me. She's under some crazy notion that you're investigating her. She thinks you've deluded yourself into thinking that you're some big-shot detective. She thinks you suspect her of committing some of our old unsolved murders. I told her that she was imagining things. I told her that you're not investigating anything. I told her that you're not even a detective and that you're fully aware of your status in life. I told her that you're an insignificant, little night-bug. You haven't deluded yourself into thinking that you're a detective, have you, Gabe? You're not investigating anything, are you, Gabe? You're sitting in your hole like a good little boy and keeping your nose clean, aren't you, Gabe? You're doing just what I told you when I lifted your police powers, aren't you?"

Gabe thought for a second, then shook his head. He looked Garrison in the eye and said, "No, Chief. No, I'm not keeping my nose clean. I've been reading through the dead files and I've made some interesting discoveries."

Garrison looked suspiciously at him and asked, "Like what?"

"I'm not prepared to say right now, but let's just say that Loar is not as clean as she pretends. The problem for you is that I've found evidence that you knew that. You've even made her privy to inside information that she's not entitled to. As a matter of fact, you've even gone so far as to become a co-conspirator with her. I can't disclose what evidence I've uncovered, but you're going to have some embarrassing questions to answer if my investigation ever goes public."

Tears of anger boiled up in Garrison's eyes. He leaned over his desk and growled through gritted teeth, "Are you threatening me?"

He was confused by Gabe's confidence, and glared at him. Gabe finally broke the silence. "Enough said, Chief. You're the

340

boss, but let me suggest something to you. You can do anything you want to me right now and I can't stop you, but think about this. I can release my investigation to the FBI or attorney general whether I'm employed or not. My status with the department in no way diminishes the credibility of the evidence that I've found. It will stand on its own merit. Now, I promise you, there will come a day in the near future when you'll come to me with your hat in your hand, begging me to bury the evidence that I've uncovered. My treatment of you then will be dictated by your treatment of me now."

He stood and walked to the door. Before exiting the chief's office, he turned and said, "I'll wait to hear from you, sir. Thank you for your time."

Garrison slumped back in his chair and thought long and hard about Gabe's revelation. He picked up his phone and punched Major Richey's extension. When Richey answered, Garrison said, "Get in here. We have to talk."

Ben Hire couldn't wait for Gabe to talk to Lindsey Schaff. He called her at home after hours, hoping she would talk freely if she couldn't be overheard. "Lindsey, Ben Hire. I'm calling for Gabe. He's busy right now. We got the impression that you have some information for us."

"Yes, Mr. Hire. Thanks for calling. Before I say anything, you have to promise to keep me out of this whole mess. I don't want anyone to know that I've talked to you."

Ben tried to reassure her. "I can't promise you that, Lindsey. If it ever becomes necessary to put you on the stand in court to verify what you've told us, you may have to testify. Why don't you tell me what you know? I'll do my best to keep it confidential."

There was a long silence, then Lindsey said, "Well, I guess I can tell you, but please try to keep me out of the investigation. I could lose my job for divulging confidential patient information."

Ben agreed and Lindsey continued, "I've known Ives ever since he first came to the Institute. I think I can safely say that he's the most dangerous man that I've ever met. He's evil incarnate. If Satan ever occupied a mortal body, it would be Ives."

341

Ben encouraged Lindsey to continue. She said, "Ives is a sadomasochist. He engages in painful acts with some of the other patients here. He's also very manipulative. He changes his personality like a chameleon. He's even having an affair with one of the staff so she'll do things for him. She's the female orderly who delivered your message to Ives the other day. She thinks he's the most powerful man in the world. She's convinced that he's some sort of god. She sneaks him things from the outside that he's not allowed to have. We can't catch her, and Ives won't burn her because he doesn't want to lose his link to the outside. We know she's having sex with him during her tour of duty, but everyone is too afraid of Ives to turn her in."

Ben wanted to clarify something that Lindsey had said earlier. "Lindsey, you said that he engages in sadomasochism with the other patients. Do you think he confides any information about his past to them or the orderly?"

"Oh, I don't think so. I've asked them about what Ives has told them. They deny any knowledge of his past. He's too smart for that. I'm positive that he's not told his girlfriend about his past or she'd never have anything to do with him. She's really a nice person, and he's an absolute monster."

Ben pushed Lindsey further. "Lindsey, what does he do to the other patients?"

"They hurt each other. They tattoo and pierce each other's bodies. One of the patients told me that they even engage in autoerotism. They will use a ligature to constrict the blood supply to their brain while they masturbate. As they ejaculate, they tighten the ligature, then release it just before they lose consciousness. I guess it produces some euphoric sensation. They do it in the presence of each other. It's the sickest thing I've ever heard of."

Ben agreed. "Yes, I know. I've heard of it. I hope I never have to see anything like that. Listen, Lindsey, what can you tell me about Dr. Loar?"

"Please don't tell anyone that I said this, but she's just as evil as Ives. I'm terrified of her. If she knew I was talking about her, I'd wind up like all her other enemies. She writes letters to Ives. Dr. Rhinehart has banned her from the institute. I'm afraid for Dr. Rhinehart. I'm afraid she'll wind up dead like everyone else who's ever crossed Dr. Loar. Anyway, she's manipulated Ives like a puppet. He's so madly in love with her that he'd do anything for her. I think he loves her because they're so much alike."

"Hey listen, Lindsey, I don't suppose you could get your hands on some of those love letters, could you?"

"Yes, I think so. I can get in Ives's room when he goes to his therapy session. I'll have to make copies. If Ives thinks that someone has stolen his letters, he'll be an absolute maniac."

Ben finished jotting down notes of the conversation. "Thanks, Lindsey. Listen, I'm pretty tied up with other cases right now. Would you get those letters to Detective Kinnett? He'll have more time to read them."

"Okay, sure, I can do that."

"Anything else?"

"Not that I can think of right now. I'll get copies of Loar's letters to Detective Kinnett. Oh yes, there is one more thing."

"What?"

"That young detective that was with you, Detective Kinnett?"

"Yes, what about him?"

Lindsay hesitated, then said with a sad tone in her voice, "Please warn him. He's going to be killed."

Ben sat in shock for a few seconds, then realized that he shouldn't be surprised. Gabe had been kicking the sleeping monster ever since he'd become obsessed with Loar.

Faithful to her word, Lindsey Schaff delivered copies of Loar's love letters to Gabe. He pored over them with intense interest. One name was casually mentioned in her letters and jumped out at him. He focused on Sarah Bethard as the one person who seemed approachable.

The name Sarah Bethard stood out in Gabe's mind. When he looked her up in Dr. Loar's patient files, he learned that she had been in the same group therapy sessions for domestic abuse victims as Linda Boreman. Sarah was a thirty-eight year-old housewife and mother of three. He hoped she would be the most approachable member of the group.

He knocked on Sarah's door unexpectedly about eight the next evening. He didn't want to forewarn her with a phone call. He

343

hoped a surprise visit would compel her to tell him the truth without any prompting by Dr. Loar.

Sarah was not at all intimidated and asked her kids and husband to leave them alone in the kitchen. After sitting at the kitchen table, she asked, "How can I help you, detective?"

Her congenial demeanor lowered Gabe's guard. "Well, Sarah, I'm looking over some of our old homicides and saw that you were in the same group therapy sessions as Linda Boreman. Her husband, Swede, was killed a few months ago. I'd like to ask you some questions if you don't mind."

Linda never allowed her pretentious smile to droop. She shifted in her chair nervously, then said, "Well, I guess it's okay. I knew Linda and was so sorry for the abuse she'd been going through. I didn't know her husband though."

Gabe listened intently, then asked, "Why were you in that group, Linda?"

She grew frightened as she looked past Gabe into the living room. When she was sure that her husband wasn't listening, she replied, "Well, detective, my husband and I were going through some marital discourse, but we're working things out now."

Gabe read between the lines and deduced that Sarah herself had been abused. He wisely chose to take another line of questioning. "So, Sarah, what types of abuse was Linda going through?"

Sarah grew more nervous and stopped the interview. "Listen, detective, this isn't a good place to talk. Is there any way that I could contact you at your office?"

He was thrilled at the prospect of Sarah opening up to him. "Sure, Sarah. How about tomorrow? I'll wait for you in the detective unit."

"Ten is good for me."

Gabe stood and shook her hand. "I'll see you tomorrow morning then. Thanks." As she closed the door behind him, she reached for the phone on the wall and immediately called Dr. Loar.

Gabe was ecstatic. He hurried home to call Ben and tell him that Sarah would open new doors for them. Ben was thrilled with the good news. He said, "That's great news, Gabe. I'll be there, too. We'll both work on her. I think Boreman's killer was in that therapy group. He or she probably sympathized with Boreman's wife and became indignant when they saw the pain that she was going through. This is the break that we've been waiting for. See you then."

Gabe could no longer stand being away from Beck. As he exited his building he looked up and down the street to make sure Kerse wasn't watching. He then carefully made his way to Beck's apartment building.

After dinner, they retired to the living room. Predictably, the petting escalated to a frenzy and they found themselves in the bedroom with their clothes strung along the path from the living room sofa. Again, Beck stopped short of intercourse. She sent him home before her resolve weakened any further.

The anticipation was more than Gabe could stand. He arrived at the detective unit about 9:45 and bounced into Ben's office. Ben said, "Hey, killer, ready to break this thing wide open?"

"Sure am. I probably won't be employed long enough to see it, but you'll keep me informed."

"Nah, you'll be around. Just keep you mouth shut to Garrison and quit pissing him off. Come on, let's go."

Gabe led the way to the first floor lobby. As he looked out to the street, he pointed and said, "There she is, Ben. Good looking woman, huh?"

"Yes, but let me do the talking, kid."

"Sure thing, boss."

Sarah stepped through the door and Gabe extended his hand to greet her. "Good morning, Sarah, I'd like to introduce you to Ben Hire. He's going to be sitting in on the interview."

Gabe turned his attention to Ben and pointed to him. With his attention on Ben, he couldn't see Sarah. He was surprised as Ben's pleasant smile dissolved and panic overtook his face. Not knowing why Ben was frightened, he looked back at Sarah.

He hadn't seen her remove the long-bladed knife from her jacket. Before he could react, she plunged it deep into his chest with an overhand thrust.

Gabe looked at Sarah in total shock. Her once congenial smile now looked sadistic and demonic. He quivered as he looked at the handle of the knife sticking out of his chest. He felt his head spin as his orientation and balance faded.

The pain was excruciating. His left lung instantly collapsed and he could no longer breathe. Aside from the pain, the loss of air threw him into respiratory arrest. Fortunately, he lost consciousness when he hit the floor.

The receptionist screamed and Ben threw the tail of his sport coat aside, exposing his pistol. He drew it with every intention of killing Sarah on the spot. The other officers who were milling around the lobby also drew their weapons. All were prepared to carry out the department's unwritten policy that anyone who killed an officer drew the ultimate sanction.

Ben thrust the muzzle of his pistol at Sarah and squeezed the trigger. Suddenly, he realized that he needed her alive. He released the tension on the trigger and looked around. The other officers were not so concerned about her testimony.

He turned to the other officers and yelled for them to stop. Sarah made no attempt to run or avoid her fate. He jumped in front of her to shield her. The other officers halted and raised their muzzles in a safe direction.

After holstering his pistol, he knelt beside Gabe. He could hear Gabe's desperate gasps and yelled for him to hold on. Without prompting, the secretary had called for an ambulance.

The sirens wailed in the distance as the officers charged Sarah. She offered no resistance, but they picked her up and slammed her face-first to the floor. She screamed in pain as an officer dropped his knee in the back of her neck and another handcuffed her. She was jerked to her feet and hustled off to the jail. She couldn't understand why she was being treated so brutally.

Gabe managed to inhale enough air into his good lung to stay alive. He clung to life as the paramedics stabilized him and rushed him to the emergency room. The doctor made a small slit in his right side and rammed a chest-tube through his ribcage so the blood in his chest cavity could drain. He thought nothing the doctor would do could hurt more than Sarah's knife. He was wrong. Again, he lost consciousness.

Ben sat in the waiting room until Gabe came out of surgery. By the time he was rolled into the recovery room, Beck had joined Ben in his vigil. When the nurse gave approval for visitors, the entire waiting room was filled with officers.

Ben and Beck went in first. Gabe was still under the affects of anesthesia and couldn't talk. Ben closed the door so no one could hear. He gripped Gabe's hand and leaned in close. "Hi, kid. We're here for you. Sorry I didn't react quicker."

Tears dripped from the corners of Gabe's eyes as he shook his head. He couldn't talk, but wanted Ben to know that it wasn't his fault. Ben patted the back of his hand and said, "We'll talk later, pal. You hang in there. I'm going to interview Bethard. We're going to break her down. She's got kids. She'll roll over on Loar in a heartbeat to shorten her jail sentence."

He stepped away from the bed and Beck stepped in. She leaned over and kissed Gabe's sweaty forehead. She grabbed a tissue from a box on the nightstand and wiped the tears from his face. She wiped her own and said, "Well, I warned you. I know you don't want to hear that right now, but this was what I was afraid of. The doctor said you're going to be all right. You have to back off of Loar. She isn't worth all this."

Gabe reacted with anger. He squeezed Beck's hand and shook his head. She got the message. She choked with emotion as she lowered her head. She looked back into his eyes, unable to hide her emotions any longer. "You stubborn fool! I love you, but I can't go on like this! You're lucky to be alive! The next time might kill you! It will surely be the end of me! If I mean anything to you, don't put me through this!"

He saw the torment that Beck was going through. He couldn't talk, so discussion was out of the question. He was in too much pain to argue anyway. He simply squeezed her hand to signal that he loved her.

The attending physician bumped into Ben as he was leaving Gabe's room. Ben thanked him for saving Gabe and was preparing to move on when the doctor stopped him. He said, "You might want to know something about Officer Kinnett's attacker."

Ben stopped in his tracks. "What?"

"Either she was coached or she's had some training in the use of a knife. Most people who have never killed with a knife make their downward thrust with the blade vertical. That's how the knife feels most natural in their hand. When that happens, the blade is usually so broad that it doesn't pass between the ribs, unless the attacker is very strong. The trauma seldom extends much deeper than the rib cage. Officer Kinnett was stabbed with a broad blade. This lady turned the blade horizontal so it would pass between his ribs. She was coached or had some training in the art. Just thought you'd want to know." Ben stared as the doctor walked on. He knew who had coached Sarah Bethard.

Ben had Sarah placed in a secure interview room. Before talking to her, he'd looked through her property, which had been collected by the detention officer. He adjusted his glasses as he read the label on her pill bottle. The name, *Amitriptylline,* didn't sound familiar. He hurried to his office and pulled the *Physician's Desk Reference* from the bookshelf.

As he'd suspected, *Amitriptylline* was indicated for treatment of depression. It was a trycyclic antidepressant with a sedative affect. The caution warned that schizophrenic patients may develop increased symptoms of psychosis, and patients with paranoid symptomology may have an exaggeration of such symptoms. The prescribing physician was Maura Loar.

Sarah was a changed person in the interview room. She was not the stoic picture of serenity that she'd presented in the lobby. She was crying softly and wringing her hands in fear. The effects of her medication were wearing off.

Ben was glad to see that she was going to pieces. This interview was going to be easier than he'd thought. She was vulnerable and at his mercy. "Good afternoon, Sarah. You and I have some serious business to settle. You've stabbed a police officer. Fortunately for you, he's going to recover, but you're still facing an attempted murder charge."

Sarah sighed in relief when she heard that Gabe was going to survive. She buried her face in her hands and wept. She finally wiped her eyes and said, "I'm so glad he is going to be okay. I wish I hadn't done that."

Ben read Sarah's body language and knew she was sincere. "Sarah, answer this question for me. Why did you feel that you had to stab the officer?"

She cried softly, then shook her head. She lowered her gaze to the floor and whispered. "I'd thought about it all night. I went from periods when I was courageous to times when I couldn't imagine why I would even contemplate such a thing. I know my moods swing, and I feel braver when I take my medication. I wish now that I'd never showed up for the interview."

The momentum of the interview was going Ben's way. He encouraged her to talk, hoping she would implicate Loar. She said, "I brought the knife with me in case I had the nerve to do it. I was hoping I would lose my nerve and leave the knife in my coat. I remember thinking that the officer was going to put me and Dr. Loar in jail, and I just couldn't let him do that."

Ben leaned into Sarah and asked, "What have you done to deserve to go to jail, Sarah? And what's Dr. Loar got to do with this?"

She looked suspiciously at Ben, then suddenly realized that she'd almost implicated herself in the Boreman murder. "Nothing. Nothing at all. She's just my doctor."

Ben kept the pressure on. "No, Sarah, that's not all. You were afraid Kinnett was going to put you and Dr. Loar in jail. Why?"

She clammed up and refused to answer. She could no longer look Ben in the eye. He pressed harder. "Look, Sarah, I know Loar put you up to this. I also know that this isn't your first time. You've killed before. You displayed too much expertise with that knife for a first time killer. You have too much to lose if you go to prison. You tried to kill a police officer, Sarah. You could go to prison for many years. Who's going to raise your kids? What's going to happen to them?"

As she began to cry, Ben intensified the pressure. "Sarah, listen to me. I know you wouldn't have hurt Kinnett without some pressure from Loar. She's used others to kill for her. You're not the only one. I know you're loyal to her, but she uses people. She gets them to do her dirty work, then throws them away or kills them. Even if you get out on bond, she'll kill you before you can

349

implicate her. I want to help you. Kinnett wants to help you. I talked to him today and he has no hard feelings toward you. It's Loar we want. We can get you a deal on the attempted murder charge. I'll talk to the prosecutor. You won't do a day in jail, but, Sarah, you've got to help us get Loar. And don't think that you're going to talk about this with Loar. You can talk to an attorney, but you'll never get to talk to Loar. I'll see to that."

Sarah regained her composure and sat quietly for a few seconds. She finally raised her head and said in her typical stoic tone, "I need to think. I assume I'll be incarcerated until my court date. Can I have some time?"

Ben leaned back in his chair and sighed in frustration. "Sure, Sarah. You'll go before the judge for arraignment tomorrow morning. The prosecutor will ask that you be held without bond pending a psychological evaluation. You'll have time to think, but just remember something, Sarah. Once we go to trial, it'll be too late. If we make a case on Loar through another source, you're out of luck. The first person to give us Loar gets the deal. You either help us soon or you'll rot in prison."

He stood and left the room. He signaled the detention officer to put Sarah back in her cell. With the idea of giving up Loar firmly planted, he hoped she would come to her senses. Perhaps when the psychologist examined her and adjusted her medications, she would think more clearly.

Ben had another ace up his sleeve. He'd planted the same idea in the head of Jimmy Clossan. He was still paralyzed, but would face charges for attempting to murder Angus Blauw if he ever recovered. Ben smiled. The world was closing in on Maura Loar.

Gabe's first two nights were fitful. He napped during the day and watched TV intermittently throughout the night. He was awaking from an afternoon nap when he sensed the presence of someone else in the room. Through his grogginess, he made out the form of a man sitting in the chair beside his bed. As his eyes focused, he made out the face of Ezard Lumas smiling back at him. Lumas greeted him in his usual sinister tone. "Well, good afternoon, sunshine. Did you enjoy your little beauty sleep?"

Gabe tried to raise himself to a semi-seated position. "I would have if I hadn't seen your ugly face."

Ezard laughed and slapped his knee. "That's what I like about you, Kinnett, defiant to the bitter end. Your career has just slid down the toilet and you're still trying to be a bad boy. Well, your bad boy days are over. The chief told you to back off the investigation and you disobeyed his directive. He lifted your badge and commission when he suspended your police powers, but I guess you had a spare. I took the liberty of searching your belongings. I lifted your other badge from your wallet while you were asleep. I'll be back in a day or two to take your statement. You're through, tough guy. You're just another street-bum now."

Gabe didn't respond. He knew his career was over. Apparently, his threat to Garrison hadn't been sufficient to hold him at bay. He sighed and mustered enough strength to tell Lumas, "Okay, asshole, you delivered your message, so slither your cowardly ass on out the door."

Lumas smiled as he stood and walked to the door. He reached in his pocket and removed Gabe's badge. He held it up and shook it. "Take a good look, Kinnett. You'll never carry one of these again."

As Lumas opened the door to leave, he bumped into Angus Blauw, who was coming to visit Gabe. Lumas smiled and said, "Angus! I was just leaving. Go on in and comfort the ex-cop." He shook Gabe's badge in Angus's face. "I got Kinnett's. I'll have yours someday." He laughed as he walked past Angus.

Angus stuck his head in Gabe's room and said, "I'll be back in a minute, kid. I need to talk to Ezard." He then hurried down the hall after Lumas.

Lumas was losing patience with the elevator and stepped through the stairwell door. Angus busted through the door and descended on him like a bird of prey.

Lumas heard the door slam against the wall when Angus threw it open. Angus's footsteps echoed in the stairwell, and Lumas turned just in time to catch Angus's fist in the face. He fell backward and rolled down the remaining stairs to the landing. Angus pounced on him and beat him unconscious.

Angus stood and listened for footsteps in the stairwell. He reached in Lumas's coat pocket and retrieved Gabe's badge. Lumas was regaining consciousness as Angus started up the stairs.

To make his message more emphatic, Angus trotted back to Lumas and kicked him hard in the face. Lumas's head slammed against the concrete floor and gushed blood from a laceration on the back of his head. His nose was now positioned on the side of his face in line with his broken cheekbone.

Angus dropped his knee into Lumas's chest. He grabbed Lumas by the throat and squeezed his windpipe. Lumas's eyes bulged out and his face turned red as Angus lectured. "Listen to me, you ass-sniffing weasel! You ain't getting no one's badge! If you screw with Kinnett in any way, I'll hunt your sorry ass down and kill you! You understand me, asshole?"

Lumas could only blink his eyes. Angus released his throat just before he lost consciousness again. Lumas gasped for air and rubbed his throat. He tried to talk, but could only cough. He finally managed to gurgle, "Garrison will have your ass for this, Blauw."

Blauw grabbed Lumas by the hair and raised him to his knees. He slammed Lumas's head against the wall, reached inside Lumas's coat and removed his Beretta from its holster. He drove it into Lumas's mouth until it came to rest against the back of his throat. Angus pulled the hammer back to the cocked position, inserted his finger in the trigger guard and squeezed the creep out of the trigger.

Lumas could see that Angus had squeezed the slack out of the trigger and that it was pressing against the sear. Another pound of pressure would turn out the lights forever. His eyes widened as he waited for the darkness. He lost control of his bladder as Angus said, "Go ahead and tell Garrison, Ezard. I never planned to die in a retirement home anyway. I got nothing to lose. I'll kill your ass and Garrison, too. If you think I won't, I'll kill your dumb ass right here and now just to prove that I will. There's no one else here but you and me. I'll claim that some psychopath escaped from the psych ward and jumped your ass. I'll claim that he took your gun away from you and killed you with it. I'll say I chased him down the stairs. You know how old and decrepit I am, Ezard. I barely move fast enough to make it to the toilet in time. I'll say the guy out-ran me. I'm a good liar. I'll sell it, Ezard, you know I will.

You'll be in hell with the devil jabbing a pitchfork up your ass, and me and Kinnett will be drinking beer and pissing on your grave."

Lumas frantically shook his head. Angus slowly removed the Beretta from his throat. Lumas began to cry and sputtered, "I won't talk! I'll back off Kinnett, just don't kill me!"

Angus de-cocked the pistol and tossed it down the stairs so Lumas couldn't shoot him in the back. He turned and walked upstairs, leaving Lumas on the landing gushing blood and crying like a baby. The last sound Lumas heard before the stairwell door closed was Blauw's gravelly voice laughing softly.

Gabe was almost in tears when Angus walked into his room. The combination of the medications and the loss of his job was more than he could stand. Angus flopped down in the chair beside his bed and slammed Gabe's badge down on the table. Gabe's eyes widened as he asked, "How did you get that?"

Angus smiled. "Ah, me and Ezard go way back. You just have to know how to talk to him. He's not such a bad guy when you know him as well as I do."

Gabe looked suspiciously at him. "Yeah, that's what worries me, Angus. What did you do to him? If you took it from him, he'll just be back later with Garrison and take it away from me again. You haven't done me any favors here."

"Oh, Kinnett, you cry-baby, ain't no one going to take your badge. I keep telling you, Garrison and me are tight. I got him wrapped around my little finger. Now quit worrying about those guys and tell me how you're feeling."

As usual, Gabe took comfort from Blauw's irreverent chastising. He relaxed and reminisced with Angus about the good times. Angus sat beside him and laughed with him until Gabe dozed off. He then adjusted Gabe's pillow and pulled his blanket up to his neck. He quietly eased to the door and turned out the light as he left.

16

GABE WAS AWAKENED by a phone call. He almost levitated out of bed when the caller identified himself as Lyman Ives. "Morning, Kinnett, I hope you don't mind that I called. I've been thinking about our last conversation."

Gabe cleared his throat and responded, "Yes, what about it?"

"I cooperated with you, but you left without telling me what I wanted to know."

Gabe knew what he was hinting at, but played dumb. "And what would that be, Lyman?"

Ives sighed deeply and grew impatient with the charade. He blurted out, "Your relationship with Maura, asshole! You know what I mean!"

Gabe was thrilled that Ives was still curious enough to inquire. He had to capitalize on that curiosity. "Let's meet, Lyman. Tomorrow okay with you?"

Ives hesitated for a few seconds and asked, "Tomorrow? Sure you're up to it? I heard you took a pretty hard shot."

Not wanting to give Ives any satisfaction, he played down the attack. "Nah, that wasn't a shot. I get hurt worse than that having sex with my girlfriend."

The line was instantly silent. Without intending to, Gabe had just solidified Ives's belief that he'd been sleeping with Loar.

When he realized how inadvertently he'd planted the idea, he beamed with pride.

Ives bitterly growled, "Tomorrow at one! Leave Hire there!" When the phone went dead, Gabe quickly assessed his condition. Tomorrow was going to be sooner than the doctors would accept, but the investigation came first. His drain tube had been removed yesterday, and he was taking oral antibiotics now. He could always re-admit himself if he had problems.

The next morning, he struggled out of bed and dressed. The nurse went ballistic and summoned the doctor immediately. After a heated exchange, Gabe signed an AMA (against medical advice) form, releasing the hospital of any liability, and walked out.

He knew he wasn't strong enough to walk home, so he took a cab. He also knew he could never sign out a detective car without Ben knowing why. He fired up his old wreck and drove to the institute.

Major Richey finished reading the morning tour reports and glanced at the clock on his desk. He rose slowly, picked up his reading glasses and walked out of his office. He was going to be on time for the meeting in the chief's office.

As he entered he was surprised to see several other people seated around the chief's conference table. Directly to the chief's left sat Dr. Loar. Beside her sat the D.A., Dan Baumgartan. The group was complete with Ezard Lumas and the human resource director, Leo Stackhaus.

Garrison called the meeting to order. "Good morning, everyone. I've called this meeting because we have a personnel issue to deal with. One of our officers is harassing Dr. Loar. I've instructed him to leave her alone, but he refuses to comply with my directive. I'm open to suggestions."

Everyone looked at each other for a second, then Dr. Loar spoke up. "I'll start. Your officer, Kinnett, has convinced himself that I'm somehow responsible for some murders that a few of my patients have committed. He's asking a lot of embarrassing questions, and frankly, my reputation is suffering as a result of it. I would appreciate some help with this matter. Robert has tried to help, but Kinnett remains unwavering in his pursuit of me. I've tried to counsel him, but he has erected too many barriers between us. I'm afraid something more drastic has to be done."

Dan Baumgartan jumped in and offered his support. "Yes, I've talked with the chief, and let me assure you, I will prosecute any officer who abuses his authority. You just prepare a case file and send it to me, Chief."

Richey sat quietly, but grew sick at Baumgartan's patronage. Baumgartan continued, "I would especially relish the opportunity to prosecute the officer who attacked Detective Lumas. The beating that Detective Lumas took was merciless. That officer has no business carrying a gun and badge."

Dr. Loar feigned a flirtatious smile and said, "Thank you, Dan. You're so sweet. I knew I could count on you." She then cast her lifeless eyes on Stackhaus as a cue for him to chime in with Baumgartan. Stackhaus, however, was unmoved by Loar's beauty. He didn't realize it, but he was risking her revenge by ignoring her cue.

Leo shook his head and said, "I don't know what the big mystery is here, Bob. You're the chief of police. If someone has disobeyed a directive, just document it and send it through with your recommendation for disciplinary action. You've done this in the past. What's the big deal with this one?"

Garrison stared at him for a few seconds. Apparently, he wasn't taking the hint. "Leonard, would you like to fill Leo in on our situation?"

Richey cringed. He hated being Garrison's puppet, but Garrison had long ago documented sufficient evidence to ruin his career. Garrison reminded him frequently that his sexual exploits with Carla Ellis would be enough to sink him.

As much as he hated Garrison, he performed his duty. He turned to Leo and explained the problem with Kinnett as tactfully as he could. "You see, Leo, Kinnett was transferred to the cold case unit as a disciplinary measure. We had to break up some of the troublemakers on the midnight shift, and he was the worst. By transferring him, we removed the biggest pot-stirrer and sent a message to everyone else that we wouldn't tolerate organizational terrorists. Kinnett, however, wouldn't take his discipline quietly. He began digging in some of our old murder files and came up with a common link. Some of the suspects were patients of Dr.

Loar. He made the illogical assumption that Dr. Loar was somehow responsible. An irrational leap of logic, I assure you. The chief ordered him to cease and desist, but he's refused. Clearly, we have to take more drastic measures at this point."

Stackhaus stared suspiciously at Richey. When he'd finished, Stackhaus shook his head and said, "Nah, nah, nah, there's something more here. You guys have been doing this for too many years to not know how to terminate someone. You've done it too many times. You know exactly what the process is to initiate a termination. Why am I really here? What's Kinnett got on you that's keeping you from strapping him on?"

Garrison leaned back in his chair nervously and responded, "Oh, Leo, you know how this generation X is. He thinks he has something incriminating on me. He thinks he can blackmail me to get me to back off."

Leo threw his hands up and said abruptly, "I don't want to hear that crap, Bob. He must have something on you or you'd have properly initiated formal termination proceedings like city policy requires. He's obviously scared you into backing off or we wouldn't be having this meeting. Don't get me involved in this. If you're going to terminate him, put your cards on the table and let's look at them. But I'm not getting involved in your underhanded agenda. I'm out of here." With his position clearly stated, Stackhaus stood and left the meeting. He had no idea that he'd just signed his death warrant.

Everyone stared at Garrison to gauge his reaction. Garrison just stared at the table and finally said, "Okay, folks, that was our best shot. It's up to us. We all know what Kinnett has. If I go down, we all go. Who has a suggestion?"

He looked conspicuously at Richey and asked, "Leonard?"

Richey almost exploded with anger. He hated doing Garrison's dirty work, but he'd done it for so many years that he couldn't stop now. He sighed deeply and managed to muster a civil tone in his voice. "I'll have a talk with Kinnett. I'll make him listen."

Baumgartan was not content with that approach. He blurted out, "Talk! That won't work! Bob's talked to this asshole enough already! He needs a serious dose of reality!"

Loar motioned for Baumgartan to calm down. "Relax, Dan. Robert doesn't mean that Leonard will simply talk to Kinnett. When Leonard gets involved, much more than talking takes place. We can all sleep comfortably from now on. Dear Leonard will see that Kinnett discontinues his moonlighting as a detective." Loar looked at Richey and asked, "Isn't that right, Leonard?"

Richey gritted his teeth. He truly hated Loar, even though she was the most striking woman that he'd ever seen. Since he wasn't high enough on the food chain to share her bed, and her outward beauty was dimmed by her evil persona, he had no difficulty hating her. He sighed deeply to show his disgust. "Whatever you say, Doctor."

Garrison was pleased with Leonard's loyalty. "It's agreed then. Leonard will make this whole mess go away. Any other comments?"

Baumgartan couldn't leave without having the last word. He rose and said, "Agreed! You do what you have to, Leonard. You'll get complete cooperation from me."

As everyone stood to leave, Ezard Lumas said, "We've got another problem. Kinnett has too much support. You can't quite him without quieting Blauw. And Blauw won't go away without pissing off Shelley. It will cause a chain reaction that we can't stop. We'll have the whole patrol bureau up in arms."

Richey knew Lumas was right. He looked to Garrison for direction. Garrison looked around the table, then back at Richey. "Talk to Kinnett. If Blauw raises his head, we'll cut it off for him. I'll deal with Shelley if he sticks his nose in it."

As the others left the conference room Richey remained seated. He was frustrated, so Garrison shut the door behind Dr. Loar and glared at him. "Spit it out, Leonard."

Richey slowly shook his head as the complexity and magnitude of the whole mess materialized. "We can't do this, Bob. You know we can't. We both know what we're suggesting here. We can't kill one of our own, no matter what the consequences. We're still cops, for God's sake."

Garrison leaned against the door and stared at the floor. He pulled out the end chair and sat down. After long consideration, he said, "Maybe they're not our own, Leonard. You and I come from the old school, pal. We have different values and ethics than these

359

new kids. We took care of each other in the old days. These new kids only think of themselves. When we made a mistake, we covered for each other. We wouldn't rat each other out like Kinnett's trying to do."

Richey smiled sarcastically and yelled at Garrison. "Listen to yourself, Bob! Listen to what you're saying! That's the same thing that Kinnett has done! He's only tried to take care of his fellow officers! He's loyal to his friends! That's why we buried his ass in the cold case unit! We've tried to castrate this kid for doing exactly what we did when we were young officers! Doesn't this seem a little hypocritical to you?"

Garrison nodded, then responded quietly, "Yeah. Yeah, I guess you're right, Leonard. The difference here is that it's me that he's after. If I were in his shoes, I'd probably have done the same thing, but it's my ass that's on the line here, Leonard. My ass! Do you understand that? I don't hate the kid, but he's got to learn when to shut up and back off. You had to learn it. I had to learn it. It's one of those things that you have to do to survive. This little bastard is going to press the issue until someone takes a fall. I know now that I should never have let Loar manipulate me. I wish I hadn't, but it's too late. The bitch has her hooks in me. If she goes down, so do I. I hate being under her thumb, but what can I do?"

Richey shook his head. "I don't know, Bob, I truly don't. But we have to draw the line somewhere. I've done a lot of shit for you. I just can't bring myself to drop the hammer on another cop. I don't like myself anymore. I've got to start regaining some self-respect somehow. Planting Kinnett would put me over the edge. I'd rather lose everything than spend the rest of my life hating myself for killing another cop."

Garrison sympathized with Richey, but the stakes were too high to back off now. "I'm sorry, Leonard. I know it's rough, but I can't take a hard fall this late in my career, and neither can you. We'd never recover. You've been knocking the bottom out of that little black bitch, Ellis. It's going to take some major terrorism to keep her quiet after I pass her up for sergeant. You're either going to have to swat Kinnett now or Ellis later."

He leaned over the table and pleaded with Richey. "Come on, Leonard. Just do this one thing for me, please? I'll promote the

360

incompetent bitch and get her off your back. You can dump her and put some distance between you and her. She'll go away quietly if I promote her. She won't sacrifice a set of sergeant stripes just to take a cheap shot at you. She's only screwing you to get promoted anyway. When she gets what she wants, she'll probably dump you first. We'll bury this mess with Loar and save our asses. We'll clean up our acts and survive long enough to retire. I'll never put you in a position like this again, I promise. What do you say?"

Richey stood and walked slowly to the door. He replied, "Maybe we deserve to take a fall, Bob. We've put ourselves in this position. We've forgotten how cops are supposed to act. I've forgotten who I am and where I came from. I've crossed the line so many times that I don't know what's right or wrong anymore. I just know that cops don't kill cops. It isn't right, by anyone's standards."

Garrison sat quietly as Richey opened the door. He wanted Richey's attention before he closed the door. He kept his voice low so Richey would have to stop and re-enter the room to hear. He said, "Maybe you're right, Leonard. Maybe you're right, but I'm not going to prison. Not now, not ever. If you won't do it, I will. If I have to do my job and yours, too, I don't need you. Don't make me do this, Leonard. You and I have been through too much together to go to war with each other now. You know how cities run scared of sexual harassment complaints these days. One word from her and you're toast, especially since she's black. She'll play the race card and scream discrimination. She'll claim that she's being treated worse than a white woman in the same circumstances. Stackhaus and the mayor will crucify you just to placate her. Let's not destroy each other over a couple of insignificant little shits like Ellis and Kinnett. I'll take care of you to the bitter end, pal, but you've got to get on board with me."

Richey didn't have to re-enter the room to hear Garrison. He'd heard loud and clear. All was said that needed to be said. He walked on.

Ives waited angrily with his hands folded in his lap. Gabe entered the interview room and sat on the other side of the glass screen. He fought through the pain and hoped the sweat on his brow didn't reveal his misery. "Hello, Lyman. Glad you called."

Ives sported some new scars as witness to his sadomasochism. He bitterly hated Gabe, but tried to speak civilly. "You didn't give me what I wanted last time. You left without telling me what your relationship with Maura is. Tell me now!"

The topic would have surfaced eventually, but Ives's directness caught Gabe off guard. This was a crucial point in the rapport-building stage. One wrong move and he would lose Ives. Worse yet, Ives would tell Loar what Gabe had said and cause more tension between them than already existed.

Gabe selected his words carefully. "I can't lie to you, Lyman. I find her very attractive. I can't help myself. You know how she is. She's beautiful."

Ives was unsympathetic. He unclasped his hands and leaned into the glass. "Yeah, I know how she is, but she's mine. You have no right to her. Just answer one question. Have you put your hands on her?"

Even though there was a glass between them, Gabe leaned back in his chair. Ives was the most frightening man that he'd ever seen. He tried to show no fear, but knew his emotions were written across his face.

He wasn't ready to show his hand yet. He knew that as soon as he admitted to sleeping with Loar, Ives would be lost. There would be no cooperation, and he knew what Ives was capable of when provoked. He had to string Ives along until he'd gotten enough information to support a search warrant affidavit. He thought for a few seconds and replied, "No, Lyman, not yet, but I've got to confess to you. It's been a real struggle. Surely you can understand. I'm only human. You had to feel the same weakness when you were around her."

Ives leaned back and stared at Gabe for a minute. He showed no signs of weakness. He glared deep into Gabe's eyes and growled through gritted teeth, "No, I didn't. I have no weaknesses. But you understand this. You touch her, I'll kill you. One touch and you're dead. This place can't hold me. I can tear it down to its foundation and walk out of here any time I want. I'll hound you right into hell if I have to, but I'll kill you with my bare hands if you so much look at her. You don't lay your fucking eyes on her again. You don't go to her office for counseling. You find another doctor, got me?"

Gabe realized that he was showing too much shock at the threat. His first instinct was to assume the Angus Blauw persona and respond with a challenge for Ives to climb on when he grew the balls. He caught himself and decided that the Ben Hire persona would be more appropriate. If Ives escaped and found him in his present condition, he would go through him like a chain saw through bologna.

Ives was right about the institute. The minimum-security facility was never designed to keep people like him secured. He was only there because it was a good place to hide. He could leave anytime he wanted.

He could easily be prompted to kill, so Gabe didn't want to say the wrong thing. The wrong word would provoke him to hunt down Gabe, Loar or anyone else that he'd targeted. Gabe wasn't worried about his own safety as long as his Colt was hanging under his arm, but he couldn't be responsible for Loar's murder.

A quick check of his facial expression revealed that there was too much shock on his face. He wiped his emotions from his face and said, "I don't blame you, Lyman. She's a real treasure. I know she loves you. She told me so. What am I supposed to do? She's counseling me about my depression, and I can't help myself. I can't be around her without becoming aroused."

Ives's face quivered with rage. "That's your problem, not mine! Stay away from her, Kinnett! You don't want me on your ass! I'll kill you slow and painful!"

Gabe wanted desperately to change the direction of the interview. "I'll try, Lyman. Now tell me about your relationships with Lindsey, Andoever and Rudder. How well did you know them?"

Ives was caught unprepared. He tried to remember back to his previous conversation with Kinnett and Hire. Had he talk about the three women? He couldn't remember if he'd admitted to knowing them or not. He didn't want to say the wrong thing. Kinnett might use Loar against him just to retaliate.

He sized Gabe up and decided that he'd asked the question with too much self-confidence. He must have admitted to knowing the women in their previous interview. "Not well. I just knew who they were."

Gabe pressed on, not wanting to lose the momentum. "You knew each one of them?" Ives thought for a second then cautiously nodded his head.

"Let's start with Lois Andoever. When did you meet her?" Ives studied him intently as he took notes. He didn't know if he should admit to any more than knowing them. The indecision was agonizing, but he had to make a decision quickly. Finally, the overwhelming pucker factor compelled him to reply, "I'm not sure. I'm not sure I should say anything more."

Gabe was ecstatic that Ives had even admitted to knowing the women. He hid his elation and said, "Honesty, Lyman. That's what this is all about, honesty. I've been honest with you, now you have to reciprocate. You can't clam up on me here. If we're going to have a relationship based on mutual trust, you can't hold out on me. I can't go to the judge and get your guardianship changed unless I trust you. You have to talk to me about these women, unless you've got something to hide. You're not hiding anything incriminating from me, are you, Lyman?"

Ives pondered his options for a few seconds. He studied Gabe carefully, but Gabe showed too much conviction. He lowered his stare to the table. Gabe knew he had won the power struggle. Ives tried to regain control of the interview. "Enough about the old women! Tell me about your last session with Maura!"

Gabe shook his head. "No, Lyman, I'm not ready for that yet. I'm in charge here. Tell me when you met Mrs. Andoever." Ives shook his head and remained silent.

He had planted his heels. Gabe had to assert his dominance if he were to remain in charge. He stood and gathered his pen and notebook. Ives growled, "Where are you going?"

Gabe walked to the door and opened it. He turned and said, "Home. I've got another appointment with Dr. Loar this evening."

Ives bolted out of his chair and slammed his torso against the glass as he lunged for Gabe. He screamed with all his rage, "Get back here!"

The impact vibrated the walls. Gabe turned and asked, "Mrs. Andoever?" Ives boiled inside and clenched his jaw. He could only shake his head. Seeing that he had to walk out to maintain control, Gabe turned and stepped through the door.

As he closed the door behind him, he heard Ives scream. Ives pounded his fists on the Plexiglas so hard that Gabe felt the vibration in the hall. He smiled as he reached in his coat pocket and turned off the tape recorder. He shuffled painfully to his car.

Gabe pulled up in front of his apartment building and parked the junk. He looked around as he walked to the front door. Seeing no sign of Jenna Kerse, he knew he was safe. On a good day, he thought he could take her, but he was weak and in considerable pain. She could put him down with one punch in the chest.

As he exited the elevator and approached his door, he fumbled for his keys. When he inserted the key in the lock, he realized that the door was unlocked. He was startled until he smelled Beck's perfume. He smiled and thought what a fun night this would be.

He stepped into his apartment and saw Beck sitting on the sofa. As he closed the door, Ben stepped out of the kitchen and said, "We have to talk."

His heart sank as he looked back at Beck. Anger shot from her eyes. She slid over and patted the sofa beside her. "Right here, Mister."

Ben paced in front of him, chewing him out with every step. "What are you doing? Don't you realize that your insurance and workman's comp won't pay your hospital and doctor bills if you sign yourself out against the doctor's advice? Are you trying to kill yourself?"

Gabe listened to the tirade, wondering if he should disclose his interview with Ives. Ben finished his lecture and Beck began hers. "We were worried sick about you. Where have you been?"

Again, he didn't respond. Ben now knew that he'd been up to something. He rolled his eyes and asked, "Okay, out with it. What have you done now?"

Silence would no longer work. Gabe shrugged his shoulders. "Well, I got a phone call yesterday. Ives wanted to talk. He wouldn't talk to you or I'd have called you. He wanted to talk to me alone. I wanted to see if I could get enough information to support a search warrant affidavit."

Ben stood in shock with his mouth open. He looked at Beck to make sure she'd heard the same thing. She wasn't looking back and was furious. "You fool! If Garrison gets wind that you're still investigating Loar, he'll fire you! And you're not experienced enough at interviewing to take on Ives! You have to quit freelancing this thing! You're going to screw it up so bad that we'll never get charges filed!"

Ben jumped in as soon as Beck took a breath. "Gabe, I warned you. I like you, but I'm not going to stand by and let you destroy the integrity of this investigation. I hate to see you get fired, but I'll go to Garrison if I have to. There's too much at stake here. If she walks, more people are going to die."

Gabe lowered his head and rubbed his eyes. "Too late, Ben, Lumas beat you to it. He came to my room and lifted my badge. Garrison is going to fire me."

Beck erupted in anger. "Oh, no he's not! He may think he has sufficient cause by you failing to back off this investigation, but I'll crucify him in court. He hasn't got one single ounce of documentation to support your transfer to the cold case unit. There is plenty of testimony in that department to support the premise that that unit is a disciplinary assignment. He was wrong to stick you there, but once there, you're completely justified in looking into those files. He hasn't provided you any training, supervision or policy. His actions are completely arbitrary and capricious. Trust me, Gabe, he's only bluffing. If he can't get the buy-in of the city's personnel director, he'll back off. I know Stackhaus and he's a fair man. Garrison won't try any of his underhanded crap with him."

Gabe didn't care anymore. "No matter, I think I got just what we need to flip Ives. Listen." He removed the tape recorder from his pocket and rewound the tape. He pushed the *Play* button and let Ben and Beck listen to Ives's confession that he had known the three murdered women. When finished, he pushed the *Stop* button and beamed with pride. "Well, what do you think?"

Beck stared at him apathetically, then said, "Not good enough. Just knowing them isn't enough. We have to establish a motive and put him at the scenes at the times of the murders.

366

We're still a long way from tying him to the women sufficiently to get a search warrant. We need more."

Gabe sat back and sighed heavily. The frustration of the never-ending obstacles overwhelmed him. "Okay, what more do we need?"

Ben paced back and forth for a few seconds, then said, "He called you this time. He'll call you again, unless you answered his questions about Loar."

"No, I didn't. I gave him no more information than the last time."

"Good! Good! Now here's what we're going to do. You aren't going to talk to him anymore without me. Got that?"

Gabe looked at Beck, who said, "It has to be that way, Gabe. You're not ready to engage in a battle of wits with Ives. He'll work you. You may not realize it, but he'll manipulate you like a small child. If we lose him, we lose Loar." He reluctantly agreed.

Ben said, "You get your ass back in the hospital and wait for Ives to call you again. When he does, you call me. Understand?"

"Ives said he wouldn't talk to you. How do I get around that?"

"That's part of taking control, Gabe. Ives doesn't dictate the terms of the interviews, we do. You have to make it clear that he's not in charge. I'll help you, but you have to stop leaving me out of the loop."

"Okay, Ben, you're the boss. I'll call you when Ives calls me. But I don't want to go back in the hospital. I'll be fine here." Ben shook his head in frustration and walked out the door without a word.

Beck glared at Gabe. He tried to diffuse her anger by giving her his cutest boyish grin. Her heart melted as her glare faded into a loving smile. She slid over close to him and wrapped her arms around his neck. He reclined on the sofa and raised his feet. He stretched out prone with her beside him. One kiss and the agenda for the rest of the evening was set. She paused periodically to chastise him, but he easily distracted her.

He knew he should spend this time searching the dead files for the young girl that Garrison had had sex with, but every kiss weakened his resolve more. As Beck shifted her hips over his, she was careful to not put pressure on his sore chest, and all thoughts of Garrison vanished.

17

JIMMY CLOSSAN WAS motionless as Ben walked into the room. He stared up at the ceiling and acknowledged Ben's presence without moving his head. "What do you want?"

Ben stepped beside Clossan's bed and stared down at him. Clossan growled, "I said, what do you want? Get out of here!"

Ben stood where he could see Clossan's eyes. "Hi, Jimmy, remember me?"

"How could I forget? I lie here day after day, staring at the ceiling. You fuckers are all I think about."

Ben laid his notebook on the edge of Clossan's bed and sighed deeply. "Yes, Jimmy, I bet you do. That was a pretty stupid move you made, trying to take out Angus Blauw without help. I've got to give you credit though. You've got balls. Not much brains, but lots of balls. Too bad you'll never get the chance to use them again."

Clossan looked away as his rage peaked. He yelled as he cried, "I had that old derelict! I had him on his back! If the chicken-shit had come alone, he wouldn't have stood a chance! I kicked his ass fair and square! If that prick sergeant hadn't back-shot me, Blauw would be in the ground instead of me being here!"

Ben smiled sympathetically. "Yes, Jimmy, that's how we cops are. We aren't going to take an ass-kicking if we can help it. No one ever accused us of fighting fair."

Clossan didn't respond. The tears of frustration in his eyes meant that he was vulnerable. This was a good time to twist the knife. "Listen, Jimmy, I can't do anything to change your current condition, but maybe I can help you out of the charges. You know if you ever get on your feet, you're facing attempted murder charges. With your rap sheet, you'll go back to prison for life. You'll never be the man that you once were, and prison won't be fun for you. You'll be too weak to fight off the back-door boys."

Clossan laughed cynically and mumbled, "No chance of that. I'm a quad for life. I can't move anything below my neck. Believe me. I'd gladly bend over for Bubba if it'd get me my arms and legs back. You haven't moved me, asshole. You're still after Loar. You want me to give her up to get out from under the charges. Here's a tip for you, Hire. You can't try me as long as I'm in this condition. No judge would ever put a quad in jail, no matter what they've done. I'm no threat to society in this condition and I'd be more trouble for the prison staff than it's worth. You're going to have to come up with something better than that."

Clossan was right. Ben looked around the room as he tried to think of something that would make him angry enough at Loar to give her up. He finally decided on an alternate approach. "Let me ask you something, Jimmy. Has Loar ever come to see you? Has she even called or written?"

Ben knew very well that she hadn't. He'd conspired with the hospital administrator to withhold all communication from Loar. Jimmy mumbled, "You know she hasn't. What's your point?"

"Just that she used you, Jimmy. She used you big time. You have to know that she lied to you when she said she loved you and that you were the only person that she'd ever taken to bed. That's not true, Jimmy and you know it. She's a user. She used your love for her to get you to go after Blauw. She's the reason you're here. Blauw is just an emaciated old boozehound who got a lucky shot on you. He only did what came naturally to him, which was to shoot back. Loar's the real villain here. Right now, she's riding someone else. She's giving someone else all the wonderful sex that she used to give you. She doesn't miss you. She's never missed a step. The night you went down, she had another stud waiting in the wings. She was probably humping him at the same

370

time that Blauw was taking a sight picture on the back of your head."

Clossan remained silent as Ben talked. He finally sighed and took a deep breath. "Won't work, Hire. I know you're right. If she is banging someone else, I'd hate her for it. But I hate you bastards more. I'd never give her up to the likes of you. I wouldn't sell Satan himself out to the cops."

Ben searched for more leverage. That was his best shot. He would have to try again later. He didn't mind. He had all the time in the world. Clossan wasn't going anywhere. He picked up his notebook. "Okay, Jimmy, I guess you're right."

He turned to leave, then a spark of genius stopped him in his tracks. Clossan wouldn't give Satan up to the cops, but he'd give up another cop. He turned back to Clossan. "Jimmy, how would you feel if the guy that she was banging the night you got shot was a cop?"

Clossan was unable to move, but the suggestion threw him into a rage. He yelled, "Bullshit, Hire, you lying sack of shit!"

Ben smiled like a fisherman who had just hooked a trophy bass. He stepped back to Clossan and wiped the smile from his face. "Sorry, Jimmy, I didn't mean to upset you, but it's true. It's true because I know the officer who was banging her that night. I never approved. That's one of the reasons I want Loar. Sleeping with a murder suspect and supplying her with information about the police investigation is the most unethical thing that a cop can do. I want this cop as bad as I want her. I'd offer her immunity from prosecution if she'd give up the cop."

Clossan cried openly. "You're lying your ass off!" Ben shook his head slowly. Clossan yelled, "Who is it?"

Ben reached over, caressed Clossan's shoulder and said in a fatherly tone. "It's my old partner, Kinnett. He's gone bad, Jimmy. Loar got to him and he's fallen in love with her. He's violated his oath of office. I want his ass fired and prosecuted. I need her, Jimmy. I can't get any of the evidence that I need to prosecute Kinnett without her testimony. Help me flip her, Jimmy. I've talked to the prosecutor and got him to buy into a plea bargain. She'll never do a day in jail. If she does, it'll be the best thing for her. At least Kinnett won't be pounding her. And one

371

other thing, Jimmy, I'm not your biggest worry. You've got much bigger problems than me."

Clossan sucked back his tears. "Wrong, Hire, I got nothing to be afraid of."

"Oh yes you do, Jimmy. Kinnett told another of Loar's lovers that you'd been banging her. He was insanely jealous. Does the name Lyman Ives ring a bell?"

Paralyzing fear fell over Clossan's face. He yelled, "Ives! That masochistic son of a bitch, why? Why did he tell him that?"

"He's gone bad, Jimmy. That's what I've been trying to tell you. Now you know why I want him so bad."

Clossan cried harder. "So what! Who cares, Hire? If Ives kills me, he'd be doing me a favor. Get out of here!"

Ben patted Jimmy on the shoulder and turned to leave. He gave Clossan one last scenario to ponder. "Yes, I guess you're right, Jimmy. It'd be a blessing if he did it quickly, but I hear Ives is a real pain freak. I'd sure hate to be lying there, unable to move, with that sadistic monster carving me up. So long, Jimmy. Call me if you want to talk."

Clossan looked away and gritted his teeth as he wept. As Ben stepped out the door, he smiled. He knew that Kinnett had never slept with Loar. The night that Clossan was shot, Kinnett was one of the officers poking holes in him. He didn't have a clue if Ives knew that Clossan had slept with Loar, but Clossan didn't know that.

With the ruse planted, all he had to do was wait. Clossan had nothing to do but lie there and let his mind run wild. He'd give up Loar. He'd give her up just so Kinnett couldn't have her. Ben bounced with pride as he left the hospital. He thought, *Another fine example of superb police work.*

Leeza Giovani timed in and began her rounds. She greeted her co-workers on the midnight shift and hurried to the west wing. She'd just returned from two days off and was eager to see Lyman. She idolized him and ached for his touch.

Lyman was lying on his back in bed, but he was not sleeping. He stared at the ceiling, contemplating his meeting with Kinnett. He had been in a constant state of agitation since Kinnett suggested that he was Loar's lover.

Leeza gently tapped on Lyman's door and stepped in. "Lyman, can I come in?"

Ives needed Leeza, so he erased the bitterness from his face and put on his most compassionate mask. "Leeza! Man is it good to see you! I haven't been able to sleep all weekend! I missed you terribly!"

He jumped from his bed and rushed to her. He encircled her with his arms and gave her a gentle embrace. Leeza wrapped her arms around his waist and returned the gesture. She laid her head on his chest and moaned. "Oh, darling, I've missed you, too. I can't stand to go on my days off. I go nuts before I can get back to work and see you again."

Ives rested his chin on top of Leeza's head and grimaced. He could barely force himself to touch her. Every time he did, his mind drifted to his sessions with Loar. Compared to her, Leeza meant nothing. She was simply a necessary evil that he'd resolved himself to endure. Sex with her was merely an exercise that he had to detach himself from in order to achieve his ultimate goal of being with Loar.

Leeza said, "Let me finish rounds, Lyman. When everyone settles down, I'll come back. I need you so much. See you about three." She broke their embrace and left. Ives flopped back down on the bed, sickened by the prospect of having sex with Leeza. He couldn't even have the pleasure of hurting her. She didn't like rough sex. His gentle facade had sufficiently covered his love of pain.

Four hours later, Leeza tapped on Ives's door. He jerked as he awoke. She looked up and down the hall as she slipped quietly into his room. She lunged at him, encircled his neck and kissed him hard on the lips. Ives embraced her head and returned the kiss. After a long embrace, he broke their kiss and asked, "Any luck?"

She returned to the door and locked it. She undressed as she replied, "I weaseled Dr. Rhinehart's password out of Ernie. He knows computers, but he doesn't know squat about women."

He showed no emotion as he asked, "And?"

She hurried to him and unfastened his belt buckle. "Nothing yet. I checked her desk and e-mail an hour ago. No one has written her about you. If that detective is trying to file charges on you, he hasn't written Dr. Rhinehart. Besides, baby, you're innocent. They can't charge you if you haven't done anything wrong."

Ives didn't respond. He raised his arms so Leeza could pull his shirt over his head. Once nude, he reclined back on the bed and Leeza slid in beside him. He mustered up his softest and most vulnerable voice. "That doesn't matter, lover. They've got lots of unsolved murders on their hands. I'm a convenient scapegoat. They'll charge me and make me prove that I'm innocent. They know I don't have any money, so I'll have to settle for a court-appointed attorney. He'll make a token effort, and I'll get convicted. Public defenders are never as competent as prosecutors. If they are, their not getting paid well enough to put out their best effort. It takes an experienced trial attorney to play hardball in a murder trial. I can't stay in here if they charge me. I'll have to leave the country. Will you go with me?"

Leeza snuggled closer to him and cooed softly, "Of course, baby, I'll go anywhere with you. I can't live without you, you know that. When you're ready to leave, I'll get you whatever you need. I can't imagine why your mother put you in here in the first place. You come to my house and we'll leave from there. I'll start selling my furniture so we can travel light."

That was what Ives had wanted to hear. He needed Leeza to help him escape. He could kill her later when she was no longer of any use. He caressed her head and said, "Good, baby. I'll need a master key and some clothes. Go to the army surplus store and buy me a survival knife. If they don't have one, get me a Marine Corpse K-Bar. I've got lots of enemies out there. I'd hate to get killed before I got to your house."

The knife disturbed Leeza. She stopped kissing his chest and raised her head. "Oh, baby, you won't need that. I hate knives and guns. I'll pick you up outside the gate here."

He thought for a second. "No, lover, if someone sees me getting into your car, they'll give your car description to the cops, and they'll have me in custody before we get to the city limits. No, baby, I need the knife. I'll pitch it out the window just as soon as we get out of town, I promise."

Comforted by his promise, Leeza relaxed. She slid her hand under the sheet and massaged him. She slid under the sheet and began kissing her way downward. Ives rubbed his face in disgust, leaned his head back and closed his eyes.

His mind drifted back to Loar's bedroom and focused on the sensations that he'd remembered from his nights with her. He closed his eyes tightly and put Leeza out of his mind. He replaced her with the image of Loar doing the same thing. For the next thirty minutes, he paid the dues necessary to keep Leeza's trust.

Two weeks had passed since Gabe had talked to Ives. His strength was slowly returning, but he couldn't jog yet. He went for nightly walks because he couldn't sleep. Garrison still had not returned him to work. He was wondering if Garrison intended to leave him on suspension indefinitely.

After his walk, he called Ben at home to see if anything new had developed. Ben must have been sleeping because he slurred his words. Gabe cheerfully said, "Evening, Ben. It's too early to sleep. You must be drunk."

Ben chuckled. "Nope, just dozed off in front of the TV. What's up, kid? How's that lung?"

Gabe sighed and rubbed his chest. "Oh, fair I guess. I can't believe how sore I still am. I don't see how those Hollywood types do it. They get stabbed or shot, and by the end of the show they're good as new."

Ben laughed. "Well, kid, if you got paid what they get, you'd heal up just as fast. Money has remarkable recuperative powers. Magnum's been shot lots of times. He gets paid so much money that it doesn't even leave a scar."

"Yeah, I guess you're right. If I got paid as much as him, I'd let people stab me every day. Listen, Ben, I'm getting worried. I haven't heard from Ives. I don't think he's going to call."

"Not to worry, lad. I've been checking your mailbox at work. He left you a message today. Call him, but remember, you don't talk to him without me. Don't make me hurt you."

Gabe almost jumped off of his sofa. "You're kidding! Great! I'll call him right now! I'll call you back and let you know what happens!" He slammed the receiver down without waiting for Ben's reply.

It was several minutes before Ives was brought to the phone. Gabe tried to hide his enthusiasm. "Hello, Lyman, I hear you want to talk."

Ives didn't respond right away. Gabe was about to repeat himself when Ives said, "Yeah, I want to talk. Have you seen Maura anymore?"

His ferocity was still fresh in Gabe's mind and he didn't want to set him off again. "No, Lyman, I haven't. You've got a real problem with that, and I want to work with you here."

Ives softly said, "You're smart. Have you ever touched her?"

"We're not going to go there, Lyman. Anyway, that's not material to our investigation. We've got some gaps to fill. Let's clear up some questions about some of our murder victims."

"Nice of you to call. Bye."

"Ah, ah, ah, Lyman, you don't want to do this. Hire is ready to pull the plug on this and leave you in the institute. I'm the only person who wants your help enough to talk to you. Don't screw with me."

There was a long silence. Lyman sighed and mumbled, "We'll talk."

"When?"

"First thing in the morning. Come alone."

Gabe remembered Ben's lecture. "Can't, Lyman, new rule, me and Hire are partners. It's both of us or not at all." Ives didn't respond. Gabe listened as he laid the phone down and walked away.

Ben arrived at Gabe's apartment early the next morning. The trip to Perkins-Hayes was tense. Gabe hoped they weren't wasting their time. "What do you think, Ben? He didn't say he'd talk after I told him that you were coming."

Ben shrugged his shoulders. "Don't worry, kid, he'll talk. You had to be eating at his gut something terrible for him to even call. You've got something he wants. He'll talk long enough to get answers to his questions. The key is to not give him those answers until we get what we want. Let's just string him along. Let me do the talking. If he won't talk to me, just refuse to speak to him. Make him go through me to get to you."

376

Ives was waiting with his arms crossed and a murderous glare when Ben and Gabe walked into the interview room. Ben greeted him and tried to establish a rapport. Ives refused to talk and stared at Gabe. Ben leaned back in his chair and said, "You're going to have to talk to me, Lyman. It's me or nothing."

Ives refused to acknowledge Ben and said to Gabe, "So, Kinnett, tell me about your last session with Maura."

Gabe stared at him and shook his head, then pointed to Ben. Ben asked, "You want to know something from him, Lyman, ask me and I'll ask him for you."

Ives's blue eyes cut through Gabe like a knife. He finally forced himself to look at Ben. He snarled, "Tell him to talk or we're through!"

Ben shook his head. "Nope, I'm the lead investigator here, Lyman. You're going to talk to me or no one."

Frustration finally overwhelmed Ives. He slowly rose to his feet and pressed his face against the glass. He growled, "Okay, lead investigator, here's my statement! You're trying to get me to admit to something that you can use against me! The best thing for me to do is to keep my mouth shut! So, here it is! I'm not going to say shit to either one of you! Kinnett isn't going to tell me what I want to know, so I'll find it out through other sources! I ain't talking to either of you again! If you want me, bring an arrest warrant!" With his piece said, Ives turned and stormed out of the room with his counselor in tow.

Gabe looked at Ben with inquiring eyes. Ben was quickly pondering his options before Ives got out the door. Nothing came to mind. He couldn't beg and had to watch Ives walk away.

The trip home was quiet and solemn. Gabe asked, "What now, Ben?"

Ben ran his fingers through his hair and replied, "I don't know, Gabe. We're on the ropes. Ives has clammed up and nothing we do is going to make him talk. What we have now is all we're going to get, and that's not enough. We're going to have to link him to Green and the three murdered women some other way. We're certainly never going to get him to flip on Loar without some serious charges hanging over his head. If we can't get him to flip, we're going to have to get Loar through other sources." Gabe just stared out the window.

Ben pulled to the curb in front of Gabe's apartment. "Sorry, Gabe, don't give up. Clossan or Bethard will flip. I talked to Clossan just the other day. I took a new approach with him this time. I think he'll break down soon."

"If he doesn't?"

"He will. I used you as bait."

"Thanks for asking me first."

"Don't mention it. It was my pleasure. I'm not sure, but I think you can whip his ass in his current condition."

"I don't know, Ben, as weak as I am, even a bullet-riddled quadriplegic could kick my ass. What if he doesn't give up Loar?"

"Well then, maybe Bethard will give her up rather than go to prison. I don't know, Gabe. If neither of them talks, we're going to have to wait till Loar does something else. Even if they talk, we'll still have to corroborate their testimony with some physical evidence. We'll never get her convicted with only their word against hers. Maybe she'll never take a fall at all. Some killers never do."

Gabe slowly stepped out of the car and waved as Ben drove away. As Ben drove down the street, he passed Jenna Kerse sitting in her car. Gabe stared hard at her as he walked to his front door.

Not wanting to show any fear, Kerse stared back. Gabe thought as they stared into each other's eyes, *Maybe I was too hasty getting rid of her. There's got to be some way to turn her against Loar. Maybe it's time to rekindle the spark that once burned. Maybe. Maybe when I'm healthy.*

Leonard Richey waited in the dark as Garrison pulled into the park. He was completely concealed by the darkness, except for the light of his cigar.

Garrison walked up casually and sat on the bench beside him. He leaned forward and put his face in his hands. Without talking, each knew what the other was thinking. Garrison broke the silence. "Time to fish or cut bait, Leonard. Kinnett and Hire are pressing one of Loar's former patients. He's in the Perkins-Hayes Institute. They're trying to get him to flip on Loar. She's worried that he'll implicate her somehow, even though she's done nothing wrong."

Richey was not moved. He exhaled a large puff of smoke and growled, "Oh bullshit, Bob, you know as well as I do that Loar is dirty. That evil bitch has manipulated people for years. She needs to take a fall. Who cares how it happens? Between you and me, Bob, sending that bitch to prison would be the best thing that ever happened to this town."

Garrison didn't respond. Richey knew he didn't agree, but he didn't care anymore. Garrison finally said, "I care, Leonard. I told you that the last time we talked. Loar isn't going to take a fall without taking everyone with her. That includes me. And I'm not taking a fall without taking everyone with me, and that includes you. I'm sorry to have to blackmail you, but I need your help. It's time, Major."

Richey dropped his cigar and ground it into the dirt with his foot. He shook his head. "No more, Bob. No more crooked shit. You want Kinnett? Take him yourself. I don't care what happens to me anymore. I'm drawing the line here. I don't kill cops. Hell, Bob, killing Loar would serve the same purpose and get us both off the hook. I'll gladly take that bitch out."

Garrison raged inside, but knew Richey wouldn't budge. He slapped his knees as he stood. "Okay, Leonard, I'm sorry you've made this choice. Get your office cleared out and turn in all your department-issued equipment."

Richey watched Garrison walk away. He rubbed his face and shook his head in disgust. Things were going to get bloody. He wished he'd never accepted the promotion to major. He was much happier when he was a patrol captain.

Len Shelley raced up to the scene of the bar disturbance. Blauw had the doors open on the prisoner transport wagon, and the officers were stuffing arrestees in the box like sardines. When Angus slammed the door and anchored the cross bar, Shelley said, "After you drop them off, meet me behind the ball diamonds at the park." Angus nodded as he climbed behind the wheel and sped toward the city jail.

Fifty minutes later, Angus saw Shelley's car in the dark behind the batting cages. As he pulled up he was laughing. When

379

he stepped out of the wagon, Shelley was leaning against the side of his car and asked, "What are you laughing about, old man?"

"Oh, you'll find out when you get back to the station."

Shelley stood erect and towered over Angus. He roared, "What the hell did you do this time? You get me in trouble and I'll ram your head in a gopher hole!"

Angus said calmly, "Oh hell, Len, you'll be proud of me. I had that wagon full of drunks. I almost turned it over going around corners. I skidded to a stop at every stoplight and stomped it at the green lights. I had those fools bouncing off the walls like rubber balls. There was puke six inches deep on the floor, and those idiots all rolled around in it till they were covered head to toe. They looked like a bunch of soaking-wet newborn calves."

Shelley shook his head and collapsed against his car. He growled, "Angus, you senile old fool, you know how mad it makes the jailers when you do that stuff. They have to book and handle those nasty bastards. And if the drunks come in complaining, you know you're going to get your ass burnt."

Blauw shook his head confidently. "No I won't, Len, that's the beauty of it. When they screamed that they wanted to sign complaints against me, I ran into your office and got a handful of your business cards. I passed them out so the complaints will come in on you. Ain't that a hoot?"

Shelley wanted to grab Angus by the neck, but headlights appeared at the park entrance. "I'll deal with you later, Angus. You've gone too far this time."

Angus slapped Len on the back. "Oh, Len, you worry too much. They're so drunk that they'll forget all about filing complaints by the time they wake up in the morning. They'll be so worried about their wives finding out that they were in a strip joint that they won't have the desire to come after you." Shelley could only glare at Angus and shake his head. Angus asked, "Hey, what did you want to talk to me about?"

"Two things. First, how are you and Millie doing?"

Angus smiled. "Oh, Len, fantastic. I've never met anyone like her. We can't keep our hands off each other."

Shelley laughed and said, "I knew it. I knew it, you phony old goat. I knew the right woman would throw you for a loop."

Angus tried to act tough, but his facade melted. He smiled and said, "Yeah, well, just keep your mouth shut. I don't want everyone at work pimping me about her. She's a classy lady. I don't want anyone saying derogatory shit about her. And don't let me catch you cussing around her either. I've quit, and I don't want her to hear that shit."

Shelley's belly bounced as he laughed. He slapped Angus on the back and said, "Yeah, sure you have. But that's great, Angus, I'm happy for you. We'll have you guys over for dinner this weekend. Just promise me that you'll leave your clothes on. Millie can get naked, but I can't stand the thought of seeing your wrinkled ass."

"Can't promise anything, Len. When I get around her, my pants just fall down by themselves. What was the other reason that you wanted to talk to me?"

Shelley motioned toward the oncoming headlights. "Him. I wanted you here for this. Richey wants to talk to us alone. Something to do with Kinnett. I'm really worried about that kid."

Angus sobered and growled, "This doesn't look good. Richey doesn't come out at night unless he's head-hunting someone or chasing tail."

Richey slowed to a stop and turned off his headlights. Shelley said, "Angus, you let me do the talking. You'll just piss him off if you open your mouth." Angus didn't reply, but leaned against Shelley's car and glared at Richey through his sagging eyelids.

Richey approached and greeted the two. "Evening, boys. How's life in the trenches?"

Shelley patronized him. "Oh, no worse than when you were working nights, sir. Those were the good old days, right, Major?"

Richey smiled and reminisced. "Yeah, life was simpler back then. I wish I'd never taken this position." He looked at Angus and jokingly asked Shelley, "You still babysitting this old fossil to make sure he doesn't forget to take his meds."

Angus couldn't resist an opportunity to remind the major of his worth to the organization. He interrupted Shelley and said in his low, gravelly voice, "Nah, Leonard, he doesn't have to remind

381

me to take my meds. He just wanted some backup because he knows what a two-faced, back-stabbing, dirty fucker you are."

Shelley's shoulders sank and his pretentious smile dissolved into a rage. He glared at Angus and elbowed him hard in the ribs. He lowered his head, rubbed his eyes and mentally asked himself, *When will I learn? When will I ever learn to leave this crusty old son of a bitch out of sensitive situations?*

With the tone set, Shelley knew the conversation would go downhill from here. With all facades shattered, he asked, "Okay, Major, what can I do for you? You didn't come out here this time of night to bullshit. What's up?"

Richey was smiling with his most unpretentious smile. "You know, Angus, I've been surrounded with phony ass-suckers for so long that I'd forgotten how refreshing it is to talk to people who shoot you straight from the hip. You're a lousy, no-good cocksucker, but you're just the kind of people I need to talk to tonight. Brutal honesty is refreshing from time to time. How have you been? I don't see your name come across my desk very often, so I guess you're still as slippery as ever."

Angus smiled, looked at Shelley and said, "Yep, slippery as ever, right, Len?"

Shelley frowned. "He's not as slippery as he thinks, Major. I'm sure you'll be seeing his name cross your desk any day now."

"Yeah, I know. I've been meaning to compliment you, Angus, but I haven't seen you lately. That was an outstanding job of stomping the dog-shit out of Lumas. It always humors me when a backstabbing little weasel-dick like him gets his head handed to him, especially by a broken-down old drunk. He'll never live that down. You're a useless bastard, Angus, but I'll give you credit for one thing. You're treacherous." Angus puffed out his chest and beamed with pride.

Shelley looked at Angus with a curious stare. He asked, "What did you do to Lumas, Angus? You know he's in Garrison's hip pocket. Are you trying to commit professional suicide?"

"I ain't afraid of Garrison, Len. If he were a real man, he'd do his dirty work himself instead of blackmailing others to do it for him." He looked at Richey and asked, "Right, Leonard?"

Richey smiled and said sarcastically, "Len, this man's intuition is mind-boggling. How will we ever get along when he retires?"

"I'm sure we'll all discover that things will go quite well without Angus Blauw around to throw a wrench in the gears. In the mean time, just make sure you keep your business cards locked up. What do you want with us tonight, Major?"

Richey leaned up against Shelley's car beside Angus and began. "Well, boys, I've got a big problem and I'm hoping you two can help me. Frankly, Angus, I'm glad you're here. As deranged as you are, I've always respected your opinion, prehistoric as it is. Garrison has put me over a barrel with this Loar case. Kinnett has scratched and dug until he's uncovered enough circumstantial evidence to make Loar nervous. She's put Garrison on notice that if she takes a fall, he's going with her. Now, I don't know what she's got on him, but with a body like hers, I can make a pretty good guess. Kinnett's got to back off, Len. He hasn't listened to Garrison, Ben Hire or me. He's just too hard-headed."

Angus asked, "What's wrong with that, Leonard? You ought to be happy to see that prick take a fall. He's done nothing but make your life miserable for the last five years. If he falls out of the saddle, you'll be the chief. Maybe then you can redeem yourself and show us that you're not the phony prick that we all think you are."

Shelley yelled, "Shut up, Angus, that's enough of that!"

Richey said, "Well, I'll never be chief, but you're right, he's made my life hell. The problem is that I've done so much of his dirty work that he's got my nuts in a vice. If he takes a fall, one call to the city administrator and I'm out of a job. Frankly, I don't care anymore. I'm so sick of this that I'm thinking of retiring anyway. But until then, I've got to do something with Kinnett. He doesn't threaten easily, so I guess I'm looking to you guys for suggestions."

Angus shook his head as he crossed his arms. "Nah, Leonard, that's a bunch of bullshit. You're not just facing the loss of your job. The stakes are higher than that. You'd have retired long ago is it was just the job. You're in much deeper than that. You're facing prison if you don't do what Garrison wants, aren't you?"

Richey glared at Angus and shook his head. He looked at Shelley and said, "Damn this guy is good, Len. How did we ever overlook him on the sergeant's exam?"

"You didn't overlook him, Major. He's just so obnoxious that no one but us goons can stand to be around him. You guys in the ivory tower would throw him out a window after dealing with him for five minutes."

Richey laughed sarcastically and looked back at Angus. "Well, Angus, you may or may not be right, but the fact remains. I've got to do something with Kinnett. Help me out here."

Angus looked at Shelley to gauge his reaction. Shelley stared at Richey for a minute, then asked, "What are you saying here, Major? What are you going to do to Kinnett?"

Richey lowered his head and sighed in frustration. He'd hoped he wouldn't have to go into detail. "Len, Garrison is serious about Kinnett going away. Do you understand that? He wants him to disappear! Do I have to spell it out for you?"

Shelley looked back at Angus in shock. They both fully understood Richey's hint. He said, "Major, you can't mean what I think you're saying. You mean kill him?"

Richey shrugged his shoulders. "Maybe, Len, stranger things have happened. I don't want to see that, but like I said, Garrison is serious about Kinnett fading into the woodwork."

Angus stood up straight and turned to face Richey. "I never thought I'd ever hear you say that, Leonard. I knew you were a back-stabbing prick, but I never thought you were a cop-killer."

Richey yelled angrily, "I'm not, Angus, but there are those in the organization who are! Garrison is not above anything to get what he wants! He'll bring someone in from the outside if he has to! You know that! I'm not proud of what I've done to keep my oak leafs! I'm no murderer, but there are those in the department who'll do anything to get ahead. You may not believe it, Angus, but I'm really one of the good guys!"

Shelley and Angus stared at each other. Shelley said, "Major, what do you want us to do?"

"Talk to him, Len. Terrorize him if you have to. Make him back off. You and Angus can influence him. You're his role models. He'll listen to you. He thinks bucking me and Garrison makes him some kind of hero, but he won't buck you guys."

"I'll help you, Major, but I don't see Kinnett that often. I don't have much influence over him right now. It'd be easier if you'd put him back on my shift. I could ride roughshod over him easier if he was on my shift where I could keep an eye on him. That'd also get him away from those dead files. I'd keep him so busy and worn out that he wouldn't have the time or energy to chase Loar."

"Good idea, Len. I'll talk to Garrison. I think we can work that out. But in the mean time, would you please terrorize his ass for me?"

Angus hurried to his truck and said, "I'll get Kinnett and bring him to lunch, Len. See you there." Shelley nodded. Angus then turned to Richey. "We'll talk to him, Leonard, but you understand this. Ain't no one going to put a pill in him. If he gets whacked, I'm coming after both you and Garrison, and nothing will stop me. Job or no job, neither of you two fuckers will be safe if Kinnett gets killed. I'll go to the media and the attorney general. I'll hunt you two down like the gutless sewer rats that you really are and I'll kill your sorry asses. You know me, Leonard. I mean what I say."

Richey didn't respond. As Angus drove away, he turned to Shelley. "Sorry, Len, I wouldn't have come out here if I didn't care about you guys. I know you have no respect for me, but I'm still a cop at heart."

Shelley rubbed his eyes and slowly nodded. "I know, Major. You're in a tough spot, but you put yourself there. Blauw's right. If Kinnett gets hurt, it's war. You can get one or two of us, but you can't eliminate us all. We're all tight, and we won't sleep till we get your ass. For God's sake, Major, don't let it go that far."

Richey nodded. "I know, Len. I don't want to see that. I long ago gave up on the idea of getting out of this in one piece, but I don't want any of you to get hurt. You're all in danger, you, Kinnett, Blauw, all of you. Garrison won't stop till everyone who opposes him is gone, you and Blauw especially. You guys need to be careful. You have nothing to fear from me, but Bob is dangerous. You have no idea who's working as his secret agents in the department. If you knew the number and names of the people ratting others out to Garrison, you'd be stunned."

Richey slapped Shelley on the back and walked to his car. He drove away, leaving Shelley to worry. Shelley leaned against his car and rubbed his face. He had to talk sense to Kinnett. He couldn't stand to lose one of his boys.

18

BECK EISMAN WAITED patiently in the chair across from the desk of Judge Lou Lemry. Judge Lemry suffered from arthritis, and she stood as he walked in. Judge Lemry frowned and motioned for her to sit. "Sit down, Beck, you make me feel old. I should be standing till you sit down. You've been hanging around those liberals in your office too long. Tell me, Beck, how are your parents? Good I hope."

Beck nodded graciously. "Great, Judge, they're just fine."

"Good! Give them my regards. Now, what can I do for you today?"

She smiled nervously. "Judge, I'm putting my career on the line here. Please hear me out before you bite my head off."

Lemry leaned back and frowned at her. "I'm not going to bite your head off, Beck. I've known you too many years for that. I might chew on you a little though, what are you up to?"

She took a deep breath and began. "Judge, I'm not telling you anything that you don't already know, and forgive me if I insult your intelligence, but I've got a real problem."

Judge Lemry looked suspiciously at her, then nodded and signaled her to continue. "Judge, I've been working on a covert investigation without the approval of Mr. Baumgartan. I hope you won't tell him, but if you have to, it's okay. I'm going to tell him myself in a few days. I've been working with a couple of the detectives at the P.D. on a murder investigation. We've really hit a brick wall. We've identified the killer, but we're having trouble getting enough evidence to charge her."

Judge Lemry looked sympathetically at her and asked, "Who is it, dear?"

Beck stared at Judge Lemry, then looked at the floor. He looked suspiciously at her and asked, "Don't trust me, Beck?"

She couldn't hold out on the judge if she wanted his help. She had to put him in the loop. "It's Dr. Maura Loar, Judge."

He studied Beck for a few seconds, then asked, "What leads you to believe that, Beck?"

She ran down the list of killings that were associated with Dr. Loar and her patients. She drew a crystal clear picture of a psychiatrist manipulating her patients to kill for her. When she'd finished, she watched her professional life pass before her eyes.

Judge Lemry sat quietly for a few seconds, then said, "That's a strong accusation if you can't prove it. So far, all you have is circumstantial evidence and guilt by association, hardly enough probable cause to charge her."

"I know, Judge, that's why I'm here. We've identified one of Loar's patients who's responsible for at least four of the killings. We desperately need to flip him and get him to testify against her. He won't do that without a murder charge hanging over his head. He might not even flip then."

Judge Lemry studied Beck. "And you're falling short of enough probable cause to charge your snitch, right?" She nodded. Judge Lemry asked, "What do you have on him?"

Beck told the Judge about Ives's association with Andoever, Rudder and Lindsey. She carefully linked him to Loar and Lucian Green. She went on to explain that if they could get a search warrant for blood and hair from Ives, she was sure that it would match the hair and semen left at the murder scenes.

Judge Lemry listened intently, then folded his hands as he thought. "Thin, Beck, mighty thin. Association alone is too thin for a search warrant. Can you get him to talk, maybe get him to admit to more than mere acquaintance?"

"No, Judge, the detectives have tried. He's invoked his 5th and 6th amendment rights. He's refused to talk without an attorney. We're screwed."

Judge Lemry frowned. "And you want me to give you a search warrant for hair and blood without sufficient probable cause."

She lowered her head and looked at the floor. She finally looked up at Judge Lemry and said, "Yes, Judge. Yes I do. This isn't like any other murder case that we've ever worked. This doctor has killed over a dozen people. She killed Tim Allis from our office. You remember him?"

"Yes, Beck, I remember him. Nice boy. I liked him, but do I have to remind you of the consequences of coming up empty handed after issuing a search warrant without probable cause? You're in the clear once my name goes on the warrant, but I could be in real trouble with the Oregon State Board of Judicial Review if your snitch hires an attorney and makes a complaint against me. You don't have the right to ask that of me, Beck. I love you like my own, but you're putting both of us in a tough spot. I could be impeached off the bench and you'd certainly lose your job, maybe even be disbarred. "

Beck again lowered her head and agreed. Judge Lemry said, "I can't help you, Beck, and it's not because I know Loar. Don't think I'm refusing the warrant to protect her. We're not as close as people think. She sucks up to me at social events, but I'm smart enough to recognize when someone is blowing smoke up my butt. If she's dirty, I'll give you the warrant, but you've got to bring me more."

She stood and extended her hand. Judge Lemry stood, shuffled around the corner of his desk and opened his arms. He encircled her and said, "No handshakes between us, dear, give me a hug."

Judge Lemry hugged her like a daughter and said, "Bring me more, Beck. I'll give you whatever you need."

Beck walked toward the door, then turned to Judge Lemry and asked with a disappointed smile, "Judge, would you please not tell Mr. Baumgartan I was here?"

"My lips are sealed, dear. You be careful."

Gabe was lying on his sofa watching TV when Beck knocked on his door. When he opened it, she and Ben were in the hall looking gloomy. "Come in. I can see that it's bad news again."

Ben stepped in behind Beck and said, "Now, don't go getting all upset. We're not beat yet."

Gabe flopped down on the sofa and said, "Let me have it."

Beck began. "I met with Judge Lemry this afternoon. He confirmed what I already knew. We don't have enough of a connection between Ives and the four victims to get a search warrant. Mere acquaintance isn't enough, but we already knew that."

Ben continued where Beck had left off. "Since Ives has invoked his right to remain silent and wants an attorney, we're through with him. We're going to have to wait till Loar kills again and work on whoever kills for her."

Gabe asked, "What about Machka? Did we find any evidence that would help us? I know she or one of her patients killed him."

"Not a thing, Gabe. The car was clean. The only witness was his girlfriend, but she slept through the whole thing."

Gabe rubbed his face in frustration. "So where do we go now?"

Beck replied, "Underground, boys, underground. We've run this thing into the dirt. We've put our jobs on the line. It's time to retreat back into our holes and do some damage control. Gabe, I want you to do what Garrison says and get yourself back on the road. Save your career. I'm going to stay out of Baumgartan's way, and we're going to lick our wounds. When Loar strikes again, we'll pick it up from there."

Ben said, "That's exactly right, Gabe. I'll keep you in the loop, but it's my case now. I hate to do this to you, but it's for your own good. I want all the files that you have. Garrison will fire you for sure if he knows you have them here."

Gabe slowly stood and walked to his kitchen cabinets. He opened a door and removed the stack of files. He slowly walked over to Ben and laid them in his arms. Ben stopped at the door and said, "Whatever you do, Gabe, stay out of it. Convince Garrison that you're a team player and forget Loar."

He didn't reply and Ben closed the door behind him. Beck sat quietly on the sofa and felt Gabe's hurt. She reached over and caressed his hand. "I'm sorry, Gabe, I know how much you wanted Loar. We'll get her. Someday we'll get her."

"No, Beck, we won't. Ben was right. Some killers are never caught. Some of them are just too smart. We're not going to get Loar, but that's okay. I can live with it."

She slid closer to him and said, "Let's forget her. Come on, dinner is on me. Let's go out and talk about getting you back in patrol."

"Nah, I'm not in the mood."

Both sat quietly for a few seconds. Beck gently ran her fingernail along the top of Gabe's leg and said, "I think it's time we took this to the next level. This whole investigation has been stressful for both of us. Maybe now we can concentrate on each other and see what develops."

His disappointment radiated from his face. Beck whispered, "Would you like to go to bed? I won't stop you this time."

He put his arm around her and kissed her on the forehead. "I wouldn't be any good tonight. You deserve better."

She returned his kiss and said, "There isn't anything better. I want you." He didn't respond. Sensing that he wanted to be alone, she stood and let herself out.

Gabe laid awake most of the night. He ran the evidence around in his head until he got a headache. It just wasn't there. Loar was untouchable. Everyone was right. He had to suck up to Garrison and get his job back.

Garrison had just seated himself behind his desk when his secretary stuck her head in the door and announced that Officer Kinnett wanted to talk to him. He eagerly motioned for her to bring him in.

Once seated, Gabe began. "Chief Garrison, I'd like to discuss this Loar thing with you." Garrison eagerly nodded and urged him to continue. "First of all, I'd like to apologize to you for my past incidents of insubordination. I was wrong and I want to make up for it. You were right about the Loar investigation. I wasn't qualified to investigate anything, let alone an investigation as complex as that one. I was wrong and I apologize. If you'll put me back in patrol, you won't have any more trouble out of me. I'll do the best job I can and I'll keep my nose out of things that don't concern me."

Garrison looked suspiciously at Gabe, but wasn't going to look a gift horse in the mouth. Obviously, Leonard Richey had been successful in whatever tactics that he'd used. He leaned back and said, "Good, Gabe, good. I'm glad to hear that. You're a good man, and I knew you'd come to your senses. You were wrong, you know. Maura would never hurt anyone. You had her pegged wrong."

Gabe burned inside. He thought, *Yeah, you slime-ball, and did I peg you wrong when I saw you in bed with that juvenile?* He swallowed his anger. "You're right, Chief, I dug for months and there wasn't anything there. I owe her an apology."

Garrison had already talked to Richey. Richey had urged him to transfer Kinnett back to patrol where Shelley could keep an eye on him, but he couldn't think of a way to do it without losing face. Kinnett had just made it easy for him.

He reached into his center desk drawer and pulled out Gabe's badge and commission, then stood and extended his hand as he walked around his desk. He gave them back to Gabe and shook his hand as he escorted him to the door. Garrison said, "Thanks, Gabe, you're doing the right thing. I'll have you a letter this afternoon. Report back on Sgt. Shelley's shift tonight."

A sense of relief fell over Gabe as he walked home. Maybe this was the best thing. He'd always known that he was out of his league trying to investigate Loar. This was a job for Ben.

Garrison anguished as he typed Gabe's reinstatement and transfer letter. He hoped neither he nor Richey would take a fall. He seriously doubted that Richey had persuaded Kinnett to back off. He didn't believe for one minute that Kinnett would give up on Loar. He was too determined. The Kinnett that Garrison had just seen was not the Kinnett that he'd known all too well. He was up to something. He was still a real threat to him and Loar. Something more drastic had to be done.

Gabe had to make one phone call before settling down for a few hours of sleep. He dialed Lindsey Schaff's extension at the Perkins-Hays Institute. He wanted to warn her to be careful around Ives. "Hi, Lindsey, Gabe Kinnett."

Lindsey was surprised and cheerfully replied, "Gabe! How are you? I haven't heard from you or Detective Hire for some time. Anything new with Ives?"

His tone reflected his disappointment. "No, sorry, there isn't. That's why I'm calling. We've hit a brick wall. Ives invoked his 5th and 6th amendment rights and we can't interview him anymore. He admitted to knowing some of our victims, but mere acquaintance alone isn't enough probable cause for a search warrant. We'd hoped to get samples of his hair and blood to compare with the evidence at our murder scenes. So, we're going to have to wait till Loar kills again. It rips my guts out, but we have no choice."

Lindsey said, "I'm sorry, too, Gabe. I think Ives is up to something. He's romancing a night orderly, Leeza Giovani. You must have put the fear of God in him. He's being real attentive to her. She can't see that he's only using her to get information. I think he'd leave here if he thought you were closing in on him."

He wished he could do more, but he couldn't. "Lindsey, be careful. Keep your distance and let me know if anything develops."

"I sure will, Gabe. Listen, any chance we could stay in touch anyway, maybe dinner now and then?"

He was surprised by Lindsay's suggestion. He didn't want to alienate her, but he couldn't risk losing Beck. "Sure, Lindsey, that would be nice." After he hung up, he wondered how he would get out of this mess. He should have been honest with Lindsey and told her about Beck. He would the next time he had the opportunity.

Gabe's first night back to work was strange. He felt like a fish out of water. The other officers tried to make him feel like family, but he couldn't shake the feeling that he was an outsider. Angus and Shelley met him for lunch, and Ramon picked up where he'd left off, trying to set Gabe up with his sister.

Being back in patrol on midnights had its advantages. Gabe used the opportunity to keep tabs on Jenna Kerse. He knew Ben was working on Sarah Bethard and Jimmy Clossan, but one more informant couldn't hurt.

He decided that Jenna's own tactics could work against her. He found a conspicuous vantage point near her apartment. As planned, she quickly saw him and confronted him. He used her own argument against her. He told her that it was a free country, and he was legally parked. He said he could park and write reports anywhere he wanted. He didn't realize that he'd already pushed her too far.

His first few nights were like the old days. The hectic pace made the nights pass quickly, and the camaraderie quickly returned. After the first week, he felt like one of the guys again.

Gabe awoke from his morning sleep to a growling stomach. He stumbled to the kitchen and made himself a sandwich, then popped the tab on a Coke and flopped down on the sofa. About half-way through his meal, the phone rang. He normally screened his calls, but he was hoping to see Beck. He picked up the phone and his heart almost stopped. "Hello, pretty boy, know who this is?"

He took some silent deep breaths and asked, "Should I?"

Ives chuckled in an evil tone. "Yeah, you know me. Keep up the tough act, prissy. You and I have lots to talk about. You left without answering my questions, remember?"

Gabe's mind raced as he wondered what Ben would say right now. He finally said, "No, Lyman, that's not what happened. You're the one who walked out. You exercised your right to remain silent. Let's tell it like it was. And by the way, how did you get my number?"

Ives sighed and growled, "I've got my sources. Anyway, I guess it's all a matter of perception. I wouldn't have walked out if you had done as you were told."

"You don't give me orders, Lyman."

"You and me, Kinnett! You and me! Leave Hire home and get over here! You've got something I want and I'm going to get it back!"

Gabe knew what he meant, but played dumb. "What's that, Lyman?"

Ives minced no words. "Maura! You know what I mean! You have a choice, Kinnett! You can get your ass here or I'll come to you! If you make me come to you, it won't be pleasant! It'll be

394

less painful if you to come to me! You'll have the protection of the safety glass to talk through, at least until I tear it down."

Gabe couldn't let himself be threatened, but he wanted to talk to Ives again. He had to manipulate him somehow. "Lyman, Lyman, Lyman, do you think I can be intimidated? You don't seriously think that you're someone to be afraid of, do you?"

Ives burned with anger, but composed himself enough to respond. "Yes, Kinnett, I seriously do. Listen, you need to understand something. You aren't even in my league. If I want your ass, there isn't anything you can do to stop me. No power on earth can stop me from tearing you to pieces if you touch Maura. You come to me. If you've ever had enough sense to realize when you were in deep trouble, you better realize it now. Come here, Kinnett. Don't make me come for you."

Gabe reconsidered his previous commitment to show no fear to Ives. Maybe it would be to his advantage for Ives to believe that he was frightened of him. Maybe he could use that against him later. He could always take a tough stand later if he had to. "Okay. Okay, Lyman, if you insist. Tomorrow?"

Ives growled, "Today", and hung up the phone.

Gabe rubbed his face and tried to decide what to do. He didn't dare let Ben, Beck or Garrison know that he was going against their instructions, but it would be nice to get enough evidence to support a search warrant affidavit.

He pondered his options as he finished his meal. He finally went to the kitchen, washed his dishes and got dressed. He hoped no one found out what he was doing. He hoped he could get back in time to go to work. He hoped his car would start.

Gabe drove to Perkins-Hays and parked in the rear lot so his car couldn't be seen from the street. Lindsey Schaff met him at the back door and let him in. Once inside, she took him by the arm and said, "Hi, Gabe, please don't let Dr. Rhinehart know that I'm doing this. I could get fired. All patient interviews have to be cleared through her, and she has to appoint a staff psychologist to sit in on the interview."

He needed Lindsey, so he promised that her secret would be safe with him. "No way, Lindsey. I'm worried about you being here with Ives. If he decides to leave, stay out of his way. I don't want you hurt."

Lindsey flirted as she escorted him to the interview room. "Wait here. I'll have the orderly get Ives." After five nervous minutes, Ives strolled through the door. He made himself comfortable, then immediately took control of the conversation. He leaned toward the glass and began. "Okay, Kinnett, here's the deal. I'm not playing games with you anymore. You're going to tell me what I want to know. If you don't, I'll be out of here by morning. I've put up with your con all I'm going to. You're going to tell me what I want to know. Got me?"

Gabe studied him and saw that he was teetering dangerously close to the edge of insanity. He knew it had been a mistake to come here. This was no time to get tough with Ives. Once loose on the street, he would be impossible to locate. He could move at will and kill at his leisure. With Loar's assistance, he could hide forever.

Gabe nodded slowly and replied, "I'm listening."

Ives leaned back in his chair, comfortable that he was in charge. "Now, Kinnett, you and Maura, talk."

Gabe stared at Ives, trying to decide what to say. Getting a confession from Ives was out of the question. He'd lost any dominance that he might once have had. His mind raced as he considered his options. He kept returning to the same nagging question. What would be the consequences if Ives escaped?

Ives became impatient and asked pointedly, "Have you seen Maura since our last meeting?"

Gabe pondered the consequences of his answer. He stared deep into Ives's hypnotic blue eyes and slowly nodded his head. He said softly, "I'm not the only one who's seen her."

Ives began to boil. He clinched his fists and gritted his teeth. He asked, "Who else? Who else has seen her?"

Gabe wanted to give Ben more leverage against Clossan. If he thought Ives would be calling on him, he might be motivated to flip. He said, "You wouldn't know him."

Ives growled, "Try me!"

"Clossan. Jimmy Clossan."

Ives leaned his head back in disgust and asked, "Jimmy Clossan?" Gabe slowly nodded. Ives raged inside. "I know him.

396

My sources tell me that he's paralyzed after that chicken-shit, Blauw, shot him in the back. Is that true?"

Gabe shrugged his shoulders and mumbled, "I don't know."

Ives smiled as he reveled in his dominance over Kinnett. "Yeah, it's true. I can tell by the look on your face. You're not hard to read, Kinnett. I ought to be a cop. I can read you like a book."

Ives refocused on the reason for Gabe's visit. "Are you still attracted to her?"

Again, Gabe pondered his answer. Ives could be manipulated so easily at this point. He asked himself, *Did he want to unleash a homicidal maniac on society? Did he want to turn Ives loose on Loar? Did he want to have to kill Ives when he came for him? Did he want to live his life looking over his shoulder?* He tested Ives further and slowly nodded his head.

Ives leaned into the glass and roared, "Have you been to bed with her?"

This was the point of no return. Gabe could shake his head and walk away with no harm done. He could wait for Loar to kill again, if she ever did. Or he could nod his head and set in motion events that would be irreversible. Once loosed, Ives would kill anyone who got in his way. He would kill Gabe if he got the chance. He would certainly kill Loar, if for no other reason than to keep anyone else from having her. Could Gabe do that to Loar? Was this the only way to stop her? Could he become a murderer himself?

He sat silently while his conscience screamed at him. He couldn't do it. He couldn't be a party to murder, no matter who the victim was. As bad as he wanted Loar stopped, he couldn't send Ives after her. No human being deserved to die at the hands of this monster.

Ives grew impatient. The longer Gabe remained silent, the more apparent his answer became. Ives slowly leaned back in his chair and stared at Gabe. He knew the answer to his question by the look on Gabe's face, but he had to hear it. He calmly whispered, "You have."

Gabe knew what he had to do. He had to shut this down and walk away. Loar would walk, but Ives would be in Perkins-Hays. The world would be safe from Ives at least.

He decided that Loar was the lesser of the two evils. He stared into Ives's eyes and began to shake his head. But at the last second, the nagging frustration of Loar's invincibility infuriated him.

He slid his chair out. As he stood to leave, he took his eyes out of Ives's evil stare and looked down at the floor. He could very easily put Ives back in his cage with a shake of his head, but he couldn't bring himself to do it. With no response at all, he simply turned and walked to the door.

Ives mumbled, "You don't have to answer, Kinnett. I can read your eyes. I'll see you on the outside. You're a dead man!"

Gabe turned and said, "You're too smart for me, Lyman. I can't hide anything from you. But neither of us is smart enough to spar with Loar. She's using us both. You can't be so stupid as to believe that she cares for either of us. She's used you to kill for her and she's using me to provoke you."

Ives smiled at Gabe with an evil smirk. "No, you're wrong. I can't be manipulated by anyone. I don't really believe that you're having her. She could never settle for a geek like you. If you've been with her, you know about her birthmark. Where is it and what is it shaped like?"

Gabe stared at the floor. He nodded his head and left the room without answering. He remembered vividly seeing Loar's birthmark the night he was trapped in her closet and watched her and Jenna make love. This was not the time to prove anything to Ives. He said, "If I see you on the outside, Lyman, I'll kill you on sight. No questions asked."

He paused outside the interview room and leaned against the door. He knew Ives had bought the sell. No one was safe now. He had to go back inside and deny Ives's accusation. He couldn't murder Loar like this. Murder wasn't right and he was killing her just as surely as if he'd shot her himself.

His conscience pried him off the wall. He turned to re-enter the interview room, but when he looked through the window, the room was empty. Irreversible events were now in motion. Nothing short of a bullet in the brain would stop Ives. Gabe slowly walked to the exit door and let himself out. He couldn't believe what he'd just done. The man in the mirror was eating him alive.

He drove home and dressed for work. As he dressed, he stared at himself in the mirror. He hated what he had become.

Gabe slept late the next day. He hadn't talked to anyone the night before for fear that Ben would find out that he'd talked to Ives. Beck left a message on his answering machine inviting him to dinner. With her belief that the Loar investigation was over, the relationship would move to the next level. He had fantasized for months about making love to her. Surely tonight would be the night.

Jenna finished her workout and showered. The locker room was crowded with the aerobics class, so she couldn't speak with Beck. She watched Beck shower and remained out of sight. An earlier conversation with Dr. Loar revealed that Beck was Gabe Kinnett's love interest. That revelation was relayed to Dr. Loar via Bob Garrison, who had learned it from Ezard Lumas. The club manager had pointed her out to Jenna.

Beck quickly dressed and hurried out of the locker room. She had to hurry home and start dinner. As she exited the locker room, she bumped into Jenna. Jenna acted surprised and politely excused herself. The orchestrated encounter was designed to see if Beck would recognize her from her past court appearances. She did not. She innocently accepted Jenna's apology and hurried to her car.

Jenna watched her throw her bag in the trunk and slam the lid. Jenna casually walked to her car unobserved. When Beck drove out of the parking lot, Jenna was only a few car-lengths behind.

Beck parked in the underground parking garage and hurried to the elevator, which took her to her apartment. Jenna smiled sadistically as she pulled into a parking space unnoticed. Tonight, Beck would be hers.

Her arms were full, so Beck kicked the door closed with her foot as she threw her attaché case and workout bag on the sofa. Dinner tonight would be stroganoff, simple and fast, but delicious.

She showered again while the meat was browning. She wrapped herself in a towel and added the rest of the ingredients. After turning off the heat and covering the dish to simmer, she hurried to her room to finish dressing.

Jenna took her time climbing the stairs to Beck's floor. The thought of living out her long-time fantasy made every slow, deliberate step an experience to savor. She became sexually aroused and breathed harder as she allowed her mind to drift back to the shower in Loar's apartment where she'd strangled Nat Benson.

She lost all track of time as she moved up each flight of stairs. By the time that she'd found herself standing in front of Beck's door, she was breathing heavily. She found it necessary to stand there conspicuously while she slowed her breathing so as not to alarm Eisman. The vision of Kinnett's face after seeing his murdered girlfriend brought her immense pleasure.

Beck had her underwear on. She was applying her makeup when she heard a gentle knock on her door. She glanced at the clock on her nightstand, then hurried to the door. Gabe was early, but that was okay. Lately, they couldn't be together five minutes without getting busy. An exercise that obliterated any trace of carefully applied makeup. Perhaps her makeup and dinner would be wasted effort.

Jenna applied her most amiable face when the door flew open. It was apparent by Beck's enthusiasm that she was expecting someone. The thought of that someone being Kinnett heightened Jenna's erotic intoxication.

Beck stepped back behind the door to cover herself, and erased the shock from her face. "Oh, I'm sorry, I was expecting someone else. Can I help you?"

Jenna replied, "No, I don't need help, but I've seen you at the fitness center and have wanted to meet you. I've been too nervous, but after bumping into you tonight, I decided that you weren't too threatening."

Beck looked suspiciously at her, trying to remember where she'd seen her before. The face was familiar. She had seen her somewhere before and not at the fitness center. She said, "Oh, that's nice. I'd love to, but I'm expecting company very soon, so I can't visit now."

Jenna held her hand up in a defensive posture. "Oh, that's okay, I don't want to impose. We'll visit later. I just wanted to talk to you about a mutual friend."

Jenna turned to leave, but her comment had captured Beck's curiosity. She asked, "What friend?"

Jenna turned and smiled innocently. "Gabe Kinnett."

Surprised by Jenna's revelation, Beck asked, "Oh really. How do you know him?"

Jenna stepped back up to her door and squared up to her. "Oh, Gabe and I go way back. We're not really friends in the usual sense. We're more like competitors. You see, I'm going to kill him after I kill you."

Complete and immobilizing fear overtook Beck. She couldn't believe what she'd just heard. She suddenly recognized the leathery face of Jenna Kerse. Unable to respond quickly enough to slam the door, she fell under Jenna's dominance. Jenna's superior physique left her completely helpless.

Jenna quickly extended her palm to Beck's face. The heel of her hand slammed against the under side of Beck's chin, snapping her head back with sufficient force to knock her off her feet. The blow lifted her off the floor, causing her to land flat on her back, semi-conscious.

Jenna looked around to see if anyone was watching. No witnesses meant there was no hurry to leave before the police arrived. Her friendly facade faded to a sadomasochistic lust. She stepped into Beck's apartment, closed the door and fulfilled her fantasy.

Beck regained her senses and felt herself being dragged away from the door by her hair. She struggled to her feet only to meet Jenna's backhand, which knocked her to the floor unconscious.

She had no idea how long she'd been unconscious. She opened her eyes to see Jenna straddling her. Jenna outweighed her by ninety pounds. Beck was powerless to move her, so she could only lie there and listen. Jenna asked, "Awake?"

Beck cried, "What do you want?"

Jenna smiled as she stroked Beck's hair. Her face was swollen and her eye was turning purple. Jenna said, "Pain, dear, nothing more than pain. Not just yours, I want your boyfriend to hurt, too."

Beck tried to talk to distract Jenna, but she would not be deterred. She stood and jerked Beck to her feet. This was her only chance. She swung her fist as hard as she could at Jenna's chin.

Jenna showed no emotion as she effortlessly blocked the punch. She punched Beck in the face, but Beck could not fall. Jenna held her to her feet with one hand.

She smiled as she lifted Beck off the floor and drew her close to her face. She said, "Sleep tight. I'll tell Kinnett how you died." She turned Beck around, encircled her neck with her arm and applied a later vascular neck restraint. She buried her face in the back of Beck's head and said, "Relax! It'll hurt less!"

Beck felt Jenna's powerful arms constrict the carotid artery in her neck. Her life rolled through her mind like a high-speed movie reel. She struggled, but to no avail. Her world quickly went dark.

Gabe jogged to the entrance of Beck's apartment building. He didn't go through the underground parking garage or he might have seen Jenna's car. He pushed the *UP* button of the elevator and massaged his sore chest as he ascended to Beck's floor. His heavy breathing had caused his chest to throb.

As he prepared to knock on Beck's door, he noticed that it was standing open about an inch. Thinking that she had left it open so he could let himself in, he pushed it open. As the door swung open, he was stunned. He saw Beck's lifeless body dangling by her head from Jenna's arms. Her face was blue and the lifeless expression in her glazed eyes told Gabe that she was dead.

Gabe's feet were cemented to the floor. He had to make himself move. After what seemed like minutes, he charged Jenna. Her head was buried in the back of Beck's hair, so she never saw his approach.

With all his strength, he punched her just below the ear. She instantly released Beck, who crumpled to the floor in a lifeless pile. The punch was solid and sufficient to render any normal person unconscious. After all, the same punch had turned out Herbert Winn's headlights the day he'd grabbed Beck in the courthouse.

Gabe turned to attend to Beck, but to his amazement, Jenna bounced to her feet as if dropped on a trampoline. He stared at her in shock as she glared at him with no ill effects from his punch. She said, "It's going to take better than that, tough guy. I'm glad you're here. It'll save me a trip."

She took two steps toward Gabe and leaned backward. Quick as a snake, she extended her leg and kicked him hard in the chest. He staggered backward out the open door and landed on his back in the hall.

His chest had not yet healed from Sarah Bethard's knife. Jenna's kick took all the air out of his lungs, and his chest burned as his injured lung gasped for air. He wondered if it was coincidence that Jenna had kicked him directly over the knife wound.

He struggled slowly to his feet. As he got his feet under him, Jenna grabbed him by his shirt and jerked him up. Not wanting another shot like the first one, he tried to beat her to the punch. He swung hard at her chin, but was unsuccessful. She casually blocked the punch and delivered a hard shot of her own. A left hook caught Gabe on the end of the chin and dropped him to the floor.

Jenna slowly picked him up and punched him with a hard roundhouse in the chest. Again, she hit his wound, sending him to the floor in agony. He knew now that the first shot was no coincidence.

She'd hit him where it would hurt the most. She had to know about Sarah Bethard's attack. How else could she know where to hit him to cause him the most pain? The surgeon had told Ben that Bethard must have been coached. Gabe now knew who'd coached her.

His body quivered in pain. He felt himself losing consciousness and panic overwhelmed him. He knew he was dying and felt helpless. Except when Sarah Bethard had stabbed him, he'd never felt this close to death. He prayed silently for God to save him.

He had to do something. He couldn't lie there and be a victim. Right or wrong, he had to make himself move. As he sat up, Jenna ran three steps and punted him in the face. He struck his head hard on the floor when he fell back. Just when he thought he could take no more pain, she found new ways to deliver more. He realized now just how good a teacher Dr. Loar really was.

Jenna strolled casually around Gabe. She clenched her fists and shook her arms to keep them loose. She said, "Okay, lover, want to reconsider? You want to make love or fight?" Gabe tried to inhale enough air to speak, but she didn't give him an opportunity. "Don't bother, lover. I've already decided for you. I lost interest in you long ago. Besides, you're not man enough for me."

She bent over to grab Gabe. He had to do something. He couldn't survive another shot to the chest. He turned sideways and delivered a sharp kick to Jenna's pubic bone. The blow doubled her over, so he could kick her in the face. The kick knocked her backward putting her on her back.

He struggled to his feet as Jenna sat up and shook her head. She licked the blood from her lip and nose and rolled her eyes with pleasure. "Oh, baby, I love the taste of blood. Let's don't stop now."

Gabe desperately wanted to be on his feet before Jenna, but his equilibrium was gone. He felt his strength drain, and weakness overtook his whole body. Jenna couldn't have picked a better time to take him on.

She sprang to her feet and charged him at a hard sprint. With no room to sidestep, he was forced to take the full force of her charge. Dizzy and disoriented, he couldn't muster the strength to absorb her charge. She lowered her head and raised her forearms to her chest. She head-butted him in the face and drove him backward into the wall with her arms. He crumpled to the floor semi-conscious.

Jenna reveled in her victory. She was sexually aroused and savored the pain that she was delivering. With blood streaming from his mouth and nose, Gabe could think of only one thing. He had to find the strength to unholster his Colt.

He'd never considered shooting a woman before, but his .45 was the only thing that would stop Jenna. He had no hesitation about the issue now. His only concern was finding the strength to hold onto it. In his weakened condition, she would take it away from him. He had to unholster it and get a round off before she could close the distance between them and take it away from him.

Jenna bent over and grabbed Gabe's head with both hands. She lifted as she twisted his head hard to put pressure on his spinal cord. The pain forced him to jump to his feet to relieve the pressure on his neck.

She spun him around and encircled his neck with her arm. As she applied pressure on his carotid artery, she said, "Should have screwed me when you had the chance. You should have backed away from Maura. You knew I'd never let you take her from me. See you in hell."

As she constricted Gabe's neck, he felt immense pressure inside his head. He turned blue and began losing consciousness. He realized that this was what Dutch Windsor, Roger Moesen, Nat Benson and Beck Eisman had felt just before they'd died.

Gabe was passing out, but could not surrender. He mustered enough strength and composure to reach under his left arm and grip the butt of his Colt. He fumbled with the rig until he'd clumsily broken open the thumb-snap so the cocked hammer would fall. He awkwardly pulled the pistol out of the holster far enough to slide his finger inside the trigger guard. He pivoted the muzzle toward Jenna, flipped the thumb safety down and jerked the trigger.

The .45 roared with authority and the big hollow-point tore through the back of his jacket. The shot woke up the entire apartment building. The deafening boom was music to his ears. He knew now that someone would call 911 and help would be on the way.

The shot grazed Jenna's side. Though not a solid hit, the shock knocked her down the hall where she slid to a stop on her back. She screamed from the pain as blood gushed from her side. She sat up, stared in shock at her wound and applied pressure to slow the stream of blood that was pumping out on the floor.

As she assessed her wound, her rage pushed her out of reality. She glared at Gabe and struggled to her feet as she quivered from the adrenaline rush. He raised the pistol to eye level and took a shaky sight picture on Jenna's bloody face. He squeezed the trigger, but the pistol only made a disheartening click.

He looked in shock at the hammer. It was in the down position. It had fallen on a fired round. The holster had gripped the slide sufficiently to retard the cycling of a new round into the chamber. The slide moved rearward enough to cock the hammer, but not far enough to eject the fired case.

Gabe grabbed the slide to cycle it, but Jenna would not give him time to shoot her again. With blood spurting from her wound, she sprinted to him and again punched him in his stab wound. As he staggered backward, she grabbed the pistol, twisted it out of his hand and turned it on him.

No matter what Jenna had dished out so far, nothing would compare to the devastation that a round from his own .45 would cause. He had to get his gun back at all cost. He fought through the pain, bounced off the wall and charged her. He slapped the gun with all his might. It flew from her hand and fell over the railing to the landing.

Jenna grabbed him, laughed psychotically as she spun him around and again encircled his neck. She bent him over backward to keep him from getting his feet under him, which would allow him to bend over and flip her over his shoulder. She again constricted his neck and wished him farewell.

Gabe realized that this was the end. As he was losing consciousness, he mustered one final wave of determination. Jenna was badly hurt, and he could feel that she was weakening from blood loss. She'd improperly applied the lateral vascular neck restraint and had not pressed her head against his. With all his strength, he jerked his head backward and butted Jenna in the nose. She screamed out in pain, but held on tight.

Although the floor was slippery with blood, the diversion allowed Gabe to get his feet under him and turn toward Beck's doorway. With all his strength, he put his foot on Beck's doorframe and pushed backward. He and Jenna stumbled backward and fell off the top of the staircase.

It seemed like minutes before they landed. Jenna clung tight to him, but was on the bottom. They landed hard on their backs, and Jenna bore the full load of her and Gabe's combined weight as they bounced down the final few steps. Gabe's weight on top of her face was sufficient to crush her skull as it slammed against the final few stairs.

They slid to a stop on the landing. As the blood rushed back to his brain, Gabe realized that he'd been blessed with a temporary reprieve from Jenna's attack. He rolled off her and saw that she was motionless.

He looked around and found his .45. He fumbled with it, but was finally able to pick it up and cycled the slide. The fired case flew out of the ejection port and a live round funneled its way into the chamber as the slide slammed into battery.

He quickly pointed the gun at Jenna's head and jerked the trigger. He was not going to allow her to regain consciousness and inflict more pain. Again, a deafening explosion roared through the building. The big hollow-point opened a window in Jenna's head as gray matter and blood splattered on the landing. Gabe collapsed and gasped for air. He didn't realize that his final effort was unnecessary. Jenna was already dead.

The phones in the dispatch shack were all ringing at once. Every call was the same, disturbance with shots fired. Len Shelley and Angus Blauw were parked door-to-door discussing the horsepower of the motors on their future fishing boats. When the dispatcher gave the address of the disturbance, Angus snapped to attention. "Shit, Len, that's Beck Eisman's apartment building. Kinnett's been knocking the bottom out of her! I'll bet he's in trouble!"

Shelley panicked and jerked the shift lever into DRIVE. He yelled as he drove away, "That low-life Richey! If he's hurt Kinnett, I'll kill him with my bare hands!"

Gabe caught his breath, but grew weaker by the minute. He looked at his chest and saw that Jenna had reopened his knife wound. He was bleeding profusely. He laid his head down and became sleepy as he drifted into hemorrhagic shock. As the loss of blood numbed the pain, he marveled at how peaceful it was.

He felt himself being shaken. With sirens screaming in the background, he looked up into the bloody and swollen face of Beck Eisman. She slid behind him and sat down. She cradled his head in her lap, applied pressure to his bleeding chest and cried as she begged him to hold on.

Her voice grew faint and Gabe's vision blurred. He felt no fear, only peace. The last things he heard were Beck's faint screams and a stampede of footsteps coming up the stairs. The goon squad had arrived.

19

SINCE HIS LAST conversation with Kinnett, Ives had been overcome with anxiety. He hadn't been able to participate in the institute's activities and had shut himself off from his counselors. Leeza Giovani secured the knife that he'd wanted and provided him with a master key. He could now leave whenever he wanted. Leeza lived for the day when they would be together.

Ives didn't care what happened anymore. The thought of having sex with Leeza repulsed him, and he could no longer suppress his urge to see Loar. He could walk out anytime, but he wanted to make a statement when he left. He had to see Dr. Rhinehart alone.

He wanted to visit others before taking on Kinnett. He needed Leeza to find out where Jimmy Clossan was being rehabilitated. One more session with Leeza should do it. Once he had all the information he needed, he would dispose of her.

Gabe awoke the next morning. Beck, Ben and all his friends surrounded him. The officers made small talk and congratulated him. They trickled out of the room, leaving only Ben and Beck.

Ben stepped up and said, "Hi, kid, you're making a habit of coming here. How do you feel?" Gabe nodded and whispered, "Water."

Beck quickly poured a glass of water and held his head as he drank. She said, "You've lost a lot of blood, but you're going to be okay. You saved my life. I can't thank you enough."

Ben patted him on the shoulder. "Glad you're okay, Gabe. Now, I want you to stay put this time. The doctor wants you here for at least two days. Don't be walking out of here till they say so, hear me?" Gabe simply nodded.

On his way out, Ben turned back to Gabe. "By the way, I thought you might like to know that Jimmy Clossan wants to talk to me. I told him that Ives knows he'd slept with Loar and that Loar is sleeping with a cop. I guess the bluff worked."

When Ben left, Beck pulled a chair close to Gabe's bed. She held his hand, and for the first time, he saw her weaker side. She cried as she caressed his hand. He tried to comfort her, but could only squeeze her hand. He whispered, "It's okay, Beck, I wasn't hungry last night anyway."

She looked up at him through her tears and smiled. "Well, I was, and I had special plans for afterwards, too." She composed herself and asked, "How can I thank you?"

"Dinner will be fine. You don't owe me anything, Beck."

She kissed his hand and said, "I love you, Mister. I'm glad this mess is over."

He squeezed her hand. "Me too, babe."

As Beck rambled on about their future, he stared at the ceiling. He didn't hear a word she said. It wasn't over. After his last conversation with Ives, the worst was yet to come.

In his weakened state, Jenna Kerse had gone through him like a chain saw. Ives would rip his legs off and beat him to death with them. What had he done? How could he tell Beck that they both might be dead soon?

One thing was sure now. Loar had sent Kerse after him. She would not rest until he was dead. Like it or not, this was war. Any battle that he'd previously fought with the man in the mirror was over. He would have to kill Loar first, and Ives was his only weapon. He decided that the very day he got out of the hospital he would send Ives over the edge.

Gabe was preparing to check out when Ezard Lumas walked in. Beck was helping him pack when the door opened. She glared at Lumas as he spoke. "Hey there, Gabe, how are you feeling?" Gabe didn't answer. He simply continued to pack.

Lumas had a different demeanor from their last conversation. "Listen, Gabe, I'm sorry we got crossways in the past, but I'm really on your side this time. Anytime an officer fires his weapon, we have to investigate, especially when there's a killing. I've got to take a statement from you, but I'm going to take care of you on this one. That's straight from the chief's office."

Gabe showed no emotion and ignored Lumas. Beck, however, could not remain silent. "That's a lie, Lumas. You know you're not going to take care of him. That's not your decision. There's been a killing. This is a homicide investigation. That's criminal, and Gabe's 5th and 6th amendment rights kick in. He has the right to remain silent and have an attorney. That's just what he's doing. You're not fooling anyone here. You're going to investigate this and send it to the prosecutor's office for a determination of whether charges will be filed or not. You have to. So just run back to your office and put your file together. Send it over and I'll discuss it with the lead homicide prosecutor. When he hears my version, he'll flush the whole thing down the toilet."

Lumas smiled and said, "You judge me too harshly, Ms. Eisman. At any rate, I have a job to do. The department has the right to conduct an administrative investigation to see if Gabe violated any department policies. So please, butt out before I call Mr. Baumgartan and tell him that you're using your position with his office to tamper with a police investigation and help your boyfriend."

Gabe was in no condition to wrestle with Lumas or he would have physically thrown him out of his room. He reigned in his anger and said, "Lumas, you do what you have to, but since we're telling people where to go, why don't you get out of here before I call Angus Blauw to come up here and kick your ass again."

Lumas burned as he glared at Gabe. "Okay, tough guy, have it your way. See you in the chief's office." He left and slammed the door behind him.

Gabe walked into shift change four days later. He was met with a standing ovation and requests for a speech. He waved

411

everyone off and sat down. Len Shelley greeted him and ordered everyone to shut up while he read the pass-on information. When the briefing was over, Shelley trotted up to Gabe and wrapped his huge arm around his shoulder. "Not so fast there, killer, you're with me tonight."

Gabe was surprised. "What for?"

Shelley forcefully replied, "Because I care about you! You're too weak to be on your own. You're going to chauffeur me around for a few nights till you get your strength back. I don't want you getting your ass kicked anymore than you already have. Don't argue with me. If I had my way, you wouldn't even be back to work yet."

As usual, it was useless to argue with Shelley. He was too big and overbearing. Despite his rough language, Gabe knew he loved him like a son. Shelley's affection touched him deeply. "Okay, sarge, you're the boss. To tell you the truth, I'd expected Garrison to be waiting for me tonight. I was sure that he'd suspend me pending an internal affairs investigation of the shooting."

"Normally he would, but this is a unique situation. I don't know what you said to get your job back, but whatever it was, you convinced Garrison that you two have a truce. He thinks suspending you might scratch the scab off the wound. Rest assured, boy, there is an investigation going on. He's just doing it quietly and letting you work till it's over. Besides, it was a righteous shoot. They'll go through all their gyrations and make you sweat for a few weeks. When it's all over, they won't have any choice but to put it to sleep. You got nothing to worry about. Besides, Ben Hire briefed the prosecutor and got a verbal commitment that he wouldn't file charges on you. Garrison's not taking any risk by letting you work."

"I hope you're right. I still feel bad about killing her. I feel even worse about getting my ass kicked by a woman. I never thought I'd use my gun to keep from taking an ass-kicking, but I had no choice. She was killing me."

Shelley stopped him. "I don't want to hear that kind of talk, son. Any of us can take an ass-beating at any time. None of us are Superman. If you're lying in a coffin, it doesn't matter if you were put there by a woman or a man, dead is dead. Besides, that wasn't no woman. That was the Incredible Hulk with tits. That

412

bitch could have kicked my ass, and I'm a tough old dog. Anyway, you weren't ready for a fight like that. You were recovering from a collapsed lung, for God's sake. Don't sell yourself short, boy. You were in a real war. Now, go warm up my limo. I'm going to have you crunching gizzards before the week is over."

Gabe reached over and pulled the car keys out of Shelley's gunbelt. A sense of relief came over him as he walked to the rear lot. Len Shelley was like a father to him and he was glad to be back where he belonged.

Leonard Richey eased down the old river road where Swede Boreman's body had been found. In the clearing ahead, he saw Garrison's car. He pulled up behind it and shut off his lights.

He stepped out of the car and walked up to Garrison, who was leaning against the trunk of his car with his arms crossed. He faced Garrison and said, "Not a good place, Bob. The nightshift guys check this road all the time for parkers."

Garrison looked up at the stars and said with a reminiscent smile, "Yeah, I know, Leonard. We use to sneak up on parkers and watch them screw, remember?"

Richey didn't respond. He knew Garrison hadn't called him to this desolate location just to reminisce about the good old days. Garrison continued, "I just wanted to compliment you on your job with Kinnett. He's backed off Maura and things are settling down. I'm not going to take a fall after all."

Richey knew something was wrong. Garrison could have discussed Kinnett during business hours. His suspicions heightened. "I didn't do anything with Kinnett, and you didn't have to call me out here to tell me that, Bob. Are you going to rub it in my face that you're off the hook and I'm still in trouble over Carla Ellis?"

Garrison shook his head and said sadly, "No, Leonard, I'm not going to do that anymore. It was wrong of me to blackmail you. You and I have been friends for too long. I'm truly sorry for that. I called you out here to tell you that everything is fine now and I don't need you to do any more dirty work for me. You're off the hook."

Richey looked at the ground and kicked a rock at his feet as he pondered Garrison's reprieve. He still didn't like the tone of the conversation. Garrison had never let anyone off the hook. He asked, "Okay, Bob, so where does that leave me? Ellis will still scream sexual harassment when she doesn't get promoted. You're not going to promote her, are you?"

Garrison laughed. "Hell no, Leonard! That useless bitch isn't even a mediocre policeman, let alone sergeant material. But she's not going to complain about you. She can't complain about a dead man."

He uncrossed his arms and produced a short-barreled .357. Richey's eyes opened wide as he put his hands up in a defensive posture. He yelled, "Wait! Wait, Bob! What the hell are you doing?"

Garrison stood quietly as the passenger door of his car opened. Richey hadn't seen the other person in the car when he drove up. He'd assumed that Garrison was alone. He was overcome with shock when Maura Loar stepped to the rear of the car and stood beside Garrison.

Loar leaned against the trunk of Garrison's car and spoke with no emotion. "Dear Leonard, you must know how much this grieves Robert. He loves you so. The loss of your friendship has devastated him. You abandoned him when he needed you most."

Richey spoke directly to Garrison. "Bob! I didn't turn on you! You know that! Don't listen to this conniving bitch! We've been through too much together! For God's sake, we used to be partners in patrol! We rode the same district car together!"

Garrison remained silent and allowed Loar to do the talking. "Come now, Leonard, there's no need for insults. Robert is only doing what he has to. When you refused to kill Kinnett for him, you drew the line in the sand. Robert is a compassionate man, but you can't sit on the fence in this matter. You're either with him or against him. You can't stay neutral and avoid the fray."

Richey glared at Loar. "Don't give me your psycho-babble bullshit, Loar! You think the mere fact that you say something makes it gospel! You're full of shit! You don't fool me one bit! Kinnett was right about you! That's why I didn't try to stop him! I hope he fries your phony ass!"

Angered past the point of concern for his own life, Richey again turned his attention to Garrison. "Go ahead, Bob! You've always been a back-stabbing prick! I can't stop you from shooting me, but I'm not going to kiss your ass anymore! I told you that in the park! I won't be around to see it, but you mark my words. Kinnett is going to get you, you and this manipulating little whore!"

There was a long silence as Richey waited for the muzzle-flash. He thought Garrison was reconsidering his decision to fire. If he were going to survive, he'd have to do something. If he just stood there, Loar would shoot him herself. He considered walking away, but Garrison or Loar would shoot him in the back. If he tried to run, he wouldn't get two steps. He had to lunge for Garrison and get the gun.

He had waited as long as he dared. He tried to lunge for Garrison, but Garrison knew him too well. Too many years of friendship had made him predictable.

Richey had barely shifted his weight to lunge when the .357 roared. The muzzle flash lit up the area like a flashbulb for a split second. The flash brilliantly illuminated the shock on Richey's face as the hollow-point tore its way through his throat and exploded his spinal cord. The impact threw his head back and knocked him off his feet. Both feet flew up in the air as he slammed to the ground. He didn't move a muscle and was dead before he hit the dirt.

Garrison stood quietly. The dust cloud settled back down on Richey and the gunsmoke dissipated in the cold night air. Garrison lowered the pistol and stared sadly at his old friend. After a long silence, he said, "He was right, Maura. He was always right. Kinnett isn't going to give up. We're going to have to kill him."

Loar caressed Garrison's left arm and leaned her head against his shoulder. "Dear Robert, don't be so hard on yourself. Leonard was a good friend. I know the loss will be painful, but I'm here for you. You did the right thing. He would only have haunted you in the future. With Kinnett out of the way, we're home free. Poor Leonard would never have let you live your life in peace. He would ultimately have been your downfall."

Garrison stared at Richey as Loar reassured him. He sighed deeply, then began to ramble. "You're right, Maura. You're right.

415

As much as I loved the guy, it was him or me. I gave him a chance and he threw it back in my face. But did you see how he died? What a man! I've always admired his courage. He had steel balls. He was never afraid of anything. He never backed down from a fight or walked away from a friend. I always knew he would die like this, gutsy to the end. I'm so proud of him. I hope I'm as brave as he was when it's my time to die."

Loar stepped in front of Garrison and held his face with both hands so she could look him in the eyes, then lovingly lectured him. "Now, Robert, back away from this. Don't immerse yourself in the memories. Pull yourself out of the emotion of the moment. You've just been through a traumatic experience. I can help you work through it, but this is not the place. Let's remove ourselves from the drama and discuss this in a cooler, calmer atmosphere, like my apartment."

They weighted Richey's body and threw him in the river, then took his car back to the station and parked it in the designated parking space marked: Deputy Chief. His murder would go unsolved like so many others in the city's recent history. Leonard Richey's final resting place would be a dusty cardboard box marked: DEAD FILES, in the cold case unit.

Ives was sitting in his room staring into the dark corner. The soft rap on his door was no surprise. Leeza let herself in and hurried up behind him. She encircled his neck and kissed his head. She laid a package on his bed and said, "Here, baby, this came for you today. There's no return address, but it was mailed from here in town. I'll be back for my tip later." She then hurried out the door to complete her rounds.

Ives slowly shifted his despondent stare to the package on the bed. He stared for several seconds before picking it up. With the finesse of a three year-old at Christmas, he ripped the paper from the box. He tore open the box and removed the videotape. Taped to the cassette was a note. Ives gritted his teeth and shook with rage as he read, *Loar's birthmark is shaped like a heart, left side of left breast.* He trembled and screamed through gritted teeth, "No!"

He calmed himself enough to think rationally. He looked up and down the hall before leaving his room. He hurried to the multi-media room and used his master key to enter. After locking the door behind him, he moved to the back of the room and turned on a television. He turned on the VCR directly under the TV on the portable stand, then inserted the cassette, pressed the *Play* button and watched in shock.

Within seconds, his rage peaked. He watched himself beat Lucian Green to death with a length of pipe. He now knew why Maura had insisted on waiting in the car that night. She had videotaped him without his knowledge, but why? After a brief analysis, he reached the only logical conclusion. She'd taped him to use it against him later.

He stopped the tape and pushed the *Rewind* button. Kinnett had told him the truth about everything. He had been having sex with Loar. How else could he have known about her birthmark? Loar was using both of them. Why else would she have given Kinnett the videotape?

He now had his proof. This could only mean one thing. Criminal charges were close at hand. The videotape was a slam-dunk conviction. He had no choice now. He had to leave Perkins-Hays. He closed his eyes and rocked back and forth as he swore that he'd never set foot in a prison.

Ives was completely devoid of morals or conscience and put no value on honesty, so Kinnett's admission would not save him. Now, more than ever, he was committed to holding Kinnett's severed head in his hand right next to Maura Loar's.

Len Shelley called the briefing to order. He didn't mind the chatter and laughter. It meant that his men were happy and well bonded. He roared, "Quiet! Sit your asses down and shut up! I've got a lot to read tonight, so pay attention!"

When everyone was seated, he began. "Before I get to the pass-on information, I want to update you on Major Richey. He's been missing for five days now and no one has heard from him. His car was in his parking space, but he's not been heard from. Ben Hire is working the case, but it doesn't look good. It's not like the major to disappear without contacting his wife. They were close. Ben suspects foul play, but he doesn't have any suspects at this time. So! I want you guys to check all of your back-roads and keep your eyes peeled for him. Put pressure on your snitches and dig up some leads that might help find him."

Angus blurted out in his usual cynical growl, "Why should we look for the back-stabbing prick, Len. We can all breathe easier knowing that the sneaky bastard isn't head-hunting us anymore."

The room erupted in applause and cheers. Shelley couldn't disagree too adamantly. He allowed the applause to die down on its own. "That may be, but he's still a cop. He's one of us, whether you guys like it or not. He's gone to bat for many of you and you didn't realize it. I know he's hard to take sometimes, but we could do worse. You better hope he turns up. If you think about who might take his place, I think you'll agree that we're better off with the major. I haven't always liked what he's done, but you have to remember that he can only do so much. He has a boss, too, you know."

No one could disagree. They considered Richey's possible successors and mumbled among themselves. They all sat quietly as Shelley read the pass-on book.

Angus called Shelley and Gabe to meet him at one of the shopping centers about midnight. Gabe pulled alongside and rolled down his window. Angus said. "Hey, Len, this is the first time I ever saw a nigger with a white chauffeur. Make you feel special?"

Shelley laughed. "Yes sir, it sure does. I'm making snowflake here drive me by all my friends' houses so they can see how uppity I am. And you know the best part?"

Angus quit laughing long enough to ask, "What?"

"He's not costing me a dime. The city is picking up the tab."

Gabe let the two have their fun. When they had finished, he said, "Go ahead and laugh, you old fossils. I may be a chauffeur, but look who's having to take all my reports tonight."

Angus quit laughing. He realized that the sergeant couldn't allow himself to be tied up on a report call in the event that he was needed somewhere else. Shelley laughed even harder than before. He roared, "That's right, Angus! He may be my nigger, but you're his!"

Shelley and Gabe laughed at Angus. The rare loss of words was too much for them to overlook. Shelley finally quit laughing and turned to a more serious matter. He asked, "Hey, Angus, where have you got the major hidden?"

Angus shook his head. "I wish I did. As much as I disliked Richey, I'm worried about him. He was a prick, but I wouldn't want anything to happen to him. You're right, we could do a lot worse. I don't know where he is, but I'd bet my next paycheck on two things. He's dead and Garrison is behind it."

Shelley quickly chastised Angus. "Now, Angus, you don't know that. Don't be starting crap like that. You know what Garrison will do to all of us if he finds out that we're spreading rumors about him. He wouldn't hurt Richey anyway. They used to be partners."

Angus looked past Gabe and glared at Shelley. "Len Shelley, you sit there and tell me that you don't know it's true! Go ahead, lie to me!"

Shelley grudgingly mumbled, "Well, I ain't saying it is and I ain't saying it ain't. I just don't want that rumor circulating."

Gabe lowered his head and said, "I sure hope it ain't true. If he'd do that to Richey, I hate to imagine what he'd do to me."

Shelley thumped him on the shoulder and yelled, "Ain't nothing going to happen to you or any other man on my shift! You hear me, boy! You just stay away from Garrison and don't talk to him alone! He won't do anything to you at work! Just don't meet him anywhere away from the station!"

Angus followed up Shelley's advice. "That's right, kid, he won't try anything at work. You just make sure you have me or Len with you if he wants to meet you away from the station. And always keep that hog-leg .45 with you. It saved your bacon when that big lesbian kicked your ass."

Shelley quickly came to Gabe's defense. "You shut your mouth, Angus! That muscle-dyke could have whipped everyone on the shift, except me! I'd hate to imagine what she'd have done to your old bony ass."

The entire conversation sickened Gabe. He said, "I can't believe we're talking like this. We're all cops, for God's sake. We don't go around killing each other."

Angus chuckled sarcastically as Shelley corrected Gabe. "We're cops, boy, Garrison ain't. Everyone that wears blue ain't a cop, remember that."

Garrison could wait no longer. He'd wracked his brain trying to think of someone who would kill Kinnett without betraying him. Loar had warned him to let matters take their own course, but Jenna Kerse's failure had heightened his anxiety. Loar's young Cuban admirer on the nightshift had also not performed as she'd hoped. He would have to eliminate Kinnett himself.

He couldn't think of an excuse to meet Kinnett away from the station, so he finally settled on a meeting in the cold case unit. Gabe had finished shift change when the dispatcher announced over the intercom, "Kinnett, phone call on two."

Everyone assumed it was Beck Eisman and cheered as he picked up line two. He was shocked to hear Garrison's voice. "Gabe, Bob Garrison here. Listen, I want to congratulate you on your quick transition back to patrol. It usually takes a few weeks for officers to get acclimated when they've been off the streets for a while. You're doing a great job. Keep it up."

Gabe quietly mumbled, "Thanks."

Garrison continued, "Gabe, listen, I want to talk to you about Leonard Richey. I'm really worried about him. You know we used to be partners in patrol. We were very close and his disappearance is eating me alive. I want to talk to you about it."

"Chief, I don't know what I can tell you about that."

"No, Gabe, I know you don't know anything about it, but I'm afraid Loar might have been involved. They'd had an argument a few weeks ago. I'm afraid you were right about her after all. Could we meet and talk confidentially?"

Something was up, but Gabe was confident in his ability to take care of himself. "Where?"

"Downstairs in the cold case unit." Gabe agreed and walked out of the squad room.

Garrison was waiting in the musty bunker when he walked in. The room brought back old memories and new bitterness. He asked, "Yes, Chief, what can I do for you?"

A feigned look of sorrow fell over Garrison's face. "Gabe, I'm real worried about Leonard. I'm afraid something awful has happened to him."

Gabe stood quietly as Garrison rambled. He didn't believe a word Garrison said, but didn't want to get suspended or transferred again. Garrison said, "Gabe, it isn't like Leonard to be gone this long without contacting someone. I'm sure he's dead. I'd like to know where you are with the Loar investigation. Maybe you can tell me something that will help."

Gabe didn't fall for the obvious bait. He shrugged his shoulders. "There is no investigation, Chief. I've given up on Loar and I've been focusing on my patrol duties."

Garrison frowned. "No, Gabe, you haven't. I want to know where you left off with Loar. What did you find out? Don't worry, son. We have an understanding. I only want to find Leonard."

Gabe looked down at the floor and again replied, "I don't know anything, Chief. I certainly don't have a clue where the major is. We're just as worried as you are."

An angry tone crept into Garrison's voice. "You're lying to me, Kinnett. You won't ever back off of Loar. You're too stubborn. What have you been up to?"

By the direction that the conversation was going, Gabe was certain that Garrison must be aware of his interviews with Ives, but he couldn't admit to anything now. He searched desperately for an escape. When his mind couldn't work fast enough, he simply said, "Sergeant Shelley will be wondering where I am, sir. I have to get out in the back lot for vehicle inspection."

He turned to leave, but Garrison stopped him. "Shelley will have to do without you tonight, Kinnett. Give me your gun. You're suspended until I can find out what happened to Richey."

Gabe turned around in shock and yelled, "Why? I didn't have anything to do with the major!"

"I don't believe you, Kinnett! I had Leonard tailing you! He almost had enough evidence to indict you! I think you caught him watching you and killed him!"

Gabe was stunned by the accusation and adamantly protested, "That's a lie, Chief. The major wasn't tailing me and you know it."

"Give me your gun, Kinnett! You can tell it to a judge!"

Gabe ran the scenario around in his head, but couldn't think of any options. Overwhelmed with frustration, he slowly broke open the thumb-snap on his holster and removed his Colt.

As he reluctantly handed it to Garrison, he said, "Our truce is off, Garrison. You're forcing me to go for your jugular."

Garrison smiled as he turned the muzzle toward Gabe. You're my jugular, Kinnett. When you're gone, I'll be untouchable."

For the second time in recent memory, Gabe was staring down the bore of his own gun. He immediately flashed back to the hall outside Beck's apartment when Kerse had almost beaten him to death. He brought himself back to the present and asked, "You? You're going to kill me? You'll never get away with this, Garrison, not here."

"You're right, Kinnett. I couldn't get away with it, but I'm not going to shoot you. You're so obsessed with Loar and your near-death experience with Kerse that you're going to shoot yourself. Suicidal people don't always make rational decisions, and you are suicidal. Dr. Loar told me that the first time she talked to you, remember? You were despondent over your transfer. You came down here and shot yourself because this place held some unknown significance for you. Who knows, maybe you just couldn't accept Loar's rejection of your advances. Maybe your guilt over murdering Leonard was too much to handle."

Gabe would have laughed out loud, but he didn't want to provoke Garrison any more than he already had. He yelled, "No, Garrison, no! You'll never sell that! The dispatcher knows you called me down here! The guys on the shift know I came here at your request! You can shoot me, but you need to know one thing first! Loar videotaped you screwing that underage girl in her apartment!"

His mind was now racing to find a way to drive a wedge between Garrison and Loar. He hoped that if Garrison thought that Loar was conspiring against him, he might feel less confident.

"That's right, Garrison, I watched the tape. Loar gave it to me. She's not in your corner anymore. I made another copy and gave it to a friend. You shoot me and the tape goes out to the news media and prosecutor's office. We've identified the girl and she'll testify against you."

Garrison's face suddenly lost all expression. He shook his head in shock. "You're bluffing, Kinnett. That won't save you. Maura would never turn against me."

"Then shoot, Chief. Everyone in the squad room knows I'm here with you. If I end up dead, you'll be in the lock-up within the hour. Shelley and Blauw will beat you to death if you kill me. Every officer on my shift will help them. Copies of the videotape will be delivered to the mayor and counsel tomorrow. If you survive being arrested tonight, you'll be in the state lockup for the rest of your life. And you know how convicts treat cops and child molesters in prison, so go ahead!"

Garrison could not bluff Kinnett. He slowly lowered the pistol and surrendered. "Well, it looks like you have me for now." He turned the pistol around and handed it butt first to Gabe. "Stay safe tonight, Kinnett, I'd hate for anything to happen to you."

Gabe holstered his pistol and turned toward the door. Garrison interrupted his exit. "Listen, Kinnett, I need a man like you. I hate to see us at odds with each other. You've got real potential. I'll make you a deal. You play ball with me, and I'll slide you into Leonard's position. Major Kinnett, has a good ring to it. You can even keep your blackmail tape for insurance."

Gabe turned back to Garrison in shock. He couldn't believe what he'd just heard. Suddenly, the words of Sergeant Joe Rand echoed in his head. *If you ever get an ace card, use it and get ahead anyway you can.* He now knew the pressure that Rand must have felt when he'd accepted sergeant stripes to drop his lawsuit. He couldn't think clearly. He simply turned and walked away.

As he passed the threshold, he was startled to see Angus Blauw leaning against the doorframe with his arms crossed. He escorted Gabe back up the stairs and chastised him for meeting Garrison alone. Gabe asked, "How long were you there, Angus?"

"I followed you down from the squad room. I heard everything. If you weren't bluffing about the tape of Garrison and the little girl, you're going to be the next major. Sure glad I'm your buddy, Major."

"No way, Angus, I wouldn't have that job for all the money in the world."

"Why not, kid?"

"Because I'd have to put up with misfits like you. I like you okay, but you'd be a supervisor's nightmare. I've seen what a wreck you've made of Sergeant Shelley's nerves." As they climbed the stairs, Gabe asked, "Angus, why didn't you shoot Garrison for me. He could have killed me."

"I would have, but I couldn't get a clear shot, kid. You were standing between us. Besides, when I heard you throw your ace on the table, I knew he wouldn't shoot you."

"What if he had?"

Angus chuckled in a devious tone. "Then I'd have blackmailed Garrison. He'd have made me the same offer to help him cover up your murder. Major Blauw, has a good ring to it, don't you think."

"That's a scary thought."

Ives could no longer stand the stress. Every morning, he expected the police to knock on his door and haul him off to the county jail. Once there, he would be under such a high bond that he'd never get out before his trial. No one in their right mind would co-sign a bond for him. Flight to avoid prosecution would be impossible.

After the office staff went home, Ives cautiously made his way to the wing closest to the parking lot, just as he had every evening since his last interview with Kinnett. He looked outside and saw Dr. Rhinehart's car in its designated parking space. She was working late. This was the opportunity that he'd been waiting for. He hurried back to his room and prepared to leave.

He didn't know how late Dr. Rhinehart would work, so he couldn't wait for Leeza to arrive. He looked at his watch and decided that it was time to visit the doctor.

Dr. Rhinehart was typing on her laptop when Ives quietly let himself into her office. He cleared his throat to announce his presence. Dr. Rhinehart turned slowly and masked her shock. She appeared totally unfazed by his presence. She ordered, "Explain, Lyman. What are you doing here and how did you get through the security doors?"

Ives smiled sadistically and walked toward Dr. Rhinehart. "What I'm doing here will be evident in a minute. How I got here is easy." He held up his master key.

Dr. Rhinehart asked, "Okay, Lyman, which one of my stellar employees gave you that?"

"Giovani has been infatuated with me for some time. She's kept it quiet, knowing how you felt about employees having sexual relations with patients."

The doctor's fate was sealed, but she bravely masked her fear. She turned and resumed typing on the laptop as she talked. "Okay, Lyman, you've made your point. You've shown me how clever you are. Now go back to your room."

Ives laughed. "I have no room, Doctor. I'm checking out tonight. I just want to leave you some fond memories of me, short memories for you and fond ones for me."

Dr. Rhinehart finished typing on her laptop. Her final words were:

"Lyman Ives murdered me. Leeza Giovani gave him a master key and assisted him in his escape. To my family, I love you all very much. Our separation is not permanent. I will see you in Heaven. God bless you all and keep you safe. Comfort each other. Love,
Grandma Martha."

Dr. Rhinehart saved her farewell message to the *C* drive. She then closed the laptop and turned bravely to meet her fate. "I'm going to shock you, Lyman. I know you think I'm afraid of you. You've frightened everyone who's ever known you, but you don't frighten me. I've always known that you don't belong here. You belong in a gas chamber."

"Don't flatter yourself, Doctor. There was one other woman who wasn't afraid of me. She was my greatest love. In many ways, you remind me of her. Believe it or not, I admire you, much as I admire her. I admire women who aren't afraid of me. It makes the sex more enjoyable. Unfortunately for you, you're too old for sex to be enjoyable. No, Doctor, our sex won't be love. It'll be torture and humiliation for you. I enjoy that more than sex for love. As you know, I'm not capable of love."

Dr. Rhinehart rose to her feet and glared into his eyes. "There won't be any sex between us, Lyman. You're not going to rape me. You can kill me and I can't stop you, but I won't be raped. Not by a foul-smelling pig like you. My salvation with God is secured and I'm fully prepared to die, but I'm going to die with my dignity intact."

Ives smiled. "Why, Doctor, I admire your spunk, but you don't have a choice. I'm in charge here. For the first time in our relationship, I'm in charge."

He showed his knife to Dr. Rhinehart. She walked up to him and grabbed his wrist. She directed the point of the knife to her chest. "You might as well finish it, Lyman. This will be the only pleasure that you're going to get from me."

Ives could no longer mask his frustration. It was clear that the doctor would not beg or patronize him. He could rape her, but he was afraid her screams would attract security. He simply didn't have time to torture her as he'd always wanted.

He grabbed the back of Dr. Rhinehart's head and glared angrily into her eyes. Defiant to the end, she stared fearlessly back at him. He slowly drove his knife into her heart and watched the life drain from her eyes. He helped her recline gently to the floor, then slowly stood.

He wanted to kick her to relieve his frustration, but couldn't. His anger dissipated as he looked sympathetically at her. She was serene and majestic and too grand to deface.

Ives slowly turned and walked out the door. He turned the lights off, assured that security would not find the body before morning. He'd only forgotten one thing. He forgot to view Dr. Rhinehart's laptop and delete her dying declaration.

Ives sat quietly in his room, reliving the exhilaration of his recent kill. It was reminiscent of the Andoever, Rudder and Lindsey murders, but not as fulfilling. Dr. Rhinehart hadn't satisfied his masochistic cravings. He tried to figure out why he felt a twinge of guilt. Perhaps he respected her more than he'd thought.

Leeza tapped on his door and entered enthusiastically. It was apparent by her excitement that Dr. Rhinehart's body had not yet been found. Her enthusiasm would soon die.

She locked the door behind her and said, "Hi, baby, I missed you so much." She peeled off her shirt and threw her arms around Ives's neck. He kept his right hand behind his back so she wouldn't see the knife. His breathing increased as the anticipation of another kill heightened his lust.

He brought the knife up to Leeza's stomach, but paused when she said, "I can't wait for you to get to my apartment. I'll hide you out till we can leave town. We're going to have such a good life together."

He suddenly realized that this was not the time to kill Leeza. He might need to hide at her house after killing Kinnett and Loar. Before she'd sensed the presence of the knife, he returned it behind his back.

She turned to finish undressing. He quietly put the knife on top of his dresser. He sighed dejectedly as he realized that he had to pretend one more time.

Ives grudgingly undressed and slid under the sheets. He said, "Tonight is the night, sweetheart. I'll see you at your house when you get off work. I've got to visit some people first. Any luck finding out where Clossan is?"

Leeza wrapped her legs around him and said, "No, baby, sorry. The cops have him hid too well." Ives closed his eyes and performed his duty. His mind was not on the business at hand. He couldn't wait to see the look on Dr. Loar's face as he severed her head.

An hour later, Ives strolled across the parking lot of the institute. He eviscerated the guard at the gate and twisted his head around backward. He turned at the curb and looked back at Dr. Rhinehart's office window. He shook off the twinge of guilt and disappeared into the fog.

20

THIS WAS GABE'S first night solo since he'd returned to work. He'd just begun checking his businesses when the radio crackled. The dispatcher sent Throckmorton and Schumacher to the Perkins-Hays Institute to take information on a walk-away. When the name Lyman Ives came over the radio, Gabe's heart almost stopped.

Before he could catch his breath, Shelley called everyone to meet him at the station. When he arrived, he found the rest of the shift huddled in the parking lot. Shelley was pacing back and forth and giving instructions.

Ben Hire pulled up and took over the briefing. Shelley stepped aside and allowed Ben to lead. "Okay, guys, we've got a killer on the loose. Lyman Ives has walked away from the institute. We've got to find him before he kills someone, but keep this in mind. He was only in the institute under a civil commitment. He hasn't committed any crimes, at least none we can charge him with. Ramón, you and Arvid go by his mother's house. The dispatcher can get her address for you from the C.A.D. system. Len, I need you and Ellis to go by his girlfriend's house to see if he's hiding there. I'll call our snitch inside Perkins-Hays to get her address for you. Gabe, I want you to stay here. He's looking for you. I want you here where I can keep an eye on you. Angus, I need you to cruise the streets between the institute and his mother's house. You may see him on foot. Now! Everyone

429

remember, this son of a bitch is the most dangerous man on two legs. He loves to kill and he can go through any of us like a buzz saw. None of your standard restraint techniques will work on him. He loves pain, so you won't get any pain compliance if you try to hurt him. Just contain him until the rest of us can get to you. Shoot him if you have to, but don't let him get his hands on you. He's stronger than hell and he can take your pistol away from you in a heartbeat."

Everyone got in their cars and sped to their assignments. Gabe hung out around the dispatch center, hoping someone would locate Ives. More than that, he hoped no one besides Ives got hurt. Waves of guilt made him sick to his stomach.

He perked up when Arvid Hallos yelled over the radio. His voice was shaky and cracking. He'd panicked as he reported, "Dispatch, the subject's mother is code blue. We have a crime scene here."

Ben knew what they had and instructed the dispatcher to call the evidence techs out to process the scene. He instructed Arvid to call him at the station and the phone rang within seconds. The dispatcher answered and immediately pointed to Ben. "Line two."

He jerked the phone to his ear and listened for five seconds. He hung the phone up slowly. He turned to the dispatcher and said, "Put it out to all officers. Ives is now a murder suspect. Arrest him on sight. Tell them that if he won't comply with voice commands, to shoot him. Tell them to not try to wrestle with him."

As the dispatcher broadcast the alert, Gabe eased up to Ben and asked, "Ben, what did Arvid say?"

Ben didn't have to look at him. He whispered, "He cut his mother to pieces. It's the worst butchering that Arvid has ever seen."

Within minutes, the security officer from Perkins-Hayes called. Dr. Rhinehart and the gate guard had been found. Ben sent a second team of evidence techs and detectives to the institute.

Gabe turned away so no one could see how flushed his face was. Everything was happening so fast. Within a matter of minutes, his world was in chaos and people were turning up dead all over town. Although Ives had warned him, he was not prepared for this.

As a curtain of guilt draped over him, he walked slowly to the men's room and splashed water in his face. His mind raced to figure out a way to stop the killing, but only one option jumped out at him. He had to find Ives and kill him. He looked in the mirror as he dried his face. His conscience was eating him alive. He hated what he had done and had to look away.

Ben hovered around the dispatch shack, giving orders and briefing staff officers. Gabe felt helpless, so he decided to join the hunt for Ives. He could do more good on the street than at the station. Ben was so busy that he hadn't noticed that Gabe was gone.

Maura Loar returned from a dinner engagement and found her secretary waiting at her apartment. "Sorry, Beth, I couldn't get away as soon as I'd planned. Come in and let's make ourselves more comfortable, dear."

Beth was overjoyed to be alone with Loar. After Loar had turned off her alarm, Beth followed her through her apartment door. Loar wrapped her arms around Beth's waist and led her to the bedroom.

After a brief period of heated foreplay, both women undressed. Loar tied her hair back and said, "I need a shower, dear. Would you care to join me?" Beth adjusted the water temperature, then stepped in the shower ahead of Loar.

Several minutes passed. Both women lathered each other up and engaged in sufficient foreplay to peak their excitement. When the confines of the shower became prohibitive, Loar said, "Beth, dear, let's finish this in bed." Beth nodded and rinsed off.

She stepped out of the shower and dried herself as Loar rinsed off. Beth went to the bedroom and waited. Loar took her time rinsing. She turned the hot water up until the steam fogged the shower door and the heat scalded her skin. Several minutes later, she emerged and dried off.

Loar looked in the mirror and removed the tie from her hair. As she shook her hair loose, she showed no emotion over the impending lovemaking session in the next room. She turned to join Beth, but stopped abruptly in her tracks as she entered the bedroom.

Beth was nude on the bed, as Loar had expected, but she was pale and ashy and her feet were dangling off the end of the bed. Her torso was ripped up the middle from her pelvis to her clavicle. Her intestines and vital organs were lying on the floor at the end of the bed. The majority of her blood was pooled on the bed under her. Her eyes were open wide with a look of horror on her face.

Loar showed no emotion as she stepped toward Beth. She looked down at Beth and sighed apathetically with her half-closed eyes focused on Beth's open chest cavity. She dipped her finger into Beth's blood and put it in her mouth. She rolled her eyes back and sighed as she savored the taste.

Loar looked around and stepped to her nightstand. She calmly opened the drawer and reached inside. She removed the .380 automatic from the drawer and concealed it behind her leg.

She knew immediately what had happened to Beth. She only knew of one person, besides herself, capable of such carnage. She stepped to the doorway of the living room and searched the darkness. She saw nothing, but knew he was there.

Loar stepped into the living room and said calmly, "Good evening, Lyman dear. It's so good to see you again. When did you leave the institute?"

Ives stepped out of the darkness and replied, "Tonight, Maura. I couldn't stand the thought of you riding another man."

Loar feigned a smile and reassured him. "Lyman, darling, you're so mistaken. You've been the only man for me. I love you so much. You know I love you by all the letters that I've written you. I've tried to visit you, but the director wouldn't allow me in. Come, sit, let's talk."

She conspicuously flaunted her nudity at Ives. He'd never been able to control his passion when she'd displayed herself to him. She was confident that this time would be no different and quietly cocked the hammer on her pistol.

Ives stopped her before she could step to the sofa. He knew that once he was seated beside her, he would be deterred. He would still kill her, but taking time to have sex with her first would increase his chances of meeting the police on the way out. He wanted to carry out his mission without being seduced. "No! No,

Maura, not this time. We could never enjoy a life together anyway. I've gone too far tonight."

"Nonsense, dear, nothing is irreversible. I'll hide you here and keep you out of prison. We'll clean up the mess in the bedroom and I'll call Robert Garrison. He'll bury the investigation. He's got a room in the basement of the police station where he keeps unsolved murders. Poor Beth will be just another dead file."

Ives shook his head as he stepped close to Loar. She unconsciously backed against the wall. "No, Maura, that won't do. I have other people to visit tonight, and you won't be around to help me. You seduced Kinnett and gave him a videotape of me killing Green. You've betrayed me, and I'm going to teach you a lesson about pain. I love you, but you've crossed the line. I can't let you live."

He put the palm of his left hand between Loar's breasts and pinned her against the wall as he presented the long-bladed knife to her face. To his amazement, she showed no emotion. She just looked him in the eye with her lifeless stare and said, "Pain is good, Lyman, but I'm not going to let you kill me. Be careful, dear. If you play too rough, it won't be enjoyable anymore, and I'll hurt you back. This can be fun or agony. The choice is yours."

Ives smiled sadistically. "Yes, Maura, the choice is mine. I've always wanted to teach you what real pain is. Feel this."

He placed the point of the stainless blade against the left side of Loar's forehead. He slowly drove the knife under her scalp and along the contour of her skull. He pushed the blade under her scalp until it exited the back of her head. With one hard thrust, he drove the knife into the wall behind Loar, pinning her head to the wall.

Loar never took her lifeless stare out of Ives's murderous eyes. She quivered as the blade sliced its way under her scalp and exited behind her ear. She stood upright and gasped in broken breaths as the pain drove her to the edge of unconsciousness.

Ives was amazed at Loar's pain threshold. Blood poured down her face and dripped on the floor. He stepped back and said, "I'll hand it to you, Maura, you're much more woman than I'd ever imagined. I thought you'd be blubbering like a baby by now."

Loar stabilized her breathing as she swallowed the pain. She stopped quivering and regained her focus into Ives's eyes. She

433

took a couple of deep breaths and said, "Thank you, Lyman dear, your admiration flatters me. But, Lyman dear, don't delude yourself. You're not the teacher here, I am. You're the student and school starts now."

She raised the .380 from behind her leg. She pointed it at Ives and shot him directly below his right collarbone. The muzzle-flash burned his face and the shot knocked him backward and spun him around. He landed on his stomach, then bounced to his knees and turned back toward her. He stared at her in shock as she reached up and grabbed the handle of the knife. With one hard pull, she jerked the knife out of the wall. In the same fluid motion, she pulled it out of her head and staggered slightly as she regained her balance.

Throughout the entire process, her lifeless eyes seemed to glow in the dim light and displayed no sign of pain or emotion. Ives now realized what a monster she truly was. For the first time in his adult life, he felt dominated. He struggled to his feet as he compressed his wound to slow the bleeding.

Loar regaining her balance and again focused on Ives. She said, "Lesson one, Lyman dear, never try to teach the teacher. You should have remembered your place on the evolutionary scale. You'll never teach me anything about pain. Now for lesson two."

She raised her pistol to fire again. Ives had turned and sprinted for the door, but didn't get out in time. The shot struck him in the back of his leg. The blow spun him around and again knocked him to the floor.

Loar lowered the pistol, raised Ives's knife and walked slowly toward him. "Learning anything about pain yet, Lyman dear? Lesson three."

She again raised the pistol to fire, but Ives was too fast. He jumped up and hobbled out the door before Loar could obtain a steady sight picture. Her final shot hit the doorframe as he hurried out. He knew he'd never be able to wait for the elevator, so he crashed through the stairwell door and leaped down the first flight of stairs.

Loar hurried to the door and repeatedly fired her pistol down the stairs at him. When the slide locked open, she smiled softly. Lyman's clumsy headlong-rush down the stairwell amused her. When he'd put enough distance between them, he slowed his descent until he'd reached the lobby.

Seeing that Ives had escaped, Loar calmly walked to the phone and called the security desk. She wanted Ives detained until she could get dressed and go downstairs. School was not over yet. She got no answer. The decapitated guard was slumped over his desk while the late-night reruns of The Three Stooges played on the television.

Loar pondered her circumstances and realized that she had to do something with Beth. She wanted to dial the police dispatcher and report the murder since Ives was responsible anyway. A quick assessment of her crime scene photos and incriminating videotapes ruled out that option. She would have to dispose of Beth herself.

Gabe was driving the streets around Mrs. Ives's house when the dispatcher put out the call of an intruder at Loar's apartment building. He knew instantly that the intruder had to be Ives. He lit up the night with his emergency equipment and raced there.

The security officer had called the dispatcher just before Ives encircled his neck and began cutting. Police response might have been fast enough to catch Ives in Loar's apartment, but the dispatcher had violated protocol by taking the time to enter the information into C.A.D. prior to dispatching the cars.

All the officers heard the call simultaneously and headed for Loar's office building. Angus Blauw happened to be driving by and notified the dispatcher that he was at the scene. Ben Hire panicked. He leaned over the radio console, pushing the dispatcher aside. He keyed the mike and yelled, "Angus, wait for a backup unit! Angus, don't approach the building alone!"

Ben's orders went unheeded. Angus had parked his wagon at the end of the alley and walked toward the same alley door that he'd caught Gabe stumbling out of. He had his portable radio with him, but hadn't turned it on in time to hear Ben yell.

Ben's sense of urgency was not wasted on the other officers. Simultaneously, everyone threw caution to the wind and raced to save Angus.

Angus swaggered confidently toward the door and used his flashlight to illuminate the dark areas of the alley. As he reached the door, he gently gripped the knob and turned it to see if it was locked. To his shock, the door flew open and Lyman Ives staggered though. Angus took a step back as he found himself face to face with the wounded psychopath.

Ives stopped and both men stared at each other. Angus broke the ice in his typical brutal style. "Well, well, well, Lyman Ives, you sniveling pile of shit, been up to see your slut girlfriend I see. What's the matter, Ives, did she find a real man while you were cowering under your bed at the institute?"

Ives straightened up and laughed sadistically. "Yeah, Blauw, one of your asshole buddies, Kinnett."

Angus chuckled and growled, "Ives, you stupid fucker, Kinnett wasn't banging that bitch. He can't stand the phony whore."

Ives looked suspiciously at Angus. He could understand Kinnett lying to him, but how did he know about Loar's birthmark? How did he get the videotape? Blauw had to be wrong.

While Ives was engrossed in thought, Angus decided to arrest him. He could tell that Ives was seriously hurt by the blood oozing from his chest and leg. He stepped into Ives and grabbed his arm to spin him around and push him against the wall.

When he grabbed Ives's arm, he discovered that it was no less than twenty inches in circumference and hard as a band of steel. He'd arrested Ives when he was a skinny kid, but was totally surprised at his physique now. Angus had seriously underestimated him.

Ives quickly broke Angus's grip and backhanded him across the face. Angus fell backward and was stunned by the blow. He cleared his head just as Ives reached down with one hand and jerked him to his feet. Ives said, "I'm not cowering now, Blauw."

Angus realized that he couldn't survive a blow-for-blow exchange with Ives. He punched Ives hard in the bullet-hole below his collarbone. Ives reeled and staggered back a step.

Angus stepped back and tried to unholster his pistol, but Ives was too fast. He charged Angus and grabbed his gun hand. He punched Angus in the face, knocking him back to the ground. Angus struck the back of his head and his vision blurred.

Again, Ives pulled him to his feet. Angus punched him hard as he could on the chin, which was like concrete. The blow paralyzed Angus's fist. His fingers curled up as the pain shot up his arm. The punch had no effect on Ives.

Ives kneed Angus in the groin, curling him up into a fetal position on the ground. Angus knew he was in deep trouble and hoped the goons would arrive soon. He struggled to his feet with Ives's assistance and again punched Ives in his bullet-wound.

This time, Angus kicked him in his wounded leg before he could recover. Ives dropped to one knee and grimaced in pain. Angus then kicked him hard in the face and reached for his pistol.

Angus got his pistol out of its holster, but had not retreated far enough to give himself an adequate safety zone. Ives sprang to his feet and grabbed Angus's wrist. His strength was overpowering. He forced Angus's arm up, pointing the pistol skyward. Angus jerked off one round, hoping to shock Ives into releasing his arm. It didn't work.

Ives punched him in the ribs, forcing the wind out of him. He spun Angus around and encircled his neck while holding on to Angus's gun hand. Angus could not stand and dropped to his knees and gasped for air. Ives grabbed the pistol and wrenched it from his hand. He jerked Angus to his feet by his head and put the muzzle of the Beretta to his temple. Angus was now helpless to defend himself.

The goons arrived in record time, but not soon enough. They raced up the alley as far as they dared without prompting Ives to shoot Angus. They exited their cars and formed a half circle around the two men. They leveled their pistols at Ives and yelled orders and threats. Ives merely laughed at them and hid behind his hostage.

Len Shelley arrived seconds later. He raced past the police cars to see the standoff. The officers were yelling at Ives to drop the gun, and he was laughing hysterically at them.

Shelley tried to calm the chaos, but couldn't be heard over the shouts of the other officers. He finally stepped between Angus and the officers and screamed for everyone to shut up. When the officers quit yelling, he turned toward Ives. His commands fell on deaf ears. Ives laughed at him and threatened to kill everyone after he'd finished with Angus.

Realizing that his fate was sealed, Angus tried to save the others. He yelled, "Shoot this fucker! Come on, guys, shoot him!"

Shelley panicked and yelled, "Angus, you suicidal old bastard, if you've ever listened to anyone in your life, listen to me now! Keep your mouth shut! Don't antagonize him!"

Unwilling to concede defeat, Angus refused. "Fuck this puke, Len, blow his ass off! I don't care if you hit me, just shoot the son of a bitch!"

Ives put his mouth to Angus's ear and said, "Hey, Blauw, this puke just kicked your ass."

Angus replied, "No you didn't, Ives. This old man just beat your ass, and you had to resort to a gun to win. You're a coward and I could kick your ass any day of the week. Throw the gun away and let's finish this. I'll see to it that the others stay out of it." Angus then yelled at the goons, "Somebody shoot this fucker!" The officers adjusted the grips on their pistols and looked at each other for confirmation that they should shoot.

Gabe was the last to arrive. He stopped at the end of the line of cars and raced to the fray. When he saw Angus in Ives's clutches, he sprinted and yelled, "Ives, let him go! I'm the one you want!"

Shelley knew that Gabe would make matters worse. He yelled for him to stay back, but Gabe couldn't hear for the idling car engines, wind and slow drizzle. Ives yelled, "That's right, pretty boy, I do want you! Come to me!"

He lowered his grip on Angus from his neck to his chest. He encircled Angus's body with his left arm and trapped Angus's right arm to his chest so he couldn't grab the gun. Ives extended Angus's .40 caliber Beretta and fired. The hurried shot was accidentally perfect. Ives had had very little experience with firearms and the lucky shot surprised even him.

The hollow-point struck Gabe directly in the forehead, dropping him instantly. He fell on his face and slid to a stop in a lifeless heap. It was clear to everyone that he had been killed instantly.

For a moment, time stood still as everyone stared at Gabe's body. Shelley saw the bullet strike Gabe's forehead and felt the life drain out of his own heart as he watched one of his favorite kids die. The other officers stared in shock, as did Angus.

Angus broke down as he realized that Gabe had died trying to save him. His eyes watered and his rage soared as he yelled at the top of his lungs, "Would you guys shoot this son of a bitch before he kills someone else? Don't worry about me, shoot!"

Angus's anger brought the officers back to reality. In unison, they all glared at Ives and raised their pistols. Seeing that his time was up and that Angus was no longer a viable shield, Ives prepared for his final rush of pain.

He put his mouth to Angus's ear and said, "We'll finish this in Hell, Blauw. See you there in a few minutes." He screwed the muzzle of the pistol against the back of Angus's bulletproof vest until he'd found the edge of the vest panel. He jerked the trigger and fired one round downward through Angus's chest cavity.

Angus's face went blank. He dropped to his knees and lost the focus in his eyes, then fell face-down in the mud. Again, the officers and Shelley were stunned. They stood frozen in time as they watched Angus collapse. Then, as if perfectly choreographed, they simultaneously raised their pistols toward Ives.

Ives opened his eyes wide in preparation for his exit. He'd always wanted to die in a fight to the death with the police. He was now getting his wish. Killing Kinnett and Blauw was a fair trade for his own life. He spread his arms out wide and leaned his head back to savor every impulse of pain. As the rain splattered on his face he stared up into the clouds and yelled, "Yes!"

Shelley and five officers simultaneously emptied their high-capacity magazines into Ives. He staggered back three steps, then toppled over backward like a tall tree. He dropped Angus's pistol and landed flat on his back. He bounced once and laid motionless with his glazed eyes fixed on the dark sky.

The gunsmoke slowly dissipated in the night air, revealing the riddled, lifeless body of Lyman Ives lying in a pool of blood. Again, time stood still. The officers looked at each other, then at Sgt. Shelley for direction.

Shelley knew there was no need to check Ives. He didn't care about his condition anyway. He knelt by Angus and rolled him over. He cradled Angus's head and wiped the mud from his face.

Angus had enough life in him to focus on Shelley's face. He mumbled, "It's been a hell of a ride, hasn't it, pal?"

Shelley lost his composure and cried as Angus chastised him, "Ah, you big pussy, don't go getting all female on me. No one lives forever."

Tears dripped from Shelley's eyes as he yelled, "Angus, you old fool, we might have been able to talk him down! You should have given me a chance!"

"No, Len, I told you a long time ago, I ain't gonna die in a nursing home. I ain't gonna have some fat old nurse wiping my ass. This is how I want to go."

The other officers gathered around Angus and stared in shock. They had never seen another officer die before. He looked up at them and said, "You kids be careful. You're all good friends. Take care of each other and don't ever rat each other out."

Unable to speak, most broke down and turned away. They simply couldn't watch Angus die. Shelley wiped away his tears and asked, "What can I do for you, old man?"

Angus shook his head as blood oozed from his nose and mouth. "Just tell Millie that I'm sorry we didn't have more time together. Find my son and tell him that I wish I'd been a better father. Tell him I'm proud of him and that I'll be a better dad to him in the next life."

Shelley's voice trembled. "I will, Angus, I will." He tried to say more, but Angus lost his focus. His peripheral vision narrowed to a pinpoint. He stopped breathing and his eyelids closed. Shelley stopped talking and gently laid Angus down. He slowly stood and looked at the other officers, who were choked with emotion.

When Shelley turned around, he bumped into Ben Hire. Ben patted him on the shoulder. "Sorry, Len, I know you two were close."

"Thanks Ben. This is how he wanted to go. I'm surprised he lasted this long. He's been taking chances for years."

The officers milled around the alley in shock. Ben walked over and examined Ives. As Shelley walked to Gabe, he began crying harder. He yelled, "What a shame, this boy was too young to die like this!"

He dropped to his knees and gently grabbed Gabe's shoulders. He raised his face out of the pool of blood and turned him over. Gabe's scratched and bloody face was lifeless, and the hole in his forehead oozed blood.

Shelley yelled for someone to get blankets to cover Gabe and Angus. He laid Gabe down and stood. He turned to walk away, but stopped suddenly. He bent over Gabe and stared hard at his face.

Reaves brought a blanket and looked puzzled at Shelley. He thought he was studying the bullet hole in the center of Gabe's head and asked, "What is it, sarge?"

Shelley stared at the blood pooled around Gabe's mouth. His lips were parted slightly, and Shelley saw a small air bubble swell up in the blood, then pop. He knelt to one knee and studied Gabe's mouth intently. Another bubble swelled and popped.

He furiously tore Gabe's uniform shirt open and ripped the Velcro straps from the front panel of his bulletproof vest. He shoved his hand under the vest and pressed it against Gabe's sternum. When he felt Gabe's chest rise with shallow breaths, he yelled, "Gabe! Hang on! Help is coming! Keep breathing!"

Without prompting, Reaves grabbed his portable radio and yelled for the dispatcher to roll an ambulance. One had already been summoned when the first officer saw Angus being held hostage. It had staged a block away and hadn't yet cleared. Their response time was about forty seconds.

Shelley wiped the blood and dirt from Gabe's face. He cleared the blood from Gabe's mouth and continued to shout support and encouragement. When the paramedics arrived, they dove in and worked feverishly on him.

Ben Hire had called lab techs to the scene and was standing in the crowd of officers, shouting support to Gabe. He patted Shelley on the back and said, "Don't get your hopes up, Len. He can't have much of a brain left. I know Gabe. He'd rather be dead than be a vegetable."

"Yeah, I know, Ben. Poor kid, he had so much to live for."

Ben stood by as the paramedics loaded Gabe into the ambulance and sped toward the hospital. He told Shelley, "Why don't you take your guys to the station and get them started on their reports. I'll wait for the coroner to pick up Angus."

"Are you coming to the station after that?"

"No, not yet, Len. I've got a death message to deliver. There's going to be one devastated assistant D.A. tonight."

21

THREE WEEKS PASSED after Gabe's eight-hour surgery. He had a shunt to drain fluid from his brain and more wires and hoses sticking out of him than a NASCAR engine. He came out of his coma to see Beck sitting beside him, reading. He couldn't talk or move, so he stared at her and marveled at her beauty.

She glanced over at him as she'd done hundreds of times in the past weeks. When she saw that his eyes were open, she leaped from her chair and threw her book across the room. She pressed the alarm button as she bent over him.

The nurse responded and assessed Gabe's responsiveness. She did a sternal rub and applied pressure to his nail beds, checking for a reaction to painful stimuli. When she saw dilation of his pupils and coordinated eye movement, she immediately called his surgeon. Beck turned away so Gabe wouldn't see her cry.

Gabe remained awake for several minutes. He felt as though he'd just dosed off. The incident in the alley seemed like it had happened only a few seconds ago. He was shocked when the nurse told him that he'd been asleep for three weeks.

The next time Gabe awoke, he found himself surrounded by Beck, Ben, Sgt. Shelley and the surgeon. The doctor shined his light in Gabe's eyes and spoke to him. This conversation would be different. The tubes had been removed from his nose and mouth, and he could talk back. The surgeon said, "Gabe, don't talk, you're doing fine. I want to tell you what's happened to you."

He studied Gabe's chart for a few seconds before beginning. "Gabe, can you understand me?" Gabe nodded his head. Everyone was ecstatic. The surgeon continued, "Gabe, you're progressing better than we'd hoped. You may not remember, but you were shot. You took a bullet in the forehead. Fortunately for you, the bullet didn't penetrate your skull. You were running when it hit you. It struck your forehead just high enough above center to hit the curvature of your skull. It penetrated the scalp, but didn't hit straight on. The frontal curved portion of the bullet nose struck the curved part of your skull. That caused a ricochet effect which deflected the bullet upward. Your scalp trapped the bullet against your skull and it traveled around the outside of your skull under your scalp. It exited your scalp at the rear of your head. The problem was that the bullet shattered your skull at the point of impact. We had to surgically remove bone fragments from the front part of your brain and replace the shattered part of your skull with a metal plate. You've been through a lot, but the initial assessment indicates that you're going to do very well. I'll leave you with your friends for a few minutes, then I want you to rest."

As the doctor left, Shelley stepped up and bent over Gabe. He smiled from ear to ear and said, "Hey there, hard head, glad you're among the living again. Gabe forced a slight smile and nodded. Shelley eyes watered as he gripped Gabe's hand. "I'll come see you later, son. I'll tell the guys at work that you're awake."

When Shelley stepped away, Ben and Beck stepped to Gabe's side. Beck leaned over and kissed him with tears in her eyes. She said, "You really worried us, Gabe. When you get to feeling better, you're in for a real butt-chewing." He only blinked his eyes.

Ben patted Gabe's arm and said, "We got her, kid. A lot has happened in the past three weeks. We've finally got Loar." Gabe perked up and mumbled, "How?"

Ben looked at Beck, but she was still too emotional to explain. He said, "Well, Sherlock, the night that Ives shot you, he'd attacked Loar. She shot him twice. Ives took a knife to her

444

and her receptionist. After we'd cleaned up the scene in the alley, we went in and found the guard dead. We went to Loar's apartment to check her welfare. She'd wrapped the body of her secretary in sheets and was loading her into the freight elevator when we arrived. We recovered Ives's knife in Loar's apartment, and the coroner was able to match it to the wounds on Ives's mother, Dr. Rhinehart, the guard at the institute gate, and Loar's building guard and secretary. Dr. Rhinehart wrote down what had happened on her laptop before Ives killed her. We arrested Ives's girlfriend at the institute and charged her as an accomplice in all the murders after Ives escaped. She broke down like a cheap toy and told us everything. Since we had a murder scene at Loar's apartment, Baumgartan had no choice but to give us a search warrant. Old Judge Lemry approved the search warrant without hesitation. When we searched Loar's apartment, we seized the pistol that she shot Ives with. The lab compared a sample bullet fired from that pistol to bullets recovered from our old crime scenes. Loar's pistol killed Swede Boreman, Tim Allis and Howard Wilcox. We found Loar's murder souvenirs. Garrison was supplying her with copies of our crime scene photos. We got the tape of Ives killing Lucian Green. We can tell by the tape that Loar was filming the murder. We got the videotape of Kerse killing Nat Benson. Loar had audio recordings of her conspiring with Kerse to kill Dutch Windsor, Roger Moesen and Nat Benson. She had audiotapes of her encouraging Paul Siles to kill Jared Cutchall. We have a tape of her coaching Roger Moesen on how to kill Tim Allis. There is another tape of Loar manipulating Sammy Pritchard to stab Bruce Webster. Loar recorded other therapy sessions where she'd convinced Tommy Ryan to shoot Jonathan Lynch, and Nat Benson to stab Dr. Sabre. We got a tape of her coaching Sarah Bethard on how to stab you. Jimmy Clossan and Sarah Bethard decided to talk. Sarah will testify that she was with Loar the night Loar went to Mickey Cleary's house under the pretense of making love to him. She acted as the lookout while Loar strangled him. She also admitted that she'd used Loar's gun to kill Swede Boreman. She was a member of Linda Boreman's battered women's group. Loar had put her up to killing Boreman and provided her with the gun. She'll testify that Loar also put her up to stabbing you. Clossan admitted that Loar had put him up to shooting Angus. We collected samples of Ives's hair and blood at his autopsy. His samples matched the evidence at the murder scenes of Rudder, Andoever and Lindsey. We're batting a thousand, kid. We've arrested Loar, and she's being held without bond thanks to Judge Lemry. Baumgartan couldn't take the heat. He resigned and the interim D.A. has filed multiple murder counts against Loar. The state board of psychiatric review is investigating, and we're sure they'll revoke her license. We've cleared up all those cases that you worked in the cold case unit, except one. We can't prove that she killed Val Machka."

Gabe was ecstatic. He smiled and asked, "Ben, my memory is cloudy. Has something happened to Angus?"

Ben's enthusiastic smile faded to sorrow. He looked away and couldn't answer. Beck saw that Gabe didn't understand Ben's reaction. She said, "Angus is dead, Gabe. Ives killed him. I'm sorry."

Gabe's memory instantly raced back to the image of Angus being held at gunpoint just before the lights went out. Guilt overwhelmed him. He looked away as his eyes watered. Beck squeezed his hand and said, "I'm so sorry, baby. I know you liked him. Your career is going to be easier though. Richey has never been found, and Garrison committed suicide. The midnight crew found his car out on the old river road. He'd walked to the bank of the river and shot himself. No one knows why he chose that spot. It must been a special place for him."

Gabe turned back to Beck and asked, "Did Ben find a videotape of Garrison with a young girl in Loar's apartment?" She shook her head. Garrison had negotiated it away from Loar. Gabe knew he would never learn the identity of the young girl on the tape with Garrison.

Loar was bound over for trial at her preliminary hearing. She was held without bond and retained the best trial attorney in the state. Gabe was released and underwent weeks of physical therapy to regain his strength and coordination.

Angus Blauw's funeral attracted officers from all over the state. The procession of police cars was over a mile long. Lyman Ives's funeral attracted only one. The attendees were he and the crematorium operator.

Gabe awoke in the soft light of Beck's vanilla candles. He rolled over, encircled her waist and kissed her back. She rolled over and laid her head on his chest. She finally said, "You'd better get going, baby. You know how Shelley hates it when you're late."

He threw the covers off and slid down along Beck's side. When he'd reached her abdomen, he kissed her stomach. He sat on the edge of the bed and said, "Take good care of my son." He stood and staggered to the bathroom.

He brushed his teeth, shaved and combed his hair. He did indeed remember how angry Len Shelley got when he reported late to shift briefing. As he hurried through his routine, he paused briefly to examine the scar in the middle of his forehead. He rubbed it with his finger and looked deep into his own eyes.

The memory of his struggle with Ives, Loar, Garrison and Kerse haunted him. Now, more than ever, he hated what he had done. Because of his decision to use Ives to kill Loar, five innocent people had died. The man in the mirror was unmerciful.

Beck eased up behind him and wrapped her arms around his waist. She kissed his back and said, "It gets easier, baby. Give it time."

He caressed her arms and said, "I don't see how. Nothing is going to bring Angus back. I feel so bad for Millie. If it hadn't been for me, he'd still be here."

"It's not your fault, Gabe. Ives would have killed anyone who got in his way." Further explanation was pointless. Nothing short of a full confession would explain his guilt. That would only alienate the only woman that he'd ever really loved.

After shift briefing, Gabe spotlighted all of his businesses and made a DWI arrest. When the booking was finished, he drove by Angus's grave. He saw a lone figure standing in the moonlight, so he parked his car and walked in.

The night was calm and a gentle breeze swept across the headstones. Millie was composed when Gabe walked up. She turned and greeted him. Gabe said, "You're out late, Millie."

"I know. Sometimes when I can't sleep, I come here and talk to Angus." Gabe looked at the ground as he searched for the

447

words to comfort her. He mumbled, "Millie, I'm so sorry about Angus. I wish---"

Millie stopped him. "Gabe, you don't have to say anything. Angus and I had a wonderful time, short as it was. He was the kindest, gentlest man that I've ever known. I know most people didn't like him, but I saw a side of him that no one else knew. I wouldn't have missed knowing him for anything. The few months I had with him were better than a lifetime with anyone else. We did a lot of living in those months. We both knew this was how he would die. He had a mortal fear of dying alone. I tried to assure him that I would stay with him forever, but he was afraid he'd live longer than me. He couldn't stand the thought of a slow, painful death. If he hadn't died like this, he would have committed suicide someday when he'd gotten too old to care for himself."

Gabe heaved as he broke down and wept openly. He could no longer stand the guilt. He looked deep into Millie's eyes and held her by her shoulders so she couldn't look away. His voice broke and quivered as he confessed. "Millie, I have to tell you something. If Angus were alive, I'd tell him. I'm the one who caused Ives to go on the killing spree. I could have stopped him, but I didn't. I wanted him to kill Loar because we couldn't catch her legally. Dr. Rhinehart, the gate guard, Ives's mother, Loar's building guard and secretary, Angus, all those deaths are my fault."

Gabe expected Millie to hate him. To his amazement, she showed no emotion. She waited patiently while he poured out his heart. She patted him on the chest and comforted him. "I know, Gabe, Angus told me all about it. He knew what you were going to do even before you did it. At first, I didn't agree, but after a while, he made sense. Don't feel bad, Gabe. Angus would have done the same thing if he'd been in your shoes. He used to lie beside me in bed and reminisce about the job. It was all he lived for. He used to tell me how proud he was of you. He loved you like a son. I guess he saw himself in you when he was younger. I don't think badly of you, Gabe. You only did what Angus would have done."

Tears poured from Gabe's eyes. He wiped them away and said, "That doesn't make it right, Millie. Angus and I were professionals. We're supposed to play by the rules. We have to be better than the crooks or we're just crooks ourselves. I didn't

448

believe it before, but nothing justifies breaking the law, nothing! I violated my oath of office. I went against everything that I'd ever believed in. I can't forgive myself. Everyone tried to tell me that Loar wasn't worth sacrificing my honor over, but I was too hard-headed to listen."

"That's what I used to tell Angus, Gabe, but he was right. The rules are made by crooks for crooks. There's a difference between bending the rules and breaking them. And your credibility isn't destroyed if no one knows about it. Don't tell anyone about it and your honor will remain intact. Angus had no trouble looking himself in the mirror. If you're having trouble with that, stand here alone for a while and talk to him. If you listen, he'll speak to you. Angus loved you and the guys. He had no problem with what you were doing, and neither do I. Loar is behind bars and the killing has stopped. You didn't make Ives the killer that he was. He'd killed long before you identified him as a suspect. Pitting two murderers against each other is okay. You guys use crooks to catch crooks all the time. God knows Loar did her best to kill you. You're breaking the law served a higher purpose. It saved lives, and God forgives you."

Millie stepped up and kissed him on the cheek. Tears were running down his face when she walked away. As the clouds opened up and a soaking rain poured over the cemetery, Gabe took Millie's advice and stood quietly with Angus. She was right. Angus spoke to his heart and comforted him. He'd lived and died by his own code. Even staring death in the eye, he never let the bastards see him sweat.

As rain soaked Gabe's hair and ran down his face, he slowly drew strength from Angus's persona. Angus had always had a way of making him feel better. When he caught himself smiling at Angus's warped perspective, he wiped his eyes and walked away. The ways of the old school would be passed on to one more generation of officers. Too bad the world would never appreciate the importance of those values.

The End

Mike Smitley